PLAYING HARD
TO GET

Grace Octavia

Kensington Publishing Corp.
http://www.kensingtonbooks.com

DAFINA BOOKS are published by

Kensington Publishing Corp.
119 West 40th Street
New York, NY 10018

All Kensington Titles, Imprints, and Distributed Lines are available at special quantity discounts for bulk purchases for sales promotions, premiums, fund-raising, and educational or institutional use. Special book excerpts or customized printings can also be created to fit specific needs. For details, write or phone the office of the Kensington special sales manager: Kensington Publishing Corp., 119 West 40th Street, New York, NY 10018, attn: Special Sales Department, Phone: 1-800-221-2647.

Dafina and the Dafina logo Reg. U.S. Pat. & TM Off.

ISBN-13: 978-1-4967-0106-0
ISBN-10: 1-4967-0106-2
First Kensington Trade Edition: July 2010
First Kensington Mass Market Edition: November 2012

eISBN-13: 978-7582-7869-2
eISBN-10: 0-7582-7869-1
Kensington Electronic Edition: November 2012

10 9 8 7 6 5 4 3 2

Printed in the United States of America

For every beautiful black man
who has ever driven
any woman crazy:
Thanks.

And for my first "Malik":
Orpheus "Malik" Williams,
the most pro-black teen Westbury ever knew.
So happy you're still committed to your people

Acknowledgments

First, I have to thank the Creator for seeing in me a soul that could be trusted with words and stories and secrets. This is one powerful gift and I remain humbled by the grace that allows me to share it. I am thankful that I have a God who sits high and looks low. Where others might see a frail human, my God sees my heart.

But even with divine providence from the Creator, no man is an island and no writer can exist with only her laptop and a power cord. That said, I have to thank my family, friends, literary friends, my community, and my readers around the world for lifting me up and believing in my vision for what I do. I am an artist of letters. I take that very seriously and I thank you for each and every time that you support this art thing.

To the unstoppable cheering squad at Kensington, including my editor, Mercedes Fernandez—who has been there since book one, I thank all of you for your continued support and patience.

To my agent, Tracy Sherrod, my grandmother and number one supporter, Julia Reid, and all of the other sisterfriends who I caught trying to single-handedly sell all of my books at Wal-Mart, your passionate support keeps me going when I am down to those last 200 words!

To the outlets who support writers and the publishing industry, and reviewers who have taken time to peek at my work—RAWSISTAZ, Urban Reviewers, APOOO, *Essence* magazine, *Booklist, The Romantic*

Times, etc.—I pray I continue to give you works that invigorate your literary experience.

Lastly, I must thank and speak to every person who has ever done anything toward achieving revolutionary change in their life. Be it cutting off all of your hair and going natural, paying off your credit, going back to school, or starting your own business. Know that to reach your brilliant self, sometimes you have to peel back the layers of what you're used to looking at and just peek inside at a new, lovely you.

I wrote the story myself. It's all about a girl who lost her reputation but never missed it.
—Mae West

3T Diva Dictionary

Afro-disiac: 1. A "love jones" or strong desire to be with a natural brother or sister that's sure to change everything in its path.
2. When Tamia meets Malik.

1

All the world's a stage, and all the men and women merely players . . .

—Jacques in William Shakespeare's *As You Like It*

And on this luxurious, $5 million stage, nestled on the twenty-second floor of the desirous address of One Central Park West, known to the world as Trump Towers, is an astute and determined player, a woman who, it would seem to anyone watching, was preparing for the role of her life.

No, she wasn't making good on girlhood dreams of winning an Oscar or Emmy. Nonetheless, her starring role was just as riveting, just as compelling. Simply put, the angelically divine black beauty was attempting what other tired women had been trying to do at every other place in the world for as long as time existed—go to bed without having sex.

So, in the privacy of her bathroom, beneath a $10,000 Kalco chandelier that cast a sinister light over her freshly permed *and then* pressed hair, Tamia Dinkins slid an unnecessarily thick, overnight, extra-long, winged, and superabsorbent pad into the crotch of her aqua lace panties.

"Urggh," she groaned at the prehistoric, uncomfortable weight and width of the thing between her thighs. It was so ridiculous and Tamia wondered how she ever, ever concealed these things beneath her acid-washed jeans and EnVogue-tight miniskirts when she'd gotten her period in junior high school. Happily, because of nature and the intelligent folks at Playtex, she'd outgrown these little mattresses now; however, that didn't stop her from putting one on. Charleston, her ongoing leading male for the past six months, was in the bedroom. He'd been out there waiting nearly every night for two months, and quite frankly, Tamia was tired of how comfortable Charleston seemed to be getting with coming to her place, having acrobatic sex, slipping into a coma, and waking in the morning only to leave and return hours later to do it all again. And while the leading lady kept telling herself that she needed time and space to think about things with Charleston and where they were going, really she just wanted a night alone. She'd watch some tacky old R&B music videos, have a glass of overpriced Chardonnay, and think about nothing until the morning.

"Babe, what are you doing in there?" Tamia heard Charleston excitedly calling from the bedroom. He was probably already naked, his arms and legs spread out on her silk bedspread like a honeydusted cobweb.

"I'm coming," she said. She hoped he'd noticed the Midol tablets she'd conveniently left on the nightstand.

On another stage, not too far from the last, in the pricey and historic Hamilton Heights enclave in Harlem, Tamia's best friend was preparing for a less than con-

vincing performance to achieve the same goal. Somewhere between Friday-night Bible study and walking
into her refurbished brownstone, First Lady Troy Helene Hall decided that her husband, the good Reverend
Dr. Kyle Hall, who'd come into her life like a prince in
a fairy tale, wasn't getting any either. In fact, it had
now been exactly a month since Troy and Kyle had
shared more than prayers in their antique Thomas Day
bed. And even then, it had been a Valentine's Day
"treat" (Troy actually said this).

Trying her best to escape a diva past filled with
enough Chanel and Lauren to solidify her top ranking
among any circle of purified BAPs, a newly sanctified
and debatably saved Troy prided herself on being less
dubious and creative in her method of withholding sex
than Tamia. She knew about the old "I'm on my period" maxi pad trick but thought no good Christian
wife had any business lying to her husband like that.
She thought that if she didn't want to have sex, she didn't
have to have sex. It was that simple.

"No sex," Troy rehearsed telling Kyle as she laid in
bed, dressed in a white cotton smock that, combined
with her smooth fawn skin and flaxen hair, made her
look like an eighteenth-century house girl. Worse, beneath the frock, she had on the biggest, most raggedy,
stretched-out, and faded panties she could find in the
back of her drawer.

Her knees tight and her hands crossed above a Bible
that rested atop her vagina, Troy waited in bed for Kyle
to come out of the bathroom so they could pray and go
to sleep in peace. But when the reverend did open the
bathroom door, Troy wished she'd had on that super-
absorbent maxi pad. Standing inside of the crowned
rectangle that separated their underused bed from their
underused spa tub, was her husband. Nude and oiled to
a shine, he had a silver ring clasping his erect penis.

* * *

On the third stage, the player needed no pads or
Bibles for her theatrical run, for it was a one-woman
show. Alone in a California king-size bed that came to
her Alpine, New Jersey, mansion with special measure-
ments to provide a comfortable sleep for her superstar
basketball-playing husband, Tasha LaRoche had only
two props—a waterproof, neon green vibrator that rested
in its normal place beside her in the bed and a cell phone
she held to her ear.

"You're so damn sexy, baby. I want you right now," a
stern yet mischievous voice insisted through the
phone. It was her husband. Lionel was in Miami, getting ready to play the Heat the next night in a March
matchup.

"Yeah, Daddy. I want you, too," Tasha said with her
voice as breathy and childlike as a porn star's. Her nearly
sable skin blushed with fever as she imagined her husband's big, chocolate hands grabbing for her. Lionel
knew how to handle a woman. He was forceful and demanding, yet still careful and comforting. "What are
you going to do to me?"

"I'm going to get you on the bed and kiss every inch
of your body, slowly, until you beg me to get on top of
you."

"Yes," Tasha moaned, imagining her husband's lips
brushing against her breasts. Without opening her eyes,
she reached for the other prop and pulled it to her. "I
want you inside of me right now."

"I'm coming, baby, but first I have to get you ready.
I have to move my lips down below your navel—"

"Oh, yes, Lionel. Yes!" Tasha slid the vibrator between her legs and clicked. A swift pulse buzzed beneath the sheet.

"And then I'm going to—"

"Yes!" Tasha pushed the insides of her pelvis toward

the little toy and waited to hear her husband's next command. "What are you going to . . . ? Lionel? Hello?"

Silence.

After being tackled to her bed by a nude man with five moving limbs, Tamia thought that maybe Charleston had been on the wrestling team at Dartmouth. With her legs cocked back to her sides and his middle pushed hard into her, she wondered how and when he'd managed to manipulate her body in such a way. And she was still in her nightclothes.

Charleston was a decent-looking man. He had clear, brown skin and nice teeth. He kept his bald head shaved and his ears clean. His eyes weren't crossed and he didn't have shaving bumps (Tamia's deal breakers). *Presentable* was a good word, Tamia thought the first time she saw him. He looked like someone any woman wouldn't mind taking somewhere and claiming. However, even with this, there was nothing about Charleston that made him handsome or striking or especially sexy.

But really that didn't matter. Men like Charleston seldom carried their good looks on their shoulders. They had everything they needed to be considered "handsome, striking, and especially sexy" in their pockets. A self-made millionaire, Charleston started his good looks when he won his first medical malpractice lawsuit, right out of Dartmouth Law. His clients, five transplant patients who'd contracted HIV due to receiving infected organs from the same untested donor, were awarded $25 million each. His cut was 30 percent.

"Is that a pad?" Charleston asked, stilling grinding into Tamia. "You have your period?"

"Yeah." Tamia thought she sounded convincing . . . at least confident. "I guess we can't . . . we can't have sex." She raised her eyebrows matter-of-factly and shrugged her shoulders, ready for Charleston to get his 225-pound, overly exercised body off of hers.

"That's weird—I could've sworn you had it two weeks ago."

Tamia was silent. Saying anything wrong here could get her into trouble two weeks later when she really did get her period.

"Well, what day is it?" he asked.

"What?" She was sure he couldn't mean what she already knew he did.

"Is it the first day? Because we had sex two days ago."

"What difference does it make?"

"Are you bleeding heavily or lightly?" Charleston tried to maneuver his hand into the top of her night pants, but Tamia flicked it away. "Let me check."

"Yuck," she protested, pulling away from him. "I don't do that. We've never had sex on my period."

"Stop being such a prude. Some women love having sex on their period," Charleston said, looking down at his penis. "We can put a towel down."

"Let's *not* do that and say we did." Tamia pulled away from him and groaned, finding her way to her side of the bed as he sat with a surprised look. She couldn't believe what she was hearing. Was he that desperate that he'd put his hand on her pad? Yeah, she'd had sex while on her period before, but things had changed since she was young and horny, living in a boxy walk-up in Alphabet City as she starved her way through NYU Law and dreamed of the life she now had. Now they were lying on $400 white Egyptian cotton sheets and the concierge would be there to pick up the laundry in the morning. She was one of seven black owners in the entire building and four were basketball players. The last thing she needed was the cleaners talking about how they'd found blood on her sheets. Tamia sucked her teeth at the thought before reminding herself that there would be no blood on the sheets. She didn't really have her period. Her performance was so convincing, she'd convinced herself.

Now she wanted nothing more than to ask Charleston to leave. In five minutes, he'd managed to run past the finish line in a race to get on her nerves. But then she remembered one important detail that kept her from completely losing herself in a rage—this important detail was what she'd remember sixty days later when she was standing bald and draped in a sari with a delinquent notice from the bank in her hand. Charleston, in all of his doggedness, had been paying her $10,000 monthly mortgage.

After years of countless "nos," rejected young boys with rock-hard penises eventually became rejected grown men with rock-hard penises. And most of these men, Charleston and his well-accounted-for ego excluded, learned to take this denial of sex with a shrug and walk to a private place where he and his private part could find icy water or Vaseline and a *Playboy* magazine.

Somehow, this kind of acceptance never found Reverend Dr. Kyle Hall. Maybe it was because the Morehouse alum and third-generation preacher had been a virgin when he'd met his bride at a country club just three years earlier and had never really suffered sexual rejection like most of his comrades. Maybe it was because the thirty-two-year-old had grown to love every consuming aspect of the deed he'd successfully sequestered himself from for so long. Maybe it was because Kyle's brown skin and markedly handsome features drew looks and silent promises of adventure from nearly all of the saved women he'd come across each day. Regardless, of all of these "maybes," Kyle thought, lying in bed as he touched his still-rigid penis and watched Troy sleep in the same stately position he'd found her in when he'd come out of the bathroom naked, the "maybe" that mattered the most was that he was madly attracted to his wife. While it hadn't been that long since they'd been together, most people would be surprised that the feeling he'd felt when a puffy-eyed and newly single Troy marched into the dining room at the country club where he was sharing lunch with her parents, had never left him. Her smooth, supple skin haunted him when they were apart for only hours. Her eyes, almond and darting like a doe's, were visible in his mind, calling him into her, even when she was saying no.

And just as he had so many nights before, Kyle heard Troy say no to him and his hairless, coconut-candied body again. And it hurt just as much as it had the first time she'd turned him down. Seemingly ignoring his nudity as he got into the bed beside her, Troy asked if he would pray with her and before the young reverend could answer, she started a loud and long prayer thanking God for his only "*forgotten* son." Kyle didn't have the energy to correct his wife. Instead, his mind was focused on the fact that he wasn't getting any sex. He kept thinking, if only he could get her to feel this thing he'd had in him—what made him shave his entire body and pour coconut oil to be licked and rubbed off all before he'd even thought of bedtime prayer—he'd be fine. But when he reached for Troy with his one free hand, risking another sexual denial, it was made rather clear that she wasn't feeling anything. The Bible that was hiding her vagina fell to the floor after a sleeping Troy grunted at Kyle's touch. She turned her torso toward the

window and started a deep, mannish snore that wouldn't
stop for another three hours when Troy awoke, sweating and searching for her Bible, so she could escape to
the prayer closet to pray the incubus and succubus
demons away.

This was because, like her awake husband, Troy had
sex on the brain. And while she'd struggled so hard to
hide it when she was awake, at rest and between
clouded thoughts and montages of the past, Troy was
captive to her desires.

"Oh, Reverend, you give it to me so good," Troy
whispered into Kyle's ear as he sat back in the big
black leather chair behind his desk at the church. In re-
ality, the chair sat on all fours, but in the dream, it
swiveled around in circles as she plopped down harder
and harder in her husband's lap. Papers went flying.
The phone was ringing. Knocks shook the door. Troy
and Kyle didn't stop. "Oh, Reverend! Oh, Reverend!"

Without transition, the sexy scene went from the
magically swiveling chair to the long brown couch
where Kyle counseled most of the worshippers at the
Harlem sanctuary he headed. There, a naked Troy sat
center, her legs just inches apart, her husband seated
on the floor in front of her. While he never wore a
priest's white collar, now it sat crisp and immaculate at
his neck. The rest of him was naked and quite hairy.

"I know this is what you like, Sister Troy," Kyle said,
pushing her legs open. "I'm gonna make you scream.
I'm gonna make you praise the Lord."

He lined her thighs with primitive bites and then
snapped his neck back at her middle. He licked and
pulled. Troy's body was a bubble being blown to its lim-
its. A wave of pleasure so strong it stiffened her spine
forced her legs together taut around the holy man's
neck. She grabbed his head and pulled it closer to her.

*"Wait, baby!" he said, pulling back. "I can't breathe!"
But the waves were still tossing and at the moment
adrenaline simply made Troy stronger than Kyle.*

*"Yes," she moaned. "Do it! Do it!" She pushed and
pushed. Her legs closed and closed. And soon, she
couldn't hear Kyle's muffled protests anymore. But it
was no care. Pleasure was pouring. And then it happened.*

Kyle's head popped off <u>again</u>.

*Like a Ken doll's extracted in fun by a maniacal six-
year-old girl, it came loose from his body with a snap
from Troy's legs and rolled across the floor.*

Troy watched with her mouth open.

*"You did this to me," Kyle's decapitated head said,
prosecuting Troy. "You did this."*

*"I'm sorry, Reverend," Troy cried. "I didn't know . . .
I didn't know my legs were so powerful!" She looked
down and suddenly her soft lower limbs were as firm
and muscular as Serena Williams's.*

*"Get the Bible and let's pray for your soul. Let's
pray!"*

*Just then, Kyle's rolling head began to riddle passages
from the Bible—"And it was good, and Jesus said unto
them, a time to sow, the valley of the shadow of death.
Pray. Pray. Pray. Our Father, who art in heaven . . ."—
so quick and so fast that Troy began to sweat, trying to
find the pages to keep up.*

And then, in a terror, she woke up and reached for
her Bible.

"You all right?" Kyle, who'd been awake and watching her back the entire time, asked after reaching for
Troy again.

"Don't touch me!" Troy was frantic. She found the
Bible on the floor and jumped out of the bed. "I need to
pray. Right now. I'll be downstairs."

* * *

Both of the little girls Tasha gave birth to were crying now. It was 3 a.m. and the four-month-old brown one with the dimples like her father was ready for a bottle and the two-year-old with the attitude of her soap opera–star grandmother was awake just because she liked the scene of her mother in a panic.

Toni, which was the name the dubious two-year-old had learned to answer to, was standing in her white, oval-shaped crib, wiping tears from her eyes as she wailed senselessly and watched her mother scramble to get a bottle to the screaming ball in the other crib, the one she'd heard the tall man with the deep voice call Tiara.

"Oh, Mommy's baby," Tasha sang to Tiara to calm her. Only to Toni, who'd been waking up to watch Tasha's attempts since she was as little as the brown ball, it was clear that the song was little more than a performance to get them to go back to sleep.

Naked and with her short hair running in every direction the pillow in the other room had sent it when she'd finally gone to sleep after her call with Lionel had been dropped, Tasha slid the milk bottle she'd just retrieved from the warmer into Tiara's mouth.

With the warm bottle, Tiara quickly quieted, but after two sucks, what was previously a cry was now a holler.

"What?" Tasha tried. "What, baby? The milk? It's too hot? Shit! I forgot to check it." She dropped the bottle and pulled little Tiara to her shoulder to soothe her. "Mommy's so sorry . . . so sorry. I'm just sooo tired and sooo horny. I'm dying here, girls." It was nights like this that made her wonder why she'd never added a nanny to her staff at the mansion. "Could she really get back at her mother by doing all of this on her own?" might've been an intelligent question, but Tasha wasn't yet ready to admit that that was what this was all about.

Screaming now, Tiara, who could hardly see past her hunger, looked over at the other crib to see her room-mate jumping in her crib. Tears speckled the bigger one's face, but had Tiara been able to recognize a hidden smile, she'd notice that one was there.

"What's wrong with you, Toni?" Tasha turned around. "I need to feed your sister. Can't you see Mommy's busy? You're supposed to be asleep."

An hour later, the echoes throughout the overly decorated, eight thousand–square-foot mansion had quieted and Tasha, who'd already had two glasses of red wine at the wet bar in the master suite, was sitting on the toilet, thinking of how she would urinate if she had the energy.

Her eyes closed, she was sure this was the most comfortable she'd ever been in her life. Right there on the toilet, she was in a quiet, movement-free bliss that began at her toes, which were being warmed by the heated marble floors, and ended at her middle, which was just as warm.

"Oh, God, please don't let them wake up again. Please," she prayed more honestly than she had in her entire lifetime. "I just want . . . I just want some rest. Some rest and some . . . I want my husband back." Her erratic thoughts then went to her husband. In counseling, a few months after Toni was born and Tasha had been placed on antidepressants to control the crying she did whenever she was alone in the car with the crying baby with the smart eyes, Tasha had promised never to be angry with Lionel for not being there. Basketball

was his life. It was her life. It was how they could afford the $5,000 heated toilet she was enjoying so
much. He was a good husband who tried his best and if
he could, she knew he'd be right there with her. He
loved her. There was no question about that. So she had
no reason to feel so alone.

The urine finally came and Tasha eased deeper into
relaxation as it trickled from her. She sighed and
thought of how much she'd enjoy going back to bed.

"If I can't get sex, I might as well get some sleep,"
she said aloud as she reached for the toilet paper.

She wiped herself and looked down to make sure
that the paper fell into the expensive latrine. Though
the wine was making her eyelids heavy, she could see
that the inside of the bowl and the paper weren't the
only white things in the pyramid her thighs made on
the seat. There was something else. Something pointy.
Out of place. New, yet old.

"What?" Tasha spat, reaching for the thing. "What
the hell?" She pulled at it with two fingers. She rationalized that maybe it was lint. A piece of fiber she'd
picked up in the bed or maybe it had fallen off of
Tiara's nightsuit. She pulled it, not with any strength,
because she was sure the thing would fall away, but
when it didn't, she let it go and shook her hands at it
like it was a car coming at her at 80 mph.

"Gray . . . a gray . . . ? No!"

Tasha's thirty-two-year-old cry was so loud it not
only woke the little girls in her home but also many
more for dozens of blocks in their exclusive subdivi-
sion. Only not one cried or whimpered or winced.
From the little ball, Tiara, to Toni, who'd take the
vision just as poorly as her mother thirty years later,
the girls merely opened their eyes and stared into space,
feeling in Tasha's voice the inescapable physical and
heartbreaking burden time would place on their bodies.

*   *   *

After two phone calls and a triple-flight[1] of calming Merlot later, Tasha's brave little witnesses were joined by two more mourners—Tamia and Troy.

The three best friends, who'd met and started their 3T sisterhood when they were undergrads at Howard University, stood hunched over in a half circle at the basin in Tasha's bathroom. Before them was a single spiked, white hair that Tasha forbid anyone in the room to call gray.

"So you just saw it?" Tamia asked so seriously anyone who walked in would think they were looking at a dead body. And it could've been. All Tasha had said when she'd called was that it was a Code 3T[2] at her house—that could've meant the house was on fire, or she was about to set fire to it. Either way, her girls had to get there quickly.

"Yes, it was just there," Tasha whispered for no reason above dread. "Just there. Just . . . just sticking out from all the rest of the hairs."

"It is pointy," Troy said, squinting and moving closer to the hair in a way that only a best friend would do for another best friend as horrified as Tasha. This, in fact, could be said about the entire scene.

"Who cares about it being pointy, Troy? I don't want it to be here at all, period," Tasha said. "Why is God doing this to me?"

"God has nothing to do with this," Troy said. "And don't use his name in vain."

"What? God has everything to do with this," Tasha

[1] Triple-flight: a twelve-ounce tumbler of wine (three servings).
[2] Code 3T: any important situation requiring the immediate assembly of the 3Ts.

pointed out. "He put the damn hair there. He can take it away."

"What? See, you need Jesus. I'm going to have my women's group at the church pray for you." From her pocket, Troy produced a little prayer pad she used to record all of the negative things and thoughts she encountered throughout each day.

"Well, get it right and make sure you tell them to pray that I never get another one of those fuckers."

"Tasha, give Troy a break," Tamia jumped in. "I wouldn't be here if she hadn't come to pick me up and there isn't much we can say about this . . . this gray—"

"What did you say?"

"I mean," Tamia corrected herself, "as you described it, 'platinum'-colored hair anyway."

"I'm sorry, y'all." Tasha's voice cracked and then the merlot-influenced tears came. "It's just that it came from out of nowhere." She stood up and walked to a red velvet chaise that was certainly luxurious, yet oddly placed in the middle of the bathroom floor. "And it's so long. Look at it!" The girlfriends' eyes shot from Tasha and back at the devilish hair. "I'm like, how long had this been happening to me and I didn't know? It was growing and I never noticed. It's like it wasn't there yesterday and today it's everywhere."

"Everywhere?" Troy asked, pulling the prayer pad back out of her pocket.

"No, not like that. Well, I don't know. After I plucked that one, I was afraid to look." Tasha looked at her friends expectantly.

"I am *soooo* not looking at your vagina, Tasha," Tamia said bluntly before taking a sip of the glass of Malbec she'd poured to survive the occasion. "There are limits to this friendship. And I do believe this little pilgrimage to look at a platinum hair is enough."

*   *   *

Time and situations like this one had changed the three women in the bathroom with the platinum hair. For the 3Ts were once the party girls. The "It" girls. New York's finest, with the city of all cities at their disposal. When they graduated from Howard and left DC in an agreement to make it in Manhattan, the twenty-somethings' historical lineage put them at the top of the city's "to know" and "can get in" lists. A little something Troy's elitist, half white grandmother "best blood"[3] meant that without even trying, the pretty girls were in and it.

Troy had grown up on the Upper West Side with passed-down Manhattan wealth on her mother's side and a fairy tale Harlem history filled with actresses, secret societies, and front-row seats—even at church—on her father's side.

Tamia's last name was gold in the big city even before she started NYU Law with Troy. A Dinkins, she shared powerful blood with the city's first black mayor. And while her Prince George's County upbringing meant that few NYC insiders knew Tamia directly, they all accepted her like an old friend once they realized who she was.

Hailing from LaLa Land in the West was the third T, Tasha, who was both enjoying and hating the first-generation affluence and recognition her mother's fame as a soap opera star afforded her. In Hollywood, Porsche St. Simon's name alone meant that Tasha could play in the homes of Hollywood A-listers and half-eat meals at exclusive restaurants that had reservations set for months. But little of this mattered when Tasha ran away from her mother and ended up trying to make a name for herself, first at Howard and then in New York

---

[3] Best blood: someone born to a lineage of power and wealth.

City. While the crowd was impressed, Porsche's mark
had been in Hollywood, so they weren't moved. It was
purely a black industry thing. But all that changed
when Tasha caught (out of her own admission) and
made a covenant with Lionel LaRoche, a starting player
with the New York Knicks, just months after getting to
New York. Then she found herself back on top of the
scene and never once had to ask for what was given to
her. VIP entrance and invitations to birthday parties for
celebrities she'd never met—they all wanted Tasha
there, and she, arm-in-arm with her two besties,[4] seldom let them down.

It was fun. The bright lights of the New York night
shined on the 3Ts as they chased their dreams, fell in
love with dreamy men, and dreamed of how life could
be more fantastic than the ones they now enjoyed. It
was better than the best of times in their lives and what
made it that way, for sure, was that they were there for
each other.

In the big city, the 3Ts found a little love in a group
of women that was inspired by honesty, tolerance, support, and lots and lots of tears. They had rules and regulations they'd organized to help each other along the
way. Kind of signposts each T used to stay out of the
dark—how to survive a breakup, how to tell if a man is
lying, how to help a friend in need, how to take someone's man (Troy had used that one and failed miser-
ably, but in the end, she found the man she needed).
Hell, they even had their own signature drink and an
astrological 3T wine mood chart. While other people
said the 3T rules and regulations were silly and even
childish, the Ts lived by them.

Nowadays, it seemed the sisterhood and scraps of

---

[4] Bestie: casual best friend—one can be a "bestie" for a week or a
lifetime.

paper recording rules and regulations were all the 3Ts had to remind themselves of their marvelous Manhattan moments. The parties. The best tables. The lists of hunky NY bachelors. The sushi nights. The shopping sprees at Saks, yielding $3,000 boyfriends.[5] All gone (well, maybe not the boyfriends). All history to them now. They hadn't gotten old; they'd simply gotten grown. The new Christian Louboutin heels hurt their feet and they couldn't dance until dawn anymore. The music seemed louder everywhere they went. Mortgages ate up money that was once spent on bottle service. And their once slender frames were now covered with baby bump–hiding blazers for Tasha, professional blazers for Tamia, and "Blessed is the name of Jesus" blazers for Troy.

---

[5] Boyfriends: the most delectable form of arm candy, the leather boyfriends include purses by men—Jacobs, Vuitton, Gucci, Pucci, Dolce & Gabbana, and Ferragamo.

Smart Sipping: The 3T Astrological Wine Mood Chart

You like red today and white tomorrow. Then you want it sparkling or blush . . . maybe even a fruity/country mix over ice. It might seem like you're a wine-drinking schizophrenic who can't make up her mind about her favorite glass of bottled decision making, or the two guys she's been dating who drove her to drink in the first place; however, expert(ish) barroom studies show that it's not you who's confused. Your sign and mood actually dictate what kind of wine you might need or desire. A fiery Leo might require a glass of Grenache to get and stay in the mood for love, while a wild child Cancer would enjoy a sparkling champagne cocktail while in bed with her lover.

Do some more smart sipping to protect your mood . . . or create one. *Remember that good wine is best enjoyed *with* great friends and *without* automobiles.

Earth Signs: Including Taurus, Virgo, and Capricorn, these land-loving ladies are practical taskmasters who seldom fold.
Happy—Fruity (plum) wine will break the ice and get her right.
Horny—Break her tough exterior with a mellowing Merlot.
Sad—Malbec's peppery tones will help her unlock those secrets.
Sexy—White Zinfandel is sweet enough to get the groove back.

Water Signs: Like rivers, Pisces, Scorpio, and Cancer embrace everything they touch. They're sensitive and emotional.

Happy—Rousanne's wild flowers will birth the poet within.
Horny—The honey oozing in Chenin Blanc is sure to hypnotize.
Sad—Red Nebbiolo will calm the sensitive sign.
Sexy—Pinot Noir is deep and dark enough to capture her sexy.

<u>Fire Signs:</u> Strong and full of confidence, Aries, Leo, and Sagittarius are usually hard to miss—they're running things.
Happy—Riesling is sweet enough to bring a smile to her face.
Horny—Stoke her burning fire with a spicy cabernet sauvignon.
Sad—Merlot will shake the blues away.
Sexy—Grenache's complex bouquet will have her tongue-tied.

<u>Air Signs:</u> Aquarius, Libra, and Gemini girls are known for being the life of the party. They love fun and new ideas.
Happy—Moscato will keep the party girl on tabletops.
Horny—Merlot is sure to turn this tough chick into a tigress.
Sad—Control emotions, sipping nonalcoholic cabernet.
Sexy—Rice wine/sake is the perfect aphrodisiac.

"What's happening to me?" Tasha asked.

"What do you mean?" Tamia asked, holding Tiara to her chest as the baby napped. She hadn't yet decided if she wanted children but loved the weight and heat she felt when carrying Tasha's girls in her arms. The feeling of being needed in such an innocent way by another living thing was comforting in a way that beat a full day of massages at any parlor in the city. Tasha's early emergency kept the 3Ts together until sunrise, and now they were sitting on a bench beside the sandbox at the private playground in Tasha's neighborhood. While it was March and cold northern temperatures still dominated the forecast, the high sun and crisp air made for an unusually warm day at the park. Nanny-driven Mercedes-Benz station wagons and Bentley coupes with drivers who looked like Barbie dolls whizzed by. These were common sightings in Alpine, the most expensive neighborhood in the entire country, which had in its zip code Mary J. Blige, P. Diddy, and Stevie Wonder.

"Life is happening to you, Tasha," Troy said, getting up from the bench and sitting in the sandbox beside Toni.

"Nuh-uh, speak for yourself," Tasha said. "This is *some* life, but not *mine*. Not the one I ordered. I mean, I was supposed to be . . ." Tasha stopped. In her mind's eye, and with the brazen, savvy, and edgy reputation for busting balls she'd garnered, she was expected to be the "take no prisoners" go-getter of the group. The renegade. The game-changer. Now all she was doing was changing diapers and driving to the mall to buy another outfit to stuff into the girls' closet.

"Life isn't about where you thought you'd be," Troy announced prophetically. "It's about where you are. If you'd asked me a few years ago where I'd be, I'd say I was going to be Mrs. Julian James. A doctor's wife, who had her own law firm. I would be vacationing in the Hamptons with him and my two children—"

"Little Rudy and Theo," Tamia said, laughing at Troy's unconcealed dream of the perfect Cosby life she would have shared with the man who broke her heart.

If Tasha was the ballsy 3T, Troy was the ball-less one. She was the spacey dreamer whose silliness was easily marked by the mass of natural curls that shook every time she laughed. While she'd discovered the falsehoods in much of the shady, superior social practices her grandmother had taught her, Troy still tended to measure people and situations based on a black-and-white ruler of class and order. Thus, when she met and fell in love with her father's business partner and became a preacher's wife, her role went from being a future Clare Huxtable to a present-day church lady—hat and gloves included.

"Speaking of Rudy and Theo, when are you and Kyle going to start having children? Shouldn't you be pregnant already?" Tasha asked. "Y'all have been married for two years. You can't be using protection. Christians can't do that."

"That's just the Catholics," Tamia explained. "And it's not really practiced anymore."

"We're waiting," Troy managed nervously, imagining Kyle's loose head rolling from her lap and into the sand.

"Waiting for what?" Tamia asked.

"Just time and things." Troy exhaled and tried to ignore Kyle's praying head.

"Well, take all the time you want," Tasha said, "because this is not a party. Mommy hasn't been laid in two weeks." She looked from Toni to Tiara and smiled patronizingly to hide any trace of meaning from the girls. Only Toni pushed her shovel into the sand and flicked a scoop at her mother's feet.

"Toni, no!" Tasha ordered the toddler. "Don't you throw sand at Mommy. No!"

Troy laughed and took the shovel from Toni, who was smiling.

"Lord, I swear that girl is too smart for her own good," Tasha said. "The terrible twos!"

"Something tells me she's going to have more than terrible twos," Tamia added.

"Don't be mean to my little Toni." Troy defended the little girl, kissing her on the cheek. "She's a blessing and an angel. All of God's children are angels—from the baby Jesus in the manger, all the way to baby Noah being left at the steps of the king."

"What?" Tasha said. "Noah had an ark. And don't start talking all that crazy Christian stuff out here. You'll make the white people nervous."

"Please, they need Jesus too," Troy said passionately. "Everybody needs Jesus."

Tamia and Tasha traded looks on the bench. Ever since Troy and Kyle had gotten married, they'd noticed that it was hard for Troy to be in a conversation for more than ten minutes without professing her love for the Lord. It was comical at first, but now, two years later and confident that she wasn't changing, it had become annoying. But once a T, always a T, and instead of trying to kick her out, they mostly ignored her.

"Anywho," Tasha raised her voice in an attempt to shift the conversation, "what's up with you, lawyer girl? I'm surprised you could even come out here to see me. I thought you'd be somewhere in your office, having sex with your boss."

"He isn't my boss," Tamia said tensely. "Charleston works with an entirely different team. And there's nothing new. Just us . . . same as always." She rolled her eyes.

"'Just us'?" Tasha looked at Tamia sideways. "That

man is worth eight figures. He's one of the most sought-after brothers in the city. You can't tell me you haven't been on someone's overnight trip to Paris in a private jet and reinvented some rules for the mile-high club."

"I've done all of that. That's not the problem."

"What is it?" Tamia asked.

"Well, between the trips and plans and sex, Charleston isn't saying anything about us settling down—not a peep."

"Settling down is overrated," Tasha whispered sinisterly and Troy nodded along, but Tamia shook her head.

"You two can say that because you're both married already."

"Please, do you even want to settle down with Charleston?" Tasha asked. "I haven't heard you mention this before, and you just stopped seeing that white boy—what's-his-face."

"Alex," Troy confirmed.

"I know . . . I mean, I don't know," Tamia tried. "Look, I do want to settle down. And Charleston is a great guy. We're together and he's in my space . . . drinking the milk and I'm too old to give it away for free. I feel like something should be happening. You know? Like I shouldn't be standing still. He acts like all he has to do is just show up and be Lord of the Rings and that's all. I can't let him use me."

"Well, use him," Tasha snapped. "Let that fucker pay your mortgage and fly you all around and keep it moving. What's wrong with that? Have fun. Get your hair did . . . and please do something about those nails . . . scratching my baby." She wearily looked at Tamia's three-day-old manicure as they all laughed.

"Tasha," Tamia said, "I'm serious. I need to put some fire under him."

"Look, if you really want to get him thinking, get his testicles a little tighter, you need to do some love politricking."[6]

"What's that?" Troy asked.

"If you really feel like Charleston is only monopolizing your time and not investing, you've got to find a way to control the situation before it controls you and you lose him," Tasha started, readjusting the black mink shawl she insisted on wearing to the playground, "which I cannot let you do, because I happen to know two women in this very neighborhood who are waiting for you to step down so they can step up. Charleston may not be a young Denzel, but he has old-Denzel money. And that makes him prime real estate for the thirty and up crowd. This type of man is as uncommon as good weaves."

Tamia and Troy nodded in agreement.

"But what can I do?" Tamia asked. "How do I get control?"

Tasha handed Troy a tissue to wipe Toni's nose as she thought.

"How long has it been?" Tasha asked.

"Six months."

"Damn, this is worse than I thought. . . . You're actually at the breaking point. After six months, a man his age gets lazy. He thinks he doesn't have to invest and looks at you crazy if you insist. We need to move fast. Swift. You're gonna have to back up. Get some space. Give some space."

"True, true, and very true. I'll have to do that," Tamia agreed, taking the hat Tiara had pulled from her head. She ran her hand over Tiara's smooth, nude scalp and smiled.

---

[6] Politricking: playing tricky politics.

"Oh, please put that hat back on her head," Troy insisted. "That poor baby doesn't have a single curl. She'll get H1N1 in three seconds."

They all laughed as Tiara wrestled with Tamia for the hat.

"When is little mama's hair coming in?" Tamia asked. "Toni had a head of hair by now."

"Please, I don't know," Tasha answered, rolling her eyes playfully. "I'm about to get her a little baby weave or something. Like a bang."

"You will not!" Troy said, nearly falling over in the sand with Toni, she was laughing so hard.

"It's cold out here. I can't have my baby's scalp all naked." Tasha snatched the hat and put it on Tiara's head. "Maybe I could get my hands on one of Aunty Mia's tracks."

"Whatever!" Tamia snapped. "You put a hand on one of my tracks and I'll put my hands on both you and Tiara! . . . And this is Indian hair too!" She flipped her hair over her shoulder as Tasha and Troy giggled. "It costs half of my mortgage."

2

Perfection is easy to plan for, but impossible to achieve.

A consummate planner, Tamia had yet to admit the latter part of this statement to herself or anyone else. She loved plans, lists, steps, details, earmarks, and fine points—objectives she could use to achieve any goal she set for herself. Sometimes those steps were easy, like vowing to beat Lydia Walker, the great-grandniece of Madame C.J. Walker, in a rowing competition when the girls attended camp together one summer at Cape Cod. And sometimes those steps were difficult, like vying for the number-one spot in her law school class at NYU. Paradoxically, Tamia was usually successful in achieving her plan, but the results were often far from perfect. After Tamia won the rowing competition, Lydia, who was once one of her closest friends, never spoke to her again. And her drive to be ranked number one in her law school class led to an abuse of sleep deprivation drugs and a weeklong stay in a hospital. Big and small, these imperfections faded quickly into the back of Tamia's memory as she placed out front the success of her planning. Sure, there were some bumps, but she always emerged victorious.

On a more recent list of perfect plans, Tamia had made a few promises to herself.

First, when she made it—when she graduated from law school, passed the bar exam, and was recruited by a top New York law firm, she'd never, ever set foot on a subway again.

While, like most perfect plans, this was nearly impossible in a city as populated as New York, for Tamia, it was still worth the promise. To her, it was a matter of taste and principles. Tamia loved nice things. Clean things. Crisp Bloomingdale's catalogs in the mail. A new Hermès scarf, folded and tucked into perfumed tissue paper. The opening hours at the Museum of Modern Art when the floors were freshly waxed and the halls were empty of echoes.

To her, these things had promise and class. Beauty and elegance, all of the things she wanted and expected of herself—when she made it. Perfection.

Now the subway, the aged underground railroad system that veined the city together, seemed the opposite of everything Tamia wanted in her perfect world. The onion man, who felt a need to keep his arm held high in the middle of the subway car, his hairy underarm exposed to everyone on a ride in the breezeless chamber. The toothless obese woman, begging for change to get something to eat. The wannabe rapper, who felt a need to rap louder than his already loud earphones. The near-dead snoring man leaning on her shoulder. The panty-free, transgender prostitute. Sudden stops. Dirty floors. Graffiti. Grit. Grime. Crime. Perfection—not.

If Tamia worked hard, she rationalized, she shouldn't have to be exposed to this cornucopia of bad scents and bad taste. Like the rest of her friends, who traipsed around the city in taxis and chauffeured town cars, she should be able to enjoy the life she'd worked so hard for. But unlike her friends, her hard work didn't come with Manhattan or Hollywood inheritances. Her family had money. But not *that* kind of money, so she'd have to work a little bit harder. Which she, being Tamia, certainly did. And so far, the perfectly planned subway promise had been kept.

However, on the third day of her new life far and away from her new beau, when she'd done little in the way of finding space from Charleston other than not accepting his calls, she realized that she had a problem. How was she going to get to work?

In addition to her freed-up bank account, one of the other awesome luxuries she enjoyed as Charleston's girlfriend was the chauffeured Bentley that waited at the front of her residence to whisk her (well, him) to work each morning. It was a beautiful treat that she loved to remind herself of when she was in the shower or curling her hair—"the car is waiting downstairs." It sounded like something she deserved. Something better than the subway, which was what she could afford.

But on day three . . . Charleston wasn't in her other bathroom, meticulously coiffing himself as she meticulously inspected her clothing. So when the sweet thought of the car downstairs came to mind, she realized the separation wasn't going to be as perfect as she'd planned. Her car was in a rented parking garage two blocks away and even if she bothered to take the walk to the garage, it would take her an hour to maneuver through traffic and she'd never find a parking space in midtown.

"Shit," she scoffed, knowing there was no way her new leather Prada heels would survive a minute in the packed rush hour subway. Her Tahari suit would be wrinkled and thus out of place at her afternoon team meeting.

These complaints would sound ridiculous and spoiled to anyone else, but to Tamia it was a point of recognition, of realization. She'd busted her behind to get her things, to get to this place. She deserved better. She just needed a new plan.

"Bancroft," she said into the phone when the concierge downstairs answered her call.

"Madame Dinkins, how may I be of service?"

"I'll need a taxi waiting. I'll be down in ten minutes." She counted two twenties in her purse and thought it would certainly be enough to get to the office.

"A taxi?" Bancroft's voice was as English and distinguished as his name.

"Yes."

"But we assumed you'd be taking your customary mode of transportation," he said with his voice lowered to a whisper. He always referred to himself in the manner of his entire staff, saying "we" instead of "I." "Shall we tell your driver to leave?"

"He's down there?" Tamia ran to the window before she remembered her view was of the side street.

"Present, Madame."

"Oh." Tamia would've blushed had she not been so perturbed by the news.

"Will you still be needing a taxi, Madame?"

"No. Tell the driver I'll be down in ten minutes."

It was one thing to ride to work in a chauffeured luxury automobile with her affluent boyfriend beside her, wheeling and dealing on his cell phone as the car cut through traffic. It was a big, brand-new kind of thing to ride in that kind of luxury car alone. Steamy latte in hand and seat belt free, Tamia sat like she was the Queen of

Kings County. She flipped her hair over her shoulder and ordered the driver to lower and raise the windows so many times they both laughed at her indecision. And when it was all over and she was at the office, she thought to ask him to go around the block just one more time. And then she did.

"Curtis says you enjoyed your ride to work," Charleston said, walking into Tamia's office. His navy blue suit was as impeccably tailored as his timing. A periwinkle shirt and tie picked up the shine in his platinum cuff links.

Tamia was sitting at her desk, reading through a set of comments the lead counsel on a case she was working on had left on a briefing she'd approved. She'd just thought to send Charleston a text, thanking him for thinking of her that morning.

"Charleston," she said, looking up from the red ink everywhere. "I was just thinking about you."

"Moi? I'm surprised you remember who I am."

"Please." She smiled. "Have a seat."

"Oh, I get a seat, too?" Charleston looked around as if he hadn't been in there just days ago, making love to her during a late work session.

"Don't be so silly," Tamia said.

"You don't return a brother's calls for two days and *I'm* silly? I think most people call that observant."

"I've just been busy. I told you I need to get more serious about work and focus. You've been where I'm at. Why can't you understand?"

"I do understand. But I'm a man of action. I want what I want and right now I want you."

He leaned into the desk and looked down Tamia's torso.

"Do you ever take a day off?" Tamia laughed at his

flirting. While his directness could turn to pushiness in seconds, it was Charleston's fire that added to his attraction. He wasn't shy about his desires and that only multiplied his power over people.

"Look," Tamia started, unconsciously stroking her earlobe, "I need to get back to this briefing before my meeting with the Lucas team. You know how Pelst can be."

Mrs. Phaedra Pelst was another partner at the firm. She headed most of the low-maintenance, high-profile civil rights cases. The six-foot blonde was known throughout the city for her bombshell beauty and killer courtroom antics. What wasn't known was her uncontrollable craving for bedding bald black men—one of whom was Charleston, who'd stopped sleeping with her when she implied she might want to leave her non-bald and non-black husband for him.

"Good old Phaedra and her briefing notes. Let me have a look," Charleston suggested. He'd yet to tell Tamia or anyone else about his bedroom business with Phaedra.

"No," Tamia insisted. "I can't let you do that. Pelst is my problem and I have to deal with her all on my own."

"So you're kicking me out?" Charleston winked and grinned at Tamia, changing the mood.

"See, do I come to your office with all of this drama?"

"Hell, no," he said, getting up unflappably and straightening his tie. "You'd never get past my assistant."

Tamia playfully averted her eyes as he made his way to the door.

"I'll see you after work?" Charleston asked.

"Yes," Tamia agreed. "And thanks for thinking of me this morning."

"Yeah, yeah, yeah. I couldn't leave you to your own devices in the big city. It's a jungle out there, baby."

* * *

The Empire City, Gotham, the City that Never Sleeps, the Capital of the World, the City So Nice They Named It Twice . . .

It didn't matter what the rest of the world chose to call New York City. To the Virtuous Women of First Baptist it would always be known as the Big Apple. For these "serious sisters in Christ," the moniker had nothing to do with its innocent 1920s African American origins in the *Chicago Defender,* and everything to do with its most obvious connections to the sinful temptations they were trying to escape outside the doors of their Harlem sanctuary. For, like Tamia, they too were trying to shore up perfection in this lifetime.

And while the crossed legs and pursed lips around the table at the weekly Bible study would imply that their agreed avoidance of all things sinful in the city was to protect their own innocence, they'd all been there. They'd all done that. And most had their "I Love NY" T-shirts to prove it.

Now this was something that even the most discerning eye couldn't see. For 150 years, First Baptist had been the church home to uptown's most distinguished and dignified stakeholders. While other members came and went, the inner circle was a small conglomerate of "I's"—inheritors, investors, and insiders. Going all the way back before worshippers at Convent and Abyssinia, and even those blacks with more bourgeois aspirations who'd traveled downtown to find their God in the pews at the Methodist and Catholic churches, First Baptist's original members were some of New York's first Ivy League graduates, lawyers, doctors, stockbrokers, politicians, and big-business proprietors. Slick and savvy, they believed in and portrayed an image that was far from reproach and close to godliness.

More than two centuries later, the Virtuous Women were a stagnant emblem of this persona. Only, like their predecessors, it was more pomp than particularly true.

"I told Richard that no Christian man would ask his wife to do such a thing," Sister Oliver went on. She was in the middle of a tearful testimony about her husband's recent desire for oral pleasure.

"No," a chorus of condemnation surfaced around the table of twenty-three women.

"It's just not right. It's not pure. That . . . thing shouldn't be anywhere near my mouth!" She struck the table and fell back in her seat dramatically. The sisters on either side of her leaned in to provide comfort.

"When did it start?" another sister asked after Sister Oliver gathered herself. Her voice held high a focus on disdain, but still there was a hint of sheer nosiness. "I mean, when did Deacon Oliver start asking you to . . . you know"—dagger eyes from around the table stopped her midsentence—"do that?"

"It was last month," Sister Oliver started. "He went away on his business trip to Jamaica and came back asking me to . . . do it. He tried to pull the car over on the highway on the way back from the airport. We were on the Long Island Expressway! I couldn't do that! Not on the expressway!"

While a solemn hush of shame eased about the room, across the table from Sister Oliver was one member whose snickering at the thought of the roadside romp could not be contained.

Troy was trying so hard to focus. She held her hands on her Bible and bit the inside of her upper lip whenever her mind drifted away from Christian thought. But just as it had when she had gone to church with her Grandma Lucy as a child, this technique was failing her now. Her upper lip was already numb and the thought of Sister Oliver playing headmistress[7] on the side of the expressway was . . . well . . . sinfully hilarious.

The latest Sister Oliver was the second Mrs. Oliver to a sixty-year-old widower who'd spent more time enjoying his newfound sexual freedom than mourning his wife's death before he settled on courting Mamie, the short and plump middle-age daughter of an older, well-respected deacon. Never married and ridiculously prudish, Mamie wasn't exactly the best fit for Deacon Oliver, but she was the only single woman in the church in his age group who didn't have children and grandchildren he'd have to worry about.

Sister Oliver seemed to come to each meeting with some new complaint about Deacon Oliver's bed acumen and at each meeting Troy was forced to shake her head and bite her upper lip until it bled.

"I tried it for my husband once," another sister started, "but it made my jaw hurt and I bit my tongue."

Troy's snicker blossomed into a giggle that could be heard by her neighbor, the president of the Virtuous Women, Sister Myrtle Glover.

"Now, now," Myrtle said, rolling her eyes at Troy. "We won't hear of that. We all know that such behaviors are hedonistic and we must protect our husbands from falling to these worldly desires. The penis is meant for two things—the toilet and the vagina during sex." She looked at Troy. "And that's it."

"I know, Sister Glover, and we've talked about this before, but it's easier said than done," one of the younger sisters comforting Sister Oliver declared. "How am I supposed to keep my husband from cheating on me, if I can't even keep him happy in the bedroom?"

"And what about us single sisters? What are we sup-

[7] Headmistress: one who is good at performing fellatio.

posed to do?" asked Kiona, a younger member who'd, on account of her outspokenness, long been on Myrtle's list of people to vote out of the organization. "I'm a proud Virtuous Woman and I know we don't have sex before marriage or masturbate, but it's hard. *I have needs.*"

"Sisters in Christ, let us not confuse worldly desires with Christian needs," Myrtle warned sternly. "These vile and deviant behaviors of which you speak are proof of the weakness of the flesh."

Everyone, including a salty-mouthed Troy, nodded in dreaded agreement. Troy looked at Myrtle and it seemed as if steam was billowing from her ears.

"The Bible tells us that the flesh is lustful and if you live after it, you shall die!" Myrtle added.

"That's in the Word," another sister said, opening Troy's Bible to a verse in the Book of Romans and pointing to it for Troy.

Troy nodded along and sank farther into her seat. She'd been struggling with all of these ideas, these rules of religious order and sainthood, since she'd accepted Kyle's offer of love and realized that being with a leader of men of God also meant loving his church and living that life. More often than not, she'd failed, fallen super short of what the people around her said she needed to be to wear the First Lady crown. And what made it worse was that it seemed that no matter how she went about the thing, no matter what she did, she still couldn't seem to get saved—to hear the voice of God in the way the other people in the congregation claimed she would when and if she'd been chosen. This distinction, while small in any other circle, and in a few other churches, was the ax splitting Troy from really being accepted in the church. Sadly, it allowed members to question the pastor's choice in selecting an "unsaved" mate who wasn't "equally yoked" in the Lord.

"And if you should fall, my sisters, there are demons waiting to fall with you," Myrtle went on.

"The incubus and the succubus!" cried Sister Oliver. "Demons!"

Troy's ears perked up and her eyes widened. She'd been listening to Myrtle's weekly warnings at each prayer meeting.

"That's right," confirmed Myrtle, "the demons of sexual perversion that will come into your bed and have sex with you . . . and your spouse! Sisters in Christ, you'd better beware."

Something in Troy's stomach twisted and gave way. She felt full and then ill, like something rotten was growing in her gut. She kept imagining Kyle standing naked, oiled and with the little silver ring around his penis. Had the demons been in her bedroom? Were they having sex with her and her husband? It sounded unreal, ridiculous, crazy to consider, but the women before her knew the Word, and one was sitting beside her thumping on pages of the Bible, confirming what they were saying was real.

"I need to use the bathroom," Troy said, jumping up from the table in the middle of Myrtle's continuing tirade. She saw the woman roll her eyes exaggeratedly. She felt pressure pushing through her pelvis and leaning on her bladder.

"But I was about to start the closing prayer," Myrtle warned. Everyone looked at Troy expectantly. She couldn't leave and miss the prayer.

"Okay," Troy said, squeezing her thighs tightly like a schoolgirl and getting back into her seat. She sat back and heard, at length, what remained of Myrtle's speech about the incubus and the succubus. The prayer wouldn't come for ten more minutes.

* * *

The Virtuous Women of First Baptist weren't the only residents of the Big Apple facing the presence of demons. Tamia was in the middle of a professional death match with a demon of her own.

After Tamia sat in a team meeting for two hours and took more notes than anyone else—simply to prove that she was paying the most attention—Phaedra requested a private meeting in her office. Once Tamia made it inside and was instructed to close the door, she was informed that she was no longer a part of the team and was being reassigned.

"But I've done most of the work on the Lucas case. I've had the most contact with the client," Tamia pleaded. She didn't want to be moved. It was such a big case and it would look good on her list of achievements when she was up for partner in a few months.

"So you're saying it's *your* case?" Phaedra asked, her voice pregnant with accusation. Her blond hair was blown straight and cut blunt above the shoulders. It was a conservative cut, yet her beauty made its hardness sexy. She wore a fitted black skirt suit that left little wiggle room, and no stockings.

"No, you're the lead," Tamia said apologetically. "Look, I'm not trying to step on your toes here. It's just a big case and I want in."

Tamia was correct. The Lucas case was the biggest civil rights case on the firm's list. Frederick Lucas was a former porn star who'd been dropped from his agency when word of his erectile dysfunction had been leaked to the media. The agent claimed Lucas couldn't do the work. Lucas claimed he simply needed better work conditions. It was one of those quirky cases that was sure to keep the firm's name in the news and the client list growing.

"Look, Dinkins, we just don't need so many hands

on this. A paralegal could handle some of the work you're doing."

Yeah, that was an insult.

"Is this about sharing the spotlight?"

"Sharing?" Phaedra smiled pleasantly. "I don't share anything. I'm a taker. You know that." She winked. "Look, I'm giving you something with a little buzz. It'll be enough to get you some notice."

She slid a blue folder from beneath her keyboard and handed it to Tamia.

"Richard Holder," Tamia read the name on the folder. "Who is he?" She opened the folder and fingered the pages. She wanted to put up more of a fight about the Lucas thing but knew it would only end in disaster if she made a big stink. Phaedra had the ears and eyes (literally) of the senior partners and Tamia was only the new black girl on the block.

"He's some kind of organizer in Harlem—a community leader. The police played bang-bang in his apartment one night, looking for a boy they suspected in a robbery case. Turns out the boy was an illegal from Nigeria. He was working with Holder."

"They killed him?"

"No. No one died—hence the lack of news coverage." Tamia almost heard Phaedra's sigh. "And the boy was nowhere near the robbery."

"So, what's the case?"

"Well, Holder tried to get the cops fired, citing that they had no right to enter his home. And then, all of a sudden, the state is trying to slap him with this slave labor charge. He wasn't paying the boy."

Phaedra went on to explain that Holder had a hearing coming up and that he needed a strong lead to prepare him.

"This kind of man," she kept saying, needed some-

one who could "understand him . . . work with him."
She then pointed out that he'd probably work better
with someone who was more like him . . . someone
"cultural."

"You are cultural?" Phaedra asked before standing
to suggest the meeting was over. "Keep me posted,"
she added before Tamia could answer.

"That bitch," Tamia growled in a way that scared her
usually hardened assistant. Still holding the blue folder,
Tamia was walking into her office.

Seeing the red in her boss's eyes, Naudia knew to
follow Tamia into the office and close the door.

"Pelst?" Naudia quizzed, looking at the foreign folder
Tamia was holding. An aspiring lawyer who prided herself on her Brooklyn hustle and go-getter mentality,
Naudia was the perfect fit for Tamia. She was eager
and unflappable—what any assistant would need to be
to keep up with Tamia's ambitious work ethic.

"Of course. She took me off the Lucas case and
gave me this piece of crap . . . and it's pro bono. A slop
fest. That won't get me any news." Tamia handed Naudia
the file.

"What is it?"

"My new burden," Tamia said. "Hey, after you file
that, set up a mani-pedi with Juan."

Tamia waved her hand to excuse Naudia from the
office and picked up the phone to call Tasha. She
wanted to vent and afterwork drinks with the 3Ts was
just what she needed to keep from completely losing
her mind.

"I'm sorry to hear she took you off the case," Naudia
said before exiting. "You worked really hard on it and
Lucas was lucky to have someone like you on his team.
He wasn't just a big joke to you."

Even in her anger, Tamia heard the sincerity in her voice.

"Thanks," Tamia said, lowering the phone from her ear. "Look, forget about Juan. . . . Just start a new file and contact Holder to set up a meeting. I'll need to see him as soon as possible."

"No problem, Counselor," Naudia said brightly.

Tamia was about to leave a message on Tasha's voice mail when Naudia finally walked out.

"Hey, girl!" Tamia heard a loud and familiar voice from just outside the door. "Your boss lady in there?"

In poked the head of another demon Tamia dreaded. Only this one was that of a peer.

"Hey, Tamia. You free?"

"Yes, Jones," Tamia answered wryly. "Come in."

Tasha couldn't answer Tamia's phone call because she was busy thinking about maybe holding one of her daughters in her arms. But they were getting so heavy now, even little Tiara, and she didn't want to wrinkle the silk shirt she was wearing before Lionel had a chance to see how good she looked.

She was standing in the lobby at Newark Airport, awaiting Lionel's return from Miami. Around her stood an eager crowd of drivers holding pickup cards with secret names the players had selected, in-the-know fans, a few mistresses (whom she'd identified by their ridiculously long hair weaves), and some of the other wives of Knicks players who'd also made the move to New Jersey in search of suburban sprawl and a small chance of marital bliss.

While Tasha had long separated herself from the drama and backbiting that provided the unstable backbone of the NBA wives' club, she still knew many of the faces of these women and when she'd arrived at the airport had smiled sociably at them and chatted just long enough to hear the latest gossip.

Naturally short tempered, she hated the fakeness associated with carrying on long conversations with women she considered less than associates, but knew that she had to know what they knew in order to remain an educated NBA wife. An uneducated NBA wife was sure to become a former NBA wife as an ambitious groupie with a ridiculous weave became a mistress with a more ridiculous weave, waiting for another woman's husband at the airport. There was a long list of critical rules in surviving this hoop dream universe, and something as trivial as not knowing where and how to await the arrival of one's husband at the airport could lead to a drawn-out and embarrassing demise.

"Look at my girls!" Lionel was the picture of pride, his long, lanky frame crouched down before his family. He kissed a gurgling Tiara, pinched Toni's cheek, and should've stood up to hug his wife, but instead he handed Tasha his shoulder bag and pulled Toni from the twin-seater stroller to play.

To this, Tasha smiled pleasantly. The other husbands were doing the same thing as Lionel, and their wives were looking on adoringly as the men inspected the little ones for boo-boos and gave out kisses. There was no reason to vie for attention. No reason at all. But still, behind the most pleasant of smiles, Tasha was thinking, *Do you not see me standing here? Look at my shirt. Hell, just look at me!* She'd stuffed herself into Spanx so she could fit into Lionel's favorite jeans, lifted up her sighing breasts and put them into an armorlike bra, and pushed the heavy stroller through the airport in a pair of red devils.[8] Someone had better look at her!

"You look nice, baby," she heard Lionel say. She

---

[8] Red devils: red patent-leather stilettos.

batted her eyes and looked at him to see that he was speaking to Toni. The little girl couldn't talk yet, but intelligently responded to her daddy with the one word she'd been practicing: "Dada."

"You want me to drive?" Lionel asked when they'd finished walking to the car. Tasha was quiet. Her feet were burning from pushing the stroller back across the lot as Lionel carried and played with Toni and she still held the shoulder bag. "What?" Oblivious to her condition, Lionel looked at Tasha's screwed-up face. "Why are you so quiet?"

Tasha was about to either spit or curse, but the pot of her anger wasn't fully to a boil yet. While she was annoyed, she still had missed Lionel and a tiny part of her was just happy to be reunited with his scent, a masculine mix of woodsy shaving cream and spicy cologne that never left him but dissipated to nothing whenever he went away.

Lionel stood there looking at her for a second and then put the girls into the car and got behind the steering wheel.

Halfway to the house, he tried speaking again.

"Why do you come meet me, if you know you don't like it? I can get a driver like some of the other guys."

Request a driver? Like the other guys? None of those guys were happily married. Not one of them. Their wives were either too busy being too busy for their husbands or too angry being angry about their upcoming divorces. The good, happy wives were team players, pictures of perfection, the trophies the players retrieved happily upon their return home like soldiers back from war. They weren't too busy or too angry, they were just there—at the airport, at the game, waiting with open arms, their cups running over.

But no one had cared about Tasha's open arms, and now her pot was boiling over.

"You want to request a driver? Look, I came to the airport because I'm your damn wife, but it seems you forgot that, seeing as how you haven't paid me any attention." Tasha turned to look out the window. She was too angry to put on her seat belt. "You hand me your damn bag like I'm some kind of groupie . . . and then you have the nerve to—"

"Jesus, this is exactly what I didn't want to happen. When you said you were coming to get me, I knew—" Lionel stopped and looked at his sleeping daughters in the rearview mirror.

"What? You knew what?"

"That you'd get all touchy. You always do this when you come get me from the airport."

"I always do what?"

"You always—"

"Don't tell me what I always do." She cut him off, though she had asked the question. "I'm a grown woman. I know what I do and how I do it." Tasha's voice had already been loud and now it was getting louder. "This ain't even about what I do. It's about what you don't do!"

"Can you keep your voice down? You're going to wake them up."

"Wake them up?" Tasha turned to Lionel. Her forehead was crowded with angry wrinkles. On her tired, frustrated ears, Lionel's request sounded more like an accusation. "I take care of *our* daughters all by *myself.* I don't need you or anyone else to worry about if I wake them up. They wake up when and where I choose. And if I want them up right now, then so be it!"

That must've been what Tasha wanted, because they were up, and they were crying, and later that night, when they all got back to the house, she put them to bed alone.

*   *   *

"Salt and Pepa! Finesse and Sequins! Latifah and Monie Love! We're about to be all of them." Jones was laughing, but Tamia wasn't.

She was too busy trying to remember who Finesse and Sequins were while looking at the open door of her office. She'd told Naudia too many times to close the door whenever Jones was in there and come in after ten minutes with an urgent call. Neither of those things had happened.

Jones was the firm's latest equal opportunity hire. A Howard Law School grad whose supreme understanding of the law was constantly undermined by her lack of an understanding of how to conduct herself in a law office. According to a laughing Charleston one evening over dinner, Jones had the "big/little issue" that many unpolished black females had at the firm—big mouths and little clothes. This sad stereotype stung Tamia's ears when she'd heard it, but even right now, Jones, whose full name was Da-Asia Moshanique Jones (which she insisted on having put on the nameplate on her office door), was proving him right.

"You know, I've been waiting, just waiting for this firm to finally give me a case I can sink my teeth into, something where I can help my people, you know?" Jones said, grinning.

"Know? What do you mean?"

"The case . . . with Richard Holder—the Freedom Project—us . . . We're on it together!" Jones wiggled in her seat happily. Tamia saw wide gold hoop earrings peek out from beneath the mop of wet and wavy curls Jones had braided to her scalp.

"We're what? Partners? Who told you that? Pelst?" Tamia kicked the inside of her desk.

"Yup! Aren't you excited? I mean, what are the odds

that the only black girls on the team get to work together? I needed a break from those white folks anyway! Always being all nosy. I know my job. How to do
what I do and they want to know everything other than
that—where I live, who I date, what I eat. Damn. No, I
don't want to eat no damn hummus. I ain't no bird.
Know what I mean?"

"Yes," Tamia agreed, nervously watching the door.
She really did agree with what Jones was saying, but
couldn't understand why she had to be so loud saying it
or what made her think it was cool to say it at work in
the first place. Luckily, Naudia, who Tamia was sure
could now hear Jones's speech, finally came and closed
the door.

"We can do this together and do it right. Blow everyone away. I'm ready. Know what I'm sayin'? Know
what I mean?!"

Tamia nodded her head in agreement, but she really
didn't "know what" Jones was "saying."

Class for Classy Ladies

Being a unique individual is admirable, but being an undisputed ignoramus is unacceptable. To avoid being identified as the latter in any classy situation that requires class action, it's necessary for every classy girl to know . . . how to act. Yes, we love Macy Gray, but some situations call for her to comb the dome, and while Mary J. Blige is our girl, even she had the good sense to get those tattoos covered up. Bluntly, unless you ARE prepared to be locked out and led away, don't confuse being yourself with being unprepared. It just might make the difference between making your dream a reality, or going back to bed for a lifetime of nightmares.

25 Classy-Girl Rules of Class Action

1. *Know when and where to wear flip-flops. Never to work. Always to the beach.*
2. *Don't talk on cell phones at the dinner table, in a church, or on the train.*
3. *Never get too drunk or too full. Know when to back away from the table or bar.*
4. *Don't pop your gum or blow bubbles—unless you're playing a stripper in a movie.*
5. *Wipe your sweat off the gym equipment after use.*
6. *Know who the baby's daddy is. . . . And if you don't, avoid going on* Maury *to find out.*
7. *Don't hand the checkout girl your credit card when you know you've reached your limit . . . and follow it up with another card that will be declined.*
8. *Don't get tattoos on any part of your body that*

might sag after menopause, or usually requires jewelry—the neck.

9. *Own a nice set of matching luggage—never travel with plastic bags.*

10. *Have a bank account—stay out of the check-cashing place.*

11. *Don't get loud at work or with your boss; if it's that bad, quit.*

12. *Don't wear anything to the office that requires choreographed movement, a thong, a strapless bra, no bra, or pasties.*

13. *Avoid wearing too much perfume or makeup that bleeds onto your teeth or clothing.*

14. *Don't litter.*

15. *Don't wear platform shoes to work, unless the job includes a stage.*

16. *Don't kiss and tell, or leave video footage of the encounter—Eve and Fantasia discovered this the hard way.*

17. *Don't sit down at a dinner table if you can't afford the 20 percent tip.*

18. *Don't leave traces of baby powder, deodorant, hair gel, or body oil on your body at any time—rub it in, or get it off.*

19. *Don't have more than two colors on your fingernails at one time, or try too hard to match the polish to your outfit.*

20. *Don't have fingernails that are longer than your fingers and/or a bar of soap.*

21. *Don't have sex with anyone for any reason other than having sex—intimate relations don't lead to marital relationships.*

22. *Always know the way home and have a way to get there.*

23. *Perform community service.*

24. *Don't discuss personal matters at work. No one needs to know about your breakup.*
25. *Don't wear your cell phone earpiece unless you are engaging in a conversation and not sitting near someone who can hear it.*

"It's like this woman wants me dead, or worse, fired," Tamia complained, walking behind Charleston as they entered the Blue Note, one of the city's oldest and most respected jazz clubs. Nathaniel, Charleston's college roommate and fraternity brother, who'd never completed a day's work on anyone's payroll since they'd graduated, was celebrating the release of his first jazz album and invited the pair out for a toast with his latest dinner date, Ava.

"You can't take Phaedra that personally. She wants everyone dead . . . and fired. Being on top is what drives her." Charleston was giving his comfy grin and looking at Tamia like she was an insect. He'd dated a lot of beautiful women, but Tamia, with her long, thick hair and classic beauty, was among the top ten. Plus, he always reasoned, she had a good upbringing and brains. He always loved pretty girls, but wanted the one on his arm to be the triple threat that made them the perfect pair. Tamia, he thought, even with her naive ways, fit the bill. "Look, you want me to be honest?"

"Yes."

"The case is a dog. And your partner is even worse. You can't win even if you win."

"What do you mean?" Tamia stopped him.

"It's nigger work. The two black women at the firm, one who's up for partner soon and another who won't make it three years, get the nigger case to keep them nigger busy. Basically, if you lose, they'll say they can't give you the bigger cases because you messed this one up, and, Lord, if you win . . ." He paused.

"What?" Tamia's chest tightened.

"Then you'll get all the nigger cases from now until infinity. And everyone will say it's a good thing, great, you're doing service for your people, but the only place that can lead to is an office somewhere in Brooklyn.

Six figures tops. You'll go from making headlines to hoping some community rag will give you ad space."

Tamia's mouth was hanging open. Everything she'd worked for, everything she'd sacrificed was ablaze in a tinker house in her mind.

"I knew this was a trap. I have to get out of it!"

"No way out, babe. You override Phaedra and they'll say you're not a team player."

"So what would you do?"

"I'd take the loss and work my way back up. Pray for the best." Charleston shrugged. He felt his phone vibrating in his pocket.

"You're saying lose the case? On purpose?"

"No, babe. I'm saying survive."

"Oh no," Tamia said, still processing Charleston's words as he started to walk again. "I just wish I knew why she's all over me like this."

"Buck up, grasshopper," Charleston said, navigating toward Nathaniel, who was standing up and waving toward them. "Don't let crazy Phae get you down."

"Did you just call her Phae?"

After feeding, clothing, and forcing to sleep her two little daughters, who seemed to want to have nothing to do with her and everything to do with their father, Tasha slid on her cutest boy shorts and sauntered, ever so casually, between her husband and his laser focus on *Sportscenter.* After the fight in the car, and a wordless dinner, she didn't want to come on too strong, but certainly wanted to get it on. The little shorts, hot pink and so tight they almost looked like swimming bottoms, were the perfect mix of "I'm just walking around doing housework" and "come and get it!" She really just wanted his attention, and even if he was still upset about the fight earlier, she knew he had to be missing her attention just the same.

She was hoping for a night of mind-erasing sex that could release her from the tension that was burying her, and decided that maybe it would be better not to tell Lionel, who began palming her backside as soon as she walked by, about the little platinum hair she'd plucked. There was no sense talking about getting old with the one person she wanted to see her as young, vivacious, and supple. Yes, he'd seen the stretch marks and hardened nipples that were delivered with the babies, and lifted without a word the little sack that formed atop her once taut abs, which, contrary to what any personal trainer told her, wouldn't return with any amount of crunches or sit-ups. But even with all of this, he was still grabbing at her and whispering things like "You trying to walk past Big Daddy with those shorts on?" as if they weren't married and two children in. And Tasha never wanted that to change.

Sucking in her sack and poking out her back, she responded nonchalantly, "Who, me? I'm just cleaning up." She giggled but still found her way to bend over his knee. It wasn't the most appropriate position to send up a prayer of thanks, but she did, and vowed to hide away what she was thinking, so she could feel something better. And she might have been able to keep this up had Lionel been able to keep himself up. Five minutes into the lovemaking, Big Daddy wasn't so big anymore.

Tasha wasn't the only 3T who was hiding something. On the fourth floor of her Harlem habitat, Troy was on her knees, stacking a brand-new pair of $1,500 silver Jimmy Choo water-snake pumps behind an older brand-new pair of $1,500 black Jimmy Choo water-snake pumps. Natural black curls sticking to her sweaty forehead, she was moving fast like she was hiding someone else's Christmas present, but Kyle was the only someone else who lived in the brownstone, and he had no clue who Jimmy Choo was or that his wife had over $50K worth of his shoes. And that wasn't the only thing stuffed in the back of Troy's closet.

"What are you doing?" Kyle asked, walking into the room and seeing Troy's backside and feet poking out of the closet. He'd heard rustling, what sounded like little squirrels burrowing in the walls, as he walked up the stairs.

"What?" Troy's response was fast and breathy. Something slammed and in a second she was on her feet with the closet door closed.

Kyle bent toward her to look at the door before repeating his question.

"I was just praying."

"In the closet?"

"Yeah . . ." Troy turned and looked at the closet coyly. "Praying for my clothes." She was trying to sound confident to stop Kyle from going over and opening the closet door. She felt bad, though, and reminded herself that she would need to say two prayers before bed now—one for buying the shoes (and the scarf and purse she'd already hid) and another for lying to her husband. Nervous, Troy laughed and went over to kiss Kyle on the cheek. She wouldn't and couldn't tell him all she had within that covered sliver of space. In fact, she didn't know how. The pretty little things she'd been pushing and pressing in there had come from so many places she'd loved long before she even met Kyle and she wouldn't know where to start. There was only "why?" And even that escaped Troy's knowledge.

"Oh, you're kissing me now?" Kyle said, his voice quickly turning from concern to passion. He slid his arms around Troy's waist, grabbing her buttocks. After they'd gotten married and Troy stopped working, she'd put on an extra ten pounds that he loved. A Southern gent, he liked the feeling of really holding his woman and knowing she wouldn't back away. But she did.

When Troy felt Kyle's penis hardening on her navel, she remembered the silver ring, the incubus, and the succubus, and jumped back.

"What did you come up here for? I thought you were in your study, memorizing your sermon for next week." Troy wasn't really sure about this, but that was usually where Kyle was, and that was usually what he was doing. The sturdy penis and thoughts of the sex demons who Troy believed were no doubt running free in her bedroom at that very moment made her want to be alone again so she could look at her pretty things.

"Oh," Kyle said, slapping himself on the forehead playfully. "I almost forgot. Lucy's downstairs."

"Lucy?" Troy repeated, with the ridiculous prospect of Kyle's claim laced in her tone.

"Yeah, your crazy grandmother, with her crazy dog." Kyle didn't usually label people in such a way, but Lucy and her toothless dog kept his temperance teetering.

"She's downstairs?" Troy jetted to the window and there it was, Lucy's antique white Rolls stopped in front of the brownstone, taking up half the street. Paul, her driver, was leaning against the door. "But she never comes here. She never comes to . . . Harlem."

Troy was pushing her hair back and pulling off her clothes. A new top and jeans; no, a dress; no, a purple silken lounge set was on the bed and then on her—that quickly.

"Is the house clean?" she asked.

"Clean?" Kyle replied. "It's always clean. You know we—"

"Is it *really* clean? You know what I mean!"

The newlyweds looked at each other to find understanding. As they grew older, this would turn into a telepathic ability to know what the other was thinking, but now the new groom was just too slow. Before he could remind his wife that they hadn't dusted in a few weeks, there was a call from the bottom of the steps. It was purposefully weak and highly dramatic, little more than a whisper with a Southern drawl, from a woman who hadn't lived a day in the South.

"Troy Helene, darling, you really must dust this . . . home. Ms. Pearl is liable to get a sickness in here . . . typhoid . . . or . . . swine flu." Her voice dragged and it was clear she was looking at things, frowning and certainly not touching. "Hell, *I* might get a sickness in here."

Throughout dinner, Charleston and Nathaniel kept the women laughing and the stories coming. Leaning back carefree and as pompous as princes, they'd loosened their Zenga ties and shoved platinum and mother-of-pearl cuff links into their pockets. They'd commandeered the most expensive bottle of scotch from the bar and took turns demanding ownership of the tab. How important they were and how much money they had was apparent to anyone walking past the table. It was black yuppie heaven and these two were singing like angels in the choir.

"Honestly, though, I told him, and I swear this is what I told that white boy, 'I don't care how many units this shit moves, I have the money,'" Nathaniel said coolly as he continued a rant about how he was about to be the next big thing in jazz and the world had better watch out for him. According to Charleston, Nathaniel, who was apparently a saxophone player, hadn't even played

in the band in college. But this was his new thing. He
was an artist, a jazz musician, and he'd poured his entire self into it—even picking up a few drug habits to
prove his dedication. "I want the fame," he went on.
"Just get me on the networks!" Nathaniel laughed a little louder than his joke called for. He was drunk and
Tamia had noticed two dinner dates ago that when he
got drunk he got louder and more obnoxious. While
Nathaniel was what the 3Ts called a beach ball,[9] he
had the nerve to be handsome anyway. His brown skin
was without defect. And like Charleston, he had perfect teeth and his grooming was impeccable. When
Tamia met him at some rapper's film premiere in
Chelsea, and the two shook hands for the first and last
time (it was more traditional to hug and trade dry
kisses), she'd noticed how soft and moist his palms
were. Like a newborn baby's, they felt as if he'd just
walked right out of a hospital nursery that very day. He
then whispered in her ear that she should only call him
by his full name—not Nate or Nathan. He claimed he
was the fifth Nathaniel Cecil in a line of Burris men
that predated the Civil War and it would be a shame to
dishonor this history, but really it was just because he
liked the way the formal version sounded. "Nathaniel"
was the perfect accessory. It matched his ascots, argyle
sweaters, and penny loafers.

   "You're so funny, sweetie," chimed Ava, who was smiling beside Nathaniel. Thus far, Tamia had met three of
his women, but Ava seemed to be sticking around. She
was as skinny and dainty as a dove feather. Her skin
was the color of the inside of a banana peel and there
was not a trace of a crinkle in a strand of her shoulder-
length auburn hair. It took Tamia hours of painstaking

---

[9] Beach ball: a male who has an especially round torso with im-
possibly long and skinny limbs.

pressing and perming to get hers right, and she envied just looking at Ava's slick roots. *She must be mixed,* Tamia thought, *mixed with something somewhere in her family.*

Charleston said Ava was a model, but Tamia thought she hadn't even sounded that smart. Not a day over twenty-three, she mostly agreed with what Nathaniel had to say and laughed at his jokes before he'd reached the punch line.

"I told that white boy he can keep my check. Shit, set them on fire if he wants," Nathaniel went on.

"Man, you're just talking shit now, just like at school when we pledged K-A-Psi. You know you didn't say that," Charleston insisted. "And if you don't want the $50 you're gonna make selling iTunes to me and your mama, you can send it to me. I can use it to get a haircut." Charleston rolled his hand over his head and shimmied dapperly.

"How about I cut out the middleman and just send the check directly to your mama? Pay my child support," Nathaniel jabbed and they all laughed. Unlike Charleston, he'd come from big money. His great-grandfather once sold insurance in Brooklyn, and when the business went belly up during the Depression, he spent his life savings on a dilapidated building in Greenwich Village. Only it was the '30s then and everyone thought he was crazy. The Village wasn't the big hot spot just yet. Drugs were everywhere and in just thirty years hippies would be sleeping in the streets. However, after fixing up and renting out units in the property for five decades, his son sold it and purchased another dilapidated building in midtown during the recession in the '80s. The salesman said he would need at least $5 million to fix it up in order to make any profit from renting office space. Nathaniel's grandfather spent $1 million and turned it into an indoor parking facility. Now Nathaniel's father was selling the spots for $275K a piece. The family would keep 50 percent to stay in control.

Tamia was adding up how much Nathaniel's family was making off of all the spots when she felt the table vibrating beneath her right elbow. She looked down to see that Charleston's phone was aglow and before he snatched it from the table and excused himself, she saw as clear as black lettering on a white sheet of paper the word "Phae." Before it made any sense and registered in her head in a way that would make it possible to recall when she later realized that he'd stopped paying her mortgage, Charleston was gone from the table and Tamia was looking over her shoulder.

As she listened to more about the CD and even more about Nathaniel's pending fame, time seemed to be standing still and moving fast as hell at the same time. Forever, that's how long it felt that Charleston had been away from the table. And Tamia was fighting hard with herself not to care when Ava came up with a thought of her own.

"Where's Charleston?" Ava asked. "He's been gone for a long time."

Tamia took the last sip of the third glass of wine she'd ordered to escape tasting the leathery scotch and was about to get up to see what was taking Charleston so long when he suddenly reappeared and slid back into his seat. As poised as a politician, he put his hand on Tamia's knee and kissed her on the cheek.

"Sorry that took so long. It was the office," he said in a way that left absolutely no space for Tamia to ever quiz him about what she'd seen on the phone.

"Why am I in Harlem, Troy Helene?" Lucy asked. Troy stared at her grandmother from across the mahogany table in the center of her sitting room. She didn't know why Lucy had ended up in Harlem, in her sitting room, in the Queen Anne armchair she'd purchased as a wedding gift. Ms. Pearl, Lucy's blind, deaf, and toothless bichon frise, whose once puffy white coat was now a thin, dull silver, was being stroked on Lucy's lap as she looked on with equal disgust at Troy. A two-time Westminster Best in Show, Lucy'd had the dog for as long as Troy had been alive and the two went everywhere together. Now there was a family joke that the next destination might be the pearly gates. Lucy had already purchased a plot beside hers for the dog; on the other side was Lucy's dead, rich, white husband.

Troy wanted to break the stare but had no clue as to how to answer the question. Lucy never came to Harlem—rarely crossed any of the bridges to leave Manhattan, for that matter—so even a visit to her granddaughter's home had to come with great reason.

"Brunch, Troy Helene. We were to have brunch at the Friars' Club," Lucy said sharply. As she stroked the dog, the dim light in the sitting room picked up all of the cuts in the seven-carat canary diamond she wore on her ring finger. Big and beautiful, the ring made Lucy's hand look smaller than it already was, which was why she loved it so. Lucy was a frail woman, whose white skin was as fair as fresh farm milk. Up close, the blue veins on her wrists and hands could be seen. And while anyone sitting in that living room would swear she was white, Lucy's mother and grandmother were each a shade darker than she—each, like Lucy, had married and had children with white men. The last in this line of tradition was Lucy's only daughter, Mary Elizabeth— Troy's mother—whose conception marked the end of Lucy's passing. But years ago, it came out that the white man Troy knew as her grandfather all of her life was no kin to her. Mary Elizabeth's father was a jazz musician. This revelation sent all three of the Smith women to therapy.

"Oh, brunch," Troy remembered, falling back on the couch. She saw Kyle standing in the hallway beside the chair where Lucy was sitting. He jokingly shook his hand at Troy and she sat back up. She was supposed to meet Lucy for brunch after her meeting with the Virtuous Women—well, it was really lunch, but Lucy hated that word, said it made her sound too middle American. "I totally forgot. My meeting ran over and then I . . ." Troy remembered that Kyle was standing in the hallway and thought it was best not to finish the rundown of where she'd been.

"Water, son. Can you please get my Pearl some water?" Lucy said so softly it was clear she knew Kyle was standing on the other side of the wall beside her.

"Yes, ma'am," Kyle answered quickly, walking into the room and getting the dog before disappearing into the kitchen.

"Good, they'll be gone for a while," Lucy said. "There's no way Ms. Pearl will drink a teaspoon of water in this . . . this"—she looked around at what Troy had thought was a nicely decorated room like it was a jail cell before finishing—"this place."

"I'm sorry I forgot about brunch," Troy went on. "I really wanted to go, but I had a bad day and just lost track of time, I guess."

"What happened?" Lucy got up from the Queen Anne and went to sit beside her granddaughter on the couch. The air in the room was interrupted by Chanel No. 5 as she moved.

"Nothing . . . everything." Troy tried to relax. Lucy's haughty disposition really wasn't as scary to Troy as it was to everyone else. For a long time in Troy's life, this woman, with all of her flaws, had been her best friend,

her only confidante, who took care of her as any crazy
and loving grandmother would. "I don't know, Lucy."

"I had Paul drive by that church, saw those women
there," Lucy said. Her voice was plump with contro-
versy. A retired socialite who now witnessed a new
kind of drama as she sat on philanthropic boards of
anything popular in the city, Lucy knew how to seek
and savor a matter in need of attention. "That . . . that
Myrtle Glover character . . . she was looking quite
sour."

"Oh, don't mind Sister Glover. She just has her way.
She always has." Troy remembered the near lap dance
Myrtle had given Kyle when she got the Holy Ghost
the first time Troy visited the church.

"A *way?*" Lucy repeated. "Isn't that the one who put
on like a madwoman before you and Kyle got married?
The one who broke the vase during your wedding ceremony and wore red nail polish?" Here, shining like a
star, was one of Lucy's best qualities—no matter how
small, she never forgot the dirty details.

"Now, that was a mistake. She apologized. And, yes,
she did have a thing for Kyle before I came into his
life, but who wouldn't? My husband is perfect."

"Ma cherie." Lucy stroked Troy's hair like she was a
hopeless puppy. "No woman in the history of womankind
has ever only *had* a thing for a man in the past. Either she
has a thing for him or not. Women don't get over good
men. Too few of them to go around. I tried to tell your
mother about that before she left your father . . . again,"
she added, referring to Troy's parents, who were in the
middle of their second bitter divorce. Troy hadn't seen
either of them much since she'd gotten married. When
they were together, they were alive and unhappy; when
they were apart, they were near dead, but fair.

"Sister Glover let go of the idea of getting with Kyle,

Lucy," Troy said confidently. "She's a good Christian woman. She even taught me how to be a better Christian woman . . . a better Christian wife." After Troy and Kyle had gotten engaged and Troy officially joined First Baptist, Myrtle volunteered to be her spiritual advisor and mentor in the church. Nervous about being attacked by other women for snagging the pastor, Troy thought it was the sweetest suggestion. While she'd been raised *in* the church, she wasn't exactly *of* any church. For her, church was more of a social occasion where she got to meet the right people and sit in the right pews. It was more of a lesson in power and privilege than piety and prayer. Myrtle had changed all of that for her. Showed her the right way to Jesus. And Troy was grateful.

As if she was reading her dippy granddaughter's thoughts, Lucy puckered her brow and plucked Troy upside her forehead.

"Ouch, Lucy!"

"How is someone who *isn't* a wife going to teach you to be a better wife?" Lucy asked. "Seems she has enough on her plate, trying to find what you have . . . unless she *still* wants what you have."

"Oh, Lucy." Troy laughed like she hadn't heard a word her grandmother said. "Look at you! You know God doesn't tolerate a gossip." She shook her finger as a warning.

"He also doesn't like fools."

"Who said anything about Sister Glover being a fool?"

"I didn't say anything about *that* woman. I don't even know *that* woman. I can only speak about my own."

"Lucy, did you just imply that I'm a fool?"

"I'm just saying, watch yourself, ma cherie. I know you think that because you're in the church, you left the devil outside, but he knows how to open doors, too.

I should know. You watch what those people are putting in your head, and you watch that woman."

"Don't worry about me," Troy said as Kyle came back into the sitting room with Ms. Pearl in his arms. "See"—Troy got up and stood next to Kyle—"my man is right here." She kissed Kyle on the cheek and he leaned into her.

"The dog wouldn't drink a thing," Kyle admitted, handing Ms. Pearl back to Lucy.

"I know, darling."

"You staying for dinner?" Kyle asked. "I made some pork chops . . . mashed potatoes." He was the assigned cook of the house. Troy had tried, without success, to find her way in the kitchen after they'd gotten married, but mostly things had gotten burned.

After Lucy turned down the chops and retrieved her purse, Troy insisted on walking her to the car. While Lucy was nosy and calculating, Troy felt like she was exhaling the entire time she was talking to the old woman with old ways. Troy complained that she doubted everything Lucy was saying, but what she was hiding from herself was that what Lucy said was what Troy actually felt.

"There was another matter," Lucy started as Paul opened her car door, "I hoped to chat about."

"What is it?" Troy asked.

"Nothing big. Just that Mr. Hamilton expressed that he had to put more money into your account."

"Oh, Lucy, I—"

"No matter." Lucy grabbed Troy's arm to stop her. "I don't need you to explain. We don't talk about money. It was just a matter of me signing off. See, after you got married, you said you didn't want any more money put into your account, so I told Mr. Hamilton to leave just a bit of change in case of an emergency. Well, as the emergency money, which he said was $50K, ran out last month, he put in another amount, and now there's only $5K left. You need some more?"

"I—"

"If you need money, just tell me. That's what it's for." She handed Ms. Pearl to Paul. "That's what all of my sacrificing was for. There's no sense in you living . . . on a budget."

"There's no budget. Kyle has money." Troy was ashamed. Yes, Kyle had money, but her habit had gone past anything that he wouldn't notice or would allow. And as his wife, she'd agreed to living within the means he could provide. She didn't want Kyle to feel intimidated by her family's money and as Myrtle insisted, she wanted him to feel like a man. "I don't need any money, Lucy. You can tell Mr. Hamilton to stop the deposits."

"Are you sure, dear?"

Troy kissed her grandmother on the cheek and helped her into the car.

"I love you, Grandma," she said.

"Lucy," the old woman said, full of dignity and humor. "The name is Lucy."

Someone had paid the bill. The only thing Tamia was sure of and glad about was that it hadn't been her. And judging from the fact that Ava only seemed to have lip gloss and a mirror (which she reached for whenever Nathaniel looked away) in her sparkling Judith Leiber disco-ball clutch, it hadn't been her either.

"Well, frat, I have to be honest," Nathaniel started, leaning into the table. "I didn't just call you about the CD." He reached for Ava's hand and suddenly the girl felt little cold fish jumping around in her veins.

While Tamia was still thinking about the name on Charleston's phone and how long he'd been away from the table, she noticed how quickly Ava's disposition changed. She was glowing like nothing from her past mattered that second.

"What's up?" Charleston asked.

"I . . . Ava and I . . . we're about to get married."

"What?!" Simultaneously, Tamia and Charleston's attention went from how to ask about the phone call and how to avoid answering anything about it to Nathaniel and Ava, who were now entangled like a lopsided pretzel.

"Yes." Ava smiled big and clicked the disco-ball clutch open again.

"Yeah, baby, you can show them the ring now," Nathaniel advised. "Man, I made her take the thing off so we could surprise you. It was like taking a credit card away from my mother."

"Married?" Charleston asked, looking at his friend.

From the gleaming, gem-covered sphere, Ava pulled the most perfect and precious emerald-cut diamond ring Tamia had ever seen. It was so big, so bright, Ava didn't even have to push her hand across the table once she'd put it on. Tamia could see the entire thing. No need for questions. It was a Harry Winston. Baguettes on either side of the stone. A platinum band. Flawless on every surface. The kind of ring little girls dreamed of and big boys were proud to purchase. It said something about both of them.

Ava was dancing in her seat, moving the ring from Tamia to Charleston and then back again.

"Yeah, man," Nathaniel said proudly. "I figured I'm a grown man—time for grown-up things."

"Guess so." Charleston's voice was stacked with trepidation for his friend's decision and everyone at the table, except for Ava and the dancing fish in her veins, could hear it.

While Tamia shared Charleston's anxiety, her uneasiness came from a different perspective. Knowing everything she did about Nathaniel made the announcement more than predictable. He was rich, successful, and entitled, and all the men she knew like him, including her own father, married at a certain time in their lives and married certain kinds of women. Her father, like his father and most of the men in her family, married right after law school. He'd met her mother two weeks after getting news that he'd passed the bar exam. She was celebrating the same achievement, had a similar background, knew all of the same people, and came from a good family. They were engaged in less than a year.

Tamia had seen this story repeated so many times that it seemed that if any woman with the same credentials as her mother stuck around longer than that, either she was a fool for waiting or he was a fool who was never getting married. Those kinds of men made fast, studied decisions based on high-society law and the necessity to remain a part of it. Now Ava, who seemed to have nothing in common with Nathaniel and his upbringing, and knew nothing about any of the circles Charleston and Nathaniel chatted about over dinner, presented a different kind of woman, whom more of the men in Nathaniel's position were now marrying. She was beautiful. Not just pretty. Not just lovely. Beautiful. Model beautiful. *Who cares what she has to say* beautiful. Having given up on competing with the women in their circles they now labeled "independent" like it was a curse, the men cared little about where these new breathtaking beauties were from or where they were going. They simply drew up prenuptial agreements and put a ring on it. He'd have an attractive wife, and thus attractive children, and by the time she'd gotten tired of his cheating or had an affair of her own, her looks would be fading and he would need a replacement anyway.

Tamia hated to believe this circle of selfish, predictable decision making, but she knew it was more true than false. And while she knew that Nathaniel's decision had nothing to do with her, she had to consider what it would mean for her in the future.

More out of duty than desire, Charleston ordered the best bottle of champagne for his friend and his new fiancée. They toasted and, a true sport, Charleston gave a speech as if he'd been practicing it for years. Ava was in tears, smiling and shaking her head in awe at Charleston's well wishes before she returned to her mirror for a lip-gloss retouch. This was everything she'd always wanted, and she had the face in the mirror to thank for it all. She was never going back to Memphis, not ever.

"So, what about you guys?" Nathaniel asked, putting his arm around Ava like they'd been married for twenty years. "When are you two going to get married?"

Charleston's eyes narrowed on his friend. Nathaniel knew better than to do that. It was against every man code they'd ever learned. Even mentioning the idea of marriage to another man's woman was grounds for dismissal. But Charleston knew what his old friend was up to. It was simple. If Nathaniel was going to take the chain and walk into the boneyard, he didn't want to do it alone. He wanted to take Charleston with him.

"Married? You know I don't believe in that. It just doesn't work today. It can't . . . I mean, not for me," Charleston said to burn Nathaniel's bridge. Really, he knew it was coming. He'd been a player for a long time, but it couldn't last much longer or he would risk being labeled gay or gauche.

"Ah, you know what they say—a man isn't taken seriously until he's married," Nathaniel said. "You have to do it to stay on the right side of that staircase. Or people will start to question you." He held out his hand all limp to imitate a stereotypical gay gesture.

"Please. No one will question my manhood. If they even think they should, they need only ask their wives how I'm rolling." Charleston gave a stiff punch toward the center of the table and he and Nathaniel laughed.

"Really?" Tamia asked, surprised at his brashness.

"Oh, don't get all serious," Charleston said. "We're just playing around."

"What about you, Tamia," Ava started, "do you want to get married?"

The question stung like a hot comb at the nape of Tamia's neck. While Ava wasn't her girlfriend, she had to know that in addition to the man law about questions concerning marriage, no woman should ever ask another woman how she feels about marriage in front of the man she's dating. It could and would only cause conflict. Because no matter how he felt about the topic, he'd immediately think the woman was a tramp if she said she didn't believe in marriage or was trying to manipulate him down the aisle if she said yes. Tamia couldn't win.

"Well . . . I . . . uh." She looked at her wineglass and then the champagne glass. Both were empty, so she couldn't take a sip and use the time to think. "I do want to get married," she said finally and immediately felt Charleston tense up beside her, "but not right now." She played both sides—law school was paying off.

Charleston's exhale was audible. His body seemed to melt in relief at the clause. He even put his arm around Tamia in approval. And while this was supposed to give her comfort, really she looked at the arm like the alien shelter it was. It meant so many things she hadn't wanted to think about. To consider.

Ten minutes later, Charleston's arm was still around Tamia as they rode up Sixth Avenue in the back of the Bentley. Charleston had been talking about Nathaniel and Ava since they'd gotten in the car, but Tamia was doing little more than nodding and agreeing. She was still thinking about the conversation in the restaurant. Charleston didn't want to get married. Not ever. Charleston was happy and he didn't want to get married. Not ever. It was becoming a poem.

"I'm doing that Negro's prenup," Charleston said. "It's gonna be airtight—like a virgin's legs in a fat man's bed. She won't get a dime."

"Why can't you just be happy for them?" Tamia asked.

"I am happy my man is getting married. One less hand in the pie. I'm very happy. And I'll be even happier when I finish writing that prenup."

"Oh, Lord." Tamia moved away from Charleston.

"What's wrong with you?"

"I'm just like, how could you talk about ending a marriage that hasn't even started? They're in love. That's what's important. Not when and if they split up—and who's to say that will even happen?" Tamia knew she sounded ridiculous (a betting woman would give Nathaniel and Ava three years tops—five if she had a baby once she realized he was cheating), but something in her needed to hear and believe what she was saying. Sometimes it seemed like everyone she knew who was getting married seemed more concerned about the end than the beginning.

"What is this? Are you still upset about that case?"

"The case?" Tamia looked at him. "No, it's not about the case. It's just . . . I didn't know you didn't believe in marriage. That you didn't want to get married."

"I was trying to get Nathaniel off of me. Of course I believe in marriage." Charleston's cell phone vibrated and he took it out and dismissed the call before texting a message. "I just don't see it for myself. Especially not right now. I have a lot going on. I would think you would understand that. We're in the same position."

"Yeah, I think that's something I should've known. That you should've told me." She kept thinking about all those foolish women who sat around for years with the man who was never going to pop the question.

"Look, if it makes you feel any better, Tamia, I'm not going to say that I'm never going to get married. I'm just not getting married right now."

"Hmph." Tamia shrugged her shoulders. She wasn't sure what kind of response she was supposed to give to this revelation. Really, Charleston was saying nothing new that he hadn't already said at the table. He was just saying it in a different way to a different audience. He was speaking to his jury. It was an old trick she'd learned in law school.

The phone was vibrating again when the car pulled around the drive at Trump Towers. There was another dismissal and text message.

When Curtis opened Tamia's door, she thought she felt Charleston moving along out of the car behind her, but he only pulled her arm and kissed her on the cheek.

"What's that for?" she asked, confused.

"I'm not coming up." His phone was in his hand and he was typing another message. "I have to go back to the office. Looks like it's going to be a late night."

"But it's already after nine and we're both a little tipsy," Tamia tried. "You should just come up."

"What's all this from a woman who needed her space just hours ago?" Charleston chuckled. "Look, just do your thing and I'll see you in the 'morrows. Okay? I'll send the car in the morning."

The "okay" was more of a send-off than a question. It neither needed nor required conversation. Charleston just kissed Tamia on the cheek again and she got up and out of the car and within seconds the luxurious tank was merging into the yellow ribbon of taxi cabs in front of the building.

Tamia stood there, icy. Her mind was a Dumpster and everything from the car, the dinner, the job was being tossed around in it like month-old Chinese food. Something was rotten and the smell was growing stronger by the second.

"Shall we call the elevator for you, Ms. Dinkins?" Bancroft questioned, standing beside her in his night coat and hat.

"Yes—no," Tamia answered. "Let's try a cab. I need to go by my office."

"So?" Tasha posed. She was sitting beside Tamia at the 3Ts' latest New York find, Azya. A swanky bar that specialized in fine wine and decadent chocolate, it was a depressed woman's dream. The only thing missing was an ice cream station and male strippers.

"So, he wasn't there," Tamia revealed. "I waited at the office for an hour. He never came. He lied."

"So, he lied. All men lie. You know that." Tasha forged a diabolical laugh but really her mind wasn't on Tamia's lying man, but rather the man she'd left lying in bed to come meet Tamia.

"I guess you're right." Tamia sighed. In addition to the wine she'd had earlier at the Blue Note, she was sipping on her third glass of Malbec. It was dark, peppery, complicated, all of the things she'd felt when she'd gone back to the office to see if Charleston was really returning to do work, as he'd said. "I don't know why he would lie to me . . . about something so small. He could've just kicked me out of the car and left. That would've been fine."

"Whatever, Tamia. You can cash that bad check at someone else's bank, because I know you better than that," Tasha teased. "There's no way that man would've gotten you out of that car without either hurting your feelings or getting his own feelings hurt. Two reasons men lie—to avoid tears or an argument."

As an unsteady Tamia considered this, Tasha looked over at a svelte twenty-something strawberry blonde, dressed in an all-black bodysuit, who was being hit on by a man who had to be twice her age and half as attractive. While the woman seemed disinterested at first, the man whispered something in her ear that made her perk up and giggle girlishly. The man stepped in and leered at her knowingly, like a baby pig he was about to dissect. He'd gotten in. Just that fast.

"Anyway, the real problem isn't that he lied or what he was lying about. It's what made you carry your drunk ass over to your office to spy on him," Tasha said, still watching the new couple as the man leaned his wineglass to the woman's lips so she could have a sip. "Weren't you the one saying you wanted space? What happened to you giving him space anyway?"

"I know. I know. And I do want space. I did want space."

"So why the sudden change? How do you go from wanting space one minute to stalking the office at nine o'clock at night and dragging me out of my bed at ten?"

"I know, girl, and thanks for coming," Tamia said. Her voice was so heavy it seemed to draw her head toward the bar top. "You didn't have to drive an hour out here, but you did it for your girl!"

"No biggie. I couldn't leave my girl hanging. You sounded like you were on your way to jump off the Brooklyn Bridge and I knew Troy couldn't get out of her prayer closet long enough to save you," Tasha said dutifully. "There wasn't a whole bunch going on at the house anyway . . . nothing really."

"You know what he said at dinner? He said he doesn't want to get married. That he doesn't even believe in it. What in the hell is that?" Tamia wasn't looking at Tasha. Her mind was somewhere in space, churning around in her disbelief. In the cab on the way to the office, she'd kept thinking about Ava and how snuggly and happy she seemed.

"So, you hardly like Charleston. Why do you even care?"

The numbing mix of French techno and hip-hop was replaced by a disco track, and the man and woman began to sway side to side together, just a few beats slower than the song. The woman's torso snaked into his. He slid his hand around her neck forcefully. In a second her neck went from pale to pink.

"Damn!" Tasha purred, feeling tingles at the back of her own neck.

"I know! Damn!" Ignorant to the tango beside them at the bar, Tamia thought Tasha was talking to her. "I don't know what happened. I do like Charleston. He's all right. He can be demanding. He's definitely a snob. But he's also sophisticated and successful. He has everything a woman could want."

"Yeah, but is that the everything *this* woman wants?" Turned on a bit, Tasha was swaying back and forth with the couple. Tamia felt her motion and she was swaying too.

"I'm thirty-two!" Tamia hollered suddenly, snapping herself and Tasha out of the bop. Tasha looked at her. "I know I shouldn't think about it like this, but I'm thirty-two. And I'm not married, you know?"

Tasha was silent.

"No, you don't. You're married. You've been, like, married forever, so you don't understand what it's like. . . ."

"What what's like?"

"This! This!" Tamia held her open hands out over the bar like a map of her life was on her palms. "My life. I try so hard not to care. Not to think about it. Just to focus on my career. On my goals. And I'm almost there. Almost where I want to be. But I'm getting old and I guess I just don't want to lose track and wake up one day at forty and be successful . . . and single." She paused and looked at Tasha. "What if all the good men are already gone by then? What if they're already gone now?"

"So, you thought Charleston was that good man?" Tasha rolled her eyes. Charleston was no devil, but he was no angel. She'd seen him in the box at most of the Knicks games before he and Tamia started dating. Models and video vixens climbed all over him like ants on a picnic blanket dipped in sugar water. They laughed easily at his corny jokes, happily lit his cigars, and squealed pleasantly when he tapped them on their bulbous backsides to show his appreciation. Usually this kind of treatment was reserved for visiting players and owners, but the inquiring gold diggers had long ago appraised his worth. They knew what he was, and he knew what they wanted. The champagne flutes remained filled and Tasha never once saw him walk out of the box, not even to the bathroom, alone.

"No, Charleston is who he is," Tamia said. "And I know there's a barrel of women waiting for me to kick the bucket so they can be with him."

"You got that right."

"But I know he loves me. And I guess I was thinking in the back of my mind that maybe once I got to where

I wanted to be and he was ready, we'd get married. But hearing that he doesn't even want that!—I just feel like maybe I've been wasting my time."

"Ms. Lovebird, stop being your neurotic self. You think too much," Tasha said, using the 3T name Tamia was given in college. "You haven't wasted your time. The fool hooked you up with that spot at the Towers and the sex is good." She looked at Tamia for approval on her last point.

"Yeah." Tamia nodded, noticing that her wine was wearing off. "It's good."

"Right. So, beggars can't be choosers. If that was the case we'd all be happy at home." Tasha sighed. "Just get what you got and keep it moving."

"That's the whole thing," Tamia said. "There aren't a whole bunch of black, single millionaires running around Manhattan, if you haven't noticed. Not any that want to get married."

"Good point."

"What?" Tamia frowned. "You're not supposed to agree with me. You're supposed to be cheering me up!"

"I'm just saying, beyond the ball players, business-men, bad rappers, and trust-fund babies, all of which I already know, you're left with gay dudes, grandpas, and guilty divorcés."

Tamia didn't know if she should nod or shake her head in agreement, so she just sat there, feeling the weight of her friend's words.

"The worst thing," Tamia said, remembering the heavy jewel hanging from Ava's finger, "is that the ones that are getting married are looking for models and girls that are half their age. How am I supposed to compete with that? And work on my career? Doesn't that count for something? Why can't a man who wants to get married just look for something sturdy and dependable and sweet?"

"Because they call those women grandmothers." Tasha looked toward the end of the bar again to see that the couple was gone now and only the man's empty wineglass remained on the bar. She chucked a piece of chocolate into her mouth, considering what they must be doing wherever they'd gone.

"So, what's up with you? How were you able to get out of Jersey so late at—"

"Troy?" Tasha happily cut Tamia off. She'd always been the kind of friend who preferred hearing rather than sharing dish. And she'd just seen a woman who looked like Troy walking toward the front door, only she thought it couldn't be her, because they weren't at a church and the woman wasn't carrying a pail of holy water.

"Troy?" Tamia repeated when the woman walked inside and they both saw that it was indeed her.

Before Troy could get out her prayer shawl, prayer list, prayer oil, and prayer handbook to head to her prayer closet to loosen the grip of the day's sins, a determined Kyle had been standing in the doorway of their bedroom holding her shoes, purse, and cell phone. He'd seen Tamia's frantic text inviting his wife into the city for a drink, and while it just might have been the first time in the history of all of mankind that a husband insisted that his wife get out of the house and have some fun, there he was, shuffling Troy and all of her reasons not to meet her girls to the front door. "It sounds pretty serious. They need you," he was saying as he stuffed Troy into a cab, but really he was thinking that she (and, in a way, he) needed them. Maybe Troy would come back tipsy and forget her Bible at the door. Maybe. He'd be sure to shower and get out his coconut body oil . . . just in case.

"Well, for someone who didn't expect to come out, your ass sure looks fabsie,"[10] Tasha said after Troy told the other Ts of her forced departure. "Is that a Tory Burch?"

Tamia and Tasha looked hard at the navy blue silk blouse Troy was wearing. Every woman in the city had been admiring the whimsical peasant chemise for days as an ivory mannequin donned it in the window at the midtown Bloomingdale's.

Troy nodded sheepishly and thanked the bartender for her glass of Diet Coke but when she looked back at Tasha and Tamia, they were still studying the blouse.

She started, "So, Tamia, what's going—"

"Now, that damn blouse is $795." Tasha flicked one of the perfectly tailored sleeves.

Tamia nodded.

"So, it's not a big deal. Just a T. Burch. We all gotta have it. Right?" Troy tried to chuckle the attention off, but she felt like their eyes were digging into her, asking questions and forcing answers in the way that only friends' knowing eyes can. Kyle saw her clothes every day, but to him they were just articles of fabric. He had no clue as to the value or volume. But these two bystanders were runway connoisseurs. They studied fashion shows the way other humans watched football on Sunday afternoons.

"Yeah, I gotta have it, and Tamia gotta have it, and even the old Troy I used to know had to have it." Tasha paused and looked to Tamia for a cosign.

"Sure did," Tamia confirmed.

"But not," Tasha went on, "the newly saved and sanctified First Lady of First Baptist, Troy Helene Hall. I thought you were supposed to be on some kind of new Christian wife budget, cutting your parents' money

[10] Fabsie: fabulous.

off and only living on what your husband could afford—
Payless and Pay-what-nots. Now, I know he's got a little bank, but Burch? Come on. And I know that Kors
skirt anywhere. It's a spring favo!"[11]

Troy was trying so hard to come up with a lie to tell
her friends, but while she could keep her secrets, which
seemed to be tripling these days, from the rest of the
world, she couldn't keep anything from the women sitting beside her. The pressure she'd felt in her gut earlier
in the day at the meeting was twisting itself in tight
knots in her mind now. The pressure was big, was
growing so strong, she knew she had to let it out. Troy
closed her eyes, took a deep breath, and started letting
those knots loosen.

"I have the shirt in three colors—magenta, yellow,
and blue. I have every skirt Kors put out last season.
Thirty-two . . . thirty-seven pairs of shoes, and I pre-
ordered every Be&D Hobo for the summer—I haven't
even seen them yet. I spent $7,000 this afternoon in
three hours and went by my parents' place to hide some
of the stuff in my old closet." Without inhaling or looking at either of her friends, Troy reached into her purse
and pulled out her little prayer pad. "It's all there.
Everything. Every sin I need to pray for. But I can't
stop it. I can't." She finally stopped and looked at
Tamia, wiping a tear from her eye as she banged on the
bar emphatically. "I can't stop sinning."

"Whoa, Christian chica," Tasha said as she caught
Troy's arm from hitting the bar again and attracting more
attention. "No need to put us all to shame. I still have a
reputation in this city. The only sin you've committed is
wearing Tory Burch with Michael Kors. They don't go
together. Kors can only go with Kors. No mixing."

---

[11] Favo: favorite.

"Stop it, Tash," Tamia said. "Troy is serious." She broke off a bit of chocolate she was eating and gave Troy a piece. "What's going on up there in Harlem?"

"I don't know. I don't know what it is."

"Well, let's start small," Tamia said. "You said you spent $7,000 this afternoon. What made you do that?"

"I don't know," Troy answered. "It was just like most days. I was at the church and I had a meeting with the Virtuous Women, and . . ." What little relief Troy was feeling after releasing the secret she'd been hiding for months was erased once she recalled the discussion about the incubus and succubus—the demons in the bedroom.

"Oh no, not the Virtuous Women again!" Tasha rolled her eyes. She'd run into the circle the handful of times an invitation from Troy and Kyle had forced her to attend a function at the church. While their smiles were big and welcomes came by the dozen from members, she found them completely suspicious and ridiculous. Then again, she'd found everything about every church she'd ever been in suspicious and ridiculous. A Hollywood baby with Hollywood principles, growing up she'd trusted only one church—the one on the set of her mother's soap opera. Now she felt every church in the world was reading from the same silly script.

"Do you guys think sex is a sin?" Troy asked, ignoring Tasha's disgust. "Not like the sex you have with your husband, sorry, Tamia"—she stopped and patted Tamia on the shoulder sympathetically—"but like *wild* sex . . . like *wild sex*." Her voice was lowered to a whisper, though no one else in the bar was listening to her.

"Who's having wild sex?" Tasha perked up. "Somebody's having wild sex?" She squirmed around in her seat. "I knew Pastor Hall would be tapping that ass in no time flat. He doesn't look like a missionary man.

How does he like it? Downward Facing Dog or Pigeon?"

"Those are yoga poses?" Tamia asked and they all laughed.

"Don't knock it until you've tried it. So, what kind of *wild* are you talking about, Troy?"

"Everything, anything. He has a penis ring . . . and this mask . . . I don't even know where the mask came from."

"Oh, he's a fucking freak," Tasha said, laughing.

"Oh no." Troy bowed her head and began to pray.

Tamia and Tasha looked at each other.

"Troy, stop it. Just stop," Tamia said. "There's nothing wrong with what you said and you know it."

"I'm so ashamed. I'm just so ashamed!"

"Of what?" Tasha asked. "That's your husband. Shit, he was a virgin when you two got married. Can you imagine that? He's just playing out all of the frustration he lived with for years. Shoot, there's nothing wrong with a little freakiness in the bedroom. You need to be happy he feels open enough to be that way with you. There are too many husbands out there taking their freaky sides on tour—if you know what I mean."

"I just feel like maybe it's my fault. Maybe I made him this way," Troy said. "Before he met me, he was so focused on his relationship with the Lord, and so pure. Such a good man. And here I am, just corrupting his soul."

"You sound crazy," Tasha said flatly.

"Tasha, stop it!" Tamia warned.

"No, somebody needs to tell her. That sounds crazy. Non-crazy people don't say things like 'corrupt' and 'soul.' Come on. Is this a séance? Where's Whoopi?"

"Troy, where is all this coming from? What would make you think there's a problem with you having sex with your husband?" Tamia asked.

"I know it's not those women in that group!" swore Tasha.

"Well, Sister Glover says that—" Troy tried.

"Sister Glover? She's still in the group?" Tamia looked at Troy. When the Virtuous Women was started, long before Troy joined the church, the position of president was held by the First Lady of the church. When Kyle took over and he was unmarried, Sister Glover volunteered her services. "I thought for sure she was going to leave when you took over."

"Well, I haven't exactly done that."

"What?" Tasha wasn't sure about what Tamia and Troy were talking about, but it sounded bad and she was on her third glass of wine, so she jumped right in. "Why haven't you done that?"

"She's helped me so much—with my Bible lessons and showing me how to lead a more Christian life," Troy explained. "I can't just drop her like that. And I'm not ready yet. I don't know everything there is to know about the church. She's helping me figure it all out."

"Sounds like she's also helping you mess up your marriage!" Tasha said.

"No, don't say that," Troy said. "Sister Glover has troubles like anyone else, but she's a saved woman, and we should all be so lucky."

"Snap out of it!" Tasha playfully snapped her fingers in front of Troy's face. "Snap-out-of-it."

"What are you talking about?" Troy asked.

"Girl, don't you get tired of letting these chicks run they asses all over you?" Tasha asked. "I would think that being my friend for over ten years would've given you some backbone, but Troy, it seems like you like being a skank salad."

"What's a skank salad?" Tamia asked, shaking her head at Tasha's attack.

"It's the food that skanks eat before they enjoy the

big steak—which is usually a man. Look, first Skank #1 Miata came in and took Julian, and now Sister Skank #2 is working on Kyle! And what are you doing about it? Writing some list down in a notebook." Tasha threw the prayer pad over the bar.

"I need that." Troy desperately reached for the notebook, but a rushing bartender mistakenly squashed it to a soggy mess.

"No, you need a clue. In fact, we all do," Tasha said. "You want to have sex with the man one minute, then you don't. And you, Tamia, you don't want the man around one minute and then you do. What's going on?" She looked from Tamia to Troy on either side of her. "We need to stop doing all of this complaining and take control of our lives. It's not all about these men. It's about us. We're the 3Ts, not the three lames. And look at us. We're out of control."

Troy watched as another bartender stumbled over her notebook.

"You're right, Tasha," she said. "Help me, Jesus, but sometimes I do feel I'm out of control. I just don't know what to do."

"I do," Tasha said. "We need to do a check-in, check-up, and check-out."

"A Queen Bee Competition?" Tamia and Troy's eyes glowed at the thought of the competitive sport the Ts played in undergrad to get through midterms and exam weeks. The Queen Bee Competition was how they kept one another in check, making sure the hard work they were supposed to be doing was actually getting done. No big talk without action. In one notebook, they'd check in by recording a list of goals and check up each week to see who had achieved at least some of those goals. At the end of the competition, they'd check out by seeing who'd done the most stuff and she'd be crowned the Queen Bee. The prize back then was a free dinner, but since they'd long surpassed undergraduate budgets, they'd been trading Kate Spades instead.

"I can't do all of that," Tamia said, looking at her watch. "I have a new client . . . and I'm just swamped."

"Great, then there's no better time," Tasha said. "No more complaining. We need to act." She waved down the bartender and asked him to hand her the notebook she'd just tossed on the floor. "Now let's see what goals we can write down. And who will be named the new Queen Bee of the 3Ts!"

Crowning the Queen Bee: A Little Competition Never Hurts

The difference between a dreamer and a doer is a magical word called "action." The difference between a friend and a sisterfriend is a magical word called "support." When you throw these two miraculous words together, in any situation, every sistergirl is bound to come out on top. No one can support you actively pursuing your dreams like your sisterfriends. They hug you and hold you through the process, and when they catch you slipping, they have the loving nerve to say, "Hey, sistergirl, weren't you supposed to (ENTER YOUR DREAM HERE)?"

Put this recipe for success to the test by getting some of your sisterfriends together for a little active competition. Breathe life into your dreams by openly sharing with your sisterfriends the smaller steps to achieving them and resuscitate theirs by listening and loving. The goal of the Queen Bee Competition is accountability and bragging rights. The sisterfriend who achieves the most action is the winner, and the other sisters get to say they helped her reach her goal, and continue to work on their own.

Rules of Engagement

The Check-In: Gather your sisterfriends around to chat about the things you want to do, and discuss what small things you can do to get there. For example, if you want to become the next hot ballroom dancer, it might seem impossible, but sharing smaller goals, like finding a decent class and saving $30 a week to be able to afford the class, might seem more doable. Record all of your big and small goals on a sheet of paper, date it, and agree to meet a short while (a week or a month) later.

The Check-Up: At the next meeting, go through the list to see who has put action behind words. Did you find the dance teacher and save $30? Did your bestie pay one of her speeding tickets so she can get her driver's license back? Did your sisterfriend reapply to take the LSAT so she can finally go to law school? Did Kim lose just one pound? Celebrate the small victories with a round of drinks and applause. Discuss the shortcomings with others to find out where they went wrong and how you can help. Set a list of new short-term goals, date it, and organize another short-term check-up.

The Check-Out: One pound a week can equal fifty-two pounds lost in one year! Taking the LSAT, researching schools, applying, and getting accepted can lead to a future lawyer. Paying tickets one by one will surely add up to a returned license. A class, a competition, and a trophy can make you the next ballroom dancing star. After a few short-term meetings, have a final, preplanned check-out date where the long-term goal is to be completed. The sisterfriend who has come closest to achieving her goal is the Queen Bee and must be crowned and celebrated with awe. A most luxurious gift and kind words should mark the occasion. This sister has worked hard, so don't be cheap or short on praise. Other sisters should be happy too, though. While they aren't yet Queen Bees, they've done something about getting closer to making their dreams a reality, and one more competition could put them on top.

3

Well-behaved women seldom make history.

—*Laurel Thatcher Ulrich*

Though she was only two years old, Toni was fast learning Ulrich's abovementioned astute observation. When she cried, Tasha looked upset and usually left her alone. When she hollered, Lionel looked heartbroken, and usually picked her up and held her close. For her, this pattern of events provided the two things she wanted most—to be away from her mother and alone with her father. It was emotional ecstasy—two-year-old style. And while her brain hadn't yet processed how she'd make this daily achievement a part of a permanent history, she was well on her way to developing a concrete plan.

However, one little girl behaving badly seldom topped a big girl behaving badly, and especially not when it came to the big girl's man.

The morning after the Queen Bee Competition went into official 3T effect, Tasha had one thing on her mind—

taking her husband on a date and having mistress-worthy sex with him (while on the date). And no amount of crying and hollering on the part of a little girl was going to stop her.

Toni's shenanigans started in the morning when she overheard Tasha on the phone arranging an afternoon visit from Milania, a seventeen-year-old babysitter who lived a few houses down. She remembered what happened when her mother said the name "Milania" and understood the word "come." Eating chopped bananas her father fed her with a silver spoon, Toni knew this meant one thing—he was leaving her. But he'd just gotten back. And they hadn't taken a nap on the hammock in the backyard like they always did after playtime in the pool. She hadn't smelled his spicy cologne and felt his heart beating in her ear as she drifted off to sleep.

Soon, Toni was crying, screaming, hollering, choking, and wailing on the floor.

Soon, Milania had arrived, was handed a wide-eyed Tiara, and was left standing beside Toni's tearstained face.

Soon, Tasha was pushing Lionel into the car and pulling out of the driveway.

"We can't just leave her like that," Lionel said, turning and looking at the house as his wife drove up the street. "What if she doesn't stop?"

"It's a tantrum. She has them." Tasha's voice was flat, focused. Her eyes were locked on the rolling pavement.

"But she was choking and what if—"

"Baby, trust me. She'll be fine."

"I just feel bad. Coming home and leaving her alone. Maybe we should've waited and done this tomorrow—after I spend some time with the girls."

"You have to be at practice tomorrow morning, re-member?"

Lionel nodded sadly. He'd spent so much time away from his daughters practicing when he was at home, and when he went away, only for three or four days, and returned, he noticed something different, new about them. Tiara could grab his key chain. Toni had learned a new way of laughing at the old game of peekaboo.

"Look, honey," Tasha said, "I just want to go to the spa to relax a little bit and unwind. I want to spend time with you. We can put the girls to bed together tonight. How does that sound?"

Lionel looked at Tasha.

"Okay," he agreed. "Okay."

Lionel and Tasha held hands throughout their massages. They winked and grinned like teenagers as they stole glimpses of each other's oiled, nude bodies being touched by petite ladies with large hands. The dizzying scent of lavender filled the air and hot stones dissipated every care from their bodies. Soon, as the masseuses crept from the room, they were asleep, but still holding hands. Tasha dreamed of her husband on top of her and he dreamed of his wife on top of him. Together bodily in this world, and united mentally in another time, it was the most intimate they'd been in over a year. When he woke up, he found her asleep, her arms and legs splayed on the leather table, the thick white towel slip-ping away. He let it fall to the floor and threw his on top of it. Tasha's nipples were hardened and facing the ceil-ing as she continued to dream. Lionel wrapped her legs around his head and consumed his wife in this world and in another time. She shook and writhed, calling his name so loud a collection of masseuses and clients had gathered outside the door. "How much is the couple's massage?" one woman asked. She already had her husband on the phone.

"I fucking love you," Tasha joked, sipping on cucumber water beside the indoor pool at the spa. She and Lionel were wrapped in thick, white terry-cloth robes.

"I'm sorry about the other night. It was just . . . I was stressed out and tired. You know I would've—"

"No, baby." Tasha stopped Lionel. "Let's just be in the moment and enjoy our date. I mean, maybe this is what we need. A little more us time, so we can get back . . . you know? To how things used to be."

"Get back to what?" Lionel looked past Tasha to see that a woman who was reclined in a chair with only a small towel to cover her body had noticed him and was smiling hello with her eyes.

"Us . . . like the way we were before we had the girls and moved out here to Jersey. Do you remember how it was? We were so hot and young. We couldn't keep our hands off of each other. People envied us."

"But we have a family now, Tasha. It's what we both wanted. It's why we got married. Right?"

"Yeah, and I love our life. I love our daughters. But sometimes it's so heavy. It's so much. I just want to go back to how we were."

"So that's what's wrong with you." Lionel looked away from the woman, who moved her towel down to the tips of her nipples and peered at Tasha keenly.

"Wrong?" Tasha shot up. "What do you mean 'wrong'?"

"I'm not the only one who's been coming up short. Sometimes the way you touch me isn't the same either. It's like it's good, but you're tired," Lionel said, admitting something he hadn't told anyone else. Sex with

Tasha was seldom without surprise and complete seduction, but lately, it seemed her passion had become practiced and ritualistic. She moaned and groaned, hollered and hooted, but sometimes he wondered if she even wanted to be there. If the show was more for him than anything.

"Tired? I'm fine." Tasha shifted back into her chair and tried to laugh it off, but suddenly she felt as if Tiara and Toni were sitting right on her lap.

"I was thinking," Lionel started, "maybe we should get a nanny. Like a real one. Someone to move into the house. Hell, we have seven empty bedrooms." He tried to make this idea sound as spontaneous and lighthearted as possible.

"Why would we need a nanny?" Tasha was trying to be just as lighthearted. "I'm home with the girls."

"I don't know, Tash. Sometimes when I come home, you all seem like you're just tired of each other. They're hollering. You're trying to get them to go to sleep. And why is Tiara still in the room with Toni?"

"I don't need any help, Lionel." Tasha's attempt at duplicating lightness evaporated with the last sip of her water. She'd become defensive. She slid her shades back on and crossed her arms. "They're just at an awkward place. Two babies. We'll be okay. Besides, I have to pull my own weight."

Out of the spa and in the city, Tamia was struggling with her commitment to behaving badly. Her first Queen Bee goal was to win her big-city corporate brawl by losing her small case. It was a simple plan. Pretend she cared, build an effortless case that any opposing attorney who'd tried more than three cases could pull apart in seconds, sit back and let them bury her in facts and fiction, wave the white flag, and move on with her life.

While the dramatic plot was new to her, she knew it was nothing new to top attorneys. People brought and sold cases every day in the Big Apple. Favors were used. Old frat boys from Yale and Harvard leaned on shields and no matter the verdict, both sides would meet up for drinks and jokes as soon as the gavel of judgment fell. The only uninvited party would be the client, in the dark.

Standing in the bathroom at the office, she looked for something in her reflection in the mirror. Something to speak to her and tell her that this was part of the game. How the big boys got to the top. She was a winner, always had been. And if winning this time meant losing, she would have to do what she had to do. It wasn't her proudest moment, but certainly there would be many prideful moments to follow. But what would her father, the great Judge Dinkins, think? He'd had his own life and no doubt had to make these decisions on his own about what was ethical and what was easy. Now it was her turn.

She buttoned her jacket and stepped back to look at her outfit, a charcoal gray power suit that hugged her thighs just enough.

"Please tell me that's your brother," said Maria, another attorney, bursting into the bathroom as if they were at any high school. "Your cousin . . . your nephew. Anyone but your boyfriend!"

"What? What are you talking about?" Tamia turned to her.

"That man." Maria's blush lips quivered. "He is so . . . rugged."

"What man are you talking about?"

"The one in your office. He's sitting at your desk."

"A man in my office? What?" Tamia threw a tissue she'd sat on the counter into the garbage and hustled out of the bathroom.

Outside, women were gathered in clumps she knew meant new gossip. As she walked past, they looked at her and smirked jealously.

"What?" she murmured, adjusting her jacket as she turned toward her office.

Months later, when she was on her way to becoming homeless, hairless, and wearing only a sari, she'd try to remember how this thing went. How she saw him first. Was it the smell? The sound? The face? Or just him, all of him sitting and waiting for her as if he'd always been there?

By then, with everything that led to that moment, she'd forget what came first, but really, it was the smell.

When Tamia walked into the office, her heart nearly racing with anticipation of nothing she was expecting and everything she didn't know, there was this aroma, this enveloping scent that wafted so clearly around her that she'd felt suddenly like she was standing in a field of flowers or sitting in a pew at midnight Mass as the priest walked past, shaking an incense ball filled with frankincense and myrrh. It was sugary and fiery, clean and complex. Standing in the doorway, Tamia thought it was everywhere, but there was nothing she could see to connect it to. The office was empty. Her chair was turned and facing the window, as it had been when she'd left for the restroom.

"Naudia," Tamia called, turning to see if Naudia had returned from lunch and let someone into her office.

"It's funny how they make these windows. So big and wide. Like they're daring you to go outside. I say jump." There was a laugh.

"What?" Tamia turned back to her desk, where the voice, knowing and a bit detached, maybe arrogant, was coming from.

The chair swiveled around and inside there was this

man. A dark man with dark eyes and long, dark dreadlocks that because of his complexion seemed more a
part of him than not. He was sitting back and wearing a
military jacket with a thin T-shirt beneath. He looked
like he was about to pitch a tent or start a war. She
couldn't decide which one, but knew neither activity
seemed right for her office—not in her seat either.

"Are you looking for Tamia Dinkins? This is my office."

Flat out, Tamia was put off. And she didn't know if
it was because of what she was looking at or where it
was seated. She stepped in from the doorway and saw a
tan knapsack on the floor beside the desk. Buttons and
patches with little sayings crowded every side. It seemed
like the perfect accessory for him. She'd seen men like
this before. In undergrad at Howard at poetry readings
and selling incense at the student center. They were always angry and usually high. Well, she'd never spoken
to one but that was how they looked.

"Yeah, they told me to come see you."

"They?"

"I'm Malik. I'm from the Freedom Project." Malik
stood up and his 6'5" frame seemed to erase every
available square foot of space around Tamia. He was
on the other side of the desk, but everywhere at the
same time. She tried to find her breath. Looked at the
wooden beads around his neck. Stood there.

"I apologize, sister." Malik looked confused. He
held his hands out defensively. "Did I do something
wrong?"

"Oh," Tamia tried, breathing again. "I'm just not used
to people—you know . . ." She gestured toward the desk.

"I'm sorry. My bad," Malik said, stepping back from
the desk and walking toward Tamia. They had the awkward moment of trading positions in the small space,

their bodies nearly brushing against each other. "I just wanted to see the view. See what the real people look like walking by the tower."

"It's okay really. I just . . ." Sitting down, Tamia looked at her schedule on the computer screen. "I'm sorry, my notes say I'm working with a man named Richard . . ."

"That's me. But I go by Malik." He sat down.

"Oh, well . . . then," Tamia said slowly, and had her mother not died when she was just a little girl Tamia would've known that she sounded just like her at that moment. "That's fine . . . Mal-ik." She was trying to sound welcoming, but she never understood the concept of black people with perfectly good names "going by" something else. Gerard became Little G and Taylor became Tee Tee. And then everyone in the 'hood was complaining about why they couldn't get out. It was a sad state of affairs where being unique meant being held back, and while Tamia would never let anyone hear her admit it, she always thought her own name was a little too unique.

Malik, having sized Tamia up in an equal way, felt the opposite. Tamia wasn't unique enough. The card he was given said "Da-Asia Moshanique Jones," and while he wasn't excited about taking the hookup one of his father's former employers arranged, he thought at least "Da-Asia" sounded like a sister—a real sister, who was probably coming from where he was from and could understand his situation. But what was before him, in Tamia, was a sister but not what he'd call a "real" sister. Her monkey suit was the color of the wallpaper, her hair was processed, and what was up with the way she'd said "Malik"? On her mouth it sounded like a lock or illness.

"Weren't we supposed to meet later this afternoon with Attorney Jones?"

"I was in the neighborhood and figured I'd come by earlier. Is that a problem?"

"Well, we have a pretty orderly way of running things around here," Tamia said, and while she certainly wasn't trying to sound patronizing, there was little way out of it because inside she was really thinking *who doesn't know you can't show up at a corporate office unannounced . . . or anywhere these days?* Hell, even the tiniest of downtown restaurants now took reservations.

There was silence now as the accidental adversaries sat on either side of Tamia's desk thinking things about each other they'd later share with other people. While Tamia was thinking about how clear and shiny his eyes were, big like a little boy's, she'd tell Troy about how ridiculous it was that he'd shown up for a meeting with his attorney dressed like a storm trooper, and while he was thinking of how soft and silken her wrists looked he'd complain to his neighbor about how he knew this would be a waste of his time and he'd probably be better off with some white boy than this bourgeoisie wannabe. But that would be all of the talk later. Now Malik was looking at the degrees on the wall and Tamia was swallowing spit she'd gathered from beneath her tongue. They could hear the pendulum on the clock in Maria's office next door ticking.

"Do you have any questions for me?" Malik asked. "This is an interview, right?"

"Yeah." Tamia took a pad from her desk and tried to remember what she'd read in the folder that morning on the treadmill. While she was usually prepared to meet a new client with a list of questions, a recorder, and sometimes Naudia taking additional notes, she'd planned on letting Jones lead Malik's questioning and

only half read the first few pages. "Let's see . . ." She
flipped open the case file.

"I'm just gonna come out and say this so there's no
confusion," Malik said. "I did what they said I did. It's
not what they're calling it but I did do it. And I'll do it
again."

"What?" Tamia looked at Malik like he was crazy
and this time she did nothing to hide what she was
thinking. "I don't think you need to say that right now.
Not here." Her voice was hushed. "My job is to main-
tain your innocence. You tell me what happened and
I'll decide what you did and didn't do and until then I
don't want to hear you say anything like that again."

"I know the game you're playing, but I'm saying I
don't want to play games. They say I enslaved my own
brother. I say I freed him. I'm a conscious brother and
I can't lie about something I did that I knew was right
just because a bunch of unconscious people said it's
unethical. Have you ever had to do that, sister? Put
your head out there to do something that was right,
even though the law said it was unethical?"

Tamia nervously swallowed what was inside of her
mouth again and nodded.

"Sister, are you conscious?" Malik leaned in toward
the desk as if he was saying a secret, but his voice was
still loud enough for someone walking past the office
to hear.

"Excuse me?"

"Conscious? Are you conscious?"

"As opposed to unconscious?" Tamia smiled un-
easily. "Sure I am."

"That's not what I mean. I'm asking if you're conscious about the war against African people in this
world. About how white supremacy threatens the very
existence of blackness"—his voice was getting louder
with each word and Tamia wanted to close the door to

her office but she was afraid if she got up she would have to walk farther away and he'd only get louder still—"That whiteness is a genetic mutation and—"

"Mr. . . . Mal-ik . . . I need you to stop." Tamia put her hands up crossly. "I am sure all of this stuff—"

"Stuff?"

"—is very important to you and where you're from—"

"Where I'm from?"

"—but this really isn't the place for it."

"Not the place?"

"We need to focus on your case. On the facts. Not your rhetoric about . . . whatever that was."

"Rhetoric?"

And just like that the accidental adversaries were easy enemies and Malik was on his feet.

He grabbed his knapsack and as he bent down Tamia rolled her eyes.

"I knew this was going to be a waste of my time. I'm out. Peace."

As Tamia's cautious client was making an abrupt exit in Manhattan, Troy's righteous rival had yet to arrive at the meeting of the Virtuous Women in Harlem. And it was a bad thing too, because Troy had come to the church early to meet with Myrtle and inform her of her decision to take over the organization before she told the rest of the women. This was step one of her Queen Bee competition goal and thus far, she was falling short.

She sat, quiet and nervous, in the corner of the meeting room, watching as women robed in an outdated mix of floral patterns sauntered in, thanking the Lord for the day he'd made and following up with a bit of pre-meeting rumor dispersal.

"You okay, First Lady?" asked Kiona, pulling up a

chair beside Troy. As usual, she was underdressed in jeans and a tight T-shirt—an outfit that would no doubt prompt Sister Glover to open the meeting by talking about the "proper image of a Virtuous Woman."

"I'm fine, KiKi," Troy tried to reassure her.

"I'm saying, we're just planning the next bake sale today. It's not that serious . . . well, unless Mother Wildren insists on bringing her prune pie again."

Troy and Kiona chuckled at the memory of the pie and its aftereffect stinking up the building. Over the time Troy had been at the church, she'd found Kiona to be one of the most real and hated members. It was funny, she thought, how that seemed to go together there. Sometimes she wondered why Kiona remained at the church and why they hadn't run her off yet. But the truth, Troy learned, was that while Kiona and her jeans and wild comments had made lots of enemies over the years, she loved God and worked harder than almost everyone at the church. Not one bake sale or drive or Girl Scout meeting went by without Kiona, her tight jeans, and her opinions.

"Hey, Kiona," Troy started, "you were here before my husband became the pastor, correct?"

"Sure was. Pastor Brown. Lord, that was a wonderful man of God."

"So you were also here when the Virtuous Women were started?" Troy asked, watching a few more women come in and sit at the table.

"Guilty as charged," Kiona answered. "First Lady Brown started the Virtuous Women to bring the women of First Baptist together for true fellowship and service. It was so much fun."

"What was she like? Like, how did she handle being the head of an organization with so many spiritual

women? She must've been like a saint or something."
Troy laughed, but really she was serious.

"Please, that woman was far from a saint. She was
late to most of the meetings and forgot a few events.
That woman was a trip." Kiona looked at Troy. "But,
you know, there was something about her. Something
human and real and just plain good that just made all
of us love and respect her. Women were fighting to join
this organization just to be close to her. It was like you
knew that no matter where you'd been or what you'd
done, she'd love you and embrace you. And, if you ask
me, that's what we should look for in any First Lady.
Especially one leading the Virtuous Women." Her
voice quickly went low. "Not the riffraff we have leading us right now . . . but you didn't hear that from me."

"Oh, stop it," Troy chided, playfully spanking Kiona's
hand.

The exchange between the two women quickly turned
from a conversation to a confessional, as Troy opened up
and informed Kiona of her decision to lead the Virtuous Women as she was expected to. For Troy, who
needed to let someone outside of herself and the other
Ts know of her plan, it let a bunch of guilt and anxiety
off of her shoulders. She actually felt good when the
meeting was finally opening and Kiona promised not
to tell anyone of her plan. But she immediately realized
that even the most real, most well-intentioned woman
couldn't keep a piece of hot gossip like that to herself—not for very long. And the wildest thing was that
while Troy hadn't even seen Kiona speak to any of the
other women in the room, one by one, they turned to
Troy with speculative stares. It was as if the bit of communication was being transported among these heav-
enly women telepathically . . . or via text message.

Robed in a leopard-print duster that kissed the floor

beneath her six-inch leopard-print heels, Sister Glover shifted into the room like a judge prepared to hear her next case. She greeted her jury, smiling pleasantly at their waves, took her seat, and clasped her hands on the table.

"Let us begin with prayer, sisters," she said with a weak nod to Troy, who was seated to her right.

"I need you to do something!" Tamia began rattling off her demand before she fully entered Charleston's office.

Inside, at the far end of a triangular corner enclave whose size would be the envy of any high-rolling New York office, stood Charleston beside a floor-to-ceiling window that looked out over the city. His assistant, Christina, an Irish redhead with envious, lime-colored eyes, was sitting in a chair beside his desk, typing as he spoke. Together, they looked up at Tamia.

"That'll be all," Charleston said.

"But we haven't finished the letter . . ." Christina knew better than to push. She saved the file on her laptop and hustled out of the room as quickly as her rented Prada heels would allow.

Tamia stood before the sleek chrome and glass desk, her arms crossed, her teeth tight in a grimace. There was nothing else to say. Malik and his words had ignited fire in her in some way she didn't know, couldn't explain. The nerve of him to speak to her in such a way when he needed her, Tamia kept thinking as she charged upstairs to Charleston's office. And what did he mean anyway? Her "level of consciousness"? The only thing he needed to be conscious of was keeping himself out of jail. That was the problem with men like him; they were always focused on the wrong things.

"People are going to start to believe we're sleeping

together," Charleston joked, walking around to the front of his desk and sitting before Tamia. His jacket was off, revealing matching Burberry suspenders and a bow tie. It was pretentious, but that's what he was going for.

"I'm not in the mood for games, Charleston. I just had the worst face-to-face in my career and I want out. I want you to do something. Get me out of this!" Tamia demanded. "Incense-carrying! Muslim oil–smelling! Dirty dreadlock–having! Son-of-a—"

"Whoa, girl! This is a place of business." Charleston went to close the door. "Who are you talking about? The doughnut man downstairs?"

"My new client. He's some 'hood rat with no class. He came into my office and attacked me," Tamia said. "You're right. This case is a dog. I have to get out of it and I need you to help me. I can't—no—I refuse to work with that . . . that . . . ruffian!"

"Wait, he attacked you?"

"Well, he was very nasty. Asking me questions and sitting at my desk. Whoever heard—"

"That's not the same as an attack. You know that."

"It doesn't matter," Tamia said before lowering her voice to a secretive whisper. "Look, I know how these things work. I'm with you and there has to be some benefits to that. I need you to talk to your people upstairs and pull me out of this."

"I already did that," Charleston revealed softly as he prepared to tell his tale. That morning, when he walked into the office, he'd gotten a tip from an older and nosy security guard about Tamia's suspicious night visit to the office. Just a brother looking out for another brother. The man laughed loud and long, imagining how slick Charleston would need to be to worm out of not being where he told a sister like Tamia he would be. He was sure there would be hell, but Charleston's laugh was louder and longer. He'd been there before. The trick to getting caught in that kind of lie, especially with a woman he cared about, was to tell her what she already knew before she approached him about it and cover with a better lie that was wrapped around her. It worked like a charm. It always did.

"What?" Tamia uncrossed her arms and looked at Charleston sensitively. "You already spoke to someone?"

"Look, the other night, after we had dinner with Nathaniel, I went and had a drink with someone high up to talk about the case. Someone who owes me a favor."

"Really?"

"Well, you seemed upset and I just, I couldn't let you go out like that. So, instead of coming to the office, I went and tried to pull a rabbit out of a hat. Now, I got them to drop the co-counsel so you don't have to deal with Jones anymore."

"I guess that's why Malik said reception forwarded him to my office."

"But no one wants to step on toes and they won't completely reassign the case." Charleston's tone was even and frank, like a salesman in the middle of his "I'm not pitching" pitch. He was telling the truth about not going in to the office, both he and Tamia knew that already, and he did have an important meeting with a colleague, but it was at a swingers' club and included both the colleague and two of her married, yet bored gym buddies. Needless to say, there was little talk of Tamia. Awaiting a sexy tap from the whip a nude Charleston was holding, Phaedra had agreed to remove Jones from the case if he would have sex with her.

"I can't believe you did that for me," Tamia said, feeling foolish for stalking Charleston's office and even considering that he'd lied to her. She'd been the one pushing him away.

"Yeah, well, you're my woman and I want to protect you," Charleston said, grinning at Tamia. "But it looks like the old plan is going to have to stand. Do what you have to do to get in good with this guy and just let the dog die. I'll work on my side to make sure your next case is front page."

"Really? You'd do that for me?"

"Hey, like you said, there has to be some benefits to dating a brother of my stature." Charleston pulled at his suspenders and rocked from his heels to his tippy-toes.

Lovely Lowdown Liars: Top Ten Reasons Men Lie in Love

Like navigating the Bermuda Triangle and figuring out how to best hide your weave tracks, some things will always remain a mystery. For women, at the top of this list is why men lie. For eons, sisters have met in kitchens, cafés, and coffee shops to figure it out, but really, where men are concerned, it's quite simple. The lie—the good or bad lie (which you almost always discover in the end)—is used to escape, abate, or ward off drama. Below are the top-ten reasons men lie. While knowledge certainly won't help you avoid the lies, at least you'll know why.

10. <u>*He doesn't like your family or friends:*</u> *If he suddenly has the flu the morning of your family dinner, the lie might be a sign that he simply doesn't like them. It isn't personal.*

9. <u>*He's hungry:*</u> *A man's stomach is a living, breathing thing. If over dinner he senses that saying "Of course I love your mother" will make you stop talking so he can eat, he'll do it.*

8. <u>*He's tired:*</u> *If it's 2 a.m., you've proven your point, you've thought about it from every angle, and you two still can't figure out what to do about something he can't even remember, he'll lie about, agree to, and confirm anything to avoid another "but we haven't talked about . . ." statement.*

7. <u>*He's broke:*</u> *No one likes a broke man. Even a broke man doesn't like a broke man. If his pockets are shallow and no green is coming in, he might say, "I don't want to go out." Translation: "I can't go." The lie is used to protect his ego.*

6. _He wants to sleep with you:_ This is when a man might not even know he's lying. The smaller head thinks for the bigger one and anything is liable to come out.

5. _He's already lied before:_ Sometimes he needs to cover the little lie with a medium lie and then the medium lie with a large and ridiculous lie—which is usually when he gets caught.

4. _He doesn't want you to cry:_ Crying is a man's kryptonite. It makes these natural protectors soften. If he loves you, he'll say anything to avoid seeing you cry.

3. _He's been caught:_ Some lies are told to stay out of trouble. Other lies are told to get out of trouble. If he knows that you know he's lied, a lie might be created to avoid punishment. Opening line: "I lied before, but now I'm telling the truth."

2. _He loves you:_ Love is a gift and a curse. If he loves you, he'll lie to keep you.

1. _He's a liar:_ Over time, lying can become a reflex. If he thinks the truth might cause conflict, he'll lie . . . just because he can.

After a lengthy prayer where Troy happened to open her eyes and see that she and Myrtle were the only women whose eyes had been closed—everyone else was looking directly at Troy (one woman even gave her a thumbs-up)—things went as usual at the Virtuous meeting. The bake sale was planned. They voted not to accept any contributions that included alcohol—on account of a rumor that one of the Sunday school children purposely purchased and ate an entire rum raisin pound cake to see if he could get drunk. Also, they would move ahead with plans to cosponsor a block party with the women of the Rosary Society at the Catholic church on the corner—as long as they agreed to ban alcohol and gambling (in the form of playing bingo) on site. Last year, the mixture of BYOB and seemingly Catholic-only winning at the bingo game had led to a brawl on the church steps.

"Now that we have old business out of the way," Myrtle said, shifting some unimportant papers around and handing a few to a tense Troy, "let's go ahead with any new business. Do we have anything from the floor?"

What was supposed to be a ten-second pause for additions amounted to two seconds, and without fully scanning the room, Myrtle went on to what she'd wanted to add to the new business.

"Well," she continued, "if there aren't any other—"

"Wait a minute now, girl," a gruff and defiant voice interrupted from the far end of the table. It was Eloise Perkins, a church mother whose age alone gave her the right to be feisty.

"Yes, Mother Perkins, I apologize," Myrtle said, rolling her eyes a bit. "What is it? Do you have new business? You know we've already planned the bake sale?"

"Girl, I'm old, not deaf. I've been sitting in this room just as long as you."

There were some laughs and even Myrtle dealt a courteous smile.

"Now, I think someone in here has something to say," Mother Perkins went on. "Something that we all need to hear."

Troy literally felt what little courage she'd had leave her. Quickly she'd transformed from a fierce feline pumped up on her Queen Bee mission to the cowardly lion in *The Wizard of Oz*. It was as if a microphone had been jabbed in her hand and cameras were rolling, awaiting some wise word she hadn't written yet.

"Someone? Who?" Myrtle snickered. "New business? Is there anyone?"

From her place on the other side of the table, Kiona looked at Troy and wrestled with Troy's lack of confidence with bugged-out eyes. Troy was saying, "No," and Kiona was saying, "You'd better."

Troy kept thinking she couldn't lead them. She couldn't lead all of these women. She knew half of what they knew. They needed someone else, someone like Myrtle who was saved and knew the Word. Someone who wouldn't lead them the wrong way like she'd done to Kyle, inviting the incubus and succubus into their bedroom. What was she thinking? She had no right to step in and take over. She couldn't. That was just some angry talk she'd had with her friends at a bar she probably shouldn't have visited—she'd have to remind herself to pray about that.

Finally, Kiona broke her stare.

"Well, since no one has anything, I'll just go ahead with my—I mean our—new business," Myrtle said and the groan in the room was audible, yet she ignored it. She'd been waiting for weeks to bring this suggestion to the women. "Now, I'm so excited about this new venture for us, sisters. For years, the Virtuous Women have stood for leadership, self-love, and a commitment to Christ. What we are, sisters, are strong black Christian women who humbly worship a living God."

"That's right!" Mother Wildren agreed jovially.

"Amen," someone else said and others clapped.

"Now, as we celebrate that, we must also consider how visible our image is in the church," Myrtle said as Troy and the others tried to figure out what she was adding up. "Now, I know that image might not be as important to some of you, but we must understand that if we are not known, others won't know our way. Won't be aware of just how committed we are to our worship, to our ministry. Before I get to my point, I'd like to point out that right now, more than 60 percent of our church is women. Fifteen women serve in leadership positions. And while all of this is true, no women sit at the altar on Sunday morning. Does that make any sense?"

There was silence as the women thought of who they saw sitting on either side of Kyle every Sunday. From the deacons to the assistant pastor and the head of the men's ministry, Myrtle was correct; they were all men. Even Saptosa, the secretary, who was in the room, was always instructed to sit in the first pew.

"But that's just how it is," said Elizabeth, the church treasurer and Myrtle's confidante who'd preplanned her seemingly even statement, "how it's always been. I've been here for ten years and I don't recall any woman ever sitting up there. Maybe you're right . . . maybe it is time for a change."

"Oh please, those are the rules of the house. They always have been. Why change them now?" Mother Perkins asked.

"Well, I think that's a good question," Myrtle said. "I have given it lots of thought and I think we need to change because it's time. Women don't simply sit in the pews anymore. We work, we lead, we teach. We should be recognized for that."

"Well, what are you proposing?" Kiona asked and she was probably the only person who'd figured out what exactly Myrtle was about to pull out of her metaphorical bag.

"Well, with Easter right around the corner, I'm proposing that we seek representation at the altar, at the left hand of Pastor Hall. I think Easter should be our suggestion. It's a time of resurrection and hope. And it's also a time for family and togetherness. We represent that."

"Representation at the altar? On Easter?" Elizabeth asked innocently. "Who? Who could represent us?"

"Well, it only makes sense that the person representing the Virtuous Women is the leader of the Virtuous Women—me," Myrtle said and looked straight ahead as if she was unaware of Troy's glare.

"Say what? Say what now?" Kiona quizzed, her head bopping as if she was preparing for a street fight. "You want to sit next to Pastor . . . ? On Sunday . . . ? Every Sunday . . . ?" Kiona gasped and looked at Troy. "Lord, please speak up in here."

"You know," Elizabeth said, "I think it's a good idea and maybe we should vote—"

"Vote on what? There's no motion," Kiona pointed out, trying to stall.

"Well, somebody make a motion," another sister said. "I think it's a great idea."

"I'll make the motion," Elizabeth said, smiling at Myrtle. "I move that—"

"Hold up a hallelujah minute!" Kiona stood up quickly, raising her hand. "I want to make the motion."

Both Troy and Myrtle looked at her, confused.

"You want to make the motion?" Myrtle said.

"I think that . . . I mean, I am making a motion that we formally request a seat on the left side of Pastor Hall on Sunday—"

"But—" Troy tried, but Sister Glover, excited that Kiona was supporting her appeal, dug the heel of her shoe into Troy's foot beneath the table. "Ouch," Troy said.

"With one exception to the original suggestion," Kiona added, stepping back from her seat and walking toward the top of the table, where Myrtle and Troy were seated. Everyone looked on as if they were awaiting a groundbreaking speech or a fight—it really was a toss-up. "That the representative of the Virtuous Women be the First Lady of our church."

"What?" Myrtle laughed and a few others around the table joined her, with Elizabeth's haughty snicker being loudest. "That's just ridiculous. The person that represents the group has to be the president—the leader . . . not . . . not . . . the First Lady . . . just because she happens to be the First Lady *right now.* I represent the organization and therefore I should be the appointed representative."

Hearing the retreating chatter and seeing head nods around the room, Kiona and Troy knew the battle was lost.

"Look," Myrtle went on, rising from her seat and stepping in front of Kiona, "it was my suggestion and I think it should be voted on, as is—with the leader of the organization representing us as a whole at the altar. That's the only thing that makes sense and as the president, I . . ."

As Myrtle captured the opinions of the women seated around the table, Troy's vision was growing from white, to pink, to red. The full, anxious pit she usually felt in her stomach whenever she was seated at the table was aflame. It was a moment. One that even Troy, the flighty, passive air sign, knew put a lot on the line. She knew she had to do something, but fear kept her frozen, stuck in her seat as Myrtle walked circles around her. Then she remembered the Queen Bee Competition and what she was supposed to be doing with herself that day, in that room. She saw Tasha's face and heard her command: "Snap out of it!"

". . . so, let's just vote now and stop with these ridiculous suggestions from the floor. As the president, I should—"

"Maybe you shouldn't be president anymore," Troy said. "Maybe it's my turn . . . no, it *is* my turn."

"What?" By this time, Myrtle had trolled to the other side of the table and looked over at Troy like she was crazy.

"I'm ready to be president of the Virtuous Women," Troy said confidently this time.

"Ready? But you're not even . . ." Myrtle paused and pretended she was regrouping. "Look, Troy, I know what you're trying to do, take some responsibility, get a little attention, but it's not necessary. You're not *ready*."

"Ready?" Kiona asked. "Ready for what?"

"Yeah, ready for what?" someone else chimed in.

"Well, she just joined the church, and she wasn't raised Baptist. She doesn't know how to—"

"I wasn't born Baptist either. I was raised Muslim," someone else said. "So I'm less of a member than you?"

"No, what I mean is," Myrtle tried, "she doesn't really know the Word and she's not knowledgeable about the church rules. You can ask her yourself." She looked at Troy.

"Do you know the rules of the church, First Lady?" someone asked.

IT'S ABOUT TO GO DOWN. THE FIRST LADY IS ABOUT TO LOOK LIKE AN ASS was texted from a sister at one end of the table to another.

"I don't know everything. . . . Well, I've been studying and I'm getting better," Troy said.

"Better?" Myrtle laughed. "You don't even know when the church was founded."

Everyone looked from Myrtle to Troy.

A KNIFE TO THE BACK! THAT HAD TO HURT the text messenger responded.

Over two hundred years ago . . . subtract that from 2010 . . . carry the one . . . she was so bad at math. Troy had no answer. She wanted to disappear and wished she'd kept her mouth shut.

"Well," Sister Oliver started, "haven't you been in charge of the First Lady's instruction over the last two years? Haven't you been her mentor? If she doesn't know anything, maybe it's because you haven't taught her anything."

TAG TEAM OPERATION! another text read.

"Yeah," Kiona agreed. "And who's going to know everything? I don't know when the church was founded and I've been here longer than you. And since you're so into history then, Myrtle, you should know that the original constitution of the Virtuous Women states that the president of the organization should be the First Lady and if she is new to the church, leadership of the organization should be given to her upon approval of the organization's members, or suggestion of the pastor. Basically, you have no say." Kiona walked over and was now standing in front of Myrtle.

"Hum" and "That's true" and "I don't know that either" were heard around the table, and heads that were just nodding for Myrtle were now nodding toward Troy.

"Really?" Troy asked.

"This is just stupid," Myrtle said. "So, you support this? You all want her to be your president? *Troy?*"

"Why not?" someone said. "Let's try it. I like her. She's a good person. I move that we vote on the First Lady being the new president."

"I second!" someone said quickly.

"What?" Myrtle looked to all of the faces in the group that she thought supported her, but they looked away—even Elizabeth.

"Great! So all those in favor of the First Lady being our new president, raise your hands," Kiona said and without counting, it was clear the vote was in Troy's favor.

"I can't have this," Myrtle said. "I can't let you all make this crazy decision. She's not fit. And as president I can't allow you to make this mistake. I won't and I am sure the pastor will back me on this."

"You're out of the group," Troy's heart said and her lips vocalized it before her brain could stop her. Then she was on her feet and walking toward Myrtle. "You're out of the Virtuous Women, so there's no need for you to worry about me being president."

"You can't kick me out," Myrtle said, laughing nervously.

"I just did," Troy said. "What you're doing, the way you're behaving, simply isn't a part of the image we support in this organization—the image you taught me about." Troy stood before Myrtle. "So, as the new president, I have to ask you, in a Christian way, of course, to leave."

"You can't do this," Myrtle said. "Pastor Hall won't have it."

"My husband will support me," Troy said confidently. "I know that."

Myrtle stammered across the floor and out the door like a weary two-year-old trudging out of the sandbox without her shovel. No one followed. The attention of excited eyes and lips curled up at the edges was focused on Troy.

NOW THAT WAS A COMEBACK a text read.

YEAH, SHE DID THAT!

4

*She must have been unprepared/
to accept freedom as a process/
a precious thing/
that needs to be nurtured.*

—Pamela Sneed

The Freedom Project—this was plainly written in thick black ink on a sign, which looked like a stretched-out piece of loose-leaf paper. It was literally tacked above the new doorway of an old building at the middle of a slender street a few blocks south of the Apollo Theatre.

Stepping out of a gypsy cab she had to get at the foot of the Harlem River Bridge after the yellow and black she'd rode through midtown refused to go any farther, Tamia looked from the words above the doorway to those on the card she was holding to confirm that this was the place. She stepped back and looked again, this time at the entire building and then back at the card. THE FREEDOM PROJECT.

While she hadn't really thought of what the place might look like, somehow the haphazard sign and dated brick exterior seemed like less than they should be. The

name made it sound like it would be tall and slender like
an arrow headed toward heaven, demanding freedom,
but it was actually shorter and wider than the other
buildings on the street. Sunk between two brownstones,
it looked like a pudgy child standing with its parents.

A thick brown-skinned girl with a short, fire-red
Afro walked out of the door and held it open.

"You going inside, sister?" she asked and Tamia
looked to see that the girl, who might've been fifteen or
sixteen years old, was wearing a too-tight black T-shirt
that read DAUGHTER OF A FIELD SLAVE in bold white
letters.

"Yes," Tamia said, reading the words a second and
then third time before the girl passed off the open door
to her.

"It's hot, right?" the girl said, smiling as the sets of
wooden hoops in her ears clacked together.

"What?"

"My T-shirt." The girl held out the bottom of her shirt.
"I want people to know who I am. No joke. Right?"

"Sure. It's no joke." Tamia smiled, but really she was
thinking the shirt was maybe two sizes too small and
the words just too . . . much. Distasteful. Everybody
knew her ancestors were slaves; why did she need to
remind them as she walked down the street?

"Peace, my sister," the girl said brightly, walking to
the curb to cross the street.

"Goodbye," Tamia responded.

Inside, Tamia found what was set up as a front room
or maybe a gift shop, empty of everyone, but full of
everything possible. A recording of a woman singing
in a different language above African drums provided a
soundtrack for a dizzying mishmash of African face
masks and statues, books with red, black, and green
spines, dashikis, koffis, a vat of shea butter, and racks

of incense and vials of Muslim oils. Toward the back, Tamia saw that the girl outside must've gotten her T-shirt inside, because tacked to a wall was black fabric reading in white letters SON OF A FIELD SLAVE, DAUGHTER OF A HOUSE SLAVE, WARNING: EDUCATED BLACK MAN, and $\frac{1}{10}$ OF THE TALENTED. There was even one with a picture of Malcolm X standing at a window and one of two black men Tamia didn't know were Tommie Smith and John Carlos raising gloved Black-Power fists on the podium of the 1968 Olympics. A sign revealed that the shirts were $10 apiece and Tamia thought the whole bunch of them were cheaper than her purse. If only midtown fashion was so simple. And either everyone inside of the Freedom Project was wearing Malik's cologne or wherever he was in the building, it was just that strong that Tamia could smell it where she was standing. The scent of frankincense and myrrh was so heavy, Tamia now thought it smelled more like a piece of wood burning in a stove.

"Can I help you, sister?" Tamia heard and she turned from the shirts to a woman who'd appeared behind a makeshift counter that was really a jewelry case. While she might've been lighter than Troy, her hair was just as red as the girl's outside, but it was locked and long; the edges brushed against her elbows. Tamia never cared for natural hair; to her it always looked dirty, wild, and just unkempt. But she was in awe of how long black women's hair grew when it was locked. No matter what she did, hers simply wouldn't go past her shoulders without an additional Indian track, but she'd seen locked hair dangling at ankles and tied up in massive buns.

"I'm looking for Richard Holder."

"Richard Holder? Ain't no Richard Holder here . . ." The woman looked vacant, as if she hadn't heard the name before and maybe Tamia was speaking another language. She adjusted the fitted red and yellow African dress she was wearing.

"He's the director—the . . ." Tamia looked down at the card and then at the same time the woman said, "Malik?!

"Oh, you mean Brother Malik. Why didn't you say that? He's upstairs teaching."

"Well, his name is," Tamia started as the woman, who was maybe ten or twelve years her senior, stepped from behind the counter, presenting shoeless feet, "Richard—"

"I'm Sister Kali," she said, shooing the card away and extending her arms.

Tamia thought she was trying to shake her hand, so she put her hand out, but Kali's arms went wider and pulled Tamia into her.

"I'm . . . Tamia . . . Tamia Dinkins," she said awkwardly with her arms at her sides in Kali's tight embrace. She looked at Kali's ear and beneath it was a tattoo of a cross with a loop at the top. Later, Tamia would notice that a golden earring of the same symbol was in her nose.

"Welcome, Sister Tamia. I can take you to him."

By the time Kali managed to lead Tamia to where Malik was finishing teaching a capoeira class to a room full of bony, brown-skinned boys, Tamia was carrying a cup of organic carrot and ginseng juice she originally had turned down and was wearing a tiny bracelet of crimson and cream beads Kali told her came from Ghana. Her hand held tight as they walked through the people-filled hallways of the building, Tamia thought of how familiar Kali seemed with her. They'd met less than fifteen minutes ago, but she'd called Tamia "sister" at least a dozen times and smiled so pointedly that Tamia saw in her eyes a reflection of herself that looked like an old friend, a neighbor. Her

energy was intrusive and annoying, almost like an old
lady's, but in her voice Tamia heard kindness, a well-
meaning she almost never heard beyond the 3Ts.

"Look at the king," Kali said. They were standing in
the doorway of Malik's classroom. In the middle of a
circle of topless boys, who were wearing white martial
arts trousers, was Malik, wielding a long oak stick so
slowly, it seemed as if he was dancing with it. He
crouched down to the floor and flipped it over his shoulders, jabbing it into the air so forcefully, Tamia could
see every muscle in his arm puckering out in submis-
sion to the movement. As he came up slowly, like moving pictures stapled together, the sweat puddled at his
brown throat ran down his chest. And while Tamia
looked most dignified in her dignity-filled suit, her
thoughts were far from it. Her open mouth and hardened
nipples told her that she shared the thoughts that every
woman who ever stood in that doorway thought of the
capoeira teacher.

The excitement Tamia was ignoring for professional
purposes was thwarted when two students who'd been
excused to carry a set of books they'd been reading before class to the library in the basement pushed past
her and Kali. She smiled at them before hearing a bang
that pulled her attention back to the center of the room.

Malik had clacked his stick against the floor and
everyone was looking back at the doorway. Quickly,
the boys stopped and turned back around.

"Excuse us, queens," they said to Tamia and Kali
before bowing.

"You're excused," Kali said and they backed away
carefully.

"Who made you come here?" Malik asked after offering Tamia a seat in his office. While the room seemed

much bigger on the outside, most of the wall space was taken up by floor-to-ceiling bookshelves. Even the tiny windowsill was burdened with makeshift shelves and books. Sitting down, Tamia thought there was no way Malik could've read each of the titles—she was wrong.

"What was that in there—what you were teaching those boys?" she asked, unconsciously ignoring his question as he slid on a black, sleeveless T-shirt bearing the image of Marcus Garvey.

Malik didn't hear her question either. He sat in his seat and continued his thought. "—because I know a woman like you probably hasn't been to Harlem since Obama was elected."

"I want to call it karate, but I'm pretty sure it wasn't— tai chi maybe? Tae kwon do?"

"—maybe not even before that . . . maybe never."

Suddenly, face to face, it was as if the two strangers could finally hear each other, and at the same time they answered above each other:

"Capoeira. It's an Afro-Brazilian art form—just people having conversations with their bodies."

"Why would you think someone had to force me to come here? You're my client."

Realizing she was getting nowhere quickly, Tamia put her purse on the chair beside her and smiled politely.

"Maybe we should start again," she said. "I'm Tamia Dinkins."

"I'm guilty," was all Malik replied.

"We've already established that, and now we can move forward with trying to gather more information for your hearing. Now, as I told you, the more I know about this place—and you—the better." She pulled a legal pad from her bag.

"What about what I need to know about you?"

"About me?" Tamia laughed a bit. Never once had a client asked her anything about herself. On their first meeting, most everything they needed to know about her was posted on the wall behind her desk. "Oh, you mean my history? I went to NYU Law. The firm recruited me before graduation." Married to this announcement was Tamia's pride at her achievements. A top law school. A top firm. It put her at the head of the very elite in America. It impressed most everyone when they heard it, and that expectation was clear in her tone.

"Excuse me, sister, but I don't care about any of that," Malik said. "What . . ." He paused and looked along the spines of the books on his desk—Molefi Asante, Cheikh Diop, Clarke, Sertima, hooks. "What do you know about the Afrocentric community?"

"The what?" Tamia asked, looking up from her pad.

"The Afrocentric community."

"You mean like black people? The black community?"

"No, the Afrocentric community."

"I'm not sure where you're going," Tamia said. "I'm black. I've been black all of my life, so of course I know about African American people."

"Okay," Malik said, "let me start somewhere else—have you read *The Souls of Black Folks*?"

"Yeah, of course." Tamia nodded, happy she had found somewhere to connect with Malik. She couldn't understand why his tone was so indicting, almost smug in the way Charleston's voice was when he realized someone he knew hadn't gone to a tier-one law school or any one of her girlfriends spotted a fake Gucci. "W. E. B. DuBois—the Talented Tenth."

"You would remember that." Malik laughed heartily. "What about *The Mis-Education of the Negro*?"

"Carter G. Woodson," Tamia shot back, still trying to figure out what he meant by his comment about the Talented Tenth.

"Ashay Ashay." Malik smiled and Tamia was sure it was the first time she'd seen his teeth. Nice.

"Okay, look, I don't understand the purpose of your questions. What do a bunch of books I read at Howard have to do with your case?"

"Sister, what I do . . . what we do here is about the Afrocentric community. About helping African people displaced in America find some semblance of freedom, understand who they were, what they could be, and who wants to stop that from happening," he said with as much pride in his voice as Tamia had when she listed her accomplishment. "And if you don't understand that, if you don't believe in that, if you're just another one of these blind niggas walking around on the plantation, thinking slavery is over, I don't think you can help me. See, I'm not interested in participating in some exercise in the American Injustice system, so they can just lock my African ass up. If that's what those devils want to do, they'll do it. It don't matter what 'case' we present. The devils run the system, the judge, the lawyers, the verdict. To them, a nigga selling five keys of crack is the same as a brother educating fifty former niggas—that's fifty years. But what they don't know is that I'm going to keep doing what I do out here in there."

"So, you don't believe in the criminal justice system?"

"Well, it's called the *criminal* justice system—not the *people's* justice system. And no, I don't. I don't see how any African could."

"You're one of those militant brothers," Tamia said.

"Militant involves the military. I'm a warrior," Malik responded. "I don't take orders. I deliver results. Every African man has to do his own part if we're going to get back to Akebulan."

Tamia didn't know what Akebulan meant and at that point, she didn't care. Malik's logic was smothering her thoughts. How could he virtually sign up to go to prison? He was correct. Black people, some of the best, went to prison every day for a number of reasons that had nothing to do with them. But most of those people simply had poor representation. The verdict was a reflection of their lack of control of their image. A guilty person with a lawyer who was in control wasn't guilty anymore. She'd seen it. She'd done it.

"So . . ." Tamia tried to put words into the silent space in the conversation. Once again, he'd shared nothing about the actual case. "You want to go to prison?"

"What?" Malik shook his head and leaned over the desk to hand Tamia a piece of paper he'd written on. There was an address.

"What's this?"

"The Royal Ankh," he said. "I'll be there tonight. Come out and see what we do. There'll be a lot of sisters from the community there."

"Oh, I don't do that—I'm not a—"

"It's not like that." Malik laughed and again there were his teeth. Later that night Tamia would think of how much she liked hearing his laugh and seeing his teeth. It would be great to find ways to make that happen more often. "Just come."

"I can't. I promised a friend I'd meet her at this party . . . and . . ." Tamia had been invited to countless events by countless clients and turned them down countless times. But somehow this one seemed different. Saying no made her uneasy. The way Malik had written the address on the sheet of paper—for her—wasn't like any other offer from a client to an attorney, hoping to get an edge, to build a relationship. He didn't seem like he was trying to get anything.

"Well, you have the address. Use it if you can."

5

*There are no good girls gone wrong, just
bad girls found out.*

—Mae West

Venus Jenkins-Hottentoten-Hoverslagen-Jackson, a
black woman with the most ridiculous last name of any
woman in the city on account of two failed marriages
to Swedish bankers and one mediocre, yet standing,
marriage to a Knicks starting player, was scanning a
crowd of beautiful people for the most beautiful victim
her eye could spy. Only, to Venus Jenkins-Hottentoten-
Hoverslagen-Jackson this beautiful somebody was not
a victim. In her mind, they were all friends, who unfortunately fell beneath her social knife from time to time.
While the Southern society snob fancied herself a socialite with friends abounding everywhere, the only
thing she was truly good at abounding was husbands.

Staring through a crowd of these beautiful friends
and possible future husbands (if the Knicks thing didn't
work out) at the annual cover party for *ESPN* magazine's

body issue in Gramercy Park, Venus spotted a familiar face she hadn't seen in a while.

"Look what the cat dragged in here!" Venus happily exclaimed as if she was greeting a best friend. People around her looked on as she sat down her glass of wine and pushed past a few couples to wrap her arms around the new find.

"Oh, Venus," Tasha cheerfully countered in the middle of the tight, overperfumed embrace. "My favorite frenemy."

"Oh, you mustn't believe that." Venus laughed a bit, using a faux European accent she'd picked up two husbands ago.

"Of course, beautiful," Venus gushed, stepping back to pretend to admire Tasha's frame, yet she'd already seen and felt the extra thirty pounds Tasha was carrying. "You know I'm everywhere that's somewhere. This city can't get nothing on without me. Wish we could say the same for you, darling."

It was a statement, said flat and to anyone not privy to Venus's tricks, void of expectation. But Tasha was no anyone and Venus had attempted to put her beneath the knife so many times that she knew the words were more of a question/indictment demoting Tasha from the former front-running socialite she'd once been to a sometime nobody who was lucky enough to have married the right man and been invited to an event she had no business actually attending. Yes, Tasha got all of that from "Wish we could say the same for you, darling."

"I'm around, bitch," Tasha said, giggling so her words sounded more friendly than feisty. "Just not around you."

The women laughed off the short spar heartily. It was a draw.

In Tasha's old life, the one before she'd been calmed by the suburban breeze and quieted by children's cries that were louder than her own, she would've won this challenge. But she was tired and actually happy to see someone she knew—even if it was a frenemy.

"How's my favorite Knicks player?" Venus asked, resting her hand on a set of stacked abs Tasha could see rippling beneath her purple chemise. More pretty than beautiful, Venus made up for the difference by working out so much that her muscular, fat-free frame that revealed nearly every bone and muscle through its casing could've been featured on the cover of *ESPN* magazine.

"Oh, I sure hope he isn't your favo," Tasha joked. "We know how you do with the men." The women laughed and quickly spied each other's purses. Tasha's Birkin, though old and passed down from her mother, won by a long shot over Venus's brand-new Gucci BoHo.

"I'm not that bad. Am I?" Venus batted her eyes innocently. "No, really. Where have you been hiding yourself, Ms. Tasha? I heard you moved to New Jersey. . . ."

"Sure did. You know I'm actually happily married and my husband and I moved there to raise our family. Do you have children yet?"

"Well, at least it's Alpine," Venus said, ignoring Tasha's question. No man she'd married had been crazy enough to get her pregnant yet. "I couldn't stand to see another family go into poverty because they couldn't afford to live in Manhattan anymore. This recession is killing everyone."

"There's a recession?" Tasha asked, faking surprise to poke fun at how ridiculous Venus's statement was. "I didn't know."

"I'll tell you what else you didn't know. . . ." Venus's voice was saturated in secret. She put her hand on her hip and her bony elbow poked out from her body like the tip of a witch's broom.

"What don't I know?"

Venus looked away. She wanted Tasha to beg. The moment had arrived in the common exchange where even the words of a frenemy became desired. While Tasha's hate for Venus was a sure thing, she was also sure that Venus knew everything that went on in the city that mattered. Her thirst for fresh blood and new friends/victims never failed to put her in the right place at the wrong time. It was the only reason Tasha ever tolerated her.

"What do you have?" Tasha demanded. She hadn't ever really learned to beg anyone for anything. It really was the best she could do. "Oh . . . tell me."

"Well, since you asked, a certain blond and blue-eyed cheerleader snuck into a certain player's hotel room last weekend."

Tasha's eyes, squinted and cautious, asked the questions she couldn't. Venus's eyes went to Tasha's wedding band. Yes, that's who she was talking about.

"Lionel!" Tasha hollered, looking around for her husband, who'd slipped away to chat with his former agent. Any couth or calm she had was exiting the building. There were two games Tasha simply didn't play—knock-off shopping and cheating.

"No, no, no, calm down." Venus grabbed Tasha's arm before she ran off to put Lionel beneath her own real knife. "Listen to me."

"Listen to what? You just said that some white slut slept with my husband. What the hell do I need to listen to? Which hoe is it? That's all I need to know." Tasha reached into her purse and pulled out her cell phone. She didn't have some ghetto hit man waiting to do damage, but she had her girls, Tamia and Troy, and they'd all take a ride at night if they had to.

"First, she isn't white. The eyes are fake and the hair is imported from Switzerland."

"So, she's black? Is it Carmen? I'll kill her! And she's from LA."

"It's not Carmen. Look, do you want to hear the rest?"

"Go ahead." Tasha paused and now her hand was on her hip.

"Apparently, a new cheerleader, Lisa Henderson—something or other—snuck into Lionel's room and, while I'm sad to say it, every single report I have says he kicked her out."

"What?"

"Right out into the hallway. Naked as a broke stripper."

"He did?"

"According to three sources who stayed on the floor . . . *and* Mamacita."

"Mamacita saw it?" Tasha said. Mamacita was the Knicks' oldest and most respected groupie. She knew the traveling schedule before it was posted on the Website and usually had her airfare and hotel room paid for by some rookie who'd fallen in love.

"That's right. She's the one who helped the girl back to her room. And you know Mamacita doesn't lie. He didn't touch the girl. Didn't say a word to her," Venus whispered.

While seconds ago Tasha was considering who would raise her children once she'd killed her husband in a room full of people and was sentenced to life in prison, now she was feeling a small sense of pride, vindication at Venus's revelation.

"You can smile, bitch," Venus said, smiling herself. "I know you want to smile. That kind of scene is as rare as a black man becoming president."

"It is kind of cool, isn't it?" Tasha smiled.

"Yeah, it's cool, but don't get too happy." Venus's smile turned to a stare. "You know what the incident means. Don't tell me you've forgotten. You haven't been out of here for that long."

"I'm slipping," Tasha admitted, her smile washing away as she spotted Lionel at the bar, laughing with his former agent and two groupies, whose status was marked by exposed torsos and tramp stamps, heart-shaped tattoos on their lower backs.

"That's right," Venus confirmed. "No cheerleader or real groupie would step to the husband of a wife who was on the scene. Out of sight, out of mind."

Tasha looked at Venus.

"I know you're over in Jersey enjoying the good life, but this is real life and the longer you're away, the sooner someone will snag him away. They're just waiting for you to slip up. And I can already see that's happening." Venus looked to the shawl Tasha was wearing to hide her belly. It was expensive, probably cost more than Venus's entire ensemble (purse and shoes included), but both women knew what it was for.

There was no recovering retort for Tasha. She rewrapped her shawl and held her Birkin out on her wrist like some security doll a child would clutch.

"Well, it's been nice chatting with you, beautiful!" Venus's smile reappeared like lightning striking a tree. She pulled Tasha into her arms and held her tight, kissing her on either cheek. "Take care of you. It's a jungle out there," she whispered in her ear before disappearing into the crowd of beautiful friends to gather another glass of wine and find a new victim.

Tasha exhaled and waved at one of Lionel's teammates. She wanted to go over to the bar to gather her husband, but knew the rule of these functions. A hanging-on wife was worse than an eager groupie. She could only come and go, smile and drift away to network in her own circles.

"Where's Tamia?" Tasha asked herself, knowing better than to look at her watch. The bored wife was worse than the hanging-on wife.

Attack of the Frenemies:
Surviving the Ultimate Extraterrestrial Expereince

Rodney King was wrong—we all can't just get along. And when the foe is also a friend, the result is even worse—we manage to get along and fall out all at the same time. Every woman is bound to have a frenemy in her lifetime. She's the woman she loves to hate, and hates to love. Her life would probably be better without the frenemy, but she needs her for something. And while the relationship might cause some bumps and bruises, she endures the enemy's pain to get the friend's pleasure. Here are tips for dealing with frenemies and surviving an encounter from out of this world.

Dos:
1. *Know your enemy and her weapon of contact (usually her mouth).*
2. *Know yourself and what weapon you have that can trump hers.*
3. *Keep your cool and kill her with kindness.*

Don'ts:
1. *Fall for her petty games.*
2. *Forget that this friend is an enemy, so keep your business to yourself and do your dirt alone.*
3. *Play frenemy if there's nothing to be gained. If the relationship is truly worthless, it isn't worth your time.*

While most men relished the idea of coming home to a freshly prepared dinner, before he even got married Kyle realized that a home-cooked meal by Troy came with a price tag—she'd usually done something wrong and after she finished crying he would have to order takeout and dispose of the garbage to get rid of the smell of whatever cut of expensive meat Troy had charred to a dry mess.

After smelling the now familiar scent of what he identified as burning beef when he walked into the house, he immediately asked his wife what the matter was and thwarted her phony half smile with an eye roll. He insisted it was something and she insisted it was nothing.

"Why can't I just do something nice for you? For my husband?" Troy asked, standing beside Kyle at the kitchen table.

"You call this nice?" He pointed to what looked like a mass of tar at the center of a silver platter.

At least the platter looked nice, Troy thought. She'd actually put fresh parsley sprigs and baby carrots on the side to dress it up.

"It's for you."

"Look, just tell me what's wrong, baby, so we can go get something to eat—"

"So you're not going to eat it? It took all day to cook that."

"Yeah, it looks like it's been cooking all day. And what is it? What *was* it?"

Troy pouted and went to the sink. How did he know something was wrong? The plan was to get him full and butter him up before she told him about what happened at the meeting. The last thing she needed was to stall and let Sister Glover get to him first. Even in her un-right mind, Troy knew that wasn't quite the right thing to do. She stared into the empty sink and tried to find the right thing to say. There was no way Kyle was going to eat that steak, or roast beef, or London broil, or whatever it was supposed to be. She might as well get on with it.

"I need you to ban Sister Glover from the Virtuous Women."

"What?" Kyle was half listening as he looked through his cell phone for the number to the Chinese restaurant. Troy hadn't left the sink.

She turned to him.

"I need you to ban her . . . from the Virtuous Women."

"That doesn't make any sense. It's a church, Troy. We don't ban anyone from anything and she's the president, isn't she? Wait." He looked at her. "What happened? Did something happen at the church, with Sister Glover?"

"No. Nothing happened. I just, I just kind of kicked her out of the group. That's all." Troy smiled composedly, plucked a bowl of rice from the counter, and sat it on the table as if they were going to eat the meal.

"You kind of did what? Troy, what happened? What did you do to her?"

"What do you mean 'what did I do to her?' I'm your wife. Don't you mean, what did she do to me?" Troy looked at Kyle hard.

"Just tell me what happened." He sat down beside the burnt meat and tried to relax his shoulders.

"She's crazy. She's just crazy," Troy blurted out. "And I told her it was time for me to take over the group and she said I couldn't, so I kicked her out of the meeting and told her she's banned. Now I just need you to agree. We're supposed to stick together. Right? 'Til death us do part. That's what you said. Right?"

Kyle looked at the dark cherry cabinet he'd drilled crooked into the wall.

"I can't believe this. Troy, I was just trying not to have any drama at the church. I can't have all this crazy stuff going on. You know folks are already acting funny about me marrying you because you didn't belong to the church . . . or any church . . . and you're not saved. This is just going to give them more wood to stoke the fire."

"Are you kidding me? I'm helping them stoke the fire?" Troy sat down angrily in the chair beside Kyle and the two were silent for a while.

"Look, I'm doing the best I can," Troy started again. "For two years I've been running around here playing Little Miss Perfect Christian First Lady Bride Saint for you and for them and for us. And you know what? It's hard. It's fucking hard to be perfect. It's so fucking hard. They make it hard on fucking purpose." Troy hadn't cursed in so long, the f-bombs were dropping all around the table like pelts of rain. It felt good and she wasn't even thinking about pulling out her new prayer pad.

"I never asked you to be perfect," Kyle said.

"No, but you and everyone else makes it clear that I should be. I mean, that's what this is all about. Being saved? Sanctified? Right? Just say it."

"Say what?"

"That you want me to be saved. That you want me to be like her."

"I didn't marry her. I married you, just the way you are. And of course I want you to be saved. Of course. Why wouldn't I want that for you?"

"It's impossible. It's just impossible. I can't do it. Just can't."

"Can't do what?"

"Because I've been doing good and acting right for so long." Troy kept talking as if she hadn't heard Kyle's question. "I walked away from my entire life to do this and nothing is happening."

"What is supposed to be happening?"

"I'm all this on the outside, but inside I'm just . . .

I'm still me. I'm still me but I'm drowning and waiting for this fucking light to shine down from heaven to say, 'Hey, Troy Helene Hall, you're saved.' Is that how it happens?"

"I don't know."

"What?"

"I don't know if anyone knows," Kyle said carefully. "And the ones that claim they do are lying. God is just a voice and salvation is a whisper. And it doesn't come to people just because they act good or right. Salvation can come to a killer, to anyone."

"So it's me." Troy wiped a tear from her cheek. "It's me. I can't get saved."

"You, Troy," Kyle said, reaching to cup Troy's face in his hands, "are one of the most genuine, funny, loving, and just real people I know. You have a good heart and whenever I see you, I hear God whisper in my ear that you're the woman that was assigned to me. And I don't want anyone else."

Troy looked at her husband, into his serious, honest eyes, and felt the whole, true weight of his love. A love she never requested, a love she never truly felt she deserved, and began, very softly, to weep.

"Sorry I'm late, Ms. Lovestrong," Tamia said, tapping Tasha on the shoulder after sneaking up on her at the party.

"Damn, I thought you weren't coming."

"Oh, I wouldn't leave you alone to endure looking at all of these beautiful men . . . not after what happened last year," Tamia said, referring to last year's body issue party, where a perfectly chiseled twenty-three-year-old football player decided to share his perfectly chiseled ass with the entire party. Luckily, Tasha had her camera phone out and was ready to record full video footage.

"I was in Harlem," Tamia added, "and would you believe that none of the cabs I stopped would bring me all the way downtown? I had to get two cabs."

"Yes, I would believe that, but the really crazy part was that you were uptown."

"What? I'm always in Harlem."

"Since when? Since Troy's last dinner party?"

"Okay, maybe I never go to Harlem. It's a new client," Tamia admitted, feeling then that "client" was such an odd word to put next to Malik's name. Nothing they'd done or discussed was like anything she'd ever experienced with a client. "So how are you holding up? Any streaks yet?"

"No streaks; just freaks," Tasha said. "I ran into Venus."

"Oh no." Tamia frowned and plucked a glass of wine from a tray passing by. "The original Cruella DeVil with fifteen last names? God, I hate that woman. Now, there's one I will never understand. How can that witch find, like, thirty husbands and I can't get one?"

"The law of opposites. Men love everything they hate. They say they need a nice girl, but they really want a bad girl."

There was laughter, loud, bold, and female, coming from the center of the room. All eyes shifted from drinks and faces that pretended to be listening to overused bar stories to discover the commotion, the party within the party, that was evidently more exciting.

"Lynn Hudson," Tasha said in two gruff words after the shoulders before her peeled back so she could see the source of fun. "The team's new publicist. The child is hardly out of elementary school and she's already head of the class."

Tasha and Tamia looked on openmouthed at Lynn, who was sipping on a glass of champagne as the handsome streaker from the year before whispered in her ear. Pretty as a honeysuckle and as sexy as a rose, she giggled and giggled like whatever he was saying was the best-kept secret in the room. Three girls at her side had the same kind of attention from other football players whose asses were probably just as nice as the one Tamia saw in the picture on Tasha's phone. They giggled too and sometimes went to share what was being whispered to another girl in the pack.

"What is this, high school?" Tasha said, annoyed. "The cheerleaders and the dumb jocks? Spare me. Wait until reality hits and the bullshit those men whisper in their ears leads to sloppy titties and tiger prints[12] on their guts."

"Oh, don't be so negative, Tasha," Tamia said. "They're just the new crop. We were them once. Right?" Tamia looked at Lynn's wispy, happily bouncy hair, her thin, slender hands, and new skin and suddenly couldn't remember ever looking like that. "You act like we're ancient or something," she tried to remind herself more than Tasha. "We're just thirty . . . and that's the new twenty . . . so we're them and they're—"

"Ten?" Tasha watched beside Tamia as a song prompted the girls to start dancing. And when their fists pumped into the air, the entire room seemed to want to join in.

"I guess so."

"Well, if I'm twenty and they're ten, then their asses should be at home and asleep. Not up in here messing up the party."

"Well, it doesn't exactly look like they're messing up the party," Tamia said as a couple pushed past her to get a better spot on the dance floor. "It looks like they're making the party." Her eyes followed the cou-

[12] Tiger prints: stretch marks

ple and she watched them encircle one of the girls on either side. She laughed and turned toward Tamia. "That's Ava."

"What?" Tasha asked.

"It's Ava. The one I told you about that's engaged to Charleston's friend." Tamia's heart was skipping beats. Suddenly, she'd gone from watching to spying.

"Who? Which one?" Tasha looked frantically, as if locating the betrothed beauty would make any difference in her level of disgust.

"Right there—dancing with that couple."

"The white couple?"

Tamia nodded and shook her head at how freely Ava danced with both the man and woman. It was a freedom she never understood about the younger It Girls. They didn't seem to notice much the difference between men and women and gyrated on anything beside them. When she was new to partying, it was only white girls hip rolling on each other, but now it was everyone. She looked to see if Ava was wearing her engagement ring. It was there.

"She *is* cute." Tasha wanted to find something nasty to say to keep her mood, but really admitting to the girl's beauty was enough to kick it up a few notches. "She looks kind of like me when I was younger." She looked at Tamia for approval.

"Yeah . . . and then you woke up."[13]

The faithfully entertaining frolics between foes who pretended to be friends provided just the right amount of social familiarity between both parties. Each foe knew what it was and if she was smart, she expected nothing more or less from the opposition. The com-

[13] And then you woke up: idiom for someone who is dreaming.

plete opposite was true when the line between foes and
friends was a bit softer and unclear. When a foe really
thought she was a friend or a friend had secretly decided to become a foe, things got messy and especially
uncomfortable.

Fifteen minutes of spying and frowning later, Tasha
and Tamia were heading to the bathroom to retouch
their highly unnecessary under-eye concealer when
one such line was blurred.

"It's Lionel LaRoche's wife . . . Natasha, right?" Tasha
and Tamia heard someone squeal after they'd turned
from the scene on the dance floor that now included one
of the football players' ass cheeks.

Tamia turned first, thinking she would help remind
the reporter or whoever it was that she was wasting her
time trying to chat with Tasha by calling her "Lionel's
wife" or "Natasha." It was like calling LisaRaye Lisa
or Lisa Raye—she hated both titles and anyone who
wanted to know her needed to know that.

"I'm sorry, Tasha—I meant to say Tasha," Lynn said
once both Tasha's and Tamia's eyes were on her. Free of
her entourage, she thrust out her arms for an embrace.
Tasha was pulled to her before she had any opportunity
to protest. Lynn whispered into Tasha's ear, "I know
you don't like that. I know a lot about you."

Tasha smiled her friendly pictures smile and pinched
Tamia's arm.

"Wow, that's something. That's really . . . something."

"Hello, I'm Tamia Dinkins," Tamia said, trying to
shake Lynn's hand, but she hugged her too.

"Yes," Lynn said, "I've heard of you. You both went
to my alma mater—Howard. You're on the alumnae
Web site in the 'Who's Who of New York.'"

"Wonderful," Tasha said dryly.

"Tasha, I was trying to get in contact with you a few weeks ago. I got last-minute tickets for a tea Michelle Obama was hosting in midtown. It was for influential wives, who also happened to be businesswomen—but then I realized you closed your artist-management firm."

Had Lynn been looking, she would've seen that Tamia was shaking her head for Lynn to stop speaking, but she just kept going. While Tasha had only managed Lionel and two overaged rappers during her brief, yet spirited tenure as a business owner, after having Toni and moving to Jersey, she had little time and lost lots of inner-city connections. So she officially had to shut down what was left of her operation. It was a painful departure from the only career choice or true private life Tasha had ever known, and to make herself feel better, she'd shoveled it beneath piles of silence and denial.

"Yeah, well, that's in my past." Tasha's voice was soft, resolute, everything Tamia hadn't expected. Tamia turned to be sure it was still Tasha who was standing beside her.

Lynn was laughing.

"It doesn't have to be in your past," she said, holding Tasha's arms at the wrists. "The city still needs you. You're hot." She bit at her lip in a way that confused how Tamia and the man who was standing behind the group listening understood "hot." Did she mean Tasha was "hot" or her work with artists was "hot"?

"Thank you," Tasha said. "I can't say I'm not."

"Look," Lynn said, sliding a shiny black card into Tasha's hand and whispering in her ear. "This is my private card. I know lots of people who would be happy to help you get started. When you're ready to come back into the city, give me a call." She kissed Tasha on the cheek and looked into her eyes. "Yeah, you're hot."

Kyle's head was spinning around on the floor again. Only, this time, it was on the living room floor of the Harlem brownstone. Troy was standing by the front door wearing a coat.

"You gonna pick me up?" the head asked a nervous Troy, who knew somehow she was naked beneath her coat.

"Pick you up?"

"Yeah . . . so we can go. We're on our way to hell. You burned the church down. Broke my head off and ate my body. We have to go to hell."

Now a Biggie Smalls song was playing in the background.

"I'm ready to die," Kyle's head sang along with Biggie.

"But I don't want to go to hell! I don't want to die," Troy cried.

"It's too late. You're already dead."

Then, in the way that waves come quickly up on sand, the woman and the head were away from the comfort of their living room and in the backseat of a funeral car. Kyle's head was wearing a top hat Troy's grandfather used to wear to funerals. Troy's once black coat was now red, matching her fingernails, shoes, and lipstick, which stained her teeth.

"Y'all going to hell?" the driver of the car asked, turning around. It was Sister Glover. She was smiling big from behind Troy's wedding veil.

"We sure are! My baby and me," said Kyle's head.

"No, we aren't. We want to go someplace else—I have money. I can pay," Troy tried, reaching into her pocket, but there was no insides and her hand went right in between her bare legs.

"Can't pay to go someplace else," Sister Glover said.

"That's right," Kyle agreed.

"Good thing y'all got together. Pastor, I was worried you would choose a good Christian wife, grow the house of the Lord, and spend your life in eternal heaven," Sister Glover added, turning completely away from the wheel of the moving car and thumbing through an old Bible with pages falling out everywhere. *"But you got her and now it's so clear, y'all are going to hell. Both of you. How wonderful. I am so proud. Here it is—here's the Scripture—"*

"No need to recite it, sister," Kyle said jovially. *"My wifey can do it. She knows the words. She knows the Word!"*

They both looked at Troy and from nowhere the words of a Bible verse she'd only skimmed came charging from her mouth.

"Who can find a virtuous woman? for her price is far above rubies. The heart of her husband doth safely trust in her, so that he shall have no need of spoil. She will do him good and not evil all the days of her life."

"Proverbs 31. Amen and hallelujah and shalom and selah and what else?" Sister Glover said.

"Umm . . . Praise the . . . Whatever . . . doesn't matter. Put the pedal to the metal and get us to hell!" Kyle's head wobbled and rolled onto the floor of the car.

Troy was awakened by a spill of sweat that slipped from her forehead to pool in her ears. Exhausted by her dream, she sat up slowly. She wasn't afraid or scared. Not rushing down to her prayer closet or racing to pick up her Bible, which had fallen into the center of the bed between her and Kyle. Her shoulders fell. She looked at Kyle and began to cry.

* * *

As Troy contemplated getting out of the bed, getting into her car, and getting as far away from her reality as possible, Tasha was getting a better look at what she swore were crow's-feet crowding the undersides of her eyes—they weren't.

"Any more concealer and you'll look like a corpse," Tamia said, standing beside Tasha as she hunched over the basin to get closer to the mirror. Both women could feel the bass from the music outside rattling through the sink top.

"They're like cracks . . . little cracks under my eyes." Pulling her eyes back from the sides of her head and then pushing them closer together, she turned to Tamia. "See them? See the difference when I do this?" She pulled her eyes back. "And when I do this?" She pushed them in.

A woman waiting to wash her hands walked out after it was clear she couldn't get past them.

"Well, when you scrunch your face up like that, I see many things." Tamia laughed, before turning to look at her own eyes.

"Maybe I need surgery. A blepharoplasty . . . maybe a whole face-lift. . . . Look at my forehead."

"Tasha, stop it," Tamia said, looking at her friend for a while. "You know, I can't believe he's going to marry her."

"Who?" Tasha pulled her forehead back from either side and pushed it back in again.

"Nathaniel—Charleston's friend," Tamia answered. "She's just so obviously a gold digger. She has no class and less history. The girl's only in because of how she looks. Did you see her out there? She's probably sleeping with one of those basketball players. I wouldn't put it past her. He could do so much better."

"Oh, who cares, Mia?" Tasha said. "A shallow man finds a shallow woman? They deserve each other, if you ask me. I thought he was a delicious,[14] anyway." She paused. "Do you think I should get cheek liposuction?"

Tamia had no language to communicate how ridiculous she thought her friend sounded. She just glared at Tasha's reflection in the mirror as Tasha pulled her cheeks in and out like a fish.

"What the fuck?" Tasha pushed her face closer to the mirror, and then closer again.

"What?" Tamia asked.

Tasha climbed up on the basin and angled her chin toward the mirror.

"A hair . . . Look! Another . . . fucking hair!"

"Where?"

"On my chin! Right here!" Tasha shrieked and turned her chin toward Tamia.

There was a curly, short gray hair poking out from the right side of Tasha's chin.

Tamia covered her mouth to stop from laughing.

"It ain't funny! It's not fucking funny at all! I'm aged. I'm old. I'm dying."

"Oh, don't be ridiculous. It's just a stupid chin hair."

The hair was so long, Tamia reached over and just plucked it from Tasha's chin.

"I get them all the time," Tamia added. "They have a cream for it."

"It's true. I'm dying . . . like an old cow out to pasture," Tasha cried dramatically.

"You've never even been to a pasture . . . probably haven't seen a cow."

"First the platinum hair in my basement[15] . . . then

---

[14] Delicious: an effeminate straight man, whom others suspect as being gay/bisexual.

[15] Basement: vagina

this one on my chin . . . next I'll have a beard and mustache. You know black women can't get electrolysis."

"You're overreacting. Bring it in and calm down. What's got you so on edge lately?"

"It's everything. Everything," Tasha admitted, looking at her reflection. "Sometimes I sit and look at myself in the mirror like this and I think I can see myself. Like I'm still me and everything, but I wonder if I'm the me I thought I would be. When I was younger I was gonna go out and take over the world. Now I feel like the world has taken over me. I'm a mother of two who lives in the suburbs. I take Pilates on Wednesday and spin on Friday. That's my life. Predictable . . . And then I die."

"No . . . and then you wake up and stop dreaming, because you are not dead yet," Tamia said. "Don't just give up. You can still have everything you ever planned for . . . you just need a new plan to get it."

And then it was like a pinch on her thigh or a prick on her thumb . . . Tasha had an idea.

"You're right," she said, amazed at what was cooking up in her head.

"Really?" Tamia was astonished her words had any effect.

"Not you . . . I mean you . . . you and her," Tasha explained quickly. "I need to move back to the city. Back to Manhattan to reclaim my life. You heard that Lynn out there . . . she said I'm still hot. She said I have it. She said people could help me."

"Whoa. I didn't mean all of that," Tamia said. "I was just suggesting maybe you switch your gym classes or add a hobby . . . knitting or Parcheesi . . . not up and moving back to the city. What about the girls? And Lionel? What are they gonna do?"

"They can come with me!" Tasha jumped off of the counter and fixed her dress. "I'm moving back to the city!" she confirmed. "I have to go get Lionel. I have to tell him."

"I don't think it's—"

"You can't talk me out of this. I know it's right. I feel it."

Tamia tried not to frown at her friend. Tasha always "felt" something.

"Okay. I guess so. . . . But—"

"Not another word!" Tasha sounded so excited. "Let me get Lionel and I'll meet you out front. You still want a ride home, right?"

"Um . . ." Tamia looked at her watch. It was a bit before 11. Late for people going to work in the morning, but early to end a New York night. "You know, I might make a stop before heading home. You two go on without me. I'll get a cab."

"You sure?" Tasha asked, picking up her purse.

"Yes."

"Well, give me a buzz when you get home. I want to be sure you got in okay," Tasha said. "It's a jungle out there."

The friends kissed and Tasha walked out of the bathroom to begin her new life . . . only by the time she would find her husband and get him alone, she would go soft and lose her courage.

"That woman is crazy." Tamia laughed, pulling the card Malik gave her from her purse and looking at the address beneath the soft bathroom light. She still hadn't decided if she was going, but something about the invitation, from Malik, and the idea of seeing him again kept it on her mind.

She pulled her purse onto her shoulder and was about to walk out of the bathroom, but there, at the lower corner of her eye, she saw twinkling, like a spinning star, in the dull darkness of the bathroom.

She turned her head a little and noticed that it was

coming from beneath the closed door of one of the two stalls she thought were empty. She looked and saw that the sparkling was actually a familiar disco-ball clutch, hanging from a metallic string.

"Is someone in there?" Tamia called, wincing at the thought of the last someone she'd seen with that purse having heard what she'd shared with Tasha moments before. Really, while the exquisite accessory was quite expensive, it wouldn't have been silly to consider that anyone else at the party might have had one identical to the one Tamia had seen. It was possible. But right then, considering the law of bad luck, it was also implausible.

The stall door clicked open and out emerged a screw-faced Ava.

She didn't look at Tamia. She headed right to the basin, where she washed her hands and replaced her lip gloss with the focus of a shooter.

Afraid to move or even speak the apology she was editing in her mind, Tamia just watched her.

"You know," Ava said, "with all of the bullshit women face, you'd think we'd be able to stop shoveling shit on other people." She looked at Tamia and a fire that long ago seared certain sides of her heart into something unrecognizable could be seen. "The young me, the one who came from the projects in Memphis and ran barefoot to the bus station with the last $20 my mother had in her pocket the night her pimp killed her, would've come out of that stall and beat your ass."

"But . . . I . . . I . . ." Tamia tried, but she was too flustered to speak. Her heart was pounding through her ears. The closest she'd ever come to a fight was with a pimp named Diamond at a strip club in Los Angeles.

"No. There's no reason to explain, or apologize. Don't be scared, because I'm not that girl anymore,"

Ava said. "See, she was easily upset when people said shit to her that she knew was true. But now I'm grown and I can accept my own shit. So, you're right. I am a gold digger."

"Ava, I didn't mean to say it like that," Tamia tried. "I don't even know—"

"You're right," Ava cut her off. "You don't fucking know me. I've seen bitches like you all my life. You don't know what it's like to starve. To be hungry and dream about shit like this. Places like this. It's all you can think about. And then some nigga is up in your face, breathing on you because your mother is dead now and he says, 'Keep yourself pretty and you'll get out of here.' I got out of there and I remembered what he said. So, you're motherfucking right I'm a gold digger. And, yes, Nathaniel probably could do better. He could probably have picked one of you stuffy-ass, fake hoes. But he didn't. He chose me."

Ava closed her purse and balled it up in her hand like a fat orange.

"You know, before you go talking about what someone else is, maybe you should figure out who you are," Ava added. "Now, you have a good night." A smile washed over her face quickly and two of the other women she was with came in.

"There you are," one said. "I thought we were going to need a plumber to come get you."

The women laughed, Ava winked at Tamia, and they left.

Like the Freedom Project, the Royal Ankh looked nothing like Tamia expected. And this time, weathering the late hour and cooler evening spring temperatures without a jacket, she did have a few solid expectations—a building with doors, windows, a roof. But none were present when her cabbie stopped.

"777—this is where the address should be," he said as they looked at a dark, empty space where a building had been hollowed out between two others.

Tamia exited and fretfully followed four shadows into the darkness. Behind a foot of bricks, which marked what was left of the old building, was a flat of fresh green grass. Everything inside of Tamia said she should be afraid and reminded her of how ridiculous this was. But something else, like a propeller tugging her navel, pulled her to something she felt she had to see. Really, she reasoned, she was just there because there was no way she'd get to bed after what had just happened between her and Ava at the party. She was afraid, angry, and ashamed. Actually, she might have felt better had Ava hit her.

The steam from the heaters in the other buildings filled the empty lot with a moist heat that softened the loose soil beneath Tamia's feet. Trying to keep up with the people in front, she cursed herself for wearing heels as they dug into the dirt. She looked down at the tip of her gray suede shoe and saw what looked like gold dust.

"Oh, crap!" she said, forgetting her leaders and pulling out her cell phone to get a little light.

She shined the light on the grass. The gold dust was everywhere around her.

"What is this?" Tamia said, holding the light higher. The cell phone's blue glow highlighted from the bottom of the cross to its loop, where Tamia stood, the outline of an ankh.

"I can't believe you came," Malik said later when

Tamia had found her way to the back of the lot where an open field hosted a crowd of what looked like a hundred people. Above them was a huge, wooden ankh, suspended in the air by chains that were linked to the surrounding buildings. A tall oak tree, whose branches seemed to reach out into the crowd, was centered beneath it.

"Really, I can't believe I came either," Tamia admitted, looking around the crowd. Men and women wore Afros and dreadlocks, head wraps, and some even had short buzz cuts with Adinkra symbols etched into the napes of their necks. They were all adorned with nose rings and intricate African neckwear. Some wore gold and bronze; others had silver and wood. While they all seemed like they were at a party, dancing to a set of African drummers and smiling at each other, it was quite different than the one Tamia had left in the city. "I thought I'd be too late," she added.

"We're just getting started," Malik said. "Brothers and sisters will be coming out here all night."

"So, what is this? Why are all of these people here?" Tamia asked as an older man who had one huge dreadlock spiraling down his back walked past beating a drum and chanting as if in a trance.

"It's the crescent moon." Malik pointed to the sliver of a bright white moon above them. "In our itan, our history, it meant fertility—the line between life and death. It is time for the Erena for some brothers who are being reborn to the purpose of their spirits, elevated to a higher spiritual consciousness—the ori orun."

"You do realize that I don't know what you're talking about when you say things like that?" Tamia chuckled. "I mean, you have to know that."

"Yeah." Malik smiled back at her. "Basically, it's a rite-of-passage ceremony."

"Thank you for the translation."

Suddenly all movement and chatter from the increasing crowd of onlookers around them stopped.

Behind the drummer's syncopated beat trailed seven men dressed in so much white, the moon, the clouds, and stars seemed more luminous above them. They were all bald, and ancient Kemetic symbols and markings Tamia didn't yet understand were penciled into their scalps, cheeks, and foreheads in white paint. Tamia watched intently as they organized into a circle and chanted a complicated rite to the ancestors before libations were poured into the soil around them. The drummer continued chanting what was becoming a song, as he led them around the tree.

"They died and now they're alive," Tamia heard. She turned and now Kali was standing beside Malik, draped in a beautiful red sari. Her eyes were locked on the men.

Tamia turned back around. Their composure and steady focus defied the bitter March wind that was numbing her toes. Their eyes were focused east as they called out with the chanting drummer.

"Eshu?" Tamia repeated one of the words she could make out. "Eshu? Elegbua?"

"They're calling for the Orisha, or safe travel," Kali said, grabbing Tamia's hand, "of the crossroads."

This went on for hours. Sweat poured from the men's heads, but they went on chanting. The wind swept up icy dirt from the fields around them, soiling their white clothes, but they went on chanting. The frigid temperatures sank lower with the moon as it crossed the sky, yet they went on chanting into the night.

And while Tamia had thought of every ill-informed comment she could consider about what she was seeing, watching the men fight so dedicatedly to change, be so connected with a culture she didn't know or understand that seemed so inextricably connected to other things she knew, her innocent, clear mind was moved, opened in a way a twister of a Rubik's Cube feels after turning the toy to its final position of completion. There was something about what they were doing, what the people gathered around them to observe, what she was seeing, that seemed more real, more natural, more intelligent than anything she'd ever witnessed in her entire life.

"Ayo," Malik said and Tamia's stare was broken by the vision of a woman standing between her and Malik. Kali had left long ago when the crowd encircled the group of men after it was clear the night could hear no more of their chanting. The rite was over.

"Malik," the woman said, hugging him in a familiar way that showed more than the two had said in their greeting. Ayo's light brown skin, high cheekbones, and sultry, slanted eyes provided the ingredients of a beauty that usually stunned both men and women into gazing at her before they really saw her. She looked unreal, like the spray painting of a person in a Benetton ad. Even the little golden pin earring that sat on her nose seemed perfectly in place. Not one ginger-colored dreadlock on her head was out of place.

"Tamia," Malik said like he was introducing his prom date, "this is Ayodele. She teaches poetry arts at the Freedom Project."

"Poetry arts?" Ayo laughed and playfully plucked Malik. "It's just poetry. Why do you have to be so dramatic, Malik?" The two laughed at what wasn't a joke and Tamia realized that she was the third wheel in a conversation. It was like she wasn't even standing there. "I'm so sorry, my sister," Ayo said, turning to Tamia and then she was just beside Malik, her skin the perfect contrast to his. "It is a pleasure to meet you."

"Mine too." Again, Tamia was pulled into a hug. She noticed that Ayo also smelled of frankincense.

"So, are you a . . ." Ayo looked from Tamia to Malik. "You two are like . . ."

"I was invited by Malik," Tamia said.

"This isn't her thing," Malik added. "She's my attorney. I invited her here so she could learn more about what we do."

While everything Malik revealed to Ayo was true, Tamia didn't like the way it sounded. Like she was simple. Uninformed. A visitor. At once, Tamia's shoes, clothing, purse, hair, earring-less nose were stacked up against everything opposite Ayodele was and had.

"Well, many thanks and blessings to you, Sister Tamia, for helping us. Brother Malik is a leader in our community and we couldn't do what we do without him."

Malik looked at Ayo like she was reciting marriage vows or giving him a check for $1 million. Tamia thought that she hadn't ever seen any grown man look at any woman with such respect, such love, such schoolboy wonder.

"Well, I'm going to get inside," Ayo said. "My toes are freezing in these boots. I know your feet are cold too, sister." They all looked down at the gold dusting the tips of Tamia's shoes.

After Ayo hugged both Tamia and Malik and walked off into the crowd, Tamia playfully chided, "You sure you don't want to go with her?"

"She's just my friend," Malik said. "Just someone who works with me."

Hours later, as Tamia lay in bed wondering at how the scent of frankincense and myrrh hadn't yet left her body and feeling the steady pulse of the African drum still thumping in her stomach, the phone rang and Troy was on the other end.

While some other sisterfriends might have been alarmed by the time of the call, Tamia rolled over and answered as if it was noon and not far after midnight. The friends had never been very good at limitations.

Whispering from her position in the corner of the inside of the bathroom door where she could still see Kyle in bed sleeping, Troy told Tamia about the triumph at the meeting, the pressure on her heart, and the fear she'd been keeping secret for a long time. Both friends cried as Tamia admitted how Troy had been changing and how sometimes she felt the best friend she'd pledged a sorority with in undergrad was absent even when she was present, and she couldn't understand why.

"I don't know why he married me," Troy said. "I just can't figure out why. This isn't me. This place. These people. I can't do this."

"Kyle loves you, Troy. That's why he married you."

"What if his love isn't enough? What if we can't make it on that?"

"I'm not going to lie to you, Ms. Lovesong, and say love is always enough to make it. Both of us know that sometimes love can be beat down and look just as ugly as hate," Tamia said sincerely. "But I do know you have to take the chance. And what makes you think you're not worth the chance? That Kyle wasn't lucky to find you?"

Troy looked at Kyle's sleeping body, watching his chest rise and sink. He reached out to her side of the bed.

"He's not like me, and I don't want to change him," Troy said. "Before he met me, he didn't know the dif-

ference between Polo and Purple Label. He didn't curse.
He didn't even watch television."

"People can't live like that—all shut in from the
world," Tamia said. "Did you ever think that maybe he
likes that about you? That you know about the world
and can share it with him?"

"What is there to share? And what if everything I'm
sharing with him will take him further from who he is?
Further from being a man of God?"

"You can't punish him for being a man of God and
you can't punish yourself for living your life. If you
two are going to make it you have to try to live in both
worlds, with both histories." Tamia tried not to sound
like she was still crying, but she was. It hurt her to hear
her friend in so much pain. Troy had changed her entire
life to try to make her marriage work. "Troy, you're
one of the most godly women I know. Forget about the
church and all of that stuff. If God is love, then you've
got more than most people. You love your family and
you love your friends. And even when you've fallen
short, I've seen you fight for all of us and remind us
how to love one another. Now, I'm not one of those sisters in the club at the church. I'm not sanctified"—
Tamia and Troy laughed—"but I know that kind of
love is good and godly, and Kyle is lucky to have it."

The next time Pastor Kyle Hall reached for his wife
in the night, she was there and reaching back to him.
While he was asleep, her touch immediately and fully
woke him. He opened his eyes and saw her nude breasts
facing him and leaning toward the sheets. He moved his
hand from Troy's open palm to her and looked at her
face. And while any other night when he'd touched her
in this way, his mind tried to recall if it was a holiday or

what he'd done to deserve this, this time, all he thought
was "beautiful."

"I love you," his wife said, her arm crisscrossing his
and reaching beneath the sheet.

"I love you too."

It's one amazing thing when a woman is born lumi-
nescent. It's another amazingly spectacular thing when
the same woman forgets how bright and dazzling she is
for a very long time and then, through some kind of in-
tervention, is reminded.

Two weeks after the Queen Been Competition led
Troy to inspire the biggest coup d'état in First Baptist
history, the Virtuous Women's annual bake sale raked
in its biggest profit ever and just like that Troy had a
palpable reminder of the significance of her own brand
of luminosity. While she dared not contribute a cake of
her making, she used her connections and wit to lead a
fierce marketing campaign throughout the surrounding
neighborhood that led to a line of eager customers waiting outside the church the morning of the sale. "What
are all these people waiting for?" Sister Julia asked
Troy, who was busy walking down the line to offer
guests hot tea as they waited. "You," Troy responded.
She handed Sister Julia, whose Five-Flavor Bundt was
the sweetest and softest she'd ever had, a flyer with the
woman's image on it as she held one of her cakes. Realizing that the women of the church presented the
most compelling and memorable branding behind the
products they were selling, Troy created flyers featur-
ing the images of each of the women with the cakes. So
they weren't just selling this cake and that cake—it was
Mother Beulah's Sock-It-to-Me Cake, Sister Sarah's
Sweet Potato Pie, Sister Mildred's bread pudding, Sis-

ter Junnie Mae's pineapple upside-down cake, and Sister Lena's 7Up Cake. Everyone in line had an order—they wanted the entire cake, wanted to meet the women who'd made them, and even when everything was gone the Virtuous Women were still taking orders. Needless to say, the mothers and sisters, who'd been reminded of their own luminosity as customers argued about who'd get their cakes and begged for pictures and secret recipes, had nothing but smiles and kind words for their First Lady. "First Lady is smart," Sister Julia said, smiling after a reporter from the *Amsterdam News* Troy invited begged her for the recipe for the Five-Flavor Bundt. "I'm humble . . . but my cake is good."

Sister Julia Reid's Five-Flavor Bundt
(As Passed Down at a Card Party . . .
Before Sister Julia Got Saved)

If you have a sweet tooth, this sweet cake is sure to satisfy. Invite a few friends over and indulge with vanilla bean ice cream.

Cake Ingredients:

2 sticks butter
3 cups sugar
½ c. vegetable oil
5 large eggs (well beaten)
3 cups flour
½ tsp. baking powder
½ tsp. salt
1 c. milk
1 tsp. each almond, lemon, vanilla, coconut, and rum extract

Directions:
Cream butter, sugar, and vegetable oil until light and fluffy. Add eggs (which have been beaten until lemon in color). Combine flour, baking powder, and salt in a separate bowl. Add to butter and egg mixture and beat approximately 1 ½ minutes, adding milk for smooth batter consistency. Fold in the five flavors. Bake at 350 degrees Fahrenheit for approximately 1 to 1 ½ hours. Stick toothpick in to make sure it's done. Leave in pan.

Topping Ingredients:

1 tsp. each almond, lemon, vanilla, coconut, and rum extract
1 cup sugar
½ cup water

Directions:
Combine in a saucepan and bring to a boil for 2 minutes. Make sure cake is cool; then, pour ½ mixture over cake, wait 10 minutes, and turn cake out of pan onto a plate. Pour remaining mixture over cake.

A thin and uncomfortable white leather couch sitting atop a red shag carpet was the only piece of recognizable living room furniture in Tasha's old bachelorette pad in Tribeca. The chairs were elongated shoes Tasha had styled in honor of her favo MoBos[16] and the tables, glass and close to the floor, looked like frosted ice cubes. White koi fish, as thick as bass, played in a pool beneath the table in front of the couch.

"I just can't believe you kept this place for this long," Tamia shouted to Tasha as Toni banged at the fish through the tabletop. She left Tiara at home rapping with Lionel.

"Every girl needs a quick exit," Tasha answered from the only bedroom in the tiny fifth-floor apartment.

Tamia looked at Troy, who was sitting beside her on the couch, and frowned.

"From your husband?" Troy asked.

Tasha came out of the room wearing a pair of MoBos she hadn't seen in the eight years since Lionel had refused to let her leave his SoHo loft and proposed marriage as the new friends lay naked in bed eating Froot Loops and watching reruns of *Law & Order*.

"Pack light and always have a Plan B," Tasha said after explaining that marrying a ballplayer was risky and while she knew Lionel loved her, sometimes love isn't enough to keep a millionaire connected to one woman for a lifetime.

"So you come here to water the plants?" Troy said, snatching a leaf Toni pulled from a little bonsai tree on the table.

"Of course not. I hire people to do that. Someone

[16] MoBos: Manolo Blahniks.

comes to water the plants, clean the linen, feed the fish, and adjust the temperature."

"I have to be the one to bring some reason to this madness," Tamia started. "I can't believe you've been paying rent for this apartment for the last eight years—and you didn't tell anyone. Not even us." She looked at an Andy Warhol–style series of rainbow fauves of Tasha in her twenties and a bottle of Dom on the table beside the kitchenette. "This place is like an homage to our twenties. A museum."

"I know," Tasha said. "It's cool."

"No, I didn't mean that in a good way. It's wrong. You can't move your family here."

Toni looked at her mother.

"Well, we're not gonna live here. Not for long." Tasha pulled a hot pink chinchilla jacket she'd worn to a Foxy Brown party from the closet. "Just until we find another place."

"All four of you?" Troy asked.

"It's not that small, ladies. Not for Tribeca. Look, you have to trust me. When I was in the bathroom with Tamia I realized that this is just what we need as a family to keep it interesting. Jersey is boring. Jersey is country. Jersey is like . . . like a pasture where rich people go to die. New York keeps you young. It keeps you hot. It keeps you sexy." Tasha had the coat on now and she danced around to Foxy Brown music in her head.

"I don't think babies are supposed to be sexy," Troy said, trying unsuccessfully to hand Toni over to Tasha. "Did you go to the bathroom on yourself?" She looked at the little girl as she patted her soggy diaper. Toni smiled.

"Oh, God." Tasha grimaced. "Someone change her."

* * *

An hour later, after Troy left to meet with the Virtuous Women uptown, Tamia, Tasha, and Toni went down to Chinatown for a steamer of pork dumplings at Joe's Ginger. Though Tamia wanted to continue to debate Tasha about her ridiculous move back into the city, she knew better than to push her friend. She and Troy had seen their prying in Tasha's life blow up in their innocent faces so many times that they'd learned to simply ask Tasha the important questions and move on. Tasha was born stubborn and made self-centered, and no amount of meddling was going to change that. Besides, this was the one time when Tamia actually thought her wild friend had a point. While there were lots of positives to leaving the city, what was left behind turned to negatives she knew made her friend lonely and bored. With her friends far away and her man, at times, farther away, the big house and babies were bound to drive Tasha crazy after a while. Now, here was crazy in front of her, trying to teach a two-year-old to use chopsticks.

"Do you know about the Afrocentric community?" Tamia asked, grabbing a chopstick from Toni before she jabbed her mother in the eye.

"The what? Is that one of those new neighborhoods in downtown Brooklyn? You know I'm not moving my babies there."

"No, crazy." Tamia laughed and imagined what kind of tirade Malik would go on had he heard her friend's response. He'd probably send her a whole box of books. "I said 'Afrocentric,' as in African-centered culture and tradition, history . . ."

Tasha looked at Tamia blankly.

"You know . . . the stuff we learned in school . . . in our history class. I know you know . . . because we took that class together."

Tasha was still looking.

"Oh yeah," she finally said, but her eyes were still blank. "I remember."

"No, you don't. You're lying." Flabbergasted, Tamia laughed again.

"Okay, I don't. Whatever." Tasha shrugged her shoulders and broke up a noodle for Toni. "Why? Why are you asking me this? And is there a quiz afterward? Because I paid for my grade in that class. . . . I'm just gonna be honest."

"No, Tash. There's no quiz. I was just thinking about this case I'm working on. Well, I guess it's not just a case. I've become kind of involved in this place and I was thinking maybe—"

As Tamia said much about nothing and it seemed she was never getting to a point, Toni and Tasha looked at her in the way friends look at other friends who are newly in love and thus stuck in the labyrinth of their own desires. This, of course, was exactly what the mother and daughter thought they were looking at.

"I'm sorry," Tasha interrupted. "Is there a man involved in this? Because you just look like . . . there's a man involved."

"No," Tamia lied. "Look, I have to get out of here. I need to stop by the office on my way home."

"Work, work, and work," Tasha said.

"A sister has to work hard for the money." Tamia slid a twenty onto the table and signaled for the waitress, saying, "I need a box."

"Keep the twenty and leave the dumplings," Tasha said, pulling Tamia's bowl toward her.

"You sure have an appetite," Tamia said. "What about your ever-going Halle Berry plan?"[17]

"That's on hold right now," Tasha said quickly, looking away from Tamia.

"Cool. I love you two," Tamia said before kissing Tasha and then Toni goodbye and walking out of the dark restaurant.

"And we love you back," Tasha said. She turned to Toni and grinned. "And Auntie Tamia will have to love less of us after Mommy's operation. Won't she, Toni?"

Toni, seemingly indifferent to her mother's plans, reached for a piece of noodle on her plate and stuffed it into her mouth.

"Much less," Tasha confirmed for herself. "That's what full-body liposuction is all about . . . much less." She looked at Toni. "Now let Mommy get one of her last good meals in before Dr. Miller makes her all perfect again. Your daddy is gonna love this surprise."

The BAP Declaration of Independence

We, the Black American Princesses of the universe, do hereby hold these truths to be self-evident—that black women are created to be fabulous, that they are endowed by their Creator with certain unalienable powers, that among these are intelligence, strength, beauty, and courage.

Henceforth, each sovereign BAP shall remain in charge of her own destiny, in tune with her true spirit, and empowered by her God-given strength.

---

[17] Halle Berry: Named in honor of Halle Berry's quick physical recovery after having a baby, the diet includes one small meal of anything, two veggie/fruit snacks, and three light workouts a day.

She shall honor her Declaration of Independence by following these basic rules:

1. *Always know the way home and have a way to get there.*
2. *Never let anyone extract you from the love and support of your family and friends.*
3. *Have a passport and a nice set of luggage.*
4. *Have a relationship with your Creator; when all else fails you, that's what will keep you alive.*
5. *Have secret "get up and go" cash that will last a year; make sure there's enough to support your children.*
6. *Protect and honor your mother at all costs.*
7. *If you're sick, see a doctor; worry about the bill later.*
8. *Learn how to do a breast exam.*
9. *Use condoms—always.*
10. *Get your education; your grandmother was right.*
11. *Have at least one girlfriend who knows your secrets.*
12. *Don't settle for seconds. He's not going to leave her.*
13. *If he hits you, leave and never return.*
14. *If you hit him, leave and get some help.*
15. *Even if you don't own a gun, know how to use one.*
16. *Pack light and never stay where you're not wanted.*
17. *If he has bad credit, don't let him use yours.*
18. *Get a professional massage at a real spa.*
19. *If you need therapy, go and keep going.*
20. *Buy an expensive candle and burn it.*
21. *Write down your master plan.*
22. *Have a great resume, amazing cover letter, and three wonderful references.*

23. *Have a savings account.*
24. *Plan to retire, or you won't.*
25. *Know how to pleasure yourself—yes, in bed.*
26. *Let it all go.*
27. *Establish friendships with a doctor, lawyer, and politician.*
28. *Get and cherish a mentor.*
29. *Be nice to your hair; it's beautiful the way it is.*
30. *Write a kind letter to yourself, about yourself, and believe every good word.*

After successfully conducting her third meeting of the Virtuous Women, Troy was finding her bearings. Instead of taking over everything and remaining in charge of most of the club like Myrtle did, she confided in the sisters that she knew she had weaknesses and couldn't do it all on her own. While a few sisters said it was poor taste for a First Lady to admit she needed help, others found Troy's style refreshing and provided a hand when and where needed. They took turns leading prayer, allowed others to make suggestions about events, and put all talk about the incubus and succubus on hold. The biggest achievement the women made was a formal recommendation to the pastor that the president of their organization be allowed to sit on the altar on the fifth Sundays when the mass women's choir sang. They thought it was a good petition, as it didn't require too much shifting, at first.

"Do you want me to wait outside?" Kiona asked, walking out of the church library with Troy. After the meeting, Troy invited Kiona to a special treat in the city to thank her for her support.

"Sure, I just need to hand over the petition to Pastor Hall!" Troy said, holding the paper, which carried the signatures of all of the organization's members.

"You mean your boo?"

Kiona and Troy embraced as they chuckled.

"He's that too. . . ."

Troy left Kiona and walked to Kyle's office, where she was sure he was either editing his sermon for an upcoming guest visit to a church in Staten Island or playing computer solitaire, which he did from time to time to clear his head. While they hadn't talked much about her new position, she knew he'd gotten lots of compliments from the church and sometimes she saw him walking very slowly past the open door of the library where the Virtuous Women met. She felt him reaching to hold her hand more than once as they stood in line after service to receive members and visitors, and once or twice, he'd turned to her and said, "This is my First Lady. She leads the top women's organization at the church."

Troy winked at Saptosa, Kyle's assistant, as she made her way past her desk.

"Oh, First Lady!" Saptosa said. "I was hoping you'd come by."

"Well . . . I'm happy you're happy." Troy smiled, noticing that Saptosa seemed a bit too elated to see her. It was far from uncommon for her to visit Kyle's office before she left for the day. And each time she did this, she saw Saptosa's friendly, yet busy smile. Something was very different.

"Is he in?"

"He sure is. Go right on in."

Malik was placing a daisy in the fold of Tamia's ear. Though she was busy saying how crazy he was for doing it, complaining that the stem was wet, she really liked the attention and how the activity itself forced Malik to lock his eyes on her face. In most of their conversations he'd been the militant man, the book reader, the cultural critic, but now, as they sat on the patio of a coffee shop, going over the specifics of his work with the Freedom Project, he was softening in a way that made her unintentionally lean into him.

"You should wear that in your hair for the rest of the day," Malik said.

"A daisy? In my hair? To the office? Are you kidding me?" Tamia laughed. "I'm on company time, and if I want to remain on company time, it would be best if I don't convince my employers that I'm crazy."

"Crazy for wearing a daisy in your hair?"

"Yes!" Tamia exclaimed. "Unlike you, I can't wear

dashikis and cowrie shells to work. We have rules, standards."

"I think one of those standards should be that you're crazy if you don't wear a daisy in your hair," Malik said, snatching a daisy from another table and putting it in the fold of his ear. Both he and Tamia laughed.

"Always the rebel," Tamia said as if she'd known Malik and his ways for years. And she felt that way. "So, tell me, rebel, how did you get mixed up in this situation?"

"Well—"

"And, before you start with your 'I did it; I'm guilty' revolutionary rap, I have to tell you, I've been watching you these past few weeks and it doesn't seem like you would do that. The way you are with those kids, with the other people at the center, I just don't believe it."

Malik looked down at the table and folded his hands humbly before him.

"When Simeon came to me, he was homeless and hungry, robbing people on the street," he said. "He tried to stick me up, but all I had to offer was the cowrie shells in my pocket and a chew stick."

"No wallet?" Tamia asked.

"I don't need a piece of animal skin and some cards to remind me of who I am and how I fit into the world," Malik answered. "Anyway, Simeon was sure I was lying. He felt my pockets himself and then he tried to hit me with a gun. I grabbed his arm and asked him a question."

"What?"

"I asked him if he was hungry. If he wanted something to eat," Malik said. "And then he called me every name in the book and accused me of being gay. I snatched his gun and repeated my question. Three hours later, we were in the basement of the Freedom Project cleaning out a space where he could sleep."

"Did you tell him he'd have to work and that you wouldn't pay him?" Tamia asked, nervous about the answer, as she was now wrestling with the idea of purposefully losing Malik's case.

"He's a man. And men need to work for the things they have—that's the only way they can appreciate it."

"What did you say? What did you tell him?"

"Three hots and a cot. He could live in the basement of the project as long as he helped out during the day—cleaning and helping keep the place nice," Malik explained. "He could take classes with the other boys and as soon as he found somewhere else to go, he could leave."

"So, you never told Simeon he had to stay at the Freedom Project or forced him to do anything he didn't want to do?"

"Never."

There are few things that could prepare a wife for the psychological shock and awe of seeing another grown woman sitting in her husband's lap. Auntie, grandmama, mother, sister, cousin who just got her legs cut off in a street fight—it doesn't matter who or why, the situation is bound to break the bride down in some way she didn't think was possible. And while Myrtle wasn't exactly sitting in Kyle's lap when Troy came pushing in the door, she may as well have been. Her rump was beside his on the couch that Troy had designated for her dreams of Kyle, his arm was around her shoulder, and her hands were clasped in his crotch . . . right in his crotch.

"Why does she hate me?" she cried into his lap, seeking comfort. Next, in the schedule in Myrtle's mind, she was to collapse in a fit of sadness, bury her head there, and cry until Kyle lifted her. Then she'd lock eyes with him and go for a kiss. The plan was to make Troy look crazy and irrational, while she was the victim in need of Kyle's support.

Troy heard Myrtle's cries before Myrtle and Kyle realized she was standing there. She quickly rationalized that she could kill someone and Myrtle could be her first victim. Any fantasies she'd had about Myrtle being her friend were erased in that instant. Troy was silly, but she wasn't slow. She knew seduction when she saw it and this woman was putting the moves on her husband.

"Hate is a strong wor—Oh, Troy!" Kyle looked to Troy and inched away from Myrtle a bit before she sat up.

"What's this? What's going on?" Troy stood before the pair on the couch, her arms crossed over her chest. Myrtle didn't even acknowledge her. She looked off toward the window in a show of anger.

"Sister Glover just came in for some counsel," Kyle tried.

"She's taken everything from me. I put everything I had into that organization and she just . . . ran me off!" Myrtle began crying again, but this time she managed to keep her hands and face away from Kyle's lap.

"Ran you off? I—" Troy couldn't believe how helpless Myrtle was acting. She was a witch on Rollerblades most days and now she was playing lamb.

"Honey, why don't you come and sit down so we can talk about this? See if you two can come to a compromise?" Kyle pointed to a chair beside the couch, but Troy just stood there.

"We already talked about it, *honey.*" Troy cut her eyes at him. "Why revisit it? The Virtuous Women voted on it three weeks ago."

"See? She hates me. And I didn't even do anything. I'm just a good Christian woman, trying to be a better—"

"Troy, please." Kyle cut Myrtle off as he tried to show uneasiness in his eyes. Myrtle had been in his office for over an hour talking about her relationships with the trustees and leaders of the church before she'd brought up the situation with Troy.

"Fine. I'll sit down," Troy said, walking past the seat and heading to the small space left on the couch on Kyle's right. When she sat down, Myrtle rolled her eyes and exhaled loudly. "So?"

"See what I'm talking about? She has an attitude," Myrtle pointed out.

"Hold on, ladies. Let's back up and try to come to a compromise," Kyle stressed. "Now what happened, from your point of view, Sister Glover?"

"Well, you know how I am, how I like to help people with their spiritual guidance," she said tearfully, wiping her eyes with a beat-up handkerchief. Kyle nodded as Troy frowned at the show. "Well, I've been doing that all along with Sister . . . Hall . . . since she came to this church and then all of a sudden she just says it wasn't fast enough—"

"I never—"

"And I wasn't a good enough teacher—"

"I never said that—"

"Hold on, Troy," Kyle put his hand up.

"I mean," Myrtle went on, "what did she expect? I can't turn a sinner into a saint overnight."

"A sinner? I got your sinner, you—"

"Troy!" Kyle stopped her.

"When she came to this church she was of the world, you know, and I was trying my best to pull her heart closer to Jesus. I swear I was! But then she let the evils of pride and power get in the way of her growth and— I'm just so worried about her."

Troy's stomach turned as she listened to Myrtle's

desperate emotional rant, which sounded oddly dated and somewhat Old English in tone. "Is she serious?" she kept thinking.

"Now, Troy?" Kyle looked as if he'd considered what Myrtle said and turned to Troy.

"Are you serious? You want me to respond to that? She's obviously—"

Myrtle jumped up.

"I knew she wouldn't want to talk. See, she's ruled by her anger. It's the devil."

Kyle looked at Troy sharply.

"Whatever . . ." Troy stated, crossing her arms and legs in protest. "Look, I appreciate you helping me, Myrtle, but it was time for the organization to take a new direction. You're acting like this was all my decision. We took a vote."

"That vote was poisoned and you know it!" Myrtle shouted. "That . . . that Kiosha or Kiona . . . whatever her name is, she poisoned everyone against me. And it hurt so bad. I have given everything I have to this church—to the Virtuous Women—and she just wanted to take it away from me."

"The vote wasn't poisoned. Why can't you just accept that it was time for you to move on? Or do you have other plans? Maybe this isn't about the Virtuous Women, after all. Maybe you want my—"

"Ladies!"

Kyle's head was spinning and he was praying Saptosa would step into the office and say someone else, someplace else was in need of his pastorial services pronto. But even if there was another emergency, Saptosa wouldn't be at her desk to answer the call. She was too busy at the door listening and texting all of the dirty details of the argument to her mother, grandmother, and godmother—all mothers at the church.

"Can we come to a compromise, ladies?" Kyle asked,

standing up and holding his hands out to both women. Troy jumped up too and tried to stand closer to Kyle than Myrtle. "Isn't there something that could work for both of you?" Both women looked off in opposite directions to show their disinterest.

"She could leave the church," Myrtle murmured inaudibly.

"What?" Troy puffed out her chest.

"Ladies, please!" Kyle repeated and the force in his voice was so hard it surprised and excited his company. "Can't you both find some way to get along?"

"Well," Myrtle started, peeking over at Troy, "if she'd just let me back into the organization, maybe I could help her again . . . and—"

"What?" Troy shouted.

"And I wouldn't be a bother," Myrtle went on. "It would be like I wasn't even there. I'd let her take the lead and I'd just help. I only want to serve the women of Christ."

"Wonderful," Kyle said, relieved. "That sounds perfectly reasonable to me. What do you think, Troy?"

He turned to Troy and her mouth was wide open. She couldn't believe what she was hearing. Why couldn't Kyle, in all of his wisdom, see past Myrtle's drama? She wanted to continue to probe and then protest, but she could see the irritation in her husband's face and learned, as any good wife should, that he had limitations, and there was no sense arguing with him once they were exceeded.

"Fine," Troy muttered, crossing her arms tighter over her chest. Quick as a cat, Myrtle jumped into Troy's arms like she'd been reunited with her long-lost best friend.

"I am so happy," Myrtle said excitedly. "Praise God!"

She hugged Troy tightly, her right hand cradling the back of Troy's head as she rocked back and forth.

"I am so happy," she repeated so Kyle could hear, but then, in Troy's ear, she whispered, "Watch your back. I'm coming for you."

Troy and Kiona hadn't been friends long enough for Kiona to ask if she'd had a fight with her husband, but as the pair left First Baptist on the way to a hot yoga class Troy had invited her to, it was clear that something had gone wrong in Kyle's office. Troy was silent most of the way to the studio. And as Kiona suffered in the steam that even the instructor agreed was too high, Troy hardly broke a sweat and kept a Jedi-like focus on each pose.

"Thanks for inviting me," Kiona said, dabbing her chest with a towel to sop up the pools of sweat soaking her clothes as they walked out of the class. "I've never done anything like this. Me and my friends mostly spend the afternoon in front of the TV." She laughed. "I didn't expect to sweat quite so much, but I guess that's the point."

"You get used to the heat after a while," Troy said.

They walked into the locker room and Kiona saw that her once curled hair was now a little Afro.

"I'm sure you do," Kiona said, "but until then, I think I'll stick with doing yoga in my living room. I can't afford the hair upkeep."

"Do whatever you want," Troy snapped.

"Ooookaaay . . ."

"I'm sorry," Troy said, noticing the confused look on Kiona's face. "I didn't mean to snap at you. I'm just a little stressed right now."

"Why?"

"The Virtuous Women again . . . one in particular."

"First Lady—"

"Troy," Troy stopped Kiona. "We're friends. Just call me Troy."

"Troy, you're doing a fine job. Everyone is so excited about the changes you've been making," Kiona said.

"Really?"

"I wouldn't lie to you," Kiona added as they walked out of the yoga studio. "I don't have a reason to. Now, don't let a few bad dancers ruin your soul train line. Keep the party going."

"What?" Troy laughed. "My soul train line?"

"It's an old line my big sister used to say to me," Kiona said. "The point is to enjoy yourself. The people who want to stop your line like it when you don't seem to be having fun. You've worked hard and you should be having fun."

"You're right," Troy agreed. "I should be having fun and I'm not going to let that . . . that hater ruin my good time."

"Praise God!" Kiona said. "Now, come on and let's dance!"

The two women chuckled and danced down Fifth Avenue like it was 1980 and Don Cornelius was about to ask them to unscramble VIRTUOUS WOMEN on the *Soul Train* board.

"For the Virtuous Women," Troy shouted, doing an off-step bus stop behind Kiona.

"No," Kiona started, "for the *best* leader the Virtuous Women has ever had!"

"That's right, that's right, that's right!" Troy shimmied as Kiona danced circles around her.

"Get it, girl," a random man said, coming up behind Troy and trying to dance with her. "That's my kind of lady! Wooo-weee!"

Troy and Kiona screamed and ran down the street,

laughing at the spectacle they'd caused the entire way. When they stopped and Troy gathered herself, she realized that they were standing in front of the Louis Vuitton store.

"What?" Kiona stopped too, noticing Troy's gaze. She looked in the window at the purses and mannequins dressed in Vuitton.

"You know what," Troy said, "I respect that you called me the best leader, but we both know I'm only decent, and the only reason I can be decent is because of your help."

"Thank you," Kiona said.

"I want to do something nice for you!"

"Nice?"

"Follow me." Troy pulled a resistant Kiona into the Vuitton store and in minutes she'd replaced Kiona's faux patent Surya with the real thing.

"Oh, I can't accept this," Kiona said once she realized Troy's offer. "It's much too expensive."

"Nonsense—it's a gift! It's your new boyfriend," Troy said. "You deserve it! I see how much you've done for the church. And I know what you've done for me."

"I don't do any of those things to get gifts or recognition," Kiona said. "I do it because I love it. Because it's what God called me to do."

"And that's exactly why you deserve this real bag—because you're a real woman," Troy said earnestly. "You're so busy spoiling everyone else, it's time you were spoiled."

"Thank you, Troy," Kiona said.

"I'm the one thanking you!"

Leaving Kiona to look through the other purses, Troy walked to the cashier and handed the checkout woman her card before she'd mentioned the total.

"No need to box it," Troy said casually. "I think

we're leaving the fake one here! And add a monogram wallet too . . . a wallet and a keychain."

"Well—Ms. . . . Ms. Smith—" the woman tried.

"It's Hall now, but that's my old name on the card," Troy rambled.

"Ms. Smith, your card was declined."

"What?" Troy looked as if she had no idea what "declined" meant.

"Declined—as in, funds not available."

It was like the woman was suddenly yelling over a loudspeaker.

"Funds what?"

"Do you have another card?"

"I have that one," Troy said. "Can you try it again?"

"I did it twice. The card doesn't work." The impatience in the woman's voice was mounting, yet she seemed to be getting some weird satisfaction from the turn in events.

"I—" Troy turned to see Kiona laughing with one of the salesgirls. Just then she remembered what she'd said to Lucy—that she'd told her not to put any more money into the account. "I—"

"Ms., other people are waiting," the woman said.

Embarrassed, ashamed, and nervous, Troy opened her purse and pulled out the only other card she had—Kyle's business account card from the church. He'd given it to her in case of an emergency.

"Try this one," she said. "I know it'll work."

See the World: The 3T Get-Out Guide

The weekend rut is the worst rut of all—you shop, you sleep, you meet your girls for drinks and dip and maybe a movie. It happens this way every weekend and pretty soon you get bored and mix it up by . . . just staying home. Stop limiting yourself. Stop limiting your universe. Expand your horizons by expanding your calendar.

Instead of inviting your friends out for the same old drinks at the same old place, try something new, somewhere new. Here are ten things you and your soul sisters can try that'll be sure to be added to your list of favorite pastimes.

1. *Get in the saddle:* Because horses are everywhere, dude ranches are hard to miss. Put on your leather stirrups and go for a ride on the wild side.
2. *Make your own clothes:* Believe it or not, crocheting is making a comeback. Find a local sewing circle and see what you can make. You may never wear that lopsided sweater, but you can brag about making it.
3. *Cook it up:* Yeah, you can cook soul food, but can you make chicken tikka masala? Stop paying for good Indian food and learn how to make your own by taking a cooking class next Friday night.
4. *Go hiking:* While communing with nature might leave you with a few mosquito bites, the benefits for your mind, body, and soul will be worth it.
5. *Pitch a tent:* The only thing funnier than a bunch of children in the woods is a bunch of sisters building a campfire. Make s'mores and tell relationship horror stories.

6. _Turn up the heat:_ Yoga is wonderful, but hot yoga is magnificent. It'll open your pores and leave your skin quite fab! Warning: Don't cover your hair. That'll make it worse.

7. _Go to the opera:_ From Aida to Black Orpheus, opera is full of storylines you'll enjoy and high notes you'll have fun trying to duplicate.

8. _Save a tree, save a kid:_ If you and your bestie are tired of hearing about each other's problems, try solving the problems of the world by getting involved in your community.

9. _Make beautiful art:_ Adult education programs teach everything from pottery making to sketching. Priced from $40 to $200, the weekly classes usually cost less than the bag on your arm.

10. _Support a sister:_ Find an independent sistergirl painter, poet, filmmaker, singer, or dancer and support her work on a Friday night.

6

*The great question that has never been answered
and which I have not yet been able to answer,
despite my thirty years of research into the
feminine soul, is "What does a woman want?"*

—Sigmund Freud

To the surprise of no one in the universe but the
woman wearing the second $85,000 wedding ring he'd
bought her, Lionel wasn't considering moving his bud-
ding brood back to New York City and he wasn't even
willing to talk about it. Riding in the passenger's seat
on the way home from the airport after a terrible game
that solidified his team's exclusion from the NBA fi-
nals, he'd told Tasha no so many times she'd stopped
counting.

"No. It doesn't make any sense," Lionel said after
she mentioned that they could probably find something
big and pretty and cheap in just a month or so. While
getting good property in Manhattan was like getting a
private phone call from Jesus, it was a recession and
they had the kind of money that could at least get a
Hispanic Realtor named "Hey-suess" on the line—Tasha
had come up with this joke to break the ice. "Where are

my kids?" Lionel asked. He hadn't even chuckled about the "Hey-suess" line.

"With Milania."

"Why the fuck didn't you bring them to the damn airport?" Lionel looked at Tasha like she was crazy.

"Because I wanted to talk to you about this."

"About fucking what?"

"About the move . . ."

"There's nothing to fucking talk about." Lionel held up his hands to show his puzzlement.

Tasha winced at every curse that came from his lips. Lionel wasn't a violent man. He almost never even raised his voice. But when he was upset, he cursed like a drunken sailor on weekend leave. Dropping f-bombs was his way of dealing with aggravation. The only way Tasha could get his attention after that was to drop the subject or drop more bombs than him. And she was leaning toward the latter. It was a dramatic dance any married woman knew, and while Tasha wasn't the best at it, she needed to at least be good. Good enough. Because what she wasn't telling Lionel was that she'd already packed up half of their belongings, scheduled a moving van, and redirected the mail.

She needed bombs. Canons. Howitzers. Heavy artillery.

"Fuck it. Fuck it. Fuck it! Fuck it! Just fuck it!" She hollered, banging on the steering wheel as the car jerked from left to right in the traffic on the freeway. Lionel lowered his hands and looked at her. "You know what? I was just trying to do something for this family—for our children. Get them out of this godforsaken hick-ass state and into some motherfucking culture. But just forget it. Fucking forget it! Shit! Fuck me for even trying to be a good mother."

If any of their grandmothers were alive, bars of Ivory soap would be poking out of both of the LaRoches' mouths, but in this situation clean language was the mouthwash of losers.

"Pull this motherfucker over!" Lionel shouted, pulling the steering wheel so the car jerked far to the right until Tasha got control again and charged off of the exit into a McDonald's drive-through.

"You want to tell me what's right for my damn children?" Lionel started, snatching the keys from the ignition. "What's more fucking right than what they already have—a million-dollar mansion in the best neighborhood in the country, preadmission to the best day school in the state, every piece of goddamn brand-name clothing you can find, safety, food, heat in the fucking winter, cool air in the summer. Shit, when we took Toni to the mountains last year, I realized she'd never even seen dirt. What's better than that? What could be better than the life they have?"

"If we keep them here, they're just gonna turn out like every other suburban teen—sheltered, privileged, and pretentious."

"They are sheltered and privileged," Lionel said. "And they should be pretentious. You know, I told you when I agreed to have Toni that I wanted the best for my children. Better than what I had, growing up in the damn projects, not knowing my damn daddy, thinking I was nothing. I'm not nothing anymore and my girls are something. I want them to know that. There ain't nothing in that fucking city that's gonna be good for—wait a minute." Lionel jumped out of the car and ran around to Tasha's side, pulling her from the car and standing before her like a solider in war. "Them . . . this isn't *them* going back to the city. This is about *you.* About the fucking meeting with . . . what's her name . . . Lynn."

"No," Tasha tried, but it was too late. Lionel had added up everything he thought he knew in his mind. "It's not about—"

"I fucking know you. Everything is about Tasha. Everything. You just want to get back into the city so you can be a drunk with your friends and buy a bunch of shit to make yourself feel better about the fact that you'll never be as successful as your mother."

Tasha balled up her fists.

"You know, sometimes when we fight, you take shit too far and now you have, Lionel," she said, fuming with anger. "Take that back."

"No, Tasha. Because it's time I said it to you. It's time I told you that I know you only had Toni because you wanted to prove that you could be a better mother than Porsche was to you and when Toni came and your mother came here from LA and—"

"Stop!"

"—and everything was perfect for a little while as you two pretended that you didn't still hate each other, you thought you had her. But when she left and she wasn't there anymore to watch you be the perfect mother—"

"No!" Tasha wanted to stop Lionel. His words were pouring into her ears like lava.

"—you didn't know what to do, so you had to one-up her again—and that's the only reason—"

"You stop it—"

"No!" Lionel barked, inching so close into Tasha she couldn't breathe. "That's the only reason you had Tiara. The only reason!"

"It's not true. None of it's true," Tasha cried.

"Come on. You weren't even thinking about children until it was clear your business wasn't working," Lionel said. "You weren't the hot news anymore. You were my wife and people wanted me out front."

"Putting you out front was my job."

"Not for long . . . it didn't impress Porsche for long. I wasn't enough."

"You think I married you to impress her?" Tasha asked.

"I think you think you have something to prove."

"Prove what? To whom? To Porsche? That bitch never gave two shits about me. She let the entire world raise me, her bastard daughter, as she went off and chased her dreams. What could I have to prove to her."

"That you're better," Lionel said so easily and so quickly it was clear to Tasha he'd thought about this for a long time. "That you can be better than her—even without her. That you're better than the little girl she left alone, the one she let leave."

Tasha pushed away from Lionel's hold against the car and tried to laugh it off as she walked in circles in the empty parking space beside the car. Suddenly she was seven and watching Porsche leave her in a hotel room again. Suddenly she was eleven and begging Porsche to read a poem she'd written for Mother's Day. Suddenly she was seventeen and running away from home.

"You think I didn't know how hurt you were when Porsche told you she wasn't coming when Tiara was born and that she hasn't ever been here to see her?"

"I don't care about that. I don't care about anything Porsche thinks. She chose not to see her grandchildren. She chose her career again. I didn't!" Tasha was hollering so loud the children in the playground in front of the restaurant stopped playing and watched. She wouldn't cry, though. Tears were welled up in the corners of her eyes, but she wouldn't cry.

"Yes, you do. It's obvious. It's obvious in everything you do. No nannies. No help. You have them crammed up in that little bedroom. . . ."

"That's for their own good."

"No, that's for your own good. It's so you can feel

like you're doing something for them, when you're not," Lionel said. "You're too busy doing for yourself."

"I love my children!"

"If you love them then why did you stop counseling? Why didn't you keep going to the therapist?"

"I was doing better."

Lionel looked up at the clouds like he was expecting rain, lightning, thunder, a tornado.

"You don't get it," he said, walking away from Tasha. "You just don't get it."

"Where are you going?" She went running behind him as he cornered out of the lot.

"Home."

"You can't walk home from here." She grabbed his arm. "It's too far."

"I'm not getting in that car, Tasha. I need to be alone. I need to be away from you." He stopped walking and looked at her, letting his own tears flow freely. "When we got married, I knew you were selfish. I knew I'd have to fight you and help you see the right way sometimes. And I've put up with a lot of your bullshit. A lot of it. I've let shit go and I've let you win."

"Win? This isn't a—"

"No! Listen to me. I've let you win more times than I can count. But not right now," he said. "I never fought for myself, but you're a fool if you think I'm not going to fight for Toni and Tiara. I won't let your shortcomings, your anger, ruin them the way Porsche ruined you."

Tasha pulled back her hand to slap Lionel, but he caught it.

"Fuck you," she cried.

"Fuck me? Really?"

"Fuck you."

"No. Fuck you."

Tasha snatched her hand back from Lionel and

charged toward the car. The distance between them grew from an invisible river to two tiles of sidewalk concrete. Tasha turned to see Lionel's back.

"I'm moving back to the city," she said harshly. "Just not with you."

Lionel stopped in his path on the sidewalk and turned with the ease of a beau at a debutante ball.

"That's fine with me," he replied breezily. "Just make sure you add my children to the list of people not going."

Six Male Conversation Starters to Avoid

You don't need a degree in psychology to know that women are the great communicators of the sexes. This well-recorded reality may present vindication for all of the "Chatty Cathys" of the world; however, it also adds to relationship woes where communication-craving girl-friends are left screaming mad, trying to get their dream-boats to open up. While this task is easier said than done, there are a few things you can do to win this communication coup.

1. Don't open your conversation with dreaded lead-ins like "We need to talk . . ." and "What's wrong?"
   Rationale: These words produce a "fright and flight" response.
   Easy fix: Open your talk with noncommittal language at noncommittal moments. If you're concerned about his ongoing bout with his mother, casually ask, "How's your mother?" This will open the door for discussion.

2. Don't smack him down with the biggest question on your mind: "When will you marry me?"
   Rationale: This is confrontational. Every word that follows will sound like Charlie Brown's teacher: "Wha wha wha."
   Easy fix: Instead of asking about his desires, tell him yours. If he feels the same, he'll come around.

3. Don't ask, "How do you feel about me?" after sex.
   Rationale: You can't believe anything he's saying at that moment. Hopped up on his orgasm, he might even propose.
   Easy fix: Communicate your feelings during "we

time." While listening to music, say, "I love that we enjoy the same music." This will give him a chance to express his feelings.

4. Don't begin conversations with confrontational statements: "You need to get your credit cleaned up!"

   Rationale: Unless they ask for advice, men despise being told what they should be thinking or doing.

   Easy fix: Casually state the facts and provide numbers. Men are goal-oriented. Mention that in order to move into his dream home, he'll need $60K and a FICO of 800.

5. Don't say a word leading into an emotional exchange when he's enjoying "he time."

   Rationale: From televised sports events to his beloved beer time on the couch, men have their own "me time."

   Easy fix: Wait until he's done, kiss him on the cheek, and sweetly say, "I love you."

6. Don't dominate the conversation with your own ideas if he's quiet and not responding.

   Rationale: If you become the talker, he'll become the listener.

   Easy fix: Listen and learn. If you open the conversation and he's quiet, let there be silence until he opens up. You'll learn a lot based on what he's not saying.

While 99.9 percent of the people in the universe had solid bets on Lionel saying no to New York, no one was willing to put money on Kyle saying no to Troy. For, the man of the Lord had taken the old biblical quote to heart and loved his wife the way Jesus loved the church and since the day they'd met, whenever it came to matters of the heart, he was torn between the two.

For this particular showdown, on this particularly cold evening, Troy was sitting in the first pew on the last night of First Baptist's annual revival. The pastor was at the altar, but not at the pulpit, playing host to the revival's guest speaker, the Reverend Bigsby Bigelow-Goode, a fire-and-brimstone big-tent revivalist, who'd been sent up north by Kyle's grandfather. It was Saturday evening and the last hour of the sixth night of the revival and Troy's ears were ringing from all of the tambourines chinking around her. Every time Bigelow-Goode said anything on a high note, the room shook with the noisy instruments, and Troy was five clinks away from turning around and snatching one from a church mother seated behind her. While First Baptist was a large church, sitting inside the pews every night for hours during the revival made it mid-sized. And then even smaller because every space in the aisle was taken by a metal seat to accommodate the growing crowds bused in from around the city. It was 10 p.m. and the floor was sweating, the wooden walls popping in. Children of every age, even teenagers, had given up and fallen asleep in the pews, some on the floors. It was a pressure cooker of praise and if the Holy Spirit didn't whisper in someone's ear, it might be their conscience telling them to "go outside and get some air!" before they fainted.

"An, an, an, an youa . . . youa . . . youa betta fear the Lord! Fear him!" Bigelow-Goode shouted so loud only static went into the microphone with his spit. Far into

his seventies, he was wearing a little white suit that was
two sizes too small and two decades old and two sea-
sons early. While his shoes were a mismatch in brown,
his cotton-top Afro mixed just fine with the suit. "For
the wraff of the Almightay isa comin' and i's gonna de-
stroy the devil an alla alla alla . . ." There was clinking
and cheering. "I said alla evila mena that don't knowa
the Lord!"

Troy's body was tired to the bone. She was sinking
in. Trying to pay attention, waving her handkerchief
high now and again and standing up sometimes, but really
fading. For the last six days, six different holy men had
said the same holy message in a different holy way and
she was worn down. She looked at Kyle to break her
thoughts of snatching the tambourine. He was shaking
his head along with everyone else. A believer. Not
doing like she was. He didn't seem tired. Didn't seem
pushed in and choking. He was right there with Bigelow-
Goode, and so far away from Troy.

"An evra, evra man, wombman, and chile had betta
get right in the good book before that happins!"

The lady with the tambourine behind Troy fell out.
Someone hollered, "Hallelu-JAH." Bigelow-Goode
hopped off of the altar like a rock star and ran down
the sliver of aisle left, tapping heads as he went along,
shouting mercies and prayers, saying he could save
souls and you had to be willing. Troy watched as the
heads of every single person he touched fell back hard
into the arms of people around them. They were en-
tranced. Away. In the spirit. Getting the spirit.

Kiona, who was sitting beside Troy, was crying and
grabbing onto Troy's hand.

"Praise God!" Kiona cried, her grip tightening. She
looked at Troy. "Do you feel that? Do you feel the spirit
in here? It's all around. Everywhere." Kiona was weep-
ing now, thumping her feet along, two beats faster than

the drummer, who'd caught the pacing of Bigelow-Goode as he scurried around the room.

One by one Troy watched everyone in the room fall out. Kyle was crying. And then, in a second, it seemed like everyone, everyone in the church was either on the floor, picking someone off of the floor, or jumping for joy. Everyone but Troy.

She gave show the way she knew how, but Bigelow-Goode had his eyes on her from the moment he noticed the biggest diamond he'd ever seen shining from her ring finger. Bigelow-Goode hopped like a bandleader to the front of the room with a crowd of deacons riding close behind him. He leapt and hollered out for the Holy Ghost and then he was there, in front of Troy, his hand high like a witness about to slap truth on the Bible.

"The Lord told me to come right, right now!" He pointed to the ground. "Right here with the First Lady of First Baptist."

The room went still. Kyle's shoulders raised tensely as he looked at his wife.

"Oh Jesus, oh Jesus, oh Jesus," someone cried and then prayers were mumbled lowly like ancient chants, but somehow everyone knew that all eyes and thoughts were on Troy.

Kiona's hand slipped away and Troy felt as alone as she had at birth. What she wanted more than anything, Bigelow-Goode claimed he had, claimed he was giving away. Salvation. New life. It didn't matter if she was tired or in pain, if he was speaking a Swahili she couldn't understand or saying a bunch of things she didn't even believe. She wanted it badly. Wanted to drift off the way Kiona had described. To find herself in God's hands.

His hand was still raised. Troy looked at it like a child. She wanted to know what to expect. What to feel. What to do when the moment came. She waited for him to

say something. She wanted to respond. But then, after
he screamed something in another tongue to another
someone Troy couldn't see, Bigelow-Goode's hand
came crashing into her forehead with a slap. He held it
there as the deacons took positions around her, waiting
for the fall back. And he pushed. And prayed. And
pushed again. And prayed. All of this was happening
and Troy was still waiting for something. She closed
her eyes and tried to pray. Tried to receive it. To feel something other than a sweaty, soft palm on her forehead. But
inside there was nothing but her own thoughts.

"Jesusa!" Bigelow-Goode hollered. "Jesusa, release
the demons from the woman's heart. Release the evil of
Satan from her soul. Jesusa!" Bigelow-Goode was speaking in English now and Troy understood every word, but
she didn't feel a thing. Nothing. And the harder he
pushed at her forehead, the stronger her back seemed
to become.

Troy opened her eyes and looked at Bigelow-Goode.
He was staring into her. His beady eyes red with sweat. He
released her forehead and slapped it again. This time it
was so hard, she screamed.

"Ouch!"

"Just go wait in the car," Kyle said without looking
at Troy after the service had finally ended when Bigelow-
Goode fainted and had to be carried out of the church
like James Brown.

Troy felt so empty, so empty and lost, after failing to
fall beneath Bigelow-Goode's hand that she didn't even
bother to be angry with Kyle for the dismissal. She took
a folder he handed her holding Saptosa's mock copy of
the next day's program for his approval and walked, her
head low, to the car.

While Tasha and Lionel chose fighting words to perfect the art of their war, silence was proving to be the weapon between Kyle and Troy. After Kyle returned to the car, an hour later, they drove halfway home in a quietness that was only broken by pebbles and glass crunching beneath the wheels of the car.

"I just don't know why you had to get involved," Kyle said and he didn't curse like Lionel but a "the fuck" was felt in everything he said.

"I wasn't trying to get involved," Troy said. There was no reason for her to ask what he meant. She knew. "He came to me. I was just standing there!"

"You had to look at him or something."

"Are you saying I wanted that to happen? That I wanted to embarrass you? Embarrass myself in front of all of those people?" Troy stared at Kyle but he kept his eyes on the road. "Oh, I guess I was supposed to pretend to get the Holy Ghost too! Jump around the church and scream and holler. Is that what you wanted?"

Kyle shook his head.

"I'm getting so tired of this. This whole thing is running me into the ground, Troy," he said. "My spirit. It's running me down. I can't find any peace anywhere."

"Well, I don't know what to say," Troy said. "I don't know what to do. I don't know what else I could possibly do to make this work. I've tried to impress everyone. To make everybody happy. To take care of everything. I don't know what else to do."

"I told you what to do," Kyle said weakly.

"What?"

"Take care of me." He looked at Troy and tried his best to show her everything he was feeling, thinking, missing in his eyes.

"What do you mean?"

"You're so busy worrying about the people at the church, you're not worried about me," he said, "about my needs. We haven't had sex in weeks. You run away whenever I touch you. We hardly talk anymore. Everything is about this. Everything is about the church."

"But that's what you need. That's what you want."

"I never said that. Your journey with God needs to be about you. Not what you want to do for me. Every person goes to God alone," Kyle explained and he felt so much pressure building up in his head he was beginning to see spots on the road. "Look, let's not talk about this right now. I have to get ready for my sermon when we get home. I can't do this."

Wounded, Troy sat back in her seat and looked down at the folder of programs Kyle handed her earlier. To keep her mind off of her anger and everything she wanted to say, she opened the program to read it. Under the announcements and testimonies, she saw a name that nearly snatched her eyes out.

"Myrtle? Myrtle Glover?" She looked at Kyle. "Why is her name on here? Why is she on the program?"

"It's nothing. I don't want to talk about it," Kyle answered.

"Nothing? You don't want to talk about it? I'm just asking you a question. Why is she on the program?"

"It's a testimonial. We do it every year. She asked if she could speak. I put her on the program. That's it," Kyle said sharply. "I don't want to talk about it."

Troy clapped the program closed and looked out of the window. What was Myrtle up to now?

As any good lawyer would, Tamia had immersed herself in her case, so much so that at work she remained locked up in her office for hours, at home she seldom answered the telephone—unless it was Malik, and when it was time for bed, she never once had a visitor. While she and the residents who slumbered beneath her bedroom were perfectly fine with the new arrangement, one New York baristocrat[18] wasn't quite as content. And when Tamia entered the Bentley waiting before the entrance of her posh pad one morning, she discovered just who that baristocrat was.

"Charleston!" she screeched as if the man seated in the car was a common stranger who hadn't been bankrolling her chic morning adventures.

"Whoa, don't reach for your pepper spray," Charleston said, holding his arms out defensively as Tamia got into the car.

"I'm sorry, I just didn't expect you to be . . ."

"I know; it's just my car and everything."

"You know what I mean," Tamia said. "You haven't been riding into the office with me, so I wasn't expecting you."

"I'm not the only one being incognegro."[19] Charleston accusingly peered at Tamia. "You haven't been answering my calls, and when I stop by your office you aren't there. This was the only way I could reach you—a sneak attack."

"I've just been really busy. It's nothing personal." Trying to appear relaxed, Tamia shrugged her shoulders and looked out of her window.

While she assumed this would break the ice and help them transition to another topic, seeing Tamia's back only infuriated Charleston. Three women (two of whom were together) had sexted[20] him that very morning, promising memorable trysts if he'd come by for a morning drive, and here Tamia was acting as if his

---

[18] Baristocrat: a black aristocrat.

[19] Incognegro: a black person who has become incognito.

[20] Sext: text message that is sexual in nature. Can include photos or promises of pleasures.

company was promised to her ... or anyone. He looked at the tips of his freshly manicured fingers and laughed.

"Busy?" he said. "Well, I see you weren't too busy to get that mortgage paid."

Tamia felt his words dig into her gut like a dagger. She'd hated the idea of taking money from him to buy the place. But managing both Charleston's expectations of how his lady should live, and her own needs to have something that marked her arrival in the city, she cowered and took the deal. Her father, who'd offered to provide the down payment for a two bedroom in Greenwich Village, was suspicious and said the decision would haunt her someday.

"I can give the money back, if you want it," Tamia said shortly.

"That's most of your savings." Charleston's voice was still cold. "And how will you pay it next month?"

"I don't know."

"I know you don't know."

"So, then why would you bring it up?" Tamia looked at Charleston and she was so angry now, he was the one who felt the dagger.

There was no comeback. The embarrassment in Tamia's tone made Charleston's wielding of power seem small, childish.

"I'm sorry," he said. "I'm just wondering why I can't seem to get any time with my girlfriend. I mean, Naudia tells me you've been hanging out in Harlem with that Malik character. What am I supposed to think?"

"I haven't been *hanging out* with anyone," Tamia answered. "I don't know why my assistant would tell you that. I've just been going to the center. They have yoga classes and I even took this meditation seminar. It was—"

"Meditation?" Charleston frowned. "What the hell do you need that for? That's why black people take naps or go to church."

"It's not like that." Tamia laughed and while she was looking at Charleston, she was seeing the image of Malik's bare, straight back as he demonstrated the breathing pose before her. There was no need to mention that he was the teacher . . . and she was the only student.

"Oh, that's not what it's like?" Charleston faked laughter and stopped suddenly. "Well, what is it like? No . . . what is he like?"

"Him?"

"Come on. I'm not stupid, Mia. Some ghetto nigga with dreads and a knapsack has you using your bank card to take cabs back and forth to Harlem every day. What is it? A fantasy? You wanna fuck a hoodrat? I could understand that. I really could. I've had some."

"What the hell are you talking about? Are you crazy? Wait, have you been looking at my bank statements?"

"Take this as a warning," Charleston said softly, as if he was reciting a prayer. "Don't let your fantasies fuck with your future. The case is a dog and you need to act that way. Your nose is wide open, but you can't smell your dog's shit."

The car stopped in front of the office and Tamia sat speechless as the driver came around to open her door.

"I'll be coming by later," Charleston said cheerfully when the door opened.

Top Seven Signs It's Over

If a man ever tells you that he just decided to break up with you "today," know that it's a lie. Breakups are like bread—they take time to rise to completion. Whether it's a divorce or the conclusion of a college cohabitation, the dissolution of a romance is a process—one that, unfortunately, the other party often isn't privy to. While you may not know your significant other is trying to flee the coop, there are some signs to look out for before you come home to find the locks changed, the dog missing, and an envelope from the courthouse on the steps.

7.   He wants space: If he asks for an open relationship, he already has one. If he asks for space, he needs it to put someone else in it. Translation: "I want you out of my space."

6.   You're getting two-word answers: If you suspect something's up and he says, "I'm fine" or "It's cool" without trying to make a change, pack your bags. Translation: "I'm fine . . . but you're not!"

5.   He's very busy: If he's not President Obama, he has time to see you. He can sleep over or meet you for a twenty-minute cup of coffee next to his job. Translation: "I'm too busy for you because I'm looking for a new place."

4.   She's just a good friend: And so were you! If she's calling and he's running out, pack your bags and get out of there. Translation: "She's just a friend now. . . ."

3.   He's too tired for sex: Sometimes it's true—but most times it's not. If he doesn't want to get it on, it's because he doesn't want to handle the sexual baggage when he finally gets the courage to say,

"It's over!" Translation: "I don't want to have sex . . . with you. But maybe you could call the girl from tip 4. . . ."

2. He doesn't want to go: If you don't see his friends, family, or coworkers anymore, there's a reason. Now they're collateral damage. He doesn't want to hurt them when he hurts you. Translation: "I'm not going, because I don't want you to be with me!"

1. He says, "It's over!": While this is a no-brainer, it's surprising how many women stick around after a man says she shouldn't. Refer to point 16 of the BAP Declaration of Independence—Pack light and never stay where you aren't wanted. You can't change him. Translation: "No, like, for real . . . It's over! I'm calling the police!"

After seven days of the silent treatment from her husband, Tasha and seven boxes of her most prized possessions were busy building a new relationship in an old home. Wrapped in anger at everything, Tasha spent most of her time cursing Lionel for not seeing the big picture and convincing herself that one day he would see it and come crawling back to her, a baby girl on either hip as he smiled and remembered the life they used to have in this place.

Did she miss her children? Of course she did. So much so that she dreamed of being with them and when she woke up, she wasn't ever really sure which part of her life was the dream. And she was partially sad when she realized which one was. But she kept telling herself that in order to have them with her forever the way she wanted to, she had to lose them for a little while. It was a part of her plan. Lionel's season was over and he was with them full time, alone, day in and day out. He'd never had them alone like that. Didn't know about the night feedings and fussy naptimes. How Toni would spontaneously faint if she couldn't get gum in the checkout line at the supermarket and Tiara would send vomit shooting across the room like a projectile missile if he overfed her just one ounce of milk. And once he was tired of playing Daddy Dearest, he'd realize he couldn't have the family he wanted without the wife he'd walked away from. And she was in New York.

But there was another side too. The side of free mornings, manicures that lasted more than two days, listening to music as loud as she pleased, and planning to do whatever she wanted.

Sipping on martinis at Lelabar with Lynn, Tasha thought of how chic and young and alive she must look to people walking by. Her hair in a bun and cocked to the side of the back of her head, she had on couture

jeans and a cozy cowl-neck sweater. It was under-
stated and cool. She didn't look like she was trying to
belong. She just did.

As promised, Lynn had invited her out to talk about
the idea of them joining forces and starting their own
marketing team after she built up her contacts working
with the Knicks. Tasha was so excited to have an "in"
in the industry. The way artist management and PR
went in entertainment, once you were out, you became
a dinosaur no one wanted to touch. It didn't matter
what you knew or who you knew, leaving was a sign of
defeat and no one wanted to work with the defeated.
While she didn't know why Lynn was so interested in
working with her, Tasha's ego wanted to believe it was
based on the small reputation she'd made working with
Lionel. And really she didn't have time to think about
that anyway. She had to work the opportunity. She had
to see what ideas Lynn had. What she wanted to do.
What they could do together. But so far, they'd had two
martinis and tapas and all Lynn had talked about was
other people.

"Can you believe that? That Mr. 'Put It Down on
Me' got both of those girls pregnant at the same time?
Senator Long's daughter and that actress?" Lynn said
and Tasha realized she hadn't been listening to anything
she was saying. "Now, Long won't admit the guy's the
father, but I pledged with his daughter's best friend and
she said it's true. They had pictures of him with the
baby up on Facebook!" Lynn was oozing with excitement, her eyes sparkled beneath Lelabar's dim light.
Tasha could tell that she was the kind of person who
loved to know things and share them with other people.
A gossip. Not any kind of gossip—a black gossip—a
bossip who gathered bits and pieces about every who's
who in the black "in" crowd and spread it up and down

the coast. "God, these men are a trip. If you want to get your freak on, just let your lady know. Maybe they could've shared him."

"Maybe they could've killed him."

"You're crazy!" Lynn giggled. "Things aren't that dramatic anymore."

"Dramatic? He got them both pregnant! He deserves to get his ass cut!" Tasha said.

Lynn nearly choked on her drink.

"Natasha—"

"Tasha."

"Sorry. Tasha. If you're serious about working with these people you have to know that things have changed. It's not . . . 2000 anymore."

"2000? You make it sound like that was a century ago."

"It kind of was," Lynn said, pretending to pout. "Think about it. I was in junior high school in 2000 . . . and so were the guys we want to represent. The ballplayers, the rappers, the R&B thugs . . . Hell, the ones that are just signing to the pros were hardly out of elementary school."

"So what are you saying? I'm old?" Tasha said, cocking her head to the side and looking at Lynn squarely.

"Not old . . . just not up to speed on how we've . . . how black people . . . have grown," Lynn said. "Look, like . . . you all used to vacation in Hilton Head . . . Martha's Vineyard . . . right?"

Tasha nodded.

"We're in South Beach now. We're not buying mansions in the Hamptons anymore. That's been done. We're buying yachts. We're spending the summers in South Africa, working from our laptops—if we're working at all."

"I hear you," Tasha said. "But nothing you said explained how those two women were supposed to share one man and *no man* got cut."

Tasha laughed but Lynn gave a secretive snicker.

"That's changed too. The lines are blurry. . . . Some women just get down . . . men do too."

"Get down? Like share men?"

"Share men . . . share women . . . share men and women. They party. They have a good time," Lynn explained. "We don't have all of those restrictions anymore. We're open-minded."

Tasha frowned at this explanation.

"That's just the way things are," Lynn added, sipping the last bit of Tasha's martini. "And like I said, if you're going to work with this crowd, you have to be open to it." She leaned in toward Tasha. "There's money out there. You want a yacht? Your own yacht? We can get it. We sign five or six of these young boys and we're on it. And I'm not talking pipe dreams. I'm talking real progress. You want fame? Money? Power? We can get it all." Lynn looked in her eyes. "Together."

"Well, I get that. Fine. You have to understand your clients in order to represent them," Tasha said. "But let's talk about representing them for a minute. What kind of business are we going to open? What's the plan? The projections?"

Lynn laughed and fell back in her seat, holding her chest.

"There's another thing," she said. "We don't talk business over brew. We'll get to that later. I just want us to mesh and get to know each other first."

"But you said—"

"Can you come to a party with me?"

"A party?" Tasha asked.

"Yeah, some wigs[21] are having a rooftop party. It's a great way for you to come out and meet some of the new industry people—some of my contacts."

----

[21] Wigs: women with power.

"That sounds okay," Tasha agreed. "When is it?"

"In two weeks or something," Lynn said. "I'll add you to the FB invite."

"FB?"

"Facebook . . ."

"Oh, I don't have a Facebook," Tasha said. "I don't want people all in my business. Google me if you want to see a picture."

"Tasha," Lynn called, as the waitress slid the bill onto the table, "you have to—"

"Okay, I get it," Tasha said, shrugging her shoulders and then reaching for her purse to pay the bill.

Lynn grabbed her arm.

"No," Lynn said softly. "I'll pay the bill. It's my pleasure."

There was a grown man, an old, frail man with a long gray beard, wearing nothing but what appeared to be a diaper, sitting on the floor in the middle of the room, playing a gong. Tamia wanted to explain this situation, this visual, to herself in another, more spiritual way, as she was sitting in a meditation class Malik invited her to, but really that was all she could come up with. Grandpa, in a diaper, on the floor, making a bunch of noise. Now, she was leaving out the big bird the man had painted on his chest in white paint, how ashy his knuckles were, and the fact that the rest of the empty room where Malik had been teaching capoeira the day before was full of other grown people, who were also sitting on the floor and watching and listening to this but not saying a word.

"You okay?" Malik whispered, bending over to Tamia. They were both sitting upright, with their hands placed lightly over each knee in the standard meditation pose. The man, whom the other people in the room seemed to enjoy calling "Baba" or "Babatunde," told them to search for enlightenment. And then he went off to play the gong. That was thirty minutes ago.

No, she wasn't all right.

"Is he going to do anything else?" Tamia asked. "I wanted to meditate but I need help. Isn't he supposed to be teaching us something? I could be doing this at home."

"Excuse me," a woman called from behind, rolling her eyes at the fact that they were talking.

"Peace, sister," Malik said, bowing his head and turning back to Baba.

"I just don't know what I'm supposed to be meditating on . . . the beach, the rain forest, the mountaintops . . . I need him to give me something," Tamia whispered and then as if he'd heard her, Baba jumped up like a man a quarter his age.

"Children, Afrikans, Soul Trekkers, Free People," he called, his voice more mellifluous, yet also stronger than she'd thought by looking at him. "Your body moves to the sound of the universe. The sound in space. In order to connect with your body, to create new matter, to expel illness and hatred and evil from your body, you have to be tuned in, to be plugged in to the universe. My Baba lived for 115 years because he could meditate to that sound. He cleared his body of illness and evil. Your Baba is eighty-seven and I have walked through the woods, climbed mountains, and brought more than six hundred children to their lightness."

"Baba?" Tamia repeated, leaning over to Malik and thinking of how amazed she was that Baba was eighty-seven. He didn't look two days over sixty-five. "Is that his name?"

"No. His name is Peter, but we call him Baba—Babatunde. It means 'Father,'" Malik answered.

"What is inside of you that needs healing? That

needs new matter? We die a little every day. We must replenish those dead cells. We must reconnect with the Creator of the universe. The Creator of all things. We do this by connecting our bodies to the rhythm of the universe." While he was standing, Baba bent over and hit the gong.

"Ohhmmm," everyone called out in unison. "Ohhh-mmmmm."

"What?" Tamia said.

"Ohm," Malik answered her. "It's the sound of the universe. The sound out in space."

Tamia looked at him.

"It is!" he said.

"How do you—"

Tamia hadn't realized it but Baba had walked around the circle and was kneeling behind her.

"Lean into my hand," he said, cutting her off.

She was about to say no but her back just rolled toward Baba's hand on its own.

"Ohhhhhhmmmmm," the class called out. "Ohhhm-mmmmmm."

Not knowing what else to do, and to avoid the fact that she was now laying back on the hand of an elderly man she didn't know who was wearing less fabric than she had on her bra, she hummed along.

"Ohhhhmmmmmmm."

"You have a broken heart," Baba whispered into Tamia's ear. "It has tried to kill you."

Tamia's heart flipped in the way it usually did when she'd heard bad news. But this wasn't bad news. It was just a shock. The truth.

She turned to ask Baba something, but he was already gone—back up at the gong.

"Hey, king," Ayodele said, gliding into the room as if only air carried her feet. A size two, she was wearing only a knitted bra and mudcloth harem pants—which

Tamia called MC Hammer pants. Half of her body was exposed, and Tamia kept thinking she probably had on less clothing than the hookers in the street right outside, but no one said a thing. She sat in the empty space on Tamia's other side.

"Greetings, Ayo," Malik said, straightening his back and glancing toward Ayo. Although her breasts were hanging out for all the world to see, Tamia noticed that he looked her right in her eye.

"Ohhhmmmm," everyone hummed with the gong. Yet Ayo leaned over Tamia and giggled with Malik about something that had happened in the kitchen earlier. And hahahahaha, wasn't it funny how this and that happened.

Tamia turned and looked at the woman who had shushed her, but she wasn't doing anything now.

"Why would they put soy sauce on it?" Ayo said, giggling with Malik. "Everyone knows you can't do that! Right?" She looked at Tamia.

"Oh, Ayo, do you remember my attorney? Her name is Tamia."

"Oh," Ayo said. "I thought I recognized your beautiful eyes." She kissed Tamia on the cheek and it was just enough sweetness to make Tamia know that she'd hate this woman for the rest of her life.

"Ohhhmmmmm," Tamia droned on with the rest of the people in the room to drown Malik and Ayo out. "Ohhhhmmmm!" Somehow she'd become the loudest and fastest in the room, leading everyone into an unceremonious aria.

"Wait," Baba shouted, hitting the gong like it was actually the gong show. "Someone is off-key. Someone is out of tune. Someone is not connected with the universe. Who is it?" Suddenly his voice went from African cool to Detroit ghetto.

Every head in the room turned to Tamia.

* * *

After thanking Malik for inviting her to the workshop and watching Ayo steal every stare the man had in his soul, Tamia waited around to talk to Baba about what he'd whispered in her ear.

"The sister with the broken heart," Baba said.

"That's not funny, you know," Tamia responded.

"I didn't laugh." Baba looked at Tamia. "You have come to talk to me for a reason?"

"Why did you say it? Why did you say I have a broken heart?"

"Do you?"

Tamia closed her eyes as she spoke this time and went along with the conversation on the faith of what she was feeling in her heart.

"I think you know," she said.

"I do. And I can save you. From yourself. From your death. From what killed your mother."

"You can't say that," Tamia said, her eyes filling with tears as she looked back at Baba. She paused, feeling a need to explain her emotion. "I was born with heart irregularities. The same thing that killed my mother. It almost killed me once." She wiped her tears. "So you can't just say that to me. You know? Not if you don't really know."

"What do you want me to know, child?" Baba asked, touching Tamia's heart. "What do you want me to say? You're a part of the universe. If you want to live, you have to accept that. And if you accept that, you will have to change everything about your life. That's the only way you will get free. And that's the only way your heart will continue to beat." He pressed his hand against her heart one time and released. Tamia felt an energy go through her body. It was arresting and freeing, all at once.

"What if I'm afraid," Tamia started, "afraid of freedom?"

"That's not the question you should be asking. The question is if you're more afraid of freedom than slavery," Baba said. "If you want to find that out, then join me. Join me on your next step to freedom."

"I believe in the power of God," Tamia said, "not man."

"I don't have a problem with God. We all come from the Creator. We all return to the Creator. It's what happens in the middle that matters."

"Mrs. LaRoche, I am sorry, but I simply can't make an exception for you. You're going to need to have someone here to pick you up after the surgery."

Tasha was glaring at the nurse at Dr. Miller's midtown office. One of the top plastic surgeons in the country, Miller was every New York woman's nip/tuck ninja. Three weeks earlier, when Tasha decided she was getting full-body liposuction after doing 250 crunches and nearly putting her back out, she felt she needed a little boost to her Queen Bee plan and called Dr. Miller's masseuse (a contact she'd gotten from another Knicks wife) to set up an appointment. While Miller's schedule was full for the next year, Tasha had her consultation the very next day and set up her surgery a week after that. There was no need to wait or contemplate. She knew exactly what she wanted—her old body back. And after meeting with Lynn, she felt even more sure of her decision. Lynn was right; if she was going to work with young people, she needed to understand them—to be one of them. Not this outdated and oversized bag she was becoming. Miller had the pictures and it was time for him to get to sucking and plucking until twenty-year-old Tasha emerged.

"This is New York City, for crying out loud. I don't need anyone to pick me up. There are fifty cabs waiting outside to take me wherever I want after my surgery," Tasha responded, looking at the nurse as if she was grasshopper on her arm.

"I'm fully aware of what goes on outside of the office," the nurse said sternly. "I know what goes on inside it, as well. And one thing that is going to go on is that you are going to need someone here to take you home after your surgery or there will be no surgery." While Nurse Hopkins had been a sweet, tight-mouthed Catholic girl from Connecticut when she'd started working at Dr. Miller's office six years ago, she'd been dealing with demanding Gotham girls for too long now to take Tasha's crap. This was nothing. Ivana Trump once demanded to have a Papillion in the room as she had her lip injections. That woman had a mouth on her—and she wasn't even speaking English. "Did you read the presurgical guidelines you were provided?"

"Yeah, yeah, yeah . . . and how many people does it take to screw in a lightbulb?" Tasha asked. "It's a man with a freaking vacuum, sucking the fat out of my gut . . . and my butt . . . and my back and legs, and wherever else he finds it." Tasha rolled her eyes and looked down at her purse, considering whom she could call with this. While her normal cellmate,[22] Troy, wasn't too far away in Harlem, she hadn't told her about the surgery, for fear she'd try to talk her out of it. In fact, Tasha hadn't told anyone about the surgery—Lionel included.

Tasha looked up and the nurse was looking back at her, clearly unamused with the exchange.

---

[22] Cellmate: a girlfriend someone gets into so much trouble with, the two risk getting caught and sharing a cell in prison.

"Do we need to reschedule your surgery?" she asked with a voice so impersonal one would think she hadn't handled a cup of Tasha's urine just days before.

"No . . . I need this today," Tasha said. "Damn . . . Look, now, what time do you get off? Maybe you could be my ride? Or you could take off and I could pay your salary for the day. I could pay you double."

There was no crack of concern in the nurse's face. Susan Lucci had tried that once.

"Do we need to reschedule your surgery, Mrs. Laroche?" the nurse repeated.

"No need to do that, Danielle," someone said and Tasha watched as the nurse's stern eyes went from her to someone behind Tasha and softened quickly. "I'll handle it. I'll have my driver come up and take her wherever she needs to go."

Tasha turned and Charleston was standing there smiling.

"Charleston," Tasha said. "What are you doing here?"

"Tasha, you know better than to ask such a thing at a doctor's office." Charleston's voice was as confident as the green and black argyle sweater he was wearing. It was past ugly, but both he and Tasha knew it was Ralph Lauren Purple, so there was an exception.

"Well, you're dating my girl, so I feel it's best that I ignore being politically correct and get straight to the point."

"Fiesty, Tasha." Charleston chuckled. "I love it. You should tell *my* girl to pick up on that. I like a fighter."

"No need for her to jack my style. If she needs a fighter, she has me." Tasha's grin was a full knockout.

"Touché." Charleston smiled and looked at Tasha's thighs. He'd always loved strong women, the ones who challenged and were bent on putting him in his place. It provided ambitious arguments and amazing sex. While it was hard to come by this with the women he dated and slept with now, as most were so busy vying for his love they were too afraid to challenge him, it kept him in his car, riding down to the projects to pluck-a-cluck.[23]

"So, what's your poison?" Tasha asked again.

Charleston looked at Tasha dimly.

"Look, two sinners can't meet in hell and not talk about the devil."

"A little Botox up top." Charleston pointed to his forehead.

"Botox? Your skin is perfect."

"Isn't it?" Charleston grinned. "My kind of black really don't crack . . . but it sweats. And a sweaty man doesn't cut it in my field. Something about an attorney sweating all over himself that puts people off."

"Well, just because people know you're lying doesn't mean they want evidence," Tasha said, laughing. "So, the shots stop the sweat?"

"A little poison and I'm as dry as an unsatisfied woman," Charleston said. "Speaking of unsatisfied women, what's up with your girl?"

"My girl?" Tasha looked confused but both she and Charleston knew he was talking about Tamia.

"Tamia," he said.

"Oh, yeah, Tamia." Tasha tried not to say anything to push the conversation about her friend forward. Answering any questions or telling any tales could lead to disaster. The 3Ts were good for gossip, but certainly not about one another . . . well, only in special cases . . . and only to another T.

"She's been a little distant lately, avoiding me and . . ." Charleston admitted, looking at Tasha, but she didn't budge . . . until he added: "and it's a shame, because I was about to lock it down."

[23] Pluck-a-cluck: meet/have sex with a "chickenhead."

"What?"

"I was about to ask her to marry me."

"Marry you?"

"Yes, we're in love and that's what two people in love do." While almost no one who knew Charleston would guess that he was telling the truth, he actually was being honest. If Tamia was correct about one thing during her rant about Nathaniel marrying Ava, it was that men like Charleston and Nathaniel marry in packs—once one got a ring, the others followed (reluctantly or otherwise). And as Charleston pondered Nathaniel's upcoming nuptials during a warlike game of racquetball at the gym, he decided it might be time for him to get married. With his last single friend jumping the broom, soon folks would become nosy, rumors might start, or he might accidentally get the wrong woman pregnant and have to save face by marrying her. Point: Tamia was the most decent woman standing, he loved her, she was a team player, and she didn't ask too many questions. It was time to buy a ring.

"Really?" Tasha asked, thinking about the new client Tamia had been all bug-eyed about. "Have you told her?"

"Of course not. It's a surprise. I need a ring first."

"A ring for Tamia? Oh, that's easy—the Jean Schlumberger Bud Ring with the pavé setting," Tasha blurted out as if she was recalling a grocery list. While she thought the Tiffany selection was cliché and dated, it was perfect for Tamia's whimsical, classic taste. As the two had shopped for wedding gifts for Troy, Tamia picked out the ring and nearly cried when the jeweler insisted she give it back.

"You remember all of that? Now that's a real friend."

"It's easy. I have a photographic memory—when it comes to shopping," Tasha said. "So, you're really going to ask her?"

"Yeah. I am."

* * *

For the second time in the second week in a row, Tamia had been summoned to a meeting in Mrs. Phaedra Pelst's office. Sitting on the opposite side of the desk, listening to Phaedra as she took her second phone call, Tamia thought of how ridiculous it was that she was sitting there anyway. Phaedra wasn't really her boss or direct supervisor. She had authority in that she'd been there longer than her and led many of the cases she'd helped with when she started, but now that Tamia was off the Lucas case, there was no reason for them to interact for the time being.

"Thanks for being so patient with me," Phaedra said, smiling a thin and flimsy greeting.

"No problem," Tamia replied, returning the smile. "So, what did you want to talk about?"

"Just wanted some words with you about the Holder case. Richard Holder. Ring a bell?"

That was either a stupid question or a clever way of insulting Tamia's level of commitment to her case. Likely it was the latter.

"I certainly am familiar. Holder and I have met several times and the case is progressing." Tamia could play too. "We'll be ready for his hearing."

"Yes," Phaedra said. "Well, I am not wholly concerned about the case itself, but rather some things that have come up surrounding it. Some team issues . . ."

"Team issues?" Tamia said. "There is no team. How could there be issues?"

"Well, as you know, a favor was phoned in to someone upstairs on your behalf," Phaedra said, beginning the lie she'd come up with to get information out of Tamia. There was no phone call made to anyone upstairs about the case. The favor was an exchange for sex between her and Charleston at a sex club. So far, she, Charleston, and Tamia were the only three people in the world who knew about the trade. But what Phaedra didn't know was why Charleston was so interested in helping Tamia. At first she bought the whole "she's a black woman" routine Charleston gave her one night when she was rushed out of his place because Tamia was on her way up in the elevator. But now things were out of hand. "A call to have Jones dropped from the case. Do you know about that?"

Tamia didn't shake or nod her head. She just sat there, her heartbeat quickening.

"Do you know why it was done? Do you know anything?"

"Pelst, what do you want?" Tamia asked. While rumors among the black people at the company had connected Tamia with Charleston a long time ago, he didn't want everyone to know yet.

"Well, it seems Jones found out you wanted her off," Phaedra explained.

"She what?"

"And she's pretty upset."

"Oh, my God. I didn't mean for this to get back to her."

"Don't worry about her," Pelst said. "She's about to float to the top of the water anyway."

"For this?"

"Among other things."

Tamia felt ill. Like she'd just cheated her best friend.

Phaedra knew this would be her reaction. The sensitivity among the black women in the office was so ridiculous. She didn't see how they didn't know that there was no space for such alliances in power.

"I know you don't want her feelings to be hurt, and I'm trying to fix it." Somehow Phaedra was able to make her eyes red, as if she was crying. "But I need to know who made the call upstairs."

Tamia didn't move. She didn't trust Phaedra. And it didn't matter how red her eyes got.

"Now, I heard it was Charleston," Phaedra said, watching Tamia's eyes as she threw in a name, her second-to-last resort before the question she was about to ask. "Is there something I should know about your relationship?"

Tamia still hadn't moved. She couldn't believe another person, another black woman, was losing her job because of her. Because of some advice she'd taken about how she could further her own career. She was willing to fight to get to the top, but putting people in jail, getting people fired? That wasn't the fight she wanted to make.

"Is that all?" Tamia asked, standing up.

"*Is* it?" Phaedra asked, the Howard Beach girl inside of her jumping out into the room. "Look, just tell me if you're screwing him. Are you screwing Charleston?"

"Yeah, that's it," Tamia said, Phaedra's whole plot and purpose now coming together in her mind. Jones wasn't likely anywhere near the guillotine. Phaedra was bluffing to get information. "I'll show myself out."

Good Girlfriends Guide

Men are cool. Money is okay. Wine is all right. Louis V will do. . . . But what's the sense having any of these things if, as Billy Dee said in *Mahogany,* "you don't have someone you love to share it with"? Well, Billy was talking about the comforts of the opposite sex, but most women know that a cool sisterfriend will also sweeten the ride. There's no sense having it if you can't chat about it and she's always there to lend an ear. While the rules of engaging a good girlfriend are established on the playground, it doesn't hurt to remember the top dos and don'ts to maintaining a strong relationship with your best gal pal.

Dos:
1.   Support her goals and dreams.
2.   Give her advice, but know she will follow her heart.
3.   Know that sometimes it is all about her and play second.
4.   If you know what she needs, don't ask—just do it.
5.   Good or bad, tell her about herself when she needs to hear it.

Don'ts:
1.   Judge her or give up on her.
2.   Tell her secrets to others or talk about her behind her back.
3.   Date her ex—even if she says it's okay.
4.   Support self-destructive behavior—drinking, smoking, sex, etc.
5.   Allow her to lie to you or herself.

"Are you sure this is what you want to do?" Malik asked, walking down a street in the lovely 10013 zip code of New York City, known to the world as TriBeCa and to the 3Ts as Tasha's new home.

"What do you mean, am I sure?" Tamia said, walking beside him. "I wouldn't have asked you for the number if I wasn't sure. You came all the way down here to meet me just to ask me that?"

That morning, after turning and tossing through the night with everything that happened with her at work and with Ava at the party and what she'd actually considered doing with Malik's case, Tamia had finally decided she wanted to join Baba's circle on the path to spiritual enlightenment. She'd jumped out of bed and ran to her phone to tell her client the news and ask how she could get in contact with Baba. Looking at the golden powder still sticking to the tips of her gray shoes, she thought she was ready for a change.

"Look, I know people say this all of the time and it's become cliché, but this is serious. You can't go to Babatunde if you aren't sure," Malik said. As usual, he was wearing one of his T-shirts from the Freedom Project. This one had a picture of Malcolm X on it. It had been raining that morning, so he also had on his military jacket and for the first time since Tamia had met him, he had his hair pulled back off of his face and into a headband. She'd always thought he was a beautiful man, but now, with his entire black face and sharp eyes looking at her, she saw that maybe he was more than beautiful and there was no word for that.

"The journey he's going to take you on will only work if you're open," he went on, "if you're completely open to changing."

"I've got this," Tamia assured him, thinking he seemed awfully concerned about her decision to join Baba's path.

His eyes were pleasant, smiling at her in a way that made hers smile back. "I've got me. I can handle change."

"He's going to make you cut your hair off."

"Say what?" Tamia felt something tingle at the nape of her neck. Suddenly change seemed crazy. She'd invested a lot of time, energy, money, and then more money into her hair. Not to mention the hundreds of Indians who'd also contributed to her weft.

"Your hair," Malik said. "It will have to go."

"Why?"

"Because it's not conscious. It's a shackle. A symbol that you've bought into the white man's image of beauty. That you believe your own nappy hair isn't good enough, or pretty enough, to wear just the way it is. The way it was when you were born."

"I wasn't born with nappy hair," Tamia said, stopping in front of Tasha's new/old abode. "You know it takes some time for those naps to show up."

Malik couldn't help but laugh with her.

"Why don't you cut your hair?" Tamia asked. "It's all long. . . . Isn't a man's hair supposed to be short?"

"That's the white man too," Malik said. "Dreads are the hair of the original black man. He only cuts his hair if there is great turmoil in his life. If he needs to leave something from his past behind that has been locked into his hair."

"Locked into his hair?"

"Yes. Spiritually. You carry the weight of the things around you," Malik said. "What about you? Why wouldn't you cut your hair?"

"It's too much work. Too much of a hassle," she said, but that was because she'd heard someone else say it. She'd never once worn her hair natural and had no plans of doing it. It just had no function in her world, and it wouldn't occur to her until a week later, just before Kali was shaving her head, that this was a problem.

"A hassle?" Malik repeated. "Who you are is a hassle?" He locked his eyes on hers. "I think who you are is beautiful. Without all of the hair. I think she's beautiful."

"You think I'm beautiful?" Tamia asked.

"No," Malik answered, pulling a card from his pocket and waking Tamia from a dream she didn't know she was having. "I mean, not specifically you—like, all black women. All sisters." He handed her the card. "Here's the number."

If the front of Tasha's married-and-acting crazy/bachelorette TriBeCa pad was a schoolyard, someone would've run by that particular moment and told Tamia to pick up her face.

"Thanks," she said dryly, taking the card.

"So what is this place?" Malik asked, looking up at Tasha's building. "I'm not trying to be in your business but . . ."

"It's cool. One of my best friends lives here. She has some kind of emergency. She sent me a text last night."

"Oh, I'm sorry. I didn't mean to hold you up."

"It's no problem . . . she . . . she has emergencies . . . once . . . twice a week," Tamia explained. "It's kind of been that way recently."

"Maybe she needs to call Baba," Malik suggested jokingly.

"That's probably never going to happen," Tamia said, thinking of the kind of arguments Baba and Tasha might have after sitting in the same room for five minutes.

"Why?"

"She's . . ." Tamia started, but then she saw Troy out of the corner of her eye and turned just in time to see her friend grinning and snapping a picture with her camera phone. "What?"

"Who's that?" Malik asked.

"One of my friends. One of my soon-to-be-dead friends."

"Hakuna matata . . . and whatever else they said in the *Lion King*," Tasha said, looking at the picture of Malik in Troy's cell phone. She was tucked tight in her bed with empty juice bottles and Lean Cuisine wrappers all over the floor. "Who the hell is this long-lost Ashari king, looking to save a damsel in distress?"

"Ashari?" Troy said, sitting beside her in the bed. Tamia was on the other side. "That's not an African tribe. It's Ashanti."

Tasha rolled her eyes as Tamia snatched the phone from her and handed it back to Troy.

"What's going on with you? Why did you send out a 3T text?" Tamia asked. "You're just lying in bed. What could possibly be the emergency—aside from the fact that you clearly need to clean this mess up. And frozen food? This is New York. Haven't you heard of takeout?"

"Well, if you must know, I called you two here to tell you that I . . ." Tasha stalled. "I beat both of you! I'm the queen of the 3Ts!" She stretched her arms out but then one of the muscles in her stomach jumped. "Ohhhh," she cried.

"What happened?" Troy asked, reaching for Tasha's stomach.

"My plan," Tasha said wickedly. "I got the operation."

"What operation?" Troy asked. She hadn't been at the ESPN party when Tasha mentioned liposuction to Tamia in the bathroom.

"Lipo?" Tamia said. "Your ass got freaking lipo?"

"Full body, baby," Tasha said proudly.

"I can't believe you did it. . . . I mean, I know you mentioned it, but that was like . . . like, two weeks ago," Tamia said. "Who does that? Who just gets up one day and gets liposuction . . . to their entire body?"

"Someone who wants to be Queen Bee," Tasha explained. "I'm a woman of action. A woman of power. Now, I told you I wanted my old life back and here I am . . . back on track. My old things, and soon my new body. And later, my old business."

Tamia exhaled. She couldn't even respond to her friend's craze.

"How much did this cost? Like $10K?" Tamia asked, noticing that Troy was quiet.

Hearing about surgery and thinking of how much it must have cost her friend, Troy, who once lived a life where thinking of price was passé, was busy thinking of how and when she could pay the church's credit card off without Kyle knowing about it. It had been on her mind constantly since she'd used the card in the store, and while one side of her believed if she returned the money quickly, everything would be okay, the other side knew better.

"Who cares how much it cost," Tasha said. "I won. I won and I won and I won." Though she was still a little weak, Tasha did a little dance in the bed before aggravating her stomach muscle again and hollering in pain.

"So what are you supposed to do now? How long are you going to be in bed eating bad food?" Tamia asked.

"Just a few days. Miller's surgical methods come with little to no swelling. He said I should be back on my feet in two days. In the gym in three weeks."

"Well, that's good news," Troy said, though her mind was still far away.

"So, after I get up and can get my skinny jeans back over this quarter-pounder[24]—because you know I had him leave that alone," Tasha said, "I will be expecting you chicks to take me out to celebrate my winning. And I will take cash and checks instead of gifts. Well, a new Louis Vuitton boyfriend will do too."

"Sure," Troy said, looking at Tamia and not sure what exactly Tasha thought she was winning. This was a mess.

"Now, enough about me and mine." Tasha paused and opened her eyes wide. "Ts, I have dispatch!"[25]

"What?" Tamia asked, afraid of what Tasha might say.

"One of us is about to get married . . . And I am not at liberty to say who . . . but two of us already are. . . ."

Troy looked at Tamia.

"What?" Troy shrieked. "Charleston? He came around?!"

"Wait . . . wait . . . wait," Tamia stopped her. "What are you talking about, Tasha? Are you taking too many Percocet?"

"I saw him the other day at Dr. Miller's office and he told me that he is about to pop the question," Tasha said. "Now, I know he probably wants it to be a surprise, but the Ts have a wedding to plan and that takes time. Everything in the city has to be booked for the fall by now."

"A winter wedding," Troy chimed in, oozing with delight. "White . . . white everywhere. We can pray for snow! We can have a snow machine."

"And horses," Tasha added. "Clydesdales to bring Ms. Lovebird in!"

---

[24] Quarter-pounder: nicely shaped, round buttocks.
[25] Dispatch: gossip, news.

"And doves!" Troy cried and then she and Tasha sang, *"This is what it sounds like when doves cry."*

They laughed at their merriment and went on until the guest list was complete with the Obamas and the Clintons.

"I can get the Met," Tasha said. "We can have the entire museum!"

Troy noticed that during this entire exchange, Tamia hadn't said a word. In fact, she'd gotten up from the bed and gone to the window.

"Mia," Troy called to her old roommate, "aren't you excited? Don't you want to help us plan?"

"Sure," Tamia said flatly, like she was agreeing to see an action movie.

"'Sure'?" Tasha frowned and looked at Troy. "Wait a minute . . . one day you're locking me up in a bathroom talking about a delicious and his alien fiancée and crying about how no one's going to marry you, and now after I tell you one of the richest men in the city is about to buy you that $55K Jean Schlumberger Bud Ring all you can say is, 'sure'?"

Tamia continued looking out at the people walking by in the street and shrugged her shoulders.

"Ms. Lovesong?" Tasha called Troy.

"Yes, Ms. Lovestrong?"

"Hand me that phone."

Tasha handed the phone back over to Tasha and she looked at the picture of Malik again.

"Somebody swallowed an *Afro*-disiac," Tasha said, shaking her head.

"A what?" asked Troy.

"An Afro-disiac—the jones you get for those dudes with dreads, reading poetry and whatnot," Tasha repeated. "They were all over undergrad. Looking all fine. Big, brown muscles. Knapsacks and bad attitudes. I saw many a bougie sister end up broke, bald, and selling

Muslim oil and Farrakhan tapes down on Georgia Avenue behind the Afro-disiac. Look what happened to Erykah Badu! Now it's happening to our Tamia. He put his mojo on her." She pointed to Tamia, looking out of the window. "Look at her. She's hot for him. We might as well get our Farrakhan CDs now. What's your new name? Akilah Muslimah?"

"He's just my client." Tamia wondered if Malik was back at the Freedom Project by now. Maybe he was in his office. What book was he reading? He was probably playing with one of his locks. Did he wear reading glasses?

Tasha looked at the picture again and handed the phone back to Troy.

"Look how they're looking at each other," she told Troy.

"I know. I saw it up close. That's why I took the picture."

Tamia glared at Troy.

"What?" Troy said. "You two were looking like a fake Nia Long and Larenz Tate in *Love Jones*."

"Just tell the truth, Mia," Tasha said. "We're all family here. You want him, don't you?"

"I—"

"You want to ride that red, black, and green flag until it bursts into the stars and stripes!"

"Why are you so vulgar?" Tamia asked.

"I'm high on Percocet!"

"Don't blame the drugs."

"I won't blame the drugs if you admit the truth. You want this man. You want to get with Kunta Kinte and have a little Kizzie. Tell the truth and shame the devil! Tell her, Troy!"

"I don't think that applies right now," Troy said.

"Fine, I like him," Tamia said, admitting this to herself for the first time. "I mean, you saw him."

"Yes, I did." Troy fanned herself.

"So?" Tasha pushed.

"So? So, he's fine," Tamia said.

Tasha sucked her teeth.

"Dang, I knew something would ruin my winter wedding," she said.

"Ruin?" Troy's eyes were wide. "She can't marry Charleston?"

"Who said anything about anyone getting married?" Tamia shouted.

"You did," Tasha and Troy said together.

"Now, you can still pull it off," Tasha added. "But first you have to shake it off. You have to get with Malik— well, first because I want to know if he's good in bed— and second because the only way you can marry Charleston with no regrets is if you taste the rainbow."

"Again, who said I was marrying Charleston?"

"Mia," Tasha said, "that's just the Afro-disiac kicking in on you. It's like heroin. It's made you think your new cracky life is wonderful and that you don't need the old fab you left behind, but I am here to tell you that you had a life before Nat Turner came into your life and you will when he packs up his little ginger beer and vegan brownies in his knapsack and leaves your apartment in the middle of the night."

Tamia and Troy looked at Tasha inquisitively.

"What?" she said. "I had an Afro-disiac once."

"So what should she do?" Troy asked.

"She has to try it out."

"*She* doesn't have to do anything," Tamia said. "Because *he* is my client and . . . he doesn't like me. He likes Ayo . . . Ayodele. Queen of the Nile or the gypsies or whatever."

"Is she cute?" Troy asked.

"Remarkable."

"Dang!" Tasha and Troy said, ducking as if Tamia was being knocked out.

"She's not his girlfriend . . . just some girl he looks at like she's a pan of peach cobbler."

"Oh, that's easy," Tasha said. "You can still have him. Just turn the tables."

"What?"

"You need to stop being all goo-goo ga-ga over him and play a little harder to get," Tasha said.

"I'm not goo-goo ga-ga," Tamia said.

"You didn't look at the picture," Troy said, handing Tamia the phone.

"Oh, my Lord," Tamia said, looking at her eyes practically undressing the man she was supposed to be sending to jail.

"Exactly," Tamia confirmed. "You have it bad. And the only way you're going to give it away is to get that man. You need the Dude Diet."

"The Dude Diet!" Troy said. "You mean the one I used with old Desmond Bessemer in college."

"Desmond?" Tamia quizzed.

"The sexy Kappa with the . . ." Troy stopped herself, remembering the nights she'd spent with Desmond.

"Big *cane!*"[26] Tasha laughed.

"Yes." Troy blushed.

"Oh, I remember him," Tamia said. "He practically moved into your dorm room and went to all of your classes with you, but when you asked him to be your boyfriend, he insisted you two were just having fun."

"He was crazy. But I really liked him."

"You liked his *cane*." Tasha laughed.

"I was young and full of Satan," Troy insisted. "Anyway, I did the Dude Diet—I shut him down and gave

---

[26] Cane: the penis of a man who carries a cane.

him limitations. It took him less than a week to ask me if I wanted a commitment. The boy was starving . . . wrote me a love letter and everything. It seems that living without me showed him that he wanted to be with me."

An hour later, after Troy and Tamia had cleaned the messy bedroom and ordered delivery so Tasha could have a decent home-cooked meal, they were outside the apartment, walking toward Troy's car.

"So, who's going to say something first?" Troy asked, looking straight ahead.

"I'm not saying anything to her. I've butted into her business before and ended up in the hospital," Tamia said. "Never again. If she wants to do this craziness, it's her business. She's a grown woman."

"Mia, you know that's wrong. That's not what the 3Ts are about. We can't just let her move out on her family, leaving those girls alone with Lionel, and God only knows what else she's going to do with her body."

"And who's going to stop her?"

Troy couldn't answer Tamia.

"Exactly," Tamia said. "She's not going to listen to either of us. And besides, sometimes I feel a little responsible. If we hadn't brought Porsche back into her life, maybe she'd be better off."

"I don't think so. I think it would be worse. She was going to have Toni anyway."

"Well, either way, I don't want to get burned," Tamia said. "I love Tasha, but she's going to have to work this out on her own. She'll get tired of being away from her children. And Lionel isn't going to keep her bank account full for long. This is just another one of her stunts to get some attention."

"But who's going to suffer?" Troy asked.

"Toni and Tiara will be fine," Tamia said. "I spoke to

Lionel and he's okay. You know he's not going to let those little girls go without."

"You're right," Troy said. "So, what about you? Are you going to go after your hunky client with the Dude Diet?"

"Um . . . probably not," Tamia said. "Does Tasha look like the kind of person I need to be taking advice from?"

"You have a point, but she does too. You can't marry one man if you have feelings for another. You might as well check it out. Check him out."

"Check you out, Ms. Lovesong," Tamia teased, "giving advice. What's going on with you?"

The Dude Diet: Giving Less Love to Get More Love

You lit candles at the Novena station at the church, asking God to send you a good man to save you from your boring life of <u>solotude</u>. You want to be "in a relationship" on Facebook. You want to play Scrabble in the park and drink wine as the sun sets. You want to sit at the "couples" table at the next wedding and proudly announce that you are taken when they call "all the single ladies" to the dance floor for the bouquet toss. And then, just like that, He (no, not Jesus) appears, and you're swept off your feet and into a fairy tale courtship of expensive dinners, weekends out of town, family gatherings, and sex that's so good, you proudly break up with BOB—your battery-operated boyfriend. You're in love. You give him your everything. You call. You e-mail. You put everything in your life to the side to make room for him. Then something happens. You realize that you've been having a lot of fun, a bunch of fun . . . but just fun and you want more. And then you ask an inevitable question: "Where is this going?" and your darling answers as you expected: "I'm just having fun. I wasn't looking for anything else."

Before you burst into tears, throw in the old love towel, and give up on Prince Charming, know that maybe there's a way the connection could be salvaged. Yes. You could make it work. You could get more love from that man (or any man, for that matter) by giving a little less of yourself. Basically, in your enthusiasm for finding love, you forgot one important thing—men are predators and once the prey is hunted and caught, it's time to move on. Now, he probably didn't have to hunt to get you. After enduring the desperation of lighting those Novena candles, you just fell on the floor and rolled over. Don't worry, you can reverse this history. Just get up and get ready for the chase. Try these five steps for giving less love to the men in your life, to get more in return.

1. Take notice of him: There are two things you must decide about every man you allow into your life—(a) If he's worth your time of day. (b) If he's giving you the time of day. On the first point, stop making exceptions and excuses for people you don't really like. That doesn't mean you can't love that convict. You could. But don't try if you can't and if you can, don't try to change him. Stop acting as if you need someone to choose you . . . and choose someone. Settling will only get you a settlement and we all know that's less than market value.

   Also ask yourself if the person is truly into you—if you find you are into him. Now, this is hard to do, but it simply takes honesty on your part—not his (so don't ask). Look into his eyes. Pay attention to how he's paying attention to you. Notice if he's opening up his world to you. If he's trying to impress and please you. If he watches you and anticipates your needs. See if he allows you to take your time and is vocal about what he wants. These are the signs of a man "in like." If you like him, this is good. Be sure to meet him reasonably where he's at— men like approval, but don't give the whole kit and caboodle away just yet just because he's expressing that he likes what's in the window. Let him stand there for a while and just want and just like. Men say they don't like it, but every woman knows that leaving a good date before he's ready to go will always get you a call the next day.

2. Take notice of the situation: Are you being a

bug-a-boo? Are you wide open? Do you call every day? Send texts? Sit in his row at church? Stop by his job? E-mail his mother? To be clear, you're doing too much. Know that he will like this in the beginning. He will think it's cute. Men love attention and good stories. So, he'll seem equally spellbound and even return your late-night calls, but it will get played out quick and you will be left wondering where the love went. If this is you, take notice and take a break— an unannounced break.

3. Take your time: Don't give it all away at once. Slow down and assess and reassess the situation. Accept that everyone you date or want to date doesn't need to know you—not the whole you. Accept that you shouldn't share your body, your home, your children, or your life story with just anyone. Keep it light and funny in the beginning. The best relationships take time. There's no reason to rush to love's altar.

   Note: Stop making romance where there's no romance. You can't trick him into being your man by treating him to a bunch of freebies and letting him lay up in your house. He will eat and he will lay. But he will also get up and go home when he's done.

4. Take care of you: Continue to focus on your needs and ensure that while you're dating, that's NOT ALL you're doing. Don't put all of your stock into getting a man and getting married and getting a house, and then a baby, and then a dog. Other areas of your life need attention, and focusing on them will make you more attractive because you won't be sitting by the phone or always available. You'll be too busy being busy. Focus on your mind, body, and soul. Build rela-

tionships with friends and family. Reconnect with your children. Reconnect with yourself. And your God.

5. Let it go or take the leap: If you realize that he's not taking charge or he's just not that excited about you, let it go and move on. Don't ask questions or try to figure it out. Don't accept excuses for missed calls or dates. Don't sleep with him, thinking things will change. Just move on. The diet worked and you figured out that he's not that interested. But if he is, you can—take the leap into love . . . sweet love. You've found a man worth your time and saw that he kind of liked you too. But instead of jumping all in and giving him "the best that you've got," you took your time and eased up on him! You've been taking care of yourself. You've been making it clear that you have standards and set limitations as to how far he could get with you without actually getting with you. And guess what—he liked it. And, therefore, he now likes you. . . .

Floors are hard. Not just a little hard. Really hard. Especially after three hours of sitting in silence, your bottom so confused by your position it gives in and moves over to your hips, leaving nothing but posterior bone and floorboards connected.

Tamia hadn't felt this kind of pain in her bottom since she'd pledged her sorority over ten years ago. But even then, sitting on the floor for so long wasn't as bad, as her bottom was much more firm and unable to wiggle off to the side.

It was meditation time again.

Only now Baba wasn't wearing his white cloth and there was no gong. Just three women, Baba, and his books sat in the middle of the floor at the Freedom Project breathing each other's air as they "began this long journey together," which was what Baba said. "The journey begins with a single step," Baba said in the middle of a list of proverbs. "And this one we take together— one with the other. We must hear each other's hearts beating."

Fatimah and Tanya were the women flanking her sides. Over the days they'd been spending together, preparing for their journey with Baba, Tamia had learned that Fatimah was a schoolteacher from Brooklyn. She'd started taking Swahili at the center a few weeks earlier and just like Tamia, she met Baba and her life was forever changed. While doing community service in an elder's organic garden, they laughed about how Baba spoke in constant riddles and that most of the time they were so busy trying to understand his new point, they were forgetting his last point. Tanya was the daughter of one of the men who rented the building to Malik. One day when she was collecting rent, she'd decided to sit in on one of Baba's classes. She was back the next day, and the day after that. It was like she had to have something in the building. And she was trying to figure out what it was.

While they were just beginning what Baba called their transcendence to a higher self, none of the women had eaten solid food in seven days. Baba was a strict vegan who ate a diet of only raw food. The women, or "sister circle," as the people at the project called them, were surviving on a diet of distilled water, lemons, maple syrup, and cayenne pepper. Explaining the fasting process would help them connect with their physical strength, he told them that if they passed through the initial days of hunger, by day five, they'd have clearer skin, actually feel nausea around the food they once enjoyed, and begin to see most of the things in their lives more clearly.

While Tamia could confirm that this information was correct, Baba's idea of being able to work through bodily pain during meditation was proving wrong. The longer she sat, the longer she hurt and the longer she hurt, the longer she wondered when Baba was going to call off the meditation.

By hour five, when Tamia could take no more, she realized something—in all of her anger, she'd been so busy being angry at Baba for making her sit for so long, she'd forgotten that her bottom was hurting. In fact, she couldn't feel it anymore. She couldn't feel anything. It was like her mind was just hovering. It was being held in her body, but for the first time she realized that it wasn't attached to anything at all.

"You be careful with Baba," Malik said, walking out of the project with Tamia. They were headed to a live foods bar that served a peppermint tea Baba would allow on Tamia's diet. "I once saw him convince a dog to run out in traffic."

"Did he die? Did the dog get hit?" Tamia cried. For some reason she'd been pretty sensitive lately. Beneath the African dress she was wearing, she had on a red, black, and green tank top. Though she thought it was odd that not one of the colors in the outfit matched, Tanya had put the outfit together for her and she was proud that her sister would do such a thing. She also allowed her to put wooden beads in her ears and a medallion bearing an ankh around her neck.

"No. But he was pretty messed up. I never saw him go back into traffic again."

"Maybe that was the point," Tamia concluded and with that Malik saw that she was learning one of the first rules of the circle—always protect the father.

He wanted to laugh. To smile. To sing. It was funny.

Amazing. Perplexing that someone like Tamia, like who he'd thought Tamia was, had been changing so much, so fast. While he hadn't told anyone of his doubts, when Tamia said she wanted to join one of Baba's enlightenment circles, he'd thought maybe she was just another bougie sister having a bad day. She wanted a walk on the wild side. To connect with the people. Within forty-eight hours, she'd be back on her grind. Back in the city. That was what he'd thought. But that wasn't what was happening.

Tamia stopped walking when the two of them made it to the curb in front of the project.

"Why are you stopping?" Malik asked. "The subway is around the corner."

"That subway?" Tamia repeated in a way that clarified for both of them that she had no intention of riding the underground locomotive.

"You don't ride the subway, do you?" Malik asked, ready to take back everything he was just thinking about Tamia.

"I have . . . once before."

Tamia wasn't exactly open about how long it had been since she had been on a subway, but when she and Malik were standing on the platform, she actually considered that maybe she should have said something. Baba was correct; because she wasn't eating, her body became nauseous at the idea of stuffing her mouth, but what he hadn't told her was that her senses overall would become more sensitive as the days went by. Unfortunately, she was realizing this in the subway. As trains whizzed by, so did scents. Old, new, dead, and alive and drenched in sweat. She smelled it all and by the time the train came to gather her and Malik to take them to their next stop, she couldn't imagine drinking tea, much less watching him eat anything.

"You okay?" Malik asked, looking at her as if he was wanting to protect her in some way.

"I'll be okay."

He put his arm around Tamia to keep her steady as they walked onto the crowded train. She felt she would fall right into him—and it wasn't because of the smells. It was his body.

"I can't believe you don't ride the subway. This place is the underworld of the center of the world. The blood of Gotham," Malik said.

"Gotham? Did you just say Gotham?" She looked up at him and prayed he wouldn't see her sudden alertness as a reason to move his arm.

"Yes. I was a big Batman fan growing up. Had the PJs. The mask," he said, laughing as the train wiggled through a tight tunnel. "My dad even bought me one of those Batman lights one year. I shined it out onto the street until it went out one night."

"Really?" Tamia laughed too. "I didn't peg you for a Batman fan." Tamia paused. "I hadn't pegged you for more than a man who loved the Freedom Project."

"Sad news alert!" he started. "I grew up like most people. My dad was a private investigator. My mom was a bread maker."

"You said was. Did they both pass away?"

"Yeah," Malik revealed. "My dad worked a lot. My mom didn't. She started seeing some man who lived around the corner behind Pop's back. The man shot drugs. He died of HIV. A year later my mother died. Two years after that my dad died. A whole circle of black folks wiped out because one brother was trying to feed his family—put his son through college."

"I'm so sorry to hear that," Tamia said.

"Don't be. It saved my life. It helped me save lives." He snatched a seat when two men dressed completely alike got up and exited the train. He didn't sit down, though. He simply stood before the seat so Tamia could have it.

"So, that's how you came to start the Freedom Project?" Tamia asked.

"Yes. After my father got really sick and he had to stop working—his last contract was with your firm— he asked me if I wanted to do something crazy," Malik said. "I was fresh out of college, bored, and angry. I said yes."

"What did he do?"

"He sold everything we owned on eBay and we started putting the plans together for the Freedom Project," he said. "At first it was supposed to be a place where brothers could come and find work. But then some sister said they wanted to get help too. Then Baba turned up one day. Then I started teaching a history class. Then my father died."

Tamia and Malik would never make it to the live food bar and they would never discuss a thing about his case that day. While days of interviews and information gathering the next week would provide Tamia with more than enough information she'd need to handle any surprises at Malik's hearing, where she was still trying to convince him to plead not guilty, on that unseasonably hot Harlem afternoon, the attorney and the client decided to stay in the coolness underground and just ride the subway all day. They were talking, building, vibing, and just stealing glimpses at each other as the world seemed to stand still for a second.

"Yo, let's get off here," Malik insisted, holding the train door open at one of the stops. "My man Badu sells incense down here. I could get some stacks for the store."

Following behind Malik as he searched the station for his friend, Tamia chuckled at the idea of Malik's knowing someone named Badu who sold incense. Tasha was a mess, but the woman was dead-on about this one.

"Brother Badu! What up, fam?" Malik hugged a man wearing a long white robe. He was carrying a crate of every kind of incense Tamia had ever seen. All colors and sizes and lengths.

"Blessings from Jah," Badu said, bowing to Malik.

"Ashay. Ashay," Malik said, bowing in return. "Brother Badu, this is Tamia."

"Greetings, sister," Badu said, bowing again, but this time his eyes were focused on something behind Malik and Tamia.

"Greetings."

Tamia turned to see an overweight Asian woman with pigtails, dancing with a hula hoop. No music, no crowd, no reason. Dressed in a blue and white sundress that made her look like Dorothy from *The Wizard of Oz,* she was dancing and hopping in and out of the hula hoop.

Tamia smiled at the odd scene, half listening to Malik and Badu talk about a conscious-living Web site.

"Who is she?" Tamia asked without turning around.

"They call her Ms. Lolly," Badu explained, his energy turning to agitation.

"She's funny," Tamia said.

"Yeah, and she's ruining my action," Badu said. "I just wish she'd move somewhere else. Find another station."

"She looks harmless."

The woman removed the hula hoop from her waist and started jumping through it like a jumprope. The pigtail wig she was wearing almost fell off. It was New York culture at its most real and Tamia could not look away.

"She rakes up on the weekend," Badu complained. "She doesn't even have music. What's the point? Man, people in New York will look at anything."

Tamia nodded. He was right.

While Tamia was wrapping her mind around an ancient rite, Tasha was trying to wrap her body in an ancient girdle. The rumors were all true: Dr. Miller had the hands of perfection. And just two weeks after her surgery, Tasha could see little swelling. In fact she was already two sizes smaller than she'd been when she'd gotten on that table. Her stomach was almost caved in and she could actually see through the middle of her legs when she looked in the mirror. It was a pure miracle and she was still achy in some places and bruised in others. Tasha's only regret was that she hadn't gotten her ankles and cheeks done.

The downside of the deal was that to keep the swelling to a minimum, she had to wear a special full-body girdle Dr. Miller ordered from Brazil. The stretched-out rubber band was like a Slinky around her body; it formed her shape into the perfect hourglass, but there was a lot of heavy lifting involved and each time Tasha struggled to get in and out of the thing, she considered leaving it on for the rest of her life.

Wrestling to get the girdle back up over her newly flat belly in the bathroom stall in the lobby of the Roosevelt Hotel, she resigned that she would have to cut a hole in the crotch when she got home. Then she could use the bathroom and not have to take the thing off. Next, she'd figure out how to take a shower.

"Everything okay in there?" Lynn asked when Tasha finally walked out of the bathroom, scratching at the tips of the girdle.

"Of course," Tasha answered. "I just needed to fix my eye concealer."

"Eye concealer?" Lynn looked amazed. "What would you need any of that for? You're beautiful. Your eyes are so sexy." She winked at Tasha playfully.

"Thank you," Tasha said, nearly purring at the string of kind words. She'd heard so many compliments from Lynn over the weeks they'd been drinking and eating and shopping in the city, she was really growing to like the girl. And not just in a casual gassociates[27] way. Tasha thought maybe she was really making a new friend.

"Now, let's get upstairs to the penthouse," Lynn insisted. "I saw some of my girls heading up there already. They said it's already jumping!" She linked her arm with Tasha's and pulled her toward the elevator. "Are you losing weight?" she said as they walked. "Your body looks amazing tonight."

Tamia kept thinking there should've been a song. Like maybe India.Arie could've come into the bathroom with a guitar on her hip singing "I Am Not My Hair." Yes, that would've been great. A song to set the tone. Set the theme. Set the stage. To take her mind off of what was about to happen. That morning, when she woke up in Kali's living room draped in mudcloth she was using to make dresses for her sisters, she ran to the mirror and saw her hair. It looked strange, pulled back off of her face. It hadn't been touched by anyone but her sisters since she'd started her process. She told herself she could let go of it. That she could take the next step in her life without it. Malik was wrong. Baba didn't

[27] Gassociate: girlfriend/associate; a cool girl who isn't really a good friend—just someone to entertain socially.

require the women to cut their hair. He only talked about the sacrifice. He spoke of how the knowledge they had now should affect them and that it was okay if these changes took place over time, but if each of them wanted to know how committed she was to change, she should start with what she held most precious. Tamia thought "precious" was an odd word to put next to hair. But when she thought about it, if it wasn't so precious to her, what was the harm in cutting it? It was just hair. And if it wasn't just hair, why?

But that was this morning and now Tamia, Fatimah, and Tanya were seated in the women's bathroom at the project, surrounded by their other sisters, getting ready to get their hair cut off. All three of them had committed to doing it and Kali was chosen to assist.

"We are taught that we must rule the physical realm in order to reach our Creator—with Oludumare, God, Allah, Jah, Jehovah," Kali said, standing before the three chairs where Tamia sat with her sisters. Behind her were most of the other women at the center whom Tamia saw each day—Nunu, the young girl she'd passed outside on her first day; Ayo; Afreu, the older woman who taught them their Adinkra lessons; Maria, who made them candles; Quin, who led their history lessons.

"Doing this selfless, brave act," Kali continued, "brings you one step closer to understanding yourself. We've all been there, baby sisters. We know what you are feeling."

The women behind Kali cheered and yipped African calls and for a second Tamia thought maybe she was in church.

"But today is yours. And today, you are our heroes." Kali and her soft hands came and brushed against Tamia. "You are our spirits and your daughters are our future."

"Yeeeyeeeyeeyeeyee," a sister cried out.

"Let us begin."

What Tamia saw in the mirror before her own eyes

was herself for once. She looked like every picture of her mother she'd ever seen. And not much was different. Just her head. Just her hair. Gone. But still everything was different. It was just her head. And her hair was gone.

She'd done it. And that knowledge alone made her feel like she'd lost her mind. But she really hadn't.

Kali kissed her scalp and whispered in her ear something she really needed to hear.

"You're beautiful."

The revelation sounded so much like what someone else in the project once said to her about natural hair that Tamia jumped up out of her seat and headed toward the place where she knew she could find him.

"Malik won't be able to believe this." Tamia laughed, touching her scalp and feeling like she just might want to wear her hair like that forever. "He'll love it. He'll love—"

She was stepping down on the last step that led to the level, but she could already see who was in Malik's office.

Ayo, who'd left the bathroom when Kali was cutting Tanya's hair, was sitting on the desk in front of Malik, reading what Tamia didn't know was one of Nikki Giovanni's love poems, one of Malik's favorites.

"He'll never think I'm as beautiful as her," Tamia said, sighing and losing every ounce of excitement she was carrying.

Tasha noticed two things when she walked into the penthouse party with Lynn: 1. The only men there were wearing thongs and serving drinks. 2. The women were plentiful, beautiful, and seemingly unaware of the trend concerning the opposite sex.

She didn't say anything, though. She kept her eyes

on the prize—the thongs—and chatted it up with each of Lynn's girlfriends as they made their rounds throughout the unusually large piece of Manhattan luxury in the sky.

It was clear either Lynn knew everyone there or they wanted to know who she was. Some women actually pushed past Tasha to get to her or pretended to like Tasha's shoes or hair or shade of lip gloss (which was clear) only to say, "Can you introduce me to Lynn?" within minutes of the exchange. It was like hanging out with the female version of Lionel at a groupie party. Lynn was clearly the queen of this buzzing group of size-four bees.

After tackling and being tackled, she was relieved when Lynn suggested they sit at a table with three other women. She'd schmoozed and smiled enough and was so tired she didn't remember anyone's name.

"Who's your friend, Lynn?" asked one of the women, who looked like she must've been half black and half Asian. "She's pretty."

"Thank you," Tasha said, leaning over and shaking the girl's hand. "I'm Tasha. Tasha LaRo—"

"I can introduce you," Lynn said, cutting her off, and the other women laughed.

"Okay . . . ," Tasha said, perplexed and thinking Lynn must've had a little too much party punch.

Lynn slid her hand onto Tasha's back.

"This is Tasha LaRoche," Lynn said pointedly. "See, I can do it!"

"I'm Jasmine."

"Bobby."

"Chris."

Tasha smiled and shook all of their hands and looked back at Lynn.

"Did you see Tanya?" asked Chris, the half black

and Asian girl asked Bobby, who kind of looked like Tamia. "She was on stage in back. Fucking porn star!"

"Giant freaking A+ on that two-piece!" Bobby said, taking a little mint box from her purse.

The women laughed at her joke and so did Tasha, though she had no idea what any of them were talking about and thought they were saying that some girl named Tanya, who was a porn star, was wearing a bikini on a stage in the back that she apparently hadn't seen. Aside from the name, all of this was wrong. Translation: Tanya, who had nice legs and thighs, was doing something freaky in the bedroom.

"Does she still work at the radio station?" Lynn asked, taking one of the mints from Bobby and handing the box to Tasha.

"Yes, she was promoted to station manager last month and she's supposed to be getting me a job there," Chris said.

"That's awesome, girl," Bobby said before kissing Chris on the cheek. "I guess it pays to know big people in big places."

"Girl fucking power!" Tasha heard someone say, but she wasn't sure who it was because she was too busy trying to get the nasty taste of the ecstasy she thought was a mint out of her mouth. Tasha was no newbie. She'd had ecstasy before and knew exactly what the pill was once it stuck to her tongue.

"You okay?" Lynn whispered to Tasha once she noticed her wiping her tongue with a tissue.

"I'm fine," Tasha said. "Just didn't know that was ex."

"Eww." Lynn frowned. "Maybe I should've said something. You want to leave?"

"No," Tasha said, thinking she was fine and not wanting to ruin her first party out with the new crowd. She didn't understand what they were talking about half of the time, but kept thinking about what Lynn told her—if she wanted to work with these people, she had to understand them. Tasha explored this thought, this desire, this idea for what she was sure was thirty seconds. Maybe a minute. She didn't know. She was watching Bobby's earrings. Big chandeliers with pink and white diamonds. How slow they sparkled when she tilted her head to the side. Then she couldn't tell if it was Bobby or her who was tilting. The room or the table. Pink and white. It was so pretty. She put her thumb in her mouth and watched them slow even more, sitting still like diamonds in the sky.

"Pretty earrings," Tasha said, reaching toward the diamonds.

"Thank you," Bobby said, catching Tasha's hand and moving it to Lynn's lap, where she held it and massaged it.

The sensation of her thumb in her mouth and the hand massage was so soothing, Tasha leaned into Lynn and rested her head on her shoulder.

"You okay?" Lynn asked, putting her arm around Tasha. "We can leave if you're not okay."

"I'm fine," Tasha said, taking her thumb out of her mouth. "I'm fine. I'm kicking it!" She laughed and looked up at Lynn. "Don't worry about me. I'm a big girl."

"Yeah, but—"

"I'm fine." She looked into Lynn's eyes.

"You sure about this, baby?"

"Yes," Tasha said. "I am."

Lynn leaned toward Tasha and all Tasha could think of was that she wanted to put her thumb back in her mouth. To put her thumb back in her mouth and look at the sparkly diamonds.

* * *

In the morning, when the sun was up and the penthouse was empty, Tasha would learn what the stage was. She was on it . . . well, in it.

She knew something was wrong before she even opened her eyes. There was snoring and neither she nor Lionel had the affliction.

Slowly, Tasha opened one of her eyes and saw a headful of black curls, white sheets, and a huge window with the sun pouring in.

"What?!" She sat up quickly, the sheet and a tired arm falling from her chest. "What the hell?" she hollered, looking around.

"You okay?" She felt someone sit up beside her and looked. It was Lynn, her little breasts sweeping against the sheets.

Tasha looked down and her breasts were out too.

"Whaaat?!" Tasha jumped up and she was standing on the bed. To her right was Lynn, sitting up and wiping her eyes. To her left was Bobby. Empty champagne bottles and glasses were all over the floor. "Oh, my God!"

"Calm down," Lynn warned, reaching out to Tasha.

"Calm down? What the fuck? What the fuck is this?" She jumped off the bed and looked around for her clothes. "I—I—"

"Tasha, calm down. You can stay," Lynn said.

"Stay? Stay? I don't know where I'm at. I can't stay here." She found her shirt and slid it on. "Look, I don't know what happened but . . . What did happen? Because I . . . you know . . . I'm not a . . ."

"Nothing happened."

"Nothing?"

"I mean, we kissed . . . we made out, but you passed out," Lynn said, her face washed in disappointment.

"But I was naked . . . and you . . . and her . . ." Tasha pointed to Bobby. "Y'all are naked too."

"You were kirking out."

"Kirking out?" Tasha asked, trying to remember what happened at the party. The last thing she recalled was looking at Bobby's earrings. "But I didn't even swallow the pill."

"I don't know. You must've swallowed a little bit," Lynn said. "You kissed me and the next thing I know, you were shaking and shoving my hands down your pants."

Tasha covered her mouth. She'd heard of people having this reaction with ecstasy before. The drug made their bodies incredibly sensitive to touch and without it, they just start rocking and shaking, sucking their thumbs.

"We didn't want to leave you alone. You were in no condition to drive home," Lynn went on, "so we had two options—take you to the hospital or give you what you wanted."

"And you thought this was it?" Tasha shouted. Bobby turned over in the bed and said some jibberish but didn't wake up.

"It sounded like a good idea," Lynn said. "Look, we were messed up. We thought if we just held you, you'd fall asleep. Shit, it worked."

"Well, it could've worked with our clothes on!" Tasha found her shoes and jeans.

"Well, Bobby said something about body heat. . . ."

"Body heat?" Tasha wrestled her jeans up and slid her shoes on. "Look, this is crazy. This is—"

"Tasha, I didn't force you to do anything. I thought you wanted to be here. You kissed me."

"I was high!"

"You said you were fine. You said you could hang."

"Look, I know you said you all get down and do the freaky, but that ain't me, honey. You got the wrong one. So, if that's what this was all about, the whole business thing, then we can stop it right now." Tasha looked at Lynn and in her face she saw a lack of registry, of care. "Oh, my God, that's what this was about? You didn't want to start a business with me. You wanted to get in my pants."

"I thought you were playing hard to get. Once a party girl, always a party girl," Lynn said as Bobby rolled over again and rested her head on Lynn's lap. "It's just a new club."

7

*Women are never stronger than when they arm
themselves with their weaknesses.*

—Madame Marie du Deffand

While Troy had sat at the altar during Sunday service
on many occasions, this Easter her presence beside her
husband atop the throne of grace was much more
sweet. This time, she'd been elected, appointed, and
approved to occupy the recently coveted seat by the
women of her church and that act made her feel, for the
first time ever, that she was truly the First Lady of First
Baptist. She had her big hat, white gloves, two-piece
violet suit with shoes and purse to match, a wide smile,
and a heart that was so full, even her few remaining enemies forgot the events of the previous evening when
she entered the church alongside Kyle and waved into
the congregation like it was a Miss America pageant.
Though some members frowned, a few did laugh and
wave back, and years later, as they recalled the experience, they'd say, "That was just our First Lady being
herself."

What made the auspicious celebration of resurrection even more marvelous for Troy was the fact that it presented one of the few times each year that she could get her grandmother to attend Sunday service at her church. In the first pew sat Lucy, arms and legs crossed, smiling congenially as if she was awaiting the opening curtain at the opera. Troy had invited her parents, but both declined for fear they'd run into the other at the church. Troy waved at Lucy and got a return wink and nod, a showing of support she wasn't aware she'd need in just a few minutes. Gravity was the only thing keeping Troy from floating to the ceiling. With Kyle happier than a squirrel in a nut house, Lucy in the front, and the church finally coming to her side, it seemed the Lord was smiling down at her and saying, "You better go, girl!"

And then it came.

After a series of readings and testimonies that almost made Lucy forget she'd had three mimosas before going to church and consider giving her life over to the Lord (for, like, three minutes), a tearful Sister Myrtle Glover, who was also wearing lavender, bowed before Kyle on the altar and took position at the speakers' lectern. Lucy, who'd taken to carrying a pocketknife in her purse long before she became a respectable woman of high society, moved her purse from her side to her lap.

"I asked our dear pastor if I could speak to you today, church," Myrtle started, and as she continued into an emotional address that praised the church leadership for guiding the members of First Baptist away from the snare of the devil and into the arms of the Lord, Troy actually felt bad about admonishing Kyle for giving her airtime. Myrtle's words made Kyle seem like the next Rev. Dr. Martin Luther King Jr. and First Baptist a holy ground of renewal. Members were shouting hal-

lelujah and a few walked down the aisle to lay early of-
ferings on the altar.

". . . but, church," Myrtle went on just as Saptosa
stood up to read her portion, "where there is praise,
there must also be penalty. And while I'm proud of
everything we've done in the church, in the name of
the Lord, having crawled the aisles of this sanctuary
before I could walk them, I can't sit idly by when I
know that the same evils that sent our savior to the
cross now seek solace within our midst."

Had Troy been looking at Kyle, she might've seen
his Adam's apple quiver a bit at this transition, but she
was too busy managing her own discomfort. And while
some of the other listeners seemed to share this position, a few, namely Elizabeth, pushed Myrtle on, cheering, "Say it!" and "Shame the devil!"

"Now, I'm no saint, but I know a sinner and when I
see one, I say I must say it!" Myrtle shouted in a way
that made Saptosa step up behind her and lay a hand on
her back to signal that her time was up. "Evil is here.
Right among us. And, First Baptist, I can no longer sit
back and watch."

And with that little performance, Troy's big day
ended with big problems. After ten minutes, Saptosa
had to pull Myrtle to her seat. Anyone who was in the
inner circle at the church was there and knew exactly
what Myrtle's bitter, verbal rant was about. Any members who were still upset about the pastor's decision to
marry someone from outside the church were excited
that Myrtle's less than subtle appeal was given airtime.
Others who really didn't care suspected that perhaps
the naysayers now had a point. And the few who were
beginning to like Troy and accept her as one of their
own were suspicious as to what Myrtle was talking about.
Troy and her grandmother fell into the latter group and as

Troy sat through the rest of the special sermon, she thought of what would come next.

Myrtle had said she was coming for her, and she'd selected the perfect place and time to do it. But that couldn't be it.

"You need me to make a call?" Lucy whispered in Troy's ear after the service had ended and she'd pulled Troy into the backseat of the Rolls.

"No, Lucy." Troy sighed, watching through the tinted car windows the little girls walk out of the front of the church in their new Easter dresses.

"The nerve of her!" Lucy went on. "She's hard. Much harder than I thought. You sure you don't want me to make a call? I can. Even if you say no, I can know you mean yes, but you don't want to be tied to it. I can arrange that."

Troy looked at her grandmother.

"Are you crazy?" she asked. "I can't do that. I won't even consider it. I—"

"I know," Lucy said, broken. "And I wouldn't let you. But you know you need to do something about her. I told you, you needed to do something about her before and now you have to do something about her now."

Troy wanted to lament with Lucy, but her ears were filled with Myrtle's harsh words: evil, sinner, evil, sinner. The more she replayed the tape in her mind, the more she began to believe it.

"And that husband of yours—I didn't want to say anything, but he should've done something. He should've stopped her. There's no way your grandfather would've heard of anyone speaking about me in such a way. No. No. Not in his presence."

Troy gave Lucy a look. The cat had long emerged from the bag, saying Lucy's husband was not Troy's grandfather.

"Don't get on Kyle," Troy said, watching Kyle walk out of the church with one of the deacons. His eyes were red and he looked around sadly. Troy knew he was looking for her. "He's just trying not to play sides." While Troy meant what she was saying to her grandmother, she couldn't help but feel alienated from and by her husband. She had been open with him about her issues with Myrtle and asked him not to put her on the program. He'd failed to protect her. But she couldn't say that to Lucy. Once her grandmother hated someone, that was it. And she knew sharing her hurt feelings with Lucy could only lead to the old woman making a phone call.

"Not trying to play sides?" Lucy asked. "You make it sound like he's trying to appease both of you."

"It's about me and her," Troy said, watching her husband and knowing what must be worrying him. "It's about him and the church. He knows what Sister Glover can do. He was trying to stop it."

"Well," Lucy said, grabbing her granddaughter's hand and squeezing it, "if he can't stop it, then you have to. You have to stop her. You have to confront her. Now, I know you're not a fighter. You've always chosen a smile over a fist. But you're Mary Elizabeth's child and my grandchild, and that means, dear, there's fight in you. You're going to have to find it—if you want to save your marriage, and yourself."

Nothing in Tamia's world carried weight. Everything was light. Everything had the ability to change or be changed. A pen. A pillow. A piece of Brillo pad. She would sit for hours thinking about how each thing was a part of the universe, created by the Creator and thus a part of the cycle of change.

Now she was sitting in her office, contemplating how her door was changing. It opened. It closed. It let people in and out.

"You okay?" Naudia asked, standing in the doorway.

Tamia blinked. She hadn't noticed she was there. Her focus had become so direct, her mind so encased that she could meditate anywhere for any amount of time.

"Yes," Tamia said softly.

Naudia walked into the office and sat down. She knew for a fact that it had been more than fifteen days since Tamia had eaten anything other than lemons and maple syrup. While she had to commend her driven boss for holding on for so long, she had to admit that Tamia was beginning to look a little loopy. She'd lost more than twenty pounds and had stopped shaving her legs. This certainly wasn't helping her office image. The lack of hair and abundance of colorful fabric in Tamia's life made her the official topic of the cappuccino-machine crowd. They speculated and spectated and a few even separated themselves from her. And although the chatter was plentiful, not one of them had gone to speak to Tamia about what they claimed was so worthy of their cappuccino-laced concerns. In fact, it would be two more weeks until one of the partners, noticing that Tamia was wearing moccasins, would put in a formal complaint. But by then, she'd be preparing herself for a new life.

None of this mattered now, though. It wasn't like Tamia cared or noticed anyway.

She was too busy contemplating the change of her laptop.

"I'm happy for you," Naudia said, "that you're going through with this."

"Thank you," Tamia said, grinning, but because her face had become so slender with the fast, it looked like she had the biggest smile ever.

"I mean, it's a little crazy . . . and I hope they're not serving punch at those meetings . . . but I can see how it's making you happy."

"Was I sad before?" Tamia asked.

"I don't think you were sad . . . I think you were just like the rest of us," Naudia said. "Okay."

"I was." Tamia nodded. "So, Naudia, what would make you happy? If someone said to you that you should chase bliss relentlessly, that it was the only way you'd be free, what would you do with yourself?"

"Go to law school," Naudia said quickly. It was what she thought of every day. What she researched during her lunch break. What she dreamed of. What she knew she could do in the world. "I know I have what it takes. I just need a shot."

"What's holding you back?"

"Money," Naudia revealed. "And it's so messed up that money is what's stopping me because I know I'd be a great attorney. I know the law. I know I have what it takes to take down these—"

"You don't have to tell me that." Tamia stopped Naudia.

"What?"

"I know what you're capable of," Tamia said. "Everything I can do, you can do. And probably better."

"You really think that?" This was a gargantuan statement coming from someone Naudia respected so much.

"I know so. I've seen so."

As Tamia mothered her assistant, Tasha fixed her mind on pretending her mother didn't exist. However, as every New Yorker knows, the last thing you want to do is try to hide something in the big city with the bright lights. As the old saying goes, "Whatever is done in the dark shall always come to light." Tasha, unfortunately, was doomed to learn this the hard way.

It was Porsche's birthday. Her fiftieth. The BIG 5-0. And while Tasha kept telling herself it didn't matter and she didn't care and joking that she'd wished her mother was dead anyway, doing all three of these things at one time as she ran her last mile on the tread-mill at the gym was proving impossible. Especially since she'd passed a Times Square billboard bearing Porsche's image with the rest of the cast of *Sinfully Yours* on the way to the gym and a feature on Page Six of the *New York Post* announced Porsche's fortieth birthday to the world. Turning her nose up at the Holly-wood literary lie (and the fact that if that was even true Porsche would've given birth to her at ten), she chucked the newspaper into the nearest trash can and found an escape in a television that was propped just two feet from her position on the treadmill.

Soap-Opera Kitten Turns 40 in Dubai!

It was an *Access Hollywood* story. Porsche's secre-tive smile, dipped in a luscious red lipstick came flash-ing across the screen and Tasha sucked her teeth. The woman on the treadmill beside her watched as Tasha slowed down and struggled to press the little faded re-mote button to turn the channel.

"If I had a body like hers, I'd never come to the gym," the blonde said when Tasha had successfully turned to the *Good Times* rerun when Willona adopts Penny. "I mean, these celebrities have such perfect bodies, no one can live up to it. I believe most of them have liposuction anyway."

"I guess so," Tasha said, readjusting her earphones to give the woman a signal that she wasn't in the mood for conversation. Her lipo swelling was catching up to her and in order to stay in the dozen plus pairs of couture jeans she'd purchased to run around the city as she built her management empire, she needed to lose ten pounds in a month. After two kids, it was a straitjacket-worthy idea, but she was up for the challenge. She needed to focus her mind on something other than everything that was going on. Lionel. The girls. And she hadn't told anyone about what happened at the Roosevelt Hotel with Lynn. She was determined to forget about it herself. Nothing happened, she kept thinking, so there was nothing to talk about. It was a crazy experience and now it was time to move on with plan B. She would use the contacts she'd made at the party and go out on her own. "But Porsche St. Simon doesn't have much work to do anyway," the woman went on even though she'd noticed each of Tasha's cues. "You black women have such lovely skin. She could gain fifty pounds and still look good. If I gain three, everything will start sagging and bagging. Thank God for Botox."

After finishing her workout, Tasha was in the locker room, looking at Porsche's phone number on her cell phone. She hadn't spoken to her mother since Tiara was born. Lionel was right, it had hurt her like a fresh, thin cut on her hand when Porsche, sounding rushed and tired, came up with a reason not to see her new grandchild. She'd just let Porsche back into her life when she had Toni and she'd done the same thing. Pretended to care, promised to be the perfect grandmother, and then walked away like all of Hollywood would dissipate if she took just a little bit of time to be with her daughter, with her family.

"I don't need you," Tasha said to the phone, but that was the opposite of what her heart was feeling. It didn't matter how much she said and told herself she didn't need Porsche, the emptiness she felt without her mother there, the emptiness she'd felt all of her life was unbearable. And just then, alone in the city, without any of the things she'd put in her life to fill the unbearable emptiness, it became too much for Tasha to hold inside.

"Porsche!" she hollered into the phone when she heard her mother's voice. She was ready to curse her out, dig into her and say all of the hurtful things she was thinking. But then Porsche said something her daughter had only heard from her three, maybe four times in her life.

"I miss you, baby! How are the girls?"

Tasha dropped her towel and sat down on the bench in front of her locker.

"Fine," she answered.

"Yeah, I was gonna come out there for my birthday, but—you know." It was a lie. Tasha knew it, but hearing it, hearing just the promise of it from Porsche, was like a hug she needed. And she did. What Tasha was going through, the things she couldn't control, was what she needed her mother and her words and her ears and her hugs for. She was supposed to be there. "I was thinking, why don't we all go to Jamaica this summer—me, you, the girls, even Lionel?" Porsche asked excitedly. "Won't that be great?"

"Yeah," Tasha said, though she knew it would never happen.

"Wonderful!" Porsche said. "I'll have my assistant call you to set it up. It's going right on my calendar. I promise. No excuses."

"Well, that's good, because I really want you to—"

"Look, honey, I have to go," Porsche interrupted Tasha. "I'm getting on a jet. My new boyfriend is flying me to Paris for the afternoon. We're in Dubai. Can you believe that?"

"Yeah, I was watching it on the news—"

"Gotta go, love," Porsche said quickly. "Send my love to Toni and Tiana!"

There was a click and the line went dead.

"Tiara," Tasha said to no one. "Her name is Tiara. Not Tiana."

They were Fola, Bolade, and Nijala. In that order, Fatimah, Tamia, and Tanya were given their Yoruba-based names upon how their older sisters saw them interacting within the community. Fatimah, Fola—Baba explained after their lips had been rubbed with water, palm oil, a kola nut, honey, pepper, salt, and fish—was named for always respecting her elders. Tamia, Bolade, came to the Freedom Project with great honor. Tanya, Nijala, who was always smiling and cheering for her sisters, no matter the issue was named for bringing peace.

"Ase," the big sister said, happily calling each of the women on the journey by their nicknames.

Though Malik had been keeping his distance from Tamia's process, meeting her only to discuss his case during the afternoon before she met with her sisters or afterward as they rode the subway to see Badu and Ms. Lolly—who were still in a subway turf war—Tamia often saw him waiting outside of the work room where she met with Baba.

"You could've come in," Tamia said, walking into the basement library where she found Malik studying after her naming ceremony. He was sitting at a workbench, surrounded by books. "Baba said the community was to be there."

"I was there." Malik smiled, but he didn't look up at Tamia. As she was changing how she looked, how he looked at her was changing too. He didn't notice it at first. He'd always thought she was a beautiful woman, and after she cut her hair he saw that she was even more than that. It was nice. But it was common. Most of the women who came into the project and began to accept their own beauty grew more beautiful in his eyes. He thought this was the same with Tamia. But one afternoon, as she sniffed an African musk Badu had rubbed on her wrist, Malik saw the side of her neck. As she laughed with Badu at something, she turned her head and it was there, defenseless, soft, brown. It made him feel hungry and then warm. He looked away fast. He asked Badu if he would sell him a vial of the musk. That night he would go home and smell it, thinking about Tamia again.

"But not inside," Tamia said. "You didn't come inside."

"How do you know you weren't the one outside and I was inside, my Nubian sister?" Malik joked, using the militant voice that always made Tamia laugh.

It worked.

"You're so silly," she said, giggling. "What are you reading?" She sat down beside him on the bench.

"Not reading, checking the stacks," Malik started and Tamia could tell he was about to go on one of his passionate riffs. While she'd thought they were silly before, now she found them comforting. His dedication, how he lost his mind in something he cared for so much made her believe in dreams again. "You ever hear about what happened in Philadelphia in 1985 when eleven black people were killed?"

"No," Tamia said.

"The government bombed the headquarters of Project MOVE, a militant organization," Malik said. "They used helicopters to drop bombs on the roof of the building. And when the fire started spreading, the mayor, a damn brother, said, 'Let it burn!' Eleven people died that day. Five were children."

"That's awful," Tamia said.

"You know, it is awful, but what's more awful is that most people don't know anything about it. People in Philly. Black people. Militant people," Malik said. "We can fight for freedom all we want, but if we don't record our own history, none of what we've done will matter."

"I disagree. I understand what you mean, but I have to tell you, it doesn't matter if not one book records change. If it happens, it happened."

"I think you're beautiful," Malik said suddenly.

"What?"

"A long time ago, I told you that I thought you were beautiful the way all black women are beautiful." Malik looked into Tamia's eyes. "Right now I want you to know I think you're beautiful. Not just outside. But your mind. You impress me every day."

Tamia wasn't sure how to respond to this, so she didn't. She kissed him.

She kissed him and when she tried to move away she realized Malik's hands were around her neck and holding her to him. In his lips she felt the hunger and heat he'd fought with the day she smelled African musk in the subway. When they parted, it was as if they were still together.

"What was that?" Tamia asked, covering her mouth. "What just happened?"

"I don't know," Malik said. "I kissed you."

"No, I kissed you."

"I wanted you to kiss me." Malik looked at her like he was coming in for another kiss.

"But . . ." She moved back. "But we can't. We . . . What about Ayo?"

"Ayo?"

"I know you have something with her."

"I had something with her for a very long time," Malik said. "But I think that very long time is all we have."

"I knew it," Tamia said.

"You knew what?" Malik asked. "You have somebody too. I know it. Probably some monkey-suit-wearing fraternity boy in the city."

Tamia lowered her eyes

"Now, I knew it," Malik said. "You come up here to Harlem to play, but your real thing is hidden in a high-rise. Is he paying your rent?"

"No, my mortgage," Tamia said curtly before getting up.

"I'm sorry," Malik said. "I didn't mean it like that. I'm frustrated."

"Why?"

"Because I've been thinking about that kiss for a long time. But I know we can't act on it," he explained. "We can't ruin what we have."

"What we have?" Tamia's toes were tingling just considering the idea that they had something between them.

"Our relationship," he said. "You're my attorney. You have to represent me."

"Oh, yes," Tamia said, thinking maybe her toes had just fallen off. "We wouldn't want to ruin that."

For more than a week, the flesh beneath Troy's skin was boiling with such anger, such fury at Myrtle's display at the church that it was becoming impossible for her to follow her desire to remain composed and poised as the immaculate First Lady she wanted to be. The questions Lucy had raised about Myrtle's intentions

pricked into her mind like thorns each night and she
could hardly rest without thinking about Myrtle's nerve
and what she might be planning next.

And then, one morning after a sleepless night when
the sun hit the concrete outside of the Hall brownstone,
Kyle watched his wife rise, wash, and dress in a matter
of minutes.

"Where are you going?" Kyle asked, sure he was still
dreaming. Troy wasn't exactly an early riser and her daily
coiffing routine meant that leaving the bedroom before
10 a.m. was nearly impossible.

"Nowhere," Troy said, slipping on her heels . . . and
then switching to sneakers and then back to heels. "See
you later." She kissed him on the forehead and ran out
as if she'd decided on the sneakers.

There was an early-morning line at the bank where
Myrtle was manager, but Troy's nerve pushed her past
the tired crowd, through customer support, and before
Myrtle's receptionist.

"Can I help you?" the frail assistant asked, her hands
still in position on the keyboard, her eyes peeking out
over the rims of glasses that seemed to weigh her head
down.

"I need to see the manager," Troy requested.

"Are you okay? Is there anything I can help you
with?"

"Yes," Troy snapped, "you can help me by getting
the manager. That would be what I initially requested."
While Troy wasn't ever really great at defending herself, when she finally invoked this fierce strength that
every woman in her family had before her, it came out
in great big waves of fire, threatening to burn anyone in
her path.

"I'm sorry, I mean was there something that happened
here—at the bank—that you would like—"

"Listen to me, right now," Troy started. "I need you

to get the manager. That's all I need. That's all I want. So pick up your little phone and call her up because someone is here to see her. Do you understand that?"

The phone was in the receptionist's hand and she'd pressed a button, but evidently the movement was still too slow for Troy's racing heart. She charged past the woman and opened the door to Myrtle's office.

"You can't go—" Troy heard the woman at the desk call.

Myrtle was seated at her desk, eating a bagel and chatting on the phone.

"Girl, you know I did, but I"—she stopped and looked up at Troy—"was so excited and thought maybe we should do it again." Myrtle laughed and chatted easily as Troy stood there. "No, he didn't; he is so—"

Troy stepped to the side of the desk and tried to pull the phone from the wall. And while she didn't quite disconnect the line, the set and receiver pulled from Myrtle's hand.

"Oh, shit," the receptionist said, standing behind Troy.

"You see me standing here?" Troy said.

Myrtle stood calmly and stared past Troy.

"That'll be all, Cathy," Myrtle said.

"Do you want me to get security?"

"That'll be all." Myrtle retrieved the phone from the floor and replaced the handset. "Have a seat."

"I don't need a seat," Troy said.

"Well, fine. Stand there. But make sure—"

"What was the shit you pulled at church yesterday?"

"Shit? It was merely a testimony to something that I—"

"Don't pull that crap with me," Troy said. "I'm new to this, but I'm not new to drama. I know what you're trying to do. And if you think you're gonna run me out of First Baptist with some public campaign against me you can forget it."

"Really?" Mrytle opened her drawer and produced a folded sheet of paper. She pitched it over to Troy.

Troy didn't move.

"Read it!" Myrtle demanded.

Troy opened the pages. It was a bank statement. A bank statement for First Baptist.

"Now, I know you're no financial wizard, so I'll direct your eyes to transaction 31 for last month," Myrtle said.

Troy turned to the second page, where LOUIS VUITTON was posted beside a charge for $6,189.73.

She didn't say anything. She dropped the paper and sat down in the chair before Myrtle.

"I thought so," Myrtle said wickedly. "Now, we talk."

"What do you want?" Troy said, but this time her voice was fragile, broken. She'd planned to make the deposit into the account before anyone noticed or could complain about the purchase.

"You know what I want. What I've always wanted. Your husband."

"And you think this is going to help you? A little charge from a store?" Troy tried to sound unmoved, but she knew the weight of what Myrtle was measuring. With so much already stacked against her, this could bury her, push her right into a grave and pour the dirt on top. Where she was from, the total in the margin wasn't a big deal, but being the preacher's wife, such a big charge at such a place for any reason was unacceptable. She'd pay for it. Kyle would pay for it. The church would pay for it.

"Your little show is over, Troy Smith," Myrtle said. "You're no more fit to be a preacher's wife than a pig. And now I have proof."

"So you're going to show everyone this? You'd do that just to get rid of me?"

"Not exactly. I don't think it's necessary to show everyone this little bank statement . . . just to get rid of you," Myrtle explained coolly. "I know what something like this could do to Kyle, to the church. It would ruin everything. I can't have that. Not over some silly little purchase."

Troy sat silently, her body shaking in fear as she waited for Myrtle to finish.

"Leave him," Myrtle said.

"What?"

"Leave him. If you love him. If you love the church and you don't want to ruin everything he's worked so hard for, leave him," Myrtle said. "If you don't I'll take it to the board of trustees and you'll lose him anyway. You ever see a man after you take his dream from him?"

"This is ridiculous. This doesn't make any sense," Troy rambled. "I could just pay the money back, say it was a mistake. Say I—"

"The record stands. It doesn't matter what you do now," Myrtle said. "I have the statement. I have the proof. Elizabeth knows. And it'll only be a little itty-bitty bit of time before everyone else does." Myrtle paused and looked out the window. "Now I know this is all sudden for you and you're probably going to need some time to think about it. But I'm telling you now, there's only one thing you can do. If you love that man like you claim you do, you'll leave the church and leave him. You haven't changed a bit. It's been two years and you still continue with your old games. It's time for you to make a new decision. You can't save yourself, but you can save Kyle."

Troy looked down at entry 31 again. A tear fell and stained the page, blurring the black ink. How could she have been so stupid, she thought, remembering the afternoon when she'd handed the woman at the store the card. She knew people were watching her. She knew Myrtle was watching her. She couldn't let anything happen to the church. To Kyle. And she knew in her heart Myrtle was right. This would ruin him.

"How long do I have?" Troy asked.

"I'll call you," Myrtle revealed, though inside she couldn't believe Troy had given in so easily. She'd been working on Troy for months, waiting for her to slip up and step out of line. The bank statement, when Elizabeth had brought it to her, was a total surprise. She thought for sure Troy would know not to mess with the church's money. "You'll know," Myrtle added.

8

I used to want the words "She tried" on my tombstone. Now I want "She did it."

—Katherine Dunham

Baba beat on his drum. The Royal Anhk was shining brightly. The tree was surrounded with people. There were the regulars—the dreads, the dancers, the believers, the worshippers, and the women of the earth. But in the middle—something unexpected. Two who were quite the same. One was carrying her new Ferragamo-studded clutch and red devils; the other, a pair of actual, real tennis shoes (for playing tennis) and couture jeans. Shoulder to shoulder, Tasha and Troy were the odd ones. Yet, they looked around as if surrounded by oddness.

"What the holy hell is this?" Tasha said. "She's crazy. Worshipping the devil. All of them."

She pointed to a man who was tossing a stick of fire.

"If they bring out a chicken, I'm leaving," she added.

"They are not devil worshippers," Troy said. "Right?" She pulled her sleeve down to cover a pearl bracelet.

"No need to cover up the bracelet," Tasha said. "You need to cover up those sneakers."

"What's wrong with my shoes? Tamia said to wear something comfortable. She said we'd be in the grass."

"I'm sure she didn't end with advising you to wear something that was sure to get us jumped. If they decide to do a sacrifice, you're up first."

The drumming became louder, more fierce. The crowd began to form a circle and soon Tamia and her sisters were facing the world as one. They'd come to the next stage of enlightenment and were ready to see the world.

As the brothers had been just months ago, the sisters were dressed in white, their chosen symbols painted on their chest.

Tamia was the Sankofa. The bird. The return to the Essence.

"She looks beautiful, just beautiful," Troy cried, waving to Tamia as she chanted now for guidance from the Creator.

"She's so thin," Tasha remarked, looking at Tamia's now-slender frame. "What kind of diet is she on?"

"Yeeyeeeyecycc," someone cried from the crowd and then Tamia and her sisters did a traditional West African dance that trailed around the base of a tree. It was in honor of the ancestors, of their journey and the sacrifices each of them had made so their daughters could be there.

Though her feet were kicking up the loose earth beneath her bare feet, Tamia cried so many tears the white paint was streaking her cheeks. She was dancing for her mother and prayed that wherever she was in the universe, she could hear her daughter's heart beating, wild and free.

"You guys came!" Tamia said after being rushed by Tasha and Troy when the ceremony had ended.

"Of course we did, baby," Tasha said. "Where else would we be?"

"You looked so amazing, Ms. Lovebird!" Troy said, grabbing a hug.

"Now, we must know," Tasha began, "who were those two other women?"

"Are those your new 2Ts? Are you replacing us?" Troy grimaced playfully.

"Well, those are my new sisters, but they're one T and an F," Tamia said, "and until 'the 2Ts and 1F' sounds cool, you guys can't be replaced."

"So where's Malcolm X?" Tasha asked.

Tamia frowned. She'd seen Malik in the crowd when she came in, but when Kali came over to congratulate her after everything was done, she said Malik had left early with a headache.

"He wasn't feeling well," Tamia said, wondering why he couldn't have at least stayed to cheer for her. Maybe this was just his way of handling what had happened between the two of them in the library. He was right. If they continued to connect the way they had been, it could ruin everything.

"Dang!" Troy said, feeling her cell phone vibrating in her pocket. "I was ready to take another picture."

"You and that phone!" Tamia teased.

"Wait a sec," Troy said, after pulling out her phone and seeing it was Kyle calling. "I have to get this." She clicked into the call. "Hello?"

"Hey, honey," Kyle said, his voice tired and weak. "I was just calling you because Myrtle just called here."

"What?"

"Yeah, Myrtle. She said something about the meeting you're having. That she's coming by the house next week."

"Oh," Troy said and both Tamia and Tasha saw her face fold.

"You want to call her back? She left her number."

"No," Troy answered. "I'll talk to her in the morning."

"Hey, I know I haven't given you credit on this whole thing with her and I thought that after the scene at the church you two would have it out for sure," Kyle said. "But I'm happy to see you're trying. That you're at least trying."

"Thanks," Troy said weakly. "I'll see you tonight when I get home."

"Tell the other Ts I said hello."

Troy hung up and looked up at Tamia.

"What happened?" she asked, reaching out to Troy. "Is everything okay?"

"I have to go home," Troy said. "I have to go home now."

Sometimes, late in the dark night, when even the luminous moon is hidden among clumpy clouds and the wisest people are sleeping behind the silken curtains that keep the pains of the capital of the universe from entering the rectangular openings into their worlds, others aren't quite so lucky. Awake and without any armor from the black all around, they willingly enter the darkness, and, so, it enters them.

Ever since she was a little girl, Tamia feared the unknown—what she couldn't understand, explain, and master. With no mother, no soft hand there to kiss her cheek and whisper in her little brown ear, "It's okay, baby. Take your time" when the girl came across something she didn't know, any new thing she couldn't understand became like fire in her eyes. The girl from the prayer group in college, the unruly people on the subway, marriage, love . . . Anything without boundaries that couldn't be understood. Altogether, they made her want to run away. Made her want to hide herself behind her own clumpy clouds and silken curtains.

For a long time, Malik and his whole world had been the something new in Tamia's life that she couldn't understand or explain or master. He was different. Like fire in the middle of a river. New and strange like nighttime. And while the fearful little girl inside of her still wanted to run and hide away her heart, Tamia made a decision she'd never made before—she took her time and stayed to figure him out. To figure it out. So she could save her heart. And have a new brave heart.

All of this had suddenly become clear to her when she rang Malik's buzzer. He'd been her new, unknown thing and it was okay. She wasn't hiding. She wasn't going anywhere. She just wanted him and didn't care how long it would take her to understand that or if she never did.

This, in a daytime Gotham, full of light and clarity, would've been of use. But, again, it was night, and Tamia had no clouds or curtains to shield her heart from the dark.

Over a static-filled speaker, Malik wanted to know why she was downstairs. It was 2 o'clock in morning. He had a headache.

"I want to talk to you," Tamia said, holding the black button beneath the mesh callbox that connected their wobbly voices.

"Talk . . . what?" was all she could make out from Malik's end.

"Yes," Tamia laughed. "Talk about what happened in the library. I don't care about the risks. I don't care about losing everything. Not if I have you."

"I'll be down there. Don't come up. I'm coming downstairs"—this was the clearest message the fifty-year-old intercom system had relayed in years. Crystal clear. Like Malik was standing right beside Tamia. It was easy to understand. Even easier to follow. But when another resident with a resident's key came crawling out of a cab and stumbled onto the doorstep where Tamia was standing, she quickly misheard every word. Into the building she came, helping a drunken stranger.

No time to rewrap her falling head wrap, she pulled it from her head and wrapped it around her shoulders like a shawl. She wanted him to see her. To really see what she'd become in his world. A beautiful African queen, she poked out her chest and held her head high. Instead of knocking on the door, she simply rapped one time.

"My king," she called playfully and gently to Malik. "I await."

Though she was looking high, like some empress basking in the sun over her empire, Tamia saw the door open through a side glance and poked her chest out a bit more. The inside of the apartment was dark and she couldn't see Malik standing there.

"Nice pose, Tamia," she heard and turned quickly and ashamedly back to the door. It wasn't Malik's voice. It was a woman. One she knew. Her eyes adjusted to the dark before her, and Tamia saw that it was Ayo. Standing there, she was wearing only Malik's military jacket.

"Ayo?"

"He told you to wait downstairs, didn't he?" Her voice as placid as an iceberg.

"What are you doing here?"

"He took the stairs. I'm guessing you took the elevator."

"What are you doing here?" Tamia repeated as her shawl fell to the floor. "Answer me."

"I knew it would come to this. A strong man is so weak."

The urgency in Ayo's words was empty in her stance. She leaned heavily against the door frame, making senseless circles on the floor with her nude foot. Suddenly the smell of frankincense and myrrh from Malik's apartment made Tamia nauseous. She felt silly. So silly standing there in her pieces of patterned cloth, the wooden jewelry around her neck and arms, her head without covering. This was all a joke. She was a joke.

"Malik is my soul mate. My sun," Ayo continued. "Nothing can change—"

"Tamia," Malik called, running down the hallway. "I told you to wait—"

"It's too late," Tamia screamed, tearing one of the beaded strands from her neck and throwing it to Malik's feet. "I already see."

"I—"

"No!" Tamia stopped Malik. "Don't you dare say you can explain. You can't. You can't. You can't fucking explain this!" She was hollering and tearing and throwing beads everywhere.

"Stop it!" Malik grabbed her arm.

"You were supposed to be different!" Tamia got ahold of a few of Malik's locks with her free hand. "All of this and you're a liar."

"It's not like that," Malik said and Tamia could feel his heart beating faster even though there was still space between them.

"Then what is it like?" Tamia jumped back and pointed to Ayo. "What is it like? Because it looks pretty clear to me. You know what? Both of you are just common. You're pretenders. You cover yourselves with all of this bullshit, when really there's no difference between your shit and everyone else's. You're just the same."

*   *   *

As Tamia turned to go down the stairs, Tasha was trying to go in what used to be her front door. Only her key wasn't working.

"I told you not to come here," Lionel's voice said. Only it wasn't through a decrepit buzzer in Harlem. On Tasha's third try, he'd opened the door and was standing before her like a goliath.

Like Tamia, Tasha said, "I want to talk to you."

"This ain't no time to talk. It's 2:30 in the morning."

"2:30 in the morning never stopped you before." Tasha softened her voice a bit and smiled at the man she knew still loved her.

"Tasha," Lionel started calmly, "you think this is a game. That you're just going to show up here and I'm going to let you into my house."

"Your house?"

"You're fucking right. You left before," he said, "so leave now." He tried to close the door, but Tasha pushed her $3,000 purse in the way.

"Well, let me see the girls, then," Tasha tried.

"It's the middle of the night. I'm not waking them up because you've been drinking and you suddenly want to have a moment."

"Open the damn door." She pushed herself into her husband's solid chest.

"No. You wanted to leave."

"Lionel, this isn't a fucking option. Let me into my house or I'll burn this motherfucker down." On her tippy-toes, she dug a pointed finger into his chest.

"Really, Tasha? You're gonna burn the house down with your children inside? Think about it."

Tasha sank back down to her heels.

"Let me in," she demanded.

"No."

"Let me in."

"No, Tasha."

"Let me in! Let me in! Let me in!" Tasha was pounding into Lionel with her fists, screaming and hollering so loud Toni was awake and had crawled out of her bed and made it to the top of the stairs where she sat in a space her parents couldn't see. "They're my kids. I want to see them!"

With one hand, Lionel was able to collect his wife and her things. It broke something in him to do it, but he had to keep the other parts of himself together. He dragged a fighting Tasha down the walkway and to her car.

"No," she pleaded the whole time. Now they were both crying.

Lionel opened the car door and stuffed Tasha inside.

"Why are you doing this?"

"Get out of here before the cops come," Lionel said. "I don't want to be embarrassed."

Two long and seemingly sunless days later, Troy was sitting before two puffy-eyed friends at a wine bar.

"Maybe we should've had a breakup party," Troy said. Tamia was slumped over in her seat and Tasha held such a posed pose, everyone walking by knew she was hiding something. She slid a pair of huge shades on. "You know, so you guys can get over this—"

"I cut off my hair for that fake kente cloth–wearing clown," Tamia said, shaking her head into her third glass of wine. This wasn't exactly a smooth transition for someone who hadn't had any food in more than a month. She was skin and bone, and the alcohol went right to her head and would find its final resting place in the toilet after she vomited later.

"But it's growing back, right?" Troy was padding

her voice with pleasantness, but she'd been sitting there with those two like that for two hours and was running out of sane-sounding things to say.

"I can't believe he won't let me see them. He said I have to wait until this weekend . . . to see my own children. Who does he think he is?"

"He doesn't mean that," Troy answered Tasha. "He's just angry and he needs space. Like you did when you moved back to the city."

"I didn't want space. I wanted Lionel to follow. He was supposed to follow me."

Feeling their friend's pain, both Tamia and Troy reached out and held Tasha's hands as tears slid from beneath her sunglasses.

"Tasha, I don't know how to say this, but I think you need to know that there was nothing Lionel could do," Troy said. "You boxed him into a corner. You know he couldn't move back to the city with you. You two have children. It's not that easy for him to chase you around anymore. He has other priorities. And you should too."

"But what? What could be more important than us?"

"Your daughters," Tamia said.

"What?" She pulled the glasses off and flicked them onto the table. "Are you two accusing me of not loving them? Of not caring for them? Because I love those girls more than anything in the world. I'm just fucked up. That's all."

"I know that," Tamia said. "We both know that. But it's not so easy for everyone to see. You put these walls up and—"

"What walls?"

"It's not easy . . . I mean for other people . . . to see how good of a mother—"

"Look," Tamia broke in, "what she's trying not to say is that you abandoned them and your husband when you moved out."

"I didn't abandon anyone," Tasha said.

"Really?" Tamia was frustrated and found it hard to placate her friend's feelings. Maybe a soft voice and easy opinion wasn't what she needed. It was the truth. "Tasha, you almost forced Lionel to have Toni and then after she got here and you were finally the great mother that you only wanted to be to get back at your own mother—"

"Tamia," Troy said, stopping Tamia, "you're going too far."

"No, don't stop her," Tasha said. "I want to hear everything. I want to hear what you two really think of me."

"It's not about what we think, Tasha." Tamia was raising her voice and the waitress taking orders nearby turned and came over to tell the table to quiet down. People were starting to look. "It's about what any sane person looking at your situation would think. You checked out on those girls a long time ago and now you've checked out on Lionel for this . . ." Tamia paused and looked around the room at all of the people, their glasses held in their hands as they looked at her. "For this? Look at it. Look at it! It's not everything. You know? It's nothing. You have everything with Lionel. You always have. You'd know that if you weren't so busy complaining about everything and worrying about yourself. You're too fucking selfish."

Tasha's slap was so hard and so fast Tamia didn't bother to block her or fight back. A hush fell over the room.

"You don't judge me," Tasha growled with tears so heavy coming from her eyes it was clear she was crying for both herself and what she'd just done to her friend. She got up from her seat and Troy jumped up to get between her friends, afraid of what Tamia might do next.

"Excuse us, ladies," the waitress said, standing before a much taller, male waiter. "Do you think maybe you want to take this outside?"

"Oh, we're okay," Troy answered. "We're just—"

"No," Tasha said, plucking her purse from the back of her seat, "you two stay. Enjoy the rest of your meal."

9

*Every woman is a rebel, and usually in a wild
revolt against herself. . . .*

—Oscar Wilde

Troy was embarrassed. For a woman who'd spent
most of her life having everything, she now felt like
she had nothing. And, really, aside from the touchy-
feely things people say when they're broke—love, health,
and happiness—it was true. Her pockets were so deflated,
the sides stuck together. What made it worse was that
because she'd never been in such a place and didn't know
how to ask people outside of her family for money, she
couldn't even depend on her friends for support. She
felt the shame of saying "I need" to anyone would certainly force her into a lifelong coma where Kyle was
forced to wipe the crusted drool from around her lips
while he and Myrtle made out in the bed beside her
lifeless body.

Aside from asking the other 2Ts for financial support, her other smart option might be to sell some of
her things on eBay or on the corner of Adam Clayton

and 125th Street and make double what she owed, but that never even came to her, so she appealed to the best loan agency she'd ever known.

"Troy Helene, I can't give you the money. I'm sorry," Lucy said. Ms. Pearl was up on a brunch pillow, which sat in a chair beside hers at a golden bistro set in the middle of her rooftop atrium.

"But I—" Troy tried, but Lucy only waved her off.

"I promised your mother I wouldn't give you any more money."

"You promised?" Troy repeated. "But you never keep a promise to her."

Lucy gave her a look. Even Ms. Pearl woke up from her nap to look at Troy.

"What? It's true," Troy said.

"Well, since we took that ridiculous therapy workshop—'What Mommies—'"

"'—Can Do.'" Troy finished the title of the three-week workshop she'd taken with her mother and grandmother after her true lineage was revealed.

"Whatever it was . . . Anyway," Lucy went on, "she asked me not to intrude anymore and I'm taking my hands off of it."

"But it's not intruding if I am asking you for the money, Lucy. And I am asking. It's really important. I—"

Lucy waved her off again.

"She said you'd have a story and I was to respond that if you weren't stripping or using drugs, I could say no." Lucy dropped the piece of biscotti she was holding. "Oh, my Lord, is it drugs? Did you turn to cocaine?"

"No, Lucy. It's not that."

"Troy, I know this is painful for you. And I hate to admit it, but that mother of yours is right," Lucy said. "I've spoiled you. Given you too much for too long.

Now it's time for you to get your own. You went to college. Law school too. I didn't do either of those things. I had to depend on people all of my life to get the things I have. The things I've given you. But the point wasn't for you to depend on me. The point was for you to be able to go out into the world and be able to depend on yourself."

Troy stared at her grandmother.

"What?" Lucy shrugged her shoulders and the extra fabric of the Yuzen floral caftan that covered her petite frame fell to the floor.

"You sound just like her," Troy protested. "Did she make you memorize that?"

"Word for word."

While she was standing in a stall with an all-black horse named Shalamar, Tasha looked like she was either going on a date or trying to find one. And this was because she wasn't simply visiting the exclusive New Jersey boarding stable to feed hay to the impulsive birthday present Lionel had bought for Toni when she'd turned one. She was indeed awaiting the arrival of a very special date—a play date. Lionel had agreed to bring the girls to the stable for an afternoon picnic. A promise of spring in the wintry overcast meant that she could wear her tan Lauren riding pants with a fitted blouse and Burberry scarf without looking cold. She looked fabulous, stunning. The only thing that could make her trip to the stables more complete was a photographer and maybe better lighting. By now Lionel had to miss her and she wanted him to see why. She'd stopped at Gray's Papaya on the way to the tunnel into Jersey. She had Lionel's favorite—three naked dogs and a grape fruit drink in the picnic basket.

Tasha was practicing how she'd run toward the girls

when she noticed a white woman pushing a stroller carrying two black babies toward her. Well, the woman wasn't white, she was Latina, but with the poor lighting and Tasha's quickly changed demeanor that wouldn't matter when she shared the details with Troy later that night on the phone.

"Who the hell are you?" Tasha demanded, walking toward the woman and leaving the basket of food on the floor where Shalamar could have a special treat. "And why the hell do you have my children? Where's Lionel?" Tasha twisted and turned her neck in every possible direction to find her husband.

Tasha snatched the stroller from the woman, shaking the girls from side to side. She felt fear in the center of her chest and then fury in the balls of her fists at even the idea of this woman touching her children, caring for them. And who was she? Toni looked up at her mother and then at the woman who'd been changing her diapers for three days. Without saying a word from Tasha, the woman pulled a cell phone from her purse.

"He's on the phone?" Tasha snatched the phone.

"No, you didn't just grab my phone," the woman snapped, reclaiming the phone with more force than Tasha. Then Tasha realized that she wasn't dealing with a stereotypical caretaker or whatever clichés she was thinking about the woman. She wasn't docile or slow or scared. She spoke perfect English. And her voice had enough snap-crackle-and-pop[28] in it to let Tasha know in a second that she was a boricua, a nuyorican[29] and while Tasha didn't know that she was on a full scholarship at Columbia University and only babysitting to keep her little sister in private school, it was clear that she was ready for whatever fight Tasha was serv-

[28] Snap-crackle-and-pop: anything with fire, force, and/shine.
[29] Nuyorican: New York Puerto Rican.

ing up. Really, that was why Lionel had chosen her of all the nannies he'd interviewed.

But Tasha had her own snap-crackle-and-pop too.

"I'll snatch whatever I want to snatch!" She took the phone back from the woman for no reason other than to prove that she could.

Again, little Toni looked from her mother to the woman.

"Oh, hell no!" The woman snatched the earrings from her ears, balled up her fists, and pushed her weight back on her right leg.

"What are you going to do?" Tasha threw the phone down and balled up her fists too. If anyone was anywhere near the stable that Shalamar shared with two other horses, which happened to be away at competition, now would be the time to step in and stop the madness, but no one was and so it was on like Elizabeth Taylor at a diamond shop.

Toni chucked her bottle onto the ground, but neither woman—her mother nor her new nanny—noticed.

"Whooooaaa! Whoa! Whoa! Whoa! Wait!" Tamia said, running up to the women and jumping between them just before the two began to tussle.

"I'll beat your little ass," Tasha said as Tamia held her and pushed back.

"That's right. Get your girl," the woman said as Tamia tried to settle Tasha.

"Don't nobody need to get me," Tasha charged.

"*Besame el culo!*"

"What you say?"

"Stop it! Just stop it!" Tamia shouted to Tasha, pulling her into the stable and a few feet from where the woman stood beside the stroller.

"How is he gonna send—"

"I don't know, Tasha," Tamia said stiffly. "But I do know that you don't need to be acting like an ass out

here in front of your children. Now let me handle this."
Tamia let Tasha go. "You stay right here."

"*Mierda! Mierda! Mierda!*"

"Here," Tamia said, brushing hay off of the phone
and handing it to the woman.

She took the phone.

"I didn't even do anything and now I'm going to
lose my job!"

"No," Tamia said. "Don't worry. She's just upset.
That's all."

"Mr. LaRoche told me to bring them. What was I
supposed to do?"

"Look, what's your name?" Tasha asked. She could
hear Tasha screaming into her cell phone at Lionel.

"Mercedes," the woman answered. "I just got this
job. I wasn't trying to fight anyone. She came at me."

"I know. I know," Tamia said. "Look, you go. I'm
here with her and the girls. Everything will be fine."

"This isn't about us," Lionel was saying to Tasha on
the other end of the phone. "It's about you spending
time with the girls. Why did I need to be there?"

"We're a family," Tasha said.

"No, we're not," Lionel said. "You changed that
when you ran off to New York to do whatever the hell
you're doing there." While Tasha thought that being
separated from her husband would make him miss her
and realize how much he loved her, it was having the
opposite effect at the moment. He did miss her. But he
was beginning to grow more angry at how childish and
self-centered she was behaving. He was so angry, in
fact, that he decided he couldn't stand the idea of looking at her. He was afraid of what he might say, or do.
And he didn't want that to happen in front of his children.

"So what are we going to do? Never see each other
again?" Tasha asked.

"Don't be so dramatic," Lionel said. "You asked to see your daughters. They're there. Spend time with them and call me when you're done. I'll have Mercedes come back to get them."

When Tasha walked out of the barn, she saw that Tamia had pushed the stroller with Toni and Tiara over to a fence where they could see a few of the other horses playing in a pen. Tamia had taken Toni out of the stroller and was holding her in her arms.

"What are you doing here?" Tasha asked Tamia flatly. The last time they'd seen each other was at the restaurant when they fought.

"I'm your attorney," Tamia said. "Lionel called me this morning to tell me what was going on."

"Bastard," Tasha said. "I can't believe he did this. Can you believe he sent that woman here with my children? They are his responsibility. And now he's passing them off on someone else. He has some nerve."

"What else was he supposed to do? He doesn't know what to do with them."

"Be a father," Tasha shouted and both Tamia and Toni jumped. Toni started to cry.

"I'm sorry," Tasha said, reaching for Toni. "I'm so sorry."

She tried to pull Toni from Tamia's chest, but the toddler wouldn't budge. She stopped crying and wrapped her arms around Tamia's neck.

"What is this?" Tasha grabbed Toni's chin and turned her face to her, but the girl wouldn't look at her. Tasha's heart sank.

"She's just—" Tamia started, but she didn't know what else to say. There was this anger, this raw anger in Toni's face.

"You hate me, don't you?" Tasha said to Toni. "You always have." She began to cry and think about Porsche, how much she'd hated her when she was so young, so angry at her mother abandoning her in the same way Tasha had done to Toni. "Oh, my God!" Tasha cried just thinking about what she'd done. How she'd left her family. "I'm sorry. I'm so sorry that I've been such an awful mother to you," she said to Toni. "But I never had a moth . . ." Her voice cracked and she knew if she finished her sentence a rage would grow so strong inside of her, she might never recover. "I'm trying my best . . . No, that's a lie. I could do better. And I'm gonna do better. For you."

Toni finally broke her grimace and looked at her mother.

"I'm so sorry," Tasha said to her again. "You can trust me. I'm not gonna let you down again. I promise. I promise."

Toni's little hands loosened from Tamia's neck and this time, when Tasha tried to hold her, she went to her.

Far away from her birth father, there was nothing more sweet to Tamia than seeing her spiritual father's face. She was upset with Malik and had vowed to keep their relationship on a professional level until his case was over. Then she wouldn't have any contact with him. After getting over her initial anger about what happened at his place, she decided that she would continue her journey with her new sisters at the Freedom Project. And when Baba called, asking to meet her for a chat in the park, she was honored and happy he'd reached out to her.

She couldn't lie to her sisters about the reason for distancing herself from the circle for a while and she was certain Baba had been given the information. Even though she agreed to meet him, she promised herself she wouldn't share any words about Malik. That was her professional life and she had to keep it that way.

However, after discussing the mating patterns of birds and how the clouds were much thicker this spring than they had been last spring—and on that very day (what a memory)—he made it clear that he had no intention of honoring this desire.

"You cannot hide from the truth. You know this, child," he said in his way. "Just the same as the clouds know they belong in the sky and the birds know they belong in the trees, you know your heart belongs to—"

"Me," Tamia said. "My heart belongs to me."

"That is the lonely way."

"Well, until I can find someone who respects me and respects my heart, it will be the only way."

"You are very wise," Baba said, waving at a baby who had seen his long beard and smiled. "It is in your eyes. One day you will lead a man to enlightenment."

"Thank you, Baba," Tamia said. She hadn't heard him say that to anyone else.

"But until you can help them, you've got to accept your own enlightenment."

"What do you mean?"

"What is the symbol of return? Of knowing your past? Your essence?"

"The bird," Tamia answered. "Sankofa."

"Is that the only symbol? The only one?"

"I—"

"The other is what Europeans call the symbol of the heart," Baba revealed. "The Adinkra. The heart and the bird. Child, you must know that your past, who you are inside, is love. There is no past without love. And without the past, there is no—"

"Me," Tamia confirmed.

"Wise," Baba said. "Without love, the Afrikaan is a bird without wings, the cloud with no sky. There is no reason."

"But, Baba," Tamia said respectfully, "please forgive me for asking, but please explain what love has to do with Malik and I?"

"In your past, you became upset when you saw something?" he asked, but it was more of a statement for Tamia to confirm.

"Yes."

"Why would you be upset, child, if you are not in love? Why would you care?"

"I . . . wasn't . . ."

"That is not for me to hear. It is for you to understand."

Baba stood up and began to walk away. Tamia turned to see where he was going.

"Baba?" she called but when she turned Malik was standing there. "Oh, no." She turned back around.

"Just listen to me," he pleaded, trying to sit beside her on the bench, but Tamia stood up.

"Listen to what? Why?" Tamia asked.

"I can explain what you saw. Why she was there."

"I'm an adult, Malik. I know why she was there. I'm not blind."

"I was confused," Malik said. "Things were the way they'd been between Ayo and I for so long that I was confused. I thought I was supposed to be with her, but when I saw you, I knew it wasn't true. I knew what I was feeling was more than just play. I didn't want to hurt you."

"Hurt me?" Tamia laughed. "Hurt me? You can't hurt me. We're just friends, right? Sister and brother? No . . . we're actually attorney and client."

"If that's all I can get, I accept it. Just talk to me," he said.

"You want me to talk? Fine. What I have to say to you is that you'd better get yourself together. Next week is your hearing and we're going to court. You need to clean yourself up—"

"You mean put on a monkey suit? You know I'm not—"

"You asked me to talk," she shouted. "Clean up. I don't care what you do but I know why you need to do it. If you don't get it tight and come into that courtroom looking like the leader everyone knows you to be, you can forget about the Freedom Project. If you go in there talking about how you're guilty and fuck the system and police and whoever, the DA is going to bury you and then the Freedom Project will be shut down. So, before you go and make any more of your empty, stupid statements, you think about that. You think about what's important to you. Your ego. Or your freedom."

Tamia picked up the bag of tulips she was carrying to plant in Kali's garden and left.

While Sister Myrtle Glover was the first woman of First Baptist Troy ever met, prune pie–making Mother Wildren was the first woman of First Baptist she'd ever met and hated. Back then, when Troy walked into an after-church dinner, Mother Wildren was still Sister Wildren and she had refused to put more than three string beans on Troy's barren dinner plate. The feisty senior promised Troy that it would be her first and last visit as Pastor Hall's special guest, explained that one of her offspring was to marry the church's single leader, and admonished Troy for wearing such a short skirt and sitting on the first pew of the balcony.

This whole bad beginning added up to Troy raising an invisible middle finger whenever Mother Wildren was in her path. She needed allies but didn't care to make Mother Wildren one of them. The old woman had made her position clear and hadn't even propped a pillow in the presence of the First Lady to prove otherwise since she had been given the invisible crown.

Saddled with the baggage of Myrtle's promised house call, which was less than five hours away, and the knowledge that there was absolutely nothing she could do to get the money to save herself, Kyle's good name, and maybe First Baptist altogether, Troy found herself in the church, trying to pray again. For no reason other than the fact that she'd seen people do it on television growing up, Troy was wearing all black and sitting in the first seat of a pew in the middle of the empty church. While First Baptist wasn't a Catholic church, she had a rosary set she'd purchased at Betsey Johnson stashed into a Bible—and she would've had a Koran if she'd seen that on television too. Her eyes were closed tight, but then she heard a door open and turned to see Mother Wildren wobbling down the aisle with her cane clacking against the ground.

Troy nodded pleasantly, hoping the old woman would keep moving—she was probably a part of Sister Glover's little scheme. Heck, she'd probably given her the idea. But after the woman stopped and sat in the pew behind her, she knew she'd have to turn around and chat.

"You know ain't nobody supposed to be in the sanctuary," Mother Wildren said, her voice wobbly with age, but still direct and demanding. "Pastor say ain't nobody supposed to be in here unless he knows it."

"Well, it might be my last time, so I don't think he'll mind," Troy rattled off what first came to mind without turning around.

"I guess that's supposed to make me feel some kind of way," Mother Wildren said. "I'm supposed to ask you why you said it and care. . . ." Now both Mother Wildren and First Lady Hall's eyes were rolling. There was silence. "I'm too old and too busy to care about what's wrong with you. I've got a husband, three kids, five grands, and seven great-grands. All of them are living. You know what that means?" Troy was quiet, but she still didn't turn around. "I've got sixteen children and ten things to care about for each and every day until I die or one of them goes first."

Troy wanted to laugh and she was sure later she would but her nerves were too tight.

She turned to Mother Wildren.

"Why are you here, child?" Mother Wildren said and just then, being called "child"—even by Mother Wildren—was the most comforting thing Troy had ever heard. It felt like a blue blanket over her chest as she napped, a can of chicken noodle soup in her stomach, her mother's hand around her shoulders. Troy started to cry. And in ten minutes Mother Wildren knew everything about the money, Troy's shopping, her failing to get saved, that she was afraid to have sex with Kyle, and Myrtle's plan of divide and conquer. While the outrageous outpouring might have worn someone else out, the woman with so many children and so much experience, who'd only walked into the church to tell Troy the sanctuary needed to be empty, just sat back and frowned.

"Sounds like a great big old circus to me," Mother Wildren said and Troy nodded. "But"—Mother Wildren looked through Troy's show of helplessness and right into her—"the good news about it all is that you're a woman."

"What do you mean?"

"I mean, the circus isn't complete with a ringmaster. You're busy in here being a part of the show, when you should be running it."

"But I am in the house of the Lord," Troy explained. "I am trying to pray. Isn't that what I'm supposed to do?"

"You ain't praying, child," Mother Wildren said. "You're putting on a show. Playing with God." She took the rosary and Bible.

"What are you doing?"

"My mama, a backwoods Mississippi girl, who picked cotton her whole life, raised fifteen children, and buried two husbands, prayed more than any person I've ever known," Mother Wildren said. "And you know what? For all of her praying, I never once saw her on her knees. See, when you have fifteen children and a field of cotton so big you can't see your way to the road, you don't have time for rosary beads and Bibles and rules about how you can and should praise your God. For my mama, prayer came in the kitchen when she was cooking. Prayer came in the fields when she was picking. Prayer came at the living room table when she was teaching each one of her kids how to read because she knew we'd never get out of there if we didn't. If we read a line from the Bible, she praised God right there. Jump and say hallelujah." Mother Wildren looked at Troy sitting in front of her. "That's how she prayed. That's how she got saved and that's how I got saved. And the only way you're going to get there, the only way you're going to hear the word the Lord has for you is to stop worrying about what other folks have to say about your relationship with your God and go to him alone. The veil is broken, child. You go alone and you lay your burdens down."

Troy turned and looked at the altar.

"Just talk," Mother Wildren urged her softly.

Troy sat back and breathed out, her chest easing into the back of the pew. She kept telling herself to relax and clear her mind but the more she thought this, the more she thought.

She felt a hand on her shoulder.

"Talk," Mother Wildren repeated.

And aloud right there, in the church for only two people and one God to hear, Troy prayed for her marriage, for her husband, for herself. She prayed for a clean heart.

For clarity. For vision. For truth. For the courage to love even those who didn't love her and worked against her. And she didn't even know she was thinking that. It just came out. Just lifted itself out of her and then her eyes closed and without her noticing, Mother Wildren's hand was gone. Tears fell from Troy's eyes. She prayed for safety. For her church. For her family. For sins. For her past. For her future.

And then she was on her feet. Rocking in space. Her hands were above her head. Her eyes were closed as she stared into a blanket of blackness that erased her worry and eased her pain.

When Troy said all she could say and she was just standing there, wrapped up in her own arms, she opened her eyes and exhaled from the bottom of her gut. She wasn't changed. She was changing. She was open.

"Amen," she said. And she heard, not in a whisper, not in a thin or faint voice, as clear as if someone was standing right beside her, "I love you."

"What?" Troy said, turning to Mother Wildren. "What did you say?"

Mother Wildren was sitting where Troy had left her, her mouth closed, holding a slip of paper in her hand.

"I didn't say anything, child," she said.

Troy didn't look around the room again. She just knew then where the voice had come from. And while, just ten minutes earlier, the Troy who was holding the rosary and Bible might have felt tingles of fear up her spine at this idea, this changing Troy said again, "Amen."

"Here," Mother Wildren said, handing to Troy the paper she was holding. It was a check for $5.

"What's this for?"

"So you can start paying back the church," Mother Wildren said. "Now you're five dollars closer."

"You don't have to—"

"I didn't ask you what I had to do. I just did it," she added. "When you were praying, I was writing. God put that on my heart."

"Thank you," Troy said, hugging her old foe.

"Now, let me tell you how to handle Ms. Myrtle," Mother Wildren said. "You go and you talk to your husband. You take this to him and you have the first and last word where that's concerned. That man loves you. There ain't many men out there that are willing to put their wives first, above all others, and he did that for you. Didn't matter what we said. And, you know, I think that's why we respect him. Now, you go and put him first and that'll put Myrtle in her place. Never let another woman tell your husband anything about you."

"Will do," Troy agreed.

"And as far as the bedroom is concerned—"

"No, you don't have to. I—"

"No, First Lady," Mother Wildren said, "I might be old, but I'm not broken yet."

"Okay."

"Now, you stop letting these old ideas run your bedroom. If your man wants to get freaky and he's acting right, get freaky. Get your freak on!"

"Mother Wildren!" Troy blushed, holding her hand over her heart.

"The Lord wants you to be fruitful and he wants you to be happy," she said. "What you and your husband do in the bedroom is between you two. Now, I want you to go downtown to West Fourth Street and see a man named Xavier. He works at the Pink—"

"Whoa, Mother Wildren, I can't!" Troy stopped her.

"Oh, you've been there?"

"Yes, ma'am . . ."

"Okay, well, I have too. How do you think I've been married for so long?"

The women laughed and Mother Wildren grabbed Troy's hand.

"Now, let's get out of here. Pastor don't want nobody in the church and I—"

"I know . . . I know."

The trouble with planting flowers in someone else's garden is that you tend to forget about your own. Tamia would find this out when she walked, using her own two feet, from the Columbus Circle subway station to her front door at Trump Towers.

Full of so much pride she was able to push her trouble over Malik out of her mind for a few minutes, she reveled in the power of her new freedom, of her acceptance of the world and the way things were—the way they really were, not how she'd wanted them to be— that she was nearly singing when she walked into the door.

Bancroft looked past her, out into the drive for a car to connect her to, but there was none.

"Finally all the way off her bloody rocker," Bancroft thought, watching the spectacle Tamia now seemed to cause every day when she walked into the building with her bald head and sari. "Walking today, madame?" Bancroft said understatedly as Tamia walked past him.

"Hopefully from now on," Tamia said, smiling. "Living things need to spend more time in the sun. Don't you think?"

"Certainly. Maybe not all of us. Those with Nordic blood . . . burn."

Tamia nodded.

"Good point." She handed Bancroft a package of incense she'd made at Kali's after planting the tulips.

"Why, thank you." Bancroft took the sticks and peered at them strangely.

"Just burn them," Tamia instructed him. "You'll love it."

"Yes, of course." From behind his back, Bancroft produced a thick envelope bearing Tamia's name. "And for you. It came today by certified mail."

"What is it?" Tamia asked, taking the envelope.

Though she read the contents of the letter sent from her bank on the elevator, Tamia wasn't able to respond to its declaration until she was upstairs and hidden in the confines of her residence.

This moment had been sixty days in the making. Tracings of its possibilities had been mounting in her life for days. Standing in the foyer, draped in a sari and as bald as the day she was born, Tamia remembered the one thing she was trying to forget—Charleston.

"Sixty days late?" Tamia said. "He stopped paying the mortgage?"

In seconds the sad twist of fate actualized itself in Tamia's mind. There was no need to consider how she could pay back the bank's missing $20,000, late fees, and taxes. She just couldn't. Instead, her mind bathed itself in a river of memory—how this moment had come to her. In flashes, she saw Charleston and then Malik and wondered how this all began. When she walked into the office that day after seeing Maria in the bathroom and then the women looking on in the hallway—was it his face, his voice, or his scent that she'd encountered first? And how had it pulled her so far and so fast away from the person she was once so confident she was?

Venus Jenkins-Hottentoten-Hoverslagen-Jackson was waiting in a chair at the back of a dark restaurant, on a questionable side of town, wearing big black glasses and a white and gold fleur-de-lis-print scarf wrapped around her head.

"Memorial Day passed without me knowing?" was all Tasha said when she took a seat before Venus at the table. "I know I've been busy, but I thought it was a week or so away."

"What are you talking about?" Venus whispered, taking the glasses off and looking around the room all suspicious.

"The white scarf . . . you look like the Flying Nun or something. What's up with the whole getup? And why did you ask me to meet you here? Why did you ask me to meet you, period?" Tasha looked around for any bugs she could find on the ground. Her get-up-and-go[30] account was far from running low and she wasn't even considering subjecting herself to this low level of culinary cracker barrel.

"Well, I guess you want to get right to it," Venus said as a waitress with three teeth and a Bon Jovi bandanna over her greasy and no doubt dirty hair placed a menu on the table before Tasha.

"You can keep the menu." Tasha handed the menu back. "And don't bother to bring water." She looked back at Venus. "Of course I want you to get to the point so I can get up out of here. God forbid someone sees me here or takes a picture. People will think Lionel lost his contract."

"How ironic you should bring up a picture," Venus said, sliding a big brown envelope onto the table.

"What's this, crazy?" Tasha picked it up and opened it. "Some silly pictures of the woman Lionel was . . ."

---

[30] Get-up-and-go: a secret bank account for women married to rich, successful men. The money is stashed to the side in case she needs to "get up and go" and can't wait for alimony payments to kick in.

Tasha's tongue stopped flapping, but her mind was whirling. Between her thumb and index finger was a hazy, black and white eight-by-ten of her snuggled in Lynn's arms in a couch at the top of the Roosevelt Hotel.

Not knowing what else to do, she slid the picture back into the envelope and looked at Venus, her eyes tunneling into her frenemy with silver-coated bullets.

"Where did you get this?"

"I knew Lynn would pull some shit like this."

"What do you want?"

"She can't just keep it simple—act right."

"Is it money?"

"Always has to test me."

"Is it Lionel?"

"Do you even love her?"

"What?" Tasha asked, sure she hadn't heard Venus. "What kind of dumb-ass question is that? I'm not a freaking lesbo. One of those hawks gave me ex and I was tripping."

"You expect me to believe that? I have proof right here." Venus's voice was strong and scarred like a woman when her heart is being broken.

"I'm sorry, Venus. . . . I'm thinking right now that maybe I'm living on another planet or realm than you, because I don't know what the hell is going on. You just gave me some crazy picture that some crazy person must've taken while stalking me. I don't have to stand for this. I should just call my attorney—maybe even David Letterman's attorney. This is extortion!" Tasha stood up and pulled out her cell phone.

"I didn't say anything about money," Venus said quickly. "Just sit down . . . sit down."

Tasha stood for a moment and looked at her.

"I can explain," Venus added. "I can explain everything."

Tasha sat and pushed the envelope back to Venus. "Get to talking."

Venus exhaled and looked up at the cracked ceiling tiles. What she was about to say was the biggest secret of her big New York life—only her husbands and her girlfriends (not friends who are girls) knew.

"She's my lover."

Kyle smelled it when he walked into the house. It was dinnertime and the scent was burnt pork. Cheap pork. Maybe a canned ham. And he didn't know what that really meant. But he didn't really care either. He was tired. A good man beaten down by an all-around bad situation. And he was told it would be this way by so many people he trusted before he married Troy, but always being his own man, he'd felt he had to trust himself first. The woman who burned all the food in his house also had his heart ablaze and he loved that fire. Fever never felt so good as it did with her and it didn't matter how many easy, great, good, and spiritually equally yoked women who would promise him a life of good times all and everyone were pushed before him. They were fire-retardant to him and he just preferred and longed to sit in the flames with his first love.

But the terror of time quells the power of even the most wicked forest fire. And terrible times were all around. Worse than the bad that was promised. Though Kyle wasn't ever worried about his heart smoldering, now his mind and soul were chucked into the fire too. While he'd thought Troy was making an effort to get along with Myrtle, now rumors of fighting were everywhere in the church. Every word of gossip and contention, every threat launched against his wife, made him feel like he was fading to ashes. He didn't know what to believe. He didn't know what cards were being played. And that was like a shackle on his neck. The church was God's house, but he'd given many bricks to build it, formed them with the broken rocks of his soul, and, save his heart, Kyle had put everything he ever had inside into glorifying that mission. First Baptist wasn't going anywhere, but the idea of fracturing even one of the bricks he'd given to God for the glory of that formidable house made him blame himself for playing with fire and then blame his wife for spreading the blaze.

"Is that you?" Troy called, hearing footsteps pad through the garage door and up the stairs toward the top floor of the brownstone.

Kyle didn't answer. He went into the bedroom, set his bag on the floor, and sat on the bed. Now was the time he was supposed to go into the kitchen to find out why his wife was burning food, what was wrong with her, and patch it all up so he could convince her to order takeout. But he didn't move. He said he was tired. But really it was because he was the one in need of patching.

"Kyle?" The call was coming from the bottom of the steps.

He didn't say anything. He looked up toward the ceiling, but even as a little boy he could see through ceilings and right into the center of his praying mind.

"Jesus," his body called without a known word, "I need you right now. I need a sign. You never led me astray. You never, ever left me. Just whisper in my ear so I know you're here. So I know I'm on the right path."

"Chinese food." It was a whisper in his ear. But it was too soft, too light to be that of the God he'd heard before. Awakened from his prayer, Kyle jumped and turned to the whisper.

"Oh, I'm sorry! I scared you?" Troy said. "I thought you saw me walk in. You were looking at the ceiling."

"What?"

"Chinese food. I was telling you I ordered Chinese food," she said, "from Mr. Stevie Foo. Your favo."

"But the food . . . I smell the food," Kyle said, looking at his wife like she was a Martian, an extraterrestrial, an angel or saint.

"Yeah, it was a ham. A canned ham I tried to jazz up with cumin," Troy said matter-of-factly. "Did you know spices burn in the oven?"

Kyle couldn't do anything but nod.

"Anyway, there was no sense saving the thing, so I just ordered your favo," Troy said. "I guess what I'm trying to say is that we need to talk."

Venus Jenkins-Hottentoten-Hoverslagen-Jackson, a black woman with the most ridiculous last name of any woman in the city on account of two failed marriages to Swedish bankers and one mediocre yet standing marriage to a Knicks starting player, was coming out of the closet. A great big old, Queen Elizabeth–Mariah Carey–sized closet. A 5,000-square-foot closet.

"I can't believe Lynn's your lover," Tasha said after she'd finally convinced Venus that she had no desire to be with Lynn and hadn't done anything at the hotel but pass out in an accidental drug-induced kirk at the party.

"We've been together for five years," Venus said sadly.

"But you're married," Tasha said. "And you're apparently robbing the cradle. That girl's only twenty-four. What, were you dating her when she was in college?"

"Yes," Venus admitted. "I paid for her to go to college—well, my ex-husband did."

"Oh, my God, I was joking." Tasha fanned herself. "This is freaky. This is too freaky for me. And I'm a freak. But not this kind of freak."

Venus crumbled onto the table and started to cry.

"Oh, no." Tasha looked around at the completely strange faces around her. Luckily she didn't notice any of them. "Girl, if you don't get up off of the table . . . You know they have roaches here!"

Venus sat up but she was still crying and sniffling.

"Oh, why do I know I'm going to regret this?" Tasha said. "What happened?"

"I love her. I really do," Venus cried. "She doesn't understand that. She's always sleeping with other women and out in the street. She doesn't even respect me. I saw her dancing with those football players at the party. And when I saw her talking to you, I knew she was just trying to sleep with you."

"That tag-tucking[31] hussy!" Tasha said and Venus began to wail again.

"Oh, stop it!" Tasha said. "How are you over here complaining about this girl cheating on you when you're clearly married and cheating on your husband?"

"We're both with her."

"With her?"

"Any man I marry knows Lynn is a part of my life and theirs too," Venus explained.

"A part like what? Y'all get together . . . like, everybody . . . and get the freak on?"

"It's more than that," Venus said tearfully. "She's my angel."

[31] Tag-tucker: the opposite of "popping tags," a tucker buys clothes and tucks tag so she can return them.

"Well, she wasn't an angel the other night. She was a pill-popping devil girl."

"Don't talk about her like that!"

"Don't yell at me," Tasha said. "You're the one all calling me out here to confront me about your little cheating . . . I don't know what to call her."

Hearing this, Venus began to cry again.

"Look, Venus"—Tasha exhaled—"you're a good . . . I mean decent . . . I mean child of God. And you and your little—"

Venus looked at Tasha.

"—Lynn are probably giving every lesbian in the world a bad name."

"We're not lesbians. We're polyamorous."

"I don't know what that means and I don't want to know." Tasha threw her hands up. "But what I was saying was that you two probably need to sit down and have a conversation and decide what you're going to do. Which probably needs to be breaking up."

"You really think so?"

"Venus, you're having a girl who's ten years younger than you followed around the city by a detective. Yes, it's time for you to break up—for all three of you to break up . . . and you might want to break up with Bobby too."

"When a man loves a woman . . . / She can do no wrong / Turn his back on his best friend / If he put her down."

The lyrics of this old Percy Sledge song were alive and kicking in a certain brownstone of a Harlem pastor and his wife. While anyone listening to their story might want Troy's telling of her troubles to her husband to be a little more difficult, a little more strenuous, that just wasn't Kyle's way with this woman. He knew how and what she was—probably better than she did—and as she went over everything she'd been thinking, pulled every pair of shoes from her closet, and cried every tear she had in her body, he just kept thinking that finally she was figuring out what he'd been trying to tell her all along. That the only person she could be, that she needed to be, was herself. And the more she tried to be someone else, the more dangerous their life together would be.

Yes, he was upset with her for the thing with the money and knew that he would need to smooth this over with many people for many months, and he was sad that there was an obvious lack of communication between him and his bride, but a gift he'd been born with, a gift he'd used to become one of the best preachers, was the gift of knowing a liar from a lost person and a lost person from someone wanting to be found. He worked with these kinds of people day and night and sometimes it meant the difference between saving a soul and saving time. And while in his wife, when he'd left her that very morning, he'd seen the eyes of someone who was lost, sitting beside her on the bed, with shoes and scarves and dresses with tags still attached, he saw the eyes of the latter. Troy was being found.

"I'm not perfect either," Kyle said, comforting Troy. "And I don't ever want to be that. To pretend to be that. It's dangerous. Yes, you've let me down. But the only way Myrtle could even believe that she could come between us is if she thought I might let you down. If she saw a crack she could dig at. If she thought I wouldn't fight for you. That I wouldn't pick you up."

"Would you?" Troy asked her groom, still crying. "Could you still fight for me even after I've done such stupid things?"

"You know that, baby," Kyle said seriously. "You don't even have to ask."

The doorbell the two had installed themselves rang and bells chimed throughout the house.

"You want to answer that?" Troy asked Kyle.

"Let's answer her together."

Kyle and Troy walked to the front door, the shorter, softer one behind the taller, masculine one, but then they opened the door and when Myrtle looked inside, they were side by side, his arm over her shoulder.

"I thought maybe you two weren't home," Myrtle said, looking at Troy, confused. She tapped the envelope she was holding and looked up at the pastor.

"Oh, we were just about to sit down to some Chinese food my wife ordered," Kyle said.

"Oh." Myrtle tried to look unmoved. "Well, Troy agreed that I could come by so we could tell you something. Right, Troy?" She looked at Troy.

"Now, I sure did agree to that." Troy nodded matter-of-factly.

"So, maybe I should come in so we can get started." She tapped the folder again before trying to push her way into the door.

"Hold up," Kyle said, standing firm and still holding on to his woman. "Baby, do you still agree to needing Myrtle here for our meeting?"

Troy looked from Kyle to Myrtle.

"Nahhhh," she said.

"Okay," he said. "Well, then, I guess we're done here. See you at church!"

Kyle tried to pull back from the door, but Myrtle stuck her foot inside.

"So you think you're slick, huh, Troy?" she said. "You think this is going to stop me? This little show? Well, you, no, the both of you, just wait until I go before the board of trustees."

"There's no need for that," Kyle said unaffectedly. "I already called a meeting with the trustees to discuss my wife's charges on the credit card. So . . . basically . . . you can shove it!" Troy pushed Myrtle's foot out of the way of the door and Kyle closed it a little more before saying, "But we will see you at church. First Baptist is a place for saints and sinners."

When the door was closed and Myrtle was left outside looking bad and sad, Kyle and Troy stayed together, laughing as they headed toward the kitchen.

"Shove it?" Troy joked. "I can't believe you said that!"

"I'm not exactly a cursing man. I don't have a whole list of foul words at my disposal," Kyle said.

"And what about that thing about having called the board of trustees? You couldn't have done that. I just told you about the credit card."

Kyle smiled.

"You lied, Pastor?" Troy said, shocked. "I can't believe it!"

"It wasn't a lie," Kyle said. "I'm going to call them right now. And you, my darling, can go and heat up my Chinese dinner. A brother is starving."

Working late, overtime, aftertime, and/or extra hours was never an issue for Tamia. Even in elementary school, she'd ask her teacher if she could stay behind in the classroom and study or complete her project after the other students jumped up and hustled out of the classroom like fire, death, and destruction were imminent if they didn't make it to their school buses in the next three seconds.

While any person who knew her would easily affix this desire to Tamia's commitment, it was more than that. Working after-hours, working late, gave Tamia more than an edge over the competition. It also gave her vision, understanding, a chance to meditate with her work and consider what her next move might be. When all the other workers had gone home, she could sit in her space and listen to the hum of the vacuum cleaners of the cleaning crew, look out over the empty cubicles, full of ideas, see the expansive hallways and staircases, and smell the leftover bagels in the break room and see her world in a new way.

Most days, this new way meant something good. But these days in Tamia's life weren't like most. And just a few atypical days after her distressing meeting with Baba and Malik, as Tamia sat in her office putting the final touches on Malik's case, working late was turning into something bad, something dark, something finite.

Simply put, though the vacuum cleaner was humming, though she could see the papers and reminders and ideas and contracts feathered out over Naudia's desk like a deck of Vegas cards, though the hallways and staircases were empty, and though there was the smell of bagels—no, muffins—in the break room, something was different. Something had changed. Whatever fire, whatever connection Tamia had that connected her to her work, to her workplace, seemed less glittery, less inviting than it had just months before. She didn't believe. After accepting and planning her idea to lose Malik's case, she thought about how many times this must've happened to other people, at other times, within the very walls she was walking. And if that was true, if the law she'd dedicated her life to came down to one man's mortal decision—if a client was being honest, a lawyer committed, a judge, jury, and justice system free of the burdens of life—then what was she doing? It was all chance. One bad law written by one racist person could put a person away for life. This wasn't justice. This was cloak and dagger. A magic show. A pipe dream sold from the powerful to the powerless. What place could she possibly have in all of it?

"Working late?" a voice called from Tamia's office door. She looked up to see Charleston standing there in a track suit.

She smiled cordially.

"Yes. Going to court in the morning."

Charleston didn't ask. He came in and sat down.

"Yeah, I know," he said. "I figured I'd be able to catch you. Since I can't seem to get you any other way."

Tamia didn't say anything. Charleston's words only presented opportunities for lies or excuses.

"It's been over a month." He said, taking another jab. "Two—going on. I haven't seen my girlfriend. We work in the same building. You'd think that's impossible." Yeah, it was pretty impossible for most people, but Charleston had always been good at keeping himself busy. He only thought of Tamia when he wondered what might be keeping her busy.

"Well, I guess you should know," Tamia said. "Your bank account should be about $30K richer. I got the notice from the bank. Thanks for letting me know you weren't paying anymore."

"All you had to do was call me and I would've given you the money."

"Charleston, I didn't ask you to pay my mortgage. You offered. I was moving somewhere else and you insisted I move into that building. And you insisted that you pay the mortgage."

"And you didn't want it?" Charleston snickered evilly. "Before you became . . . this"—he pointed at her clothes, her hair—"you were all about that shit. High class. Everything a 10. You wanted what you deserved. You wanted me to give it to you. And now I'm the bad guy because I don't want to pay for your dream. What is your dream now anyway?"

"You don't need to worry about my dream," Tamia said. "Maybe you should worry about Phae's dreams—"

"Whoa—"

"Yeah, I know about that. Maybe you should worry about her dreams and half of the other women you've been fucking in this city. I never said you had to pay for anything, but you know what you promised me and you know what you owe me. If you wanted to back out of the mortgage, that's fine, but give me time. Don't treat me like one of those tricks you trick off."

Charleston wasn't so sure he knew or understood the Tamia sitting on the other side of the desk. He knew she was strong. He knew she was smart, but this woman was coming back at him in a way that made him think maybe that was why he needed to be with one of those white girls she was calling "tricks." Maybe they could respect and accept a man like him. In charge. He didn't need Tamia and her shit. He could call any one of them right then and tell them to step out on the men they'd married and come be with him. And that's when he thought about it—they were all married.

"I didn't come in here to fight with you," Charleston said.

"You could've fooled me."

"I came here to"—he paused and reached into his pocket, pulling out a little box. He sat it on the desk—"give you another chance. It's your ring."

"What?" Tamia asked, looking at the box. And even though she hated Charleston, even though she'd sworn off diamonds and the exploitation of any jewels from nations under duress, the little girl in her wanted so badly to grab the box, pull the ring out, and dance around the room.

"I know Tasha told you," Charleston said. "It's the ring you wanted. You can have it. It's yours. If you come back to me. Be my wife." His voice was reasonable.

Flat. Clear. Like a contract attorney showing his client where the line was to sign. He was so sure of himself.

"Marry you?" Tamia looked past the ring, the wedding, the idea of marriage and saw the man sitting before her. "Marry you? You? Not even if Isis and Yemaya and Coretta Scott King and my own mama got up out of the grave and came and sat in this office and told me to do exactly that would I do such a thing."

"Excuse me?"

"No, excuse you," Tamia said with her voice reasonable, flat, and clear now, "for thinking you could come up in here, into my office, and think you could buy me like I'm some stupid, silly whore, who thinks the only way she can be free is to cling to what little of a man is left in you. I can get what I need without you. And I don't need Trump Towers or a Bentley. I might have wanted those things at one time, but I don't need them. That was a joke. And now the joke is on you."

A different man, maybe one with less money or a smaller penis, one with a smaller ego and fewer women at his disposal, might have heard and been hurt by Tamia's words. And, yeah, some of it did get through to Charleston and scratch at his surface, but he was a showman. And he specialized in not letting what others said stop his show. Luckily for Tamia, she wasn't saying what she was saying for him. It was for her.

"Fine," Charleston said coolly. He picked up the ring like it was a tennis ball and shoved it back into his pocket. "Suit yourself."

With Tamia's cold eyes on him, he stood, walked over to the door, and turned back to her.

"When he fails and you're broke and down in the gutter, you remember what you did right now," he said. "You remember the life I offered you. . . . What I am talking about . . . He won't fail you, because he won't be with you. He's just another nigger wearing a loincloth. A nigger in a suit . . . a nigger in a loincloth . . . either way, he's gonna fuck up. But you don't need to worry about that. You'll just be another sad, lonely black woman. Scarred by the world and dead-ass broke." He laughed and shook his head.

"Get out," Tamia said. "Get out of my office."

Tamia was so angry after her talk with Charleston, she didn't notice any of the looks from any of the by-standers peering at her as she got out of her taxi and walked into the doors of her posh and soon-to-be-available pad at Trump Towers. Her knapsack on her back and her flip-flops clacking against the cold marble floor, she trudged through the lobby, head lowered, and ready for sleep. What was coming in the morning? She didn't care anymore. She didn't care what was to become of any of this. It was all pointless. All a justice-free dance of chance and lies. Malik. Charleston. One and the same. More men to let her down. More men to walk away from.

"Madame," Bancroft called, rushing toward her from his office, "I'm so sorry I hadn't caught you when you arrived."

"It's fine," Tamia said. "Allejandro got the door for me." She pointed to Allejandro, the night doorman, who was assisting another resident with her Jack Russell.

"No, dear heart," Bancroft said. "It was to say thank you."

"Thank you for what?"

"For the felted sticks you left on my desk."

"The . . . ??" Tamia tried. "Oh, you mean the incense?"

"Yes, they're quite fragrant. I'd like some more," he explained, leaving out the part about his lover and him burning all of the sticks in one night to hide the smell of marijuana billowing from their apartment. And, yes, he knew dang well they were called incense.

"I'll be sure to bring some down to you." Tamia smiled and started walking toward the elevator.

"Your guests," Bancroft said, "you won't be joining them in the ballroom?"

"I'm not having any guests," Tamia said, pressing the button for the elevator.

"Certainly you are," Bancroft said, poking his chest out and pointing dramatically toward the Tower's private ballroom. "Madame Natasha and Madame Troy Helene await your presence at high tea."

Tamia's knapsack fell to her wrist.

"High what?" She tried to remain angry but had to smile. "No, those crazy chicks didn't."

Oh, but, yes, they did. And well.

Tamia walked into the ballroom to find a table set for three, surrounded by what looked like hundreds of yellow tea roses, and a string quartet and a stack of gift boxes.

"What is this?" she said, looking around for her friends. And then from behind her entered Tasha and Troy, dressed in their *Dynasty,* Diahann Carroll–worthy two-piece suits and floppy hats.

They led their friend and her flowing sari to a seat and kissed her on both cheeks.

Tamia was crying then. Her hand was holding her head up on the table and she just let everything go.

"Oh, Ms. Lovebird," Troy said, "don't cry. We came here to cheer you up!"

"That's right," Tasha chimed in. "You can't cry. This is a tea. No one cries at a tea. Not a high tea. Right, Troy? You're from bougieville. You know the answer."

"She's right," Troy concurred, reaching over and wiping Tamia's tears.

"You know, I'm supposed to say you guys shouldn't have done this, but really, you should've," Tamia cried, laughing a little while blowing her nose in the hankie Troy handed her. "I was so down—just a minute ago. Just before I walked in this door and saw all of this." She looked around again at the floors and strange-looking musicians she didn't know. "But this just, it just . . . it made me smile and I'm so happy to have friends like you."

"Awwww," Troy said. "Well, technically . . . we didn't do it. I'm broke. Tasha paid for everything."

The 3Ts laughed and joked like this, familiar and fortunate friends as a waitstaff carried out an assortment of teas and delectable desserts that birthed a sweet-smelling cloud of vanilla and cinnamon over the table. After sipping on English tea, they tasted, pie after cake after cookie until little more than crumbs remained on the table.

"I guess it was a good idea not to order dinner," Troy said.

"Who needs dinner when you can have dessert?" Tasha joked. "That's the new diet!"

Having told her friends about her meeting with Malik and how badly Charleston treated her at the office, Tamia sat full and also relieved. Her girls reminded her that she'd done her part. She'd remained honest to herself and everyone around her. Now it was time for the men to pick up the pieces. She could rise in the morning with a clear head and heart and move on with her life—wherever it took her.

"I'm sorry for snapping at you guys like that the other day," Tasha said, telling the other Ts that she was missing her family. "Lionel's coming around, I think. He agreed to let me see the girls on the weekends."

"That's a beautiful blessing," Troy said tenderly. "I

want you to know that we both love you and we only want what's best for you and your family."

Tamia nodded in agreement.

"Troy's right. I didn't mean to hurt you with the things I said the other week," she said. "I love you and I wasn't judging you. I just had to say what I had to say."

"Exactly," Troy added. "You can always come to us."

"And you can always come to me," Tasha snapped at Troy playfully. "Child walking all around the city as broke as a Brooklyn roach like she doesn't have wigs with money to burn. The next time you need a check or for me to check the asses of one of those chicks at the church, you call me!"

"Oh, no," Troy said.

"I might be a mama, but I haven't gone soft yet."

"That's not what Lynn said . . . Lynn or Bobby," Tamia joked, tossing a sugar cube at Tasha.

"See, there you go messing up our tea," Tasha said. "I'm trying to keep it classy and you're over here throwing stuff."

"Wait, wait!" Troy jumped in. "We forgot something!" She jumped up and ran to the gift boxes stacked on the floor.

"What's that?" Tamia asked.

"Just some gifts for our guest of honor," Tasha said, taking one of the boxes from Troy. "This one is from me."

"You two!" Tamia purred, opening her gift with the speed of a six-year-old. "What is this?" she asked, looking at a white box.

"Open it," Troy said.

Inside there was a wig of fine brown hair that looked in length and style just like Tamia's old hair.

"What?" Tamia shouted so loud the harpist skipped a note. "A wig!"

"Now, you were complaining about old Nelson

Mandela making you cut your hair off, and I figured that could help you get by until you grow some hair back on that beady head of yours. You know you have a dent in the back, right?" Tasha teased.

"No, I don't," Tamia said, stretching the wig out.

"We figured you could wear it to court," Troy said, handing Tamia another box. "You know, to play into the old you. Now, open this one."

She handed Tamia the gift and grinned gleefully.

"Now, I'm on a budget, so it's kind of, like, from my closet—but it's new. The tags were still on it and—"

"Lord, will you let her open the box before you tell her what's inside?" Tasha asked.

It was a sleek black suit that looked like something Tamia would've picked out for herself. Attached to the collar was a little Post-It where Troy had written: MY BEST SUIT FOR MY BESTIE.

"You're both too much," Tamia cried. "Too much."

"We know. We know," Tasha and Troy said together, taking turns providing each other applause.

After wiping her tears one last time, she looked up at the other gift boxes, still stacked and unopened and then back at her friends.

"What's in those boxes?" she asked. "Other things for me? Did you guys get me a new boyfriend?"

"Um . . . no," Tasha said frankly. "Those are for us. You didn't think you were the only one getting gifts, did you?"

3T Tea Time: Three Pinkies Up

Don't let the little girls have all the fun! Now that you can actually afford to upgrade from the plastic tea set you shared with your stuffed animals when you were five, call your girlfriends over for a high tea that's sure to soothe the soul and reconnect your circle.

Set a date and send out formal invitations to your special affair.

<u>Dos:</u>
1. Choose a theme: You can have a Victorian, Japanese, or Russian theme. The tea traditions of each culture will determine your decorations, menu, and assortment of teas.
2. Make a list and check it twice: In addition to your best friends, invite a new friend and consider having a special guest of honor—a local artist, someone new in town, or maybe a sister-friend who just did something amazing.
3. Get fancy: Big hats and bold dresses will make the tea official and the photos amazing. For a Japanese theme, require kimonos and have someone there to do makeup. You all will laugh all afternoon.
4. Have conversation starters: Break the ice and get the talkers talking by having games, a featured book, or list of current affairs available for discussion and fun.
5. High or low: Be sure to let the ladies know if you are organizing a low (afternoon) or high (afternoon or supper time) tea. This will let them know what kinds of food to expect. Low tea commonly calls for light fare and dainty desserts. High tea can combine hearty dishes and delectable desserts.

<u>Don'ts:</u>

1. Be afraid to laugh at yourself: Something will go wrong and something you thought would be so wonderful will be so . . . not wonderful. Laugh it off and learn for next time.

2. Overplan: Not every guest will want to play games. Be open to suggestions and changes in plans. If you have a special guest, ask if there's something she would like.

3. Do it alone: Ask for help and make a list of assignments for your friends. Tea might sound easy, but it's big business and letting someone clse do the small stuff will allow you to focus on the bigger battles.

4. Spike the tea: Tea is meant for tasting. While some mixes call for alcohol, by and large the plants are to do their magic on a holistic level. If your guests must have the bubbly, plan a post-dessert champagne toast.

10

*All the world's a stage, and all the men and
women merely players. . . .*

—Jacques in William Shakespeare's *As You
Like It*

What most people forget about Jacques's famous line
in this aged tale is that he concludes that players in the
unchanging setting of the world constantly enter and
exit and change. Players don't know when or why, but
even as they play their own roles, they can be certain to
learn that this is the truth.

So, on an old stage, in an old city, at a new age in her
life, one player was learning that she wasn't the best
player after all. For she'd been upstaged, outsmarted,
outperformed, and outacted by the one costar she could
never leave behind—herself.

Tasha sat in the center of her beautiful world, with
her beautiful things, looking more beautiful than she
ever had in her life, yet there was an ugliness creeping in.

While she was surrounded with every new thing
she'd wanted back from her old life, she kept thinking

of the old things she was missing from her last life. It was Sunday night and the girls were probably just getting out of the tub. Toni was running around naked, giggling herself silly as her father chased her and Tiara was trying to find a way to get the powder bottle open again so she could dump the sweet-smelling talc all over the floor. Lionel was getting tired and probably noticed that Tiara had gotten the bottle open and snatched it just in time. The boring suburban house was growing quiet with the boring suburban night as the boring suburban family got ready for bed. In a while, they'd all be asleep. And the night, for Tasha in her new, amazing, and alive life in the big and bold city was just about to begin. There was so much to do and see where she was. So many places to go. Beautiful people to see. No naked babies or powder sticking to her feet. No crying and midnight feeding. No tired husband, vibrators, and runs to the airport. Her options were endless, but her mind was frozen in time.

"I need a glass of wine," she said aloud, but she was speaking only to herself in the empty space of her apartment. There was silence. No response. Not even an echo of confirmation. She got up from her plush couch and walked to the refrigerator to retrieve what was left of her last bottle of white wine.

"Shit," she shouted, looking at the space in the refrigerator where the bottle once was. She turned and looked at the trash can to see the empty bottle resting on the lid. She exhaled and banged the door shut.

Maybe she could call the 3Ts together for a drink. Maybe she could meet up with her new girls for tapas. Maybe she could . . . She went and sat on the wide windowsill that separated her apartment from the street. A group of laughing women walked past. A homeless man pushing a cart. A man on his cell phone, walking his dog.

"What did I do?" Tasha said to all of them, though none of them could hear her. "What did I do to my life? How could I leave my family?"

In the silence of the city night, this last question marked the beginning of this player's grandest performance to date. In all of Tasha's life, only three times had she thought to consider how her actions affected someone else: when she was ten years old and set her nanny's car on fire, when she'd tripped a woman at a Barney's sale, and when she'd secretly started fertility treatments without Lionel's consent. Each time, Tasha had been so busy fighting for what she was getting, she cared nothing about what others actually got. The nanny was fired for leaving Tasha alone in the garage, the woman at Barney's lost a tooth, and Lionel was forced to realize that he had no control over his wife.

"I'll go back to therapy," Tasha said when Lionel picked up the phone. She was still looking out the window when she pulled the phone from her pocket and pressed the speed dial option "Home."

"What do you use to get this baby powder off of the floor?" Lionel asked. His voice was ragged with indecision and she knew he hadn't heard what she'd said. She could hear Toni hollering and Tiara crying in the background. She smiled as a tear rolled down her cheek.

"Don't use water," Tasha said quickly. "That'll make it worse. Get the broom and sweep."

"I can't leave them in the bathroom," Lionel said.

"Put them in their cribs and tell Toni to sing 'Twinkle Twinkle Little Star.' That'll give you five minutes to get the broom and sweep up the powder."

"Really? Wait a sec."

There was movement, Toni was singing, and then Lionel was back on the phone.

"Now, what did you say?" Lionel asked as he swept.

"I said I'd go back to therapy," Tasha repeated, her voice breaking on every word as she cried. "Whatever you want. I just want my family back. I need—"

"They need you," Lionel stopped her as his feelings made his throat swell. "*I* need you." This call wasn't supposed to go this way. Lionel was supposed to be angry. In his mind, the next time his wife called, he was to request a divorce, tell her to come get her things, and find the nastiest thing he could say to make her feel the worst she ever had. But as the days went by and he was managing nannies and appointments and his life with the lives of his children, he saw just how hard Tasha's job was. And sleeping alone in a big, wide bed made specially for him, he felt how lonely she must feel each night without him. As he played her role, he realized that much of what he'd hated her for, he could in some ways understand. She wasn't right for leaving the way she had, but she wasn't wrong for feeling the way she felt. In the images of his own beautiful life and beautiful family, the beautiful player Lionel had somehow forgotten to take care of one important thing—his beautiful wife.

"I know I need help. I'm fucking up," Tasha said.

"I think we both have things we need to work on," Lionel admitted. "But it's going to take time and we have to commit ourselves to it this time. I accept you for who you are, Tasha. And I know you have your faults—I do too, but we have to be a team on this. For our family. Do you want that?"

"I'm nothing without you all. I don't want anything else and I'm willing to do whatever it takes to keep us together. I love you," Tasha pleaded.

And then, the player and the player's wife were silent, as an ugly exit in their play was transitioning to a beautiful entrance that would surprise both of them for years to come. There was nothing else to be said. Everything they needed to hear was in the silence they felt.

"Hey," Lionel said suddenly. "I have someone who wants to say something to you."

"What?" Tasha asked.

"Hold on a sec."

"Ma! Ma! Mama! Mama!"

"That's right, baby. Say it again. Say it so she can hear you."

"Mama!" There was a gurgle and then the word Tasha had wanted to hear for so long from the one person who seemed to refuse to say it, was repeated as clear as a bell in the wind.

"Mama. Mama."

"You heard that?" Lionel asked, but Tasha couldn't respond. She slid from the windowsill to the floor and was cradling her face in her hands as she wept. "Say it again, Toni. Say it for Mommy on the phone. That's right! Your mommy is on the phone."

"Mama," the toddler said and this time even she herself wanted it to be clear that everyone could understand what she was saying. "Mama."

"Yes, baby girl," Tasha said, "it's your mommy."

"Mama," Toni repeated and then she requested in the only way her two-year-old mind could what she wanted most. "Mama . . . home . . . home."

"Yes, Mama's coming home."

Later in the night, and much closer to the morning, on another stage in another part of the city Tasha would soon leave for good, another player was also preparing for her grandest performance to date.

Troy was in the bathroom of her brownstone, sticking gold cones to the tips of her nipples to match her thong and blond Farrah Fawcett wig. "Lady She-Ra" was what the package containing this costume read when Troy had retrieved it from the shelf at a sex shop downtown. "He-Man" was the matching ensemble—a cape and a studded crotch cover, which Kyle thought was a headband—being showcased in the bedroom by her costar. He had a golden sword and golden boots. She had a golden whip and golden stilettos.

It was one of Kyle's fantasies. To save a damsel in distress. To save mankind. To save the world, using the power of his sword.

"I am the princess of power!" Troy practiced, shaking her golden nipple covers a bit to be sure they didn't fall off. "Can you save me? Do you have the power in your sword?" She toughened and softened her voice, unsure if she should sound hardened or needy. "Do you have the power in your sword? *Do you have the power in your sword?*"

"Ready!" she heard Kyle call excitedly from the bedroom. He was standing in the center of their bed wearing his crotch cover on his head and nothing beneath his cape.

Troy kicked the bathroom door open and stepped onto the threshold, her legs wide apart as the light from the bathroom pushed a shadow through her thick thighs. Kyle smiled immediately at his wife.

"I am the princess of power!" Troy said. "Can you save me? Do you have the power in your sword?" Her voice was innocent, helpless.

"Yes! I do, Queen She-Ra!" Kyle answered, pointing his sword at Troy.

"Well, save me!" Troy demanded, using a line she hadn't practiced. She cracked her whip and as it rippled, it flicked the underside of the door, slamming it suddenly against her face.

Kyle leapt from the bed, racing to her just as it cracked

against her nose and almost sent her crashing to the floor.

"Oww!" Troy cried, falling into Kyle's arms.

"You okay, baby, you okay?" Kyle asked frantically. He moved the loose blond hair from her face.

"My nose! The door hit my nose." She covered her nose with her hand.

"Let me see."

Troy moved her hand so her husband could see her nose. She looked into his eyes as he searched for bruises. His crotch headband had slipped over his eye and the right collar of his cape was poking into his cheek.

"I don't think anything is broken. There's no blood," Kyle said. "You feel okay? You want me to get some ice?"

Troy smiled at him.

"You're the most handsome He-Man I've ever seen," she said.

"What?" Kyle looked at her, confused. He'd forgotten the outfit and the occasion and was just caring for his wife.

"I'm slipping away," Troy said dramatically, resting the top side of her hand over her forehead in mock distress. "I see a light and I am slipping away into another life!"

"Really?" Kyle asked, catching on.

"Save me, He-Man! Use your sword to save me! That's the only thing that can wake me up!" She-Ra's hand fell heavy to the ground as she fainted and went limp in He-Man's arms.

Kyle stood and carried his damsel to the bed. He placed her on top of the sheets and she (while allegedly comatose) managed to arrange her body into the position of a sexy offering.

"By the *power of* Grayskull," Kyle shouted solemnly, raising the pretend sword over her body. "I must save She-Ra, the princess of power!" He dropped his weapon and proceeded to use his other sword three times into the morning to fight the forces of evil and save the damsel's life. She called his name so loud, the neighbors and theirs beside them complained of children watching cartoons too loud.

When Troy recovered from her injuries and was awakened by the sun coming in the window beside the bed, she looked to see that Kyle was awake too.

"Can't sleep?" she asked. They were naked.

"No. I don't want to wake up," Kyle answered. His eyes wide, he looked from the window to his wife. She pecked him on the chest.

"Thank you," he said, "not for the kiss. For everything."

"No," Troy started, "don't say that. Don't ever, ever say that. What you wanted was what anyone would want. What everyone has a right to want from the people they love—to be accepted for who they are, where they are, and for what they want."

"You think so?"

"I know so, honey."

Kyle kissed Troy passionately and feeling his tingling again, he turned her onto her back and ran his hand between her thighs.

"Again?" she asked.

"I said I don't want to wake up," Kyle replied as they laughed.

"But we don't have on our costumes anymore," Troy said as one of her nipple covers fell from the ceiling.

"We don't need them. We don't need anything." Kyle kissed her again. "Wait a minute!"

"What?"

"Did you know She-Ra was He-Man's sister?"

"Really?" Troy covered her mouth in shame. "So . . . we just . . . ?"

Kyle nodded.

"But the man at the store told me that . . ." Troy tried, but she was laughing again.

"Don't blame it on the man at the store," Kyle teased. "I said I wanted it freaky, but not *that* freaky."

Tasha was right. The wig was a perfect fit. It looked just like Tamia's old hair, straight and beautiful, bouncing and behaving. And the suit Troy picked out, black, a single-button jacket and classic trouser, was standout and made Tamia look like she was in charge of everything she walked past. The perfect sling-back heels, a matching bag with a golden chain-link strap, Versace perfume, freshly manicured fingernails, and a face painted to perfection, Tamia once again became the 3T they knew—and perhaps she was better, perhaps more confident, perhaps more powerful, perhaps more brilliant.

These were the things Tamia said to herself as she stood in the elevator, descending the levels of Trump Towers with a latte in one hand and an attaché case holding Malik's file in the other. The late summer sun was up now and the stage was set for a grand performance.

"No subway this morning, madame?" Bancroft asked, extending his hand to Tamia to guide her to the taxicab he was holding for her. He was surprised she'd phoned ten minutes earlier to request the car.

Tamia smiled introspectively, memories of the subway, Miss Lolly and her hula-hoop, and Badu and his incense, pulling her for a moment from her focus.

"No, Bancroft," she said. "I probably won't be taking the subway for a while now." There was no emotion in her voice.

"Duly noted." He nodded and helped her into the car. "Might I say a word?" he asked before closing the door.

"Sure." Tamia looked at him. It was the first time she'd ever heard Bancroft use the word "I," and his usual stiffened demeanor was softened.

"While I think you look lovely today, I preferred your look yesterday. The change suited you. I think it was the first time I ever really saw your beauty."

"I don't know what to say," Tamia said, stunned. His remarks were so intimate, Tamia was thinking she was hearing his real voice for the first time and she wasn't sure Bancroft was even from England. "I guess I didn't think anyone here cared about who I really am."

"We all wear costumes," Bancroft said, removing his hat and revealing a nude, red head, "but when we remove them, we see who we really are."

After riding to the courthouse, Tamia was standing in the bathroom, looking at herself in the mirror as she prepared for an exit. For the astute and determined player, who began this stage in her life pretending to be something she wasn't, realized she simply couldn't pretend anymore. In the car, she kept thinking about what Bancroft had said about costumes and remembered all of the people she'd known who'd been wearing them—by force, familiarity, fear, even fierce desire. Charleston, Malik, Phaedra, Naudia, Ayodele, even her. They were all caught up in these images of playing who the world wanted to see, when the world wanted to see it. The only way out was to stop playing. "I did what they said I did . . . And I'll do it again," she remembered hearing Malik say the day they met. And he was right. For that minute, he'd stopped being innocent, accepted his guilt, and took off his costume to do one thing he thought was right, even if it meant losing his role. And now she was making him play by the rules again. Now she was playing by the rules again. But there was something about moving forward that makes turning back impossible, she thought. While she was back in her role and playing by the rules, she couldn't unchange, unlearn, or unaccept the things she thought about her old world now. Seeing things for what they were was the ugliest thing she'd ever done and the only way she could make her world pretty again was to walk away from those things and embrace a new reality. She didn't know where that reality was or if she would ever even find it. She might even need to die again and be reborn a million times just to get closer to it. She didn't care what it took but she knew she had to do it and she'd never be able to do any of that, or embrace her newer self when she found her, if she was busy holding on to who and what she used to be. This was the last day of her old life. She pulled off the wig and stashed it into the attaché case. She looked at herself in the mirror and didn't smile a bit. She just looked. Really looked. And saw herself.

"I need to give you something," Naudia said, coming up beside Tamia as she made her way into the courtroom, unsure if Malik would even show up.

"What is it?" Tamia asked peacefully.

"Wait, what are you doing? Where's your wig?" Naudia whispered so the other people in the courtroom couldn't hear her. "I thought you were going to—"

"It's in my bag. What did you need to give me?"

"It's from Charleston. He dropped it off at the office this—"

Tamia put her hands up.

"I don't want—"

"I think you should look at it," Naudia said.

"Not right now. I'm in a place—and I can't handle his—"

"You need to look," Naudia insisted, and handed Tamia an envelope.

Tamia held the envelope but couldn't bring herself to open it. The last thing she needed was more bad news.

"Open it," Naudia said. "Just trust me."

Tamia looked at Naudia.

"Trust me."

There was a note on one of Charleston's desk cards:

> I'll never say I was wrong. But I can show
> you that you were right. 2X as right. Use
> this however you please.
> —Charleston

"What is this?" Tamia pulled the note from a clip that fastened it to another piece of paper.

"It's a check," Naudia said excitedly.

"A what?"

"$60k," she said. "A check. The money . . . !"

Tamia looked at the figures on the bank note and shook her head.

"Charleston," she said lightly as more people came into the courtroom. "That man . . ."

"You can use it to pay your mortgage . . . to get yourself back together and—"

As Naudia considered how the money might change her boss's life, Tamia thought of how it couldn't.

"You take it," Tamia said.

". . . you could use it to—What?" Naudia said. "What did you say?"

"Yeah . . . you take it," Tamia repeated, handing the check to Naudia's already shaking hand. "You take the money."

"But I . . . this is a check for $60K! I can't . . . It's—" Naudia tried. "You know this is crazy?"

"You've been my assistant for so long, trying to chase your dreams. Now here's your chance. Take the money and go to school."

"But I—"

"I've never seen anyone who works as hard as you. You know exactly what you want and you know exactly where you want to be. You deserve this money, Naudia. Take it."

"You really mean this?"

"Just promise me that when you get to where you want to be, if it's nothing like you thought, that you'll see it for what it is and you won't be afraid," Tamia said, "you won't be afraid to walk away."

"Yeah," Naudia said, knowing that in her words her boss was telling her that that was exactly what she was doing—walking away. "Thank you."

They hugged and laughed, agreeing that Naudia would actually beat Tamia by becoming the first black female Supreme Court justice.

"I guess this is it," Naudia said, looking around the full courtroom. "You think he'll show up?"

"What I think and what he'll do are two different things," Tamia answered. "I can only control myself."

"Hey," Naudia said before turning to take a seat. "I know this might be a bad time and all, but you do realize this check is made out to you. . . . I'm just trying to say I can't use—"

"Naudia, deposit it into my account and we'll get you a check in your name," Tamia said, laughing. "You're a mess."

"I'm just saying . . . No sense having a great big check I can't use."

"Hey, Ms. Lovebird," Troy said, coming up behind

Naudia. Behind her was Tasha, asking where the wig was.

"Ts, you're here!" Tamia said excitedly.

"We wouldn't have missed this," Tasha said. "We had to come out to support our favo bestie."

"Thanks, guys."

"So, where's Nelson Mandela? He here yet?" Tasha asked.

"No," Tamia said.

Fifteen minutes after Tamia took her seat at the front of the courtroom and the rows were full of every face she'd ever seen at the Freedom Project, the district attorney walked in with his case full of papers and slammed them on his table. He was confident. The case was in the bag. An easy kill. In a while, the bailiff would seat the judge, and court would be called to order. Everything was a go. Everything was together. But everyone wasn't there.

Tamia sent Naudia into the hallway to call Malik, but there was no answer.

"Have you seen him?" Kali asked, bending over the railing separating Tamia from the spectators.

Tamia only shook her head and looked at her watch. She couldn't believe that after all they'd talked about, after all they'd been through, he would pull this in the end. If he didn't show up, he'd go to jail. Bottom line. Then he'd be locked up and the Freedom Project, the place she loved so much, the place that changed her life, would be shut down. She didn't care about Malik anymore. She didn't even care about herself. But that place. What it did for her people, for all people, it had to keep on going. And if she was willing to sacrifice her feelings, to put aside her anger, so that could happen, why couldn't he? Why did his brave heart have to be so foolish?

"All rise," the bailiff said as the judge, whom Tamia had seen twice for other cases, walked into the room, "the Criminal Court for the District of Kings County is in session. The Honorable Judge Sadie Tanner is presiding."

The judge sat and as the reporter and she conferred about the day's cases, Tamia felt her palms sweating to the beat of her heart. She felt heavy, so heavy she could fall to the floor and lay there and sleep forever.

Lehman, the district attorney, looked at Tamia and then past her, a grin coming together on his face.

"Are the parties present?" Judge Tanner asked, looking down at the papers on her desk.

Tamia wiped her sweaty hands on her skirt and turned to look at the door, praying, hoping this was one of those miraculous moments in any book she'd read or movie she'd watched when the long-lost witness walks into the room at the last minute. She looked and looked, but there was nothing. The door was closed and through the glass panes she could see that no one was outside. He wasn't coming.

"Counselor," Judge Tanner called to Tamia, "is your client present?"

"Your honor," Tamia answered slowly.

"Counselor Dinkins, you know I don't have time to waste in my courtroom. Is your client present?"

Lehman was grinning again. He was squirming around in his seat looking like he wanted to announce Malik's absence himself.

"He's—"

"Counselor?" The judge removed her glasses and looked at the bailiff. She was about to issue the order of arrest.

Tamia felt the weight dragging her to the floor.

"Your Honor, I—" She tried but there was nothing to say. Then there was something. Something she knew. A smell. A spice. Frankincense. Myrrh.

"Wait," she hollered so loud the judge stopped speaking.

And then Tamia turned to the doors and the back of the courtroom where she'd seen so many miracles happen. The doors opened and in walked a brown brother in a sharp blue suit. Her hope was lost. It wasn't Malik. It couldn't be. The man had a short cut. No jewelry.

Everyone, even the judge, seemed upset when Tamia turned back around.

"Bailiff," the judge began her order again.

"Your honor," someone called and Tamia turned to see it was the man in blue. "I'm here," he added and the closer he got, Tamia saw that it was who she thought it wasn't.

Malik, looking like a different man, a new man, walked past the railing and toward Tamia.

"I'm here," he said again, peering into Tamia's eyes. "I'm here."

"Well, thank you for joining us," the judge said sarcastically.

"You cut your hair?" Tamia whispered, her eyes wide on Malik as the district attorney addressed the court with the charges. "I can't believe you did that. Why? I mean, you didn't—"

"This is war," Malik said. "And if this is the strategy I need to play to save my people, I'll do it."

Tamia smiled and grabbed Malik's hand.

"Counselor?" the judge called and it was clear she was repeating herself. "Are you deaf today? Or am I mute?"

"No, no, no," Tamia answered, standing up. "I was just conferring with my client."

"Isn't that wonderful. Now how does he plead to the charges?"

Tamia looked at Malik and he stood up beside her.

"Not guilty," he said. "I'm not guilty."

The outside of the Kings County courthouse looked like a poetry reading at the Royal Ankh. Dreads were everywhere. Dashikis lined the steps. Babatunde had his drum. In the middle of a small circle of folks, Kali had taken off her shoes and was doing a dance beneath the sun. Even Tasha stepped into the circle and was doing a little two-step—in her red devils.

While not much happened in the courtroom—Malik was only able to enter his plea and the judge set a court date—they celebrated the fact that the case was moving along. That Lehman saw, when Malik walked into the courtroom, that this wasn't actually going to be an open-and-shut case. The opposition was ready to fight, and they weren't giving in.

When Tamia and Malik emerged, everyone cheered and held their fists in the air.

"No justice! No peace!" someone yelled and then they chanted in celebration.

In the middle of it all Tamia and Malik hugged and when they let go, Malik looked at Tamia in a way she'd seen only once before. But this time, on her, it was different. New. Less in childish adoration and more in mature admiration. In his eyes she saw herself. She saw love.

"I can't believe you cut your hair," she said, running her hand over his nude scalp. "I loved it so much. It was so beautiful."

"I'm letting go. I'm moving on. It's time," he said in a way that both he and Tamia knew what he was talking about. "I've harmed you. I've hurt you and I can't continue to carry that past around with me. I had to cut it off. Because—"

"What? Because of what?" Tamia asked.

"Because I love you."

Malik pulled Tamia into his arms and wrapped his hands around the back of her bald head.

The crowd went wild as they kissed for a long time.

"Now, was the kiss a part of your original plan?" Tasha asked as she, Troy, and Tamia walked away from the courthouse. "Because it looked pretty planned to me."

"Stop hating," Tamia said, waving goodbye to Malik. He had agreed to meet her at the Freedom Project later. For now, she was off to celebrate her new beginning with her old friends.

"I'm not hating, I'm just saying," Tasha said.

"Saying? Saying what?" Troy asked. "Because you haven't said anything!"

They all laughed and linked arms, walking down the busy New York street to wherever their stilettos would take them.

Chapter 1

(Unwritten) Rule No. 9 of the Gibbons Family
Handbook: Learn from past mistakes or history is
doomed to repeat itself.

"Well, hel-*lo!*" Cynthia Gibbons uttered slowly. A smile crossed her glossy pink lips.

She spotted him instantly: the six-foot-tall dark Adonis in the dark suit with the iPhone at his ear and a gourmet coffee in his hand. She had been loading grocery bags into her black Lexus SUV when she saw him striding confidently across the shopping center parking lot.

Decades of man-hunting had taught Cynthia to scan potential prey quickly and assess in thirty seconds or less whether they were worthy of the chase. Cynthia noticed that his suit was well tailored and looked fairly expensive. Maybe it was even an Armani, though she couldn't tell for sure from this far away. She also noticed his gold watch and the lack of a wedding ring—though a ring wouldn't have been that much of a deterrent for her. Cynthia didn't care if a man was married or not; if he was, it just meant she had to change her approach, that's all.

She watched as he finished his phone conversation and pulled his car remote from his pocket. She then stood on the balls of her feet to get a better view of him as he walked between a row of cars. She waited to see what car he would unlock. If it was the Honda Civic four spaces away or the Town and Country van next to it, he probably wasn't worth her time. Instead, he unlocked, with two quick beeps, a glistening two-door Porsche roadster.

Bingo, Cynthia thought as she watched him swing open the car door and climb inside.

Cynthia could smell blood in the water, and like a circling shark she went in for the kill. She watched as he drove out of his parking space. Seconds later, she scrambled inside her car, tossed her purse into the passenger seat, and followed him. It didn't take long to maneuver in traffic so that she was in the lead. Now he was on his cell phone again, driving distractedly as he trailed behind her.

"That's right, handsome," Cynthia whispered as she adjusted her rearview mirror and gazed at him. "Almost there."

Cynthia had a plan in mind, but she had to be careful. She didn't want to hurt anyone, cause any serious damage to either of their vehicles, or—heaven forbid—cause a roadway pileup! She drove slowly for several minutes, stealthily glancing in her rearview mirror to make sure he was still behind her. Then when they drew near a stoplight, she slammed on her brakes. His Porsche came to a screeching halt behind her, but not before Cynthia heard the telltale *thump*. He had rear-ended her, which was all part of the plan.

Cynthia fought back a smile, undid two buttons on her silk blouse, and pulled open her collar. She glanced at her reflection one last time to make sure her cleavage was on full display and her makeup was perfect. She then furrowed her brows and cringed, feigning horror and disbelief. She threw open her car door.

"Oh, my God!" she cried, rushing to her rear bumper. Horns blared behind them as the light turned green again. "What happened?"

The handsome driver rushed out of his Porsche. "I don't know. I was . . . I was on the phone." He gestured to the iPhone in his hand, then tossed it onto his car seat. "I'm so sorry. Are you all right?"

She gazed at him with wide hazel eyes, nodded, and brought a hand to her breasts. "I . . . I think so."

"We should exchange insurance information." He reached for his wallet and flipped it open. He then began to dig through several credit cards. Cynthia inwardly jumped for joy when she noticed a black card in the group. He handed an insurance card to her.

"Derrick Winters?" she said, scanning the name on the paper card.

"Yeah, that's me." He pointed down at the text. "And if you call that number, they should—"

"Derrick," she interrupted, smiling ever so sweetly, "do we *really* have to get insurance companies involved in this?"

"What do you mean?"

"Well, it was an honest accident." She took another step toward him and bit down on her bottom lip. "I'd hate for this to appear on either of our insurance records. I'm willing to not let some stuffy old insurance agent get involved in this . . . if you're willing."

"So you . . . you want to do this under the table?"

She laughed and batted her lashes. "Well, that's an interesting way to put it."

"So you want me to pay for the damage in cash?" he asked, eying her suspiciously.

"Well, it's just a little old dent, isn't it?"

Cynthia swept her blond locks out of her face and leaned down to peer at her bumper. She inwardly moaned. It wasn't exactly a "little old dent." Dark Adonis had left quite a gash on her bumper, depositing a great deal of silver mica glossy paint while he was at it.

"But sacrifices have to be made," Cynthia could hear her mother Yolanda's voice say in her head. "You have to take some risks to land a big fish, honey!"

Cynthia stood upright. "Yes, it's just . . . a . . . a little old bitty thing." She breezily waved her hand. "It shouldn't cost much."

He frowned, still contemplating her offer. After some time, he nodded. "I appreciate you doing this, Mrs.—"

"Miss . . . It's *Miss* Cynthia Gibbons." She handed him back his insurance card. "But you can call me Cynthia."

"Well, I appreciate you doing this, Cynthia." He finally smiled, brightening his handsome face. "Look, why don't we move our cars out of the way of traffic. If you don't mind, I'll give a friend of mine a quick call. He does auto body work for me occasionally."

"*Occasionally?* Do you have these kinds of accidents often, Mr. Winters?" she joked.

He chuckled and shook his head. "Please, call me Derrick, and, no, I just have a few vintage cars that I'm working on. I like to restore them and my friend helps me. It's my little indulgence. I've got a 1958 Chevrolet Corvette and a 1960 Jag XK 150—both set me back a pretty penny. When you're dealing with one-hundred-thousand-dollar cars, you don't trust them to just anybody. My friend does good work."

Expensive vintage cars? Jackpot! Cynthia grinned. Oh, Derrick had *definitely* been worthy of the chase.

"My friend can make a quick drive here and give me

an estimate on the damage to your Lexus. Then I can have him take care of it for you. It shouldn't take long."

"Oh, I'm not in a hurry." She glanced at her watch. "I don't have an appointment for another few hours."

"It'll only take forty-five minutes, tops. He isn't far from here."

Cynthia didn't care if Derrick's mechanically inclined friend took until doomsday. The ice cream she had bought at the grocery store that was now sitting in her trunk would just have to melt. She had an excuse to talk to Derrick even longer and even more time to reel him in!

They pulled over to the side of Main Street and stood on the curb together, waiting for his friend to arrive.

It was a slow weekend afternoon in Chesterton, her hometown in northern Virginia. The one-mile stretch of roadway was designed to look like an old-fashioned, small-town Main Street, with scrolled Victorian street lamps and striped awnings over two-story brick storefronts. It was summertime, so the oversized ceramic flowerpots lining the sidewalks were filled with newly bloomed lilies and geraniums. The flowers alternated with each season.

Two doors down was an old favorite in Chesterton, Mimi's Coffee Shop, which was known for its freshly brewed coffee and the cinnamon buns Miss Mimi baked every morning. You knew you were near it because you could smell the delicious aroma wafting out her front door for blocks around. At the end of the block was the bridal shop where Cynthia had purchased her first wedding dress. At the other end of the block was the savings and loan bank, with a clock tower that marked the twelve o'clock hour. Its chime could be heard throughout Chesterton.

Derrick leaned against an old-fashioned mailbox

while they talked and laughed for a good half hour. Cynthia could feel she was making headway with him. She was just about to venture the topic of cooking him a meal at her home as thanks for fixing her car when he suddenly looked up and over her shoulder.

"Looks like my friend's here," Derrick said.

Cynthia turned to follow his gaze. She spotted a tow truck gliding toward them with its engine chugging loudly, drowning out the other roadway noise.

The truck was haloed by the afternoon sun. Cynthia raised her hand to her brow to block out the blinding light. She squinted. When she recognized the man in the driver's seat, her bright smile faded. Her mouth fell open, aghast.

"*That's* your friend?" she squeaked.

"Yeah, that's Korey." Derrick noticed the change in her facial expression. "Why? What's wrong?"

Cynthia glanced nervously at Derrick as the truck came to a stop not far from where they stood. Her pulse started to race. Her throat went dry. Sweat instantly formed on her brow and underneath her arms. She felt cornered, like a bank robber who had flubbed a getaway after a robbery, had hit a dead end, and now saw red and white flashing lights swirling behind her.

"Are you okay?" Derrick asked, touching her shoulder. "You look flushed."

"I'm fine," she lied, clearing her throat. She shrugged off his hand. "I'm fine . . . really. I'm just a little h-hot . . . th-that's all."

Derrick stared at her warily.

The driver of the tow truck killed the engine and threw open his car door. Cynthia fought the urge to bolt. Her car wasn't that far away. She could make it before he even reached them. Instead, she forced herself to stay put and watched as he climbed out of the truck and stepped onto the asphalt. After slamming the door shut, he casually strolled toward them.

God, he hasn't changed! Even after all these years, Cynthia thought.

Korey Walker still looked the same way he had looked almost twenty years ago when they were in high school together, except now he had a few sprinkles of gray hair on his head and in the beard stubble on his russet-brown cheeks. But he was still tall, still muscular, and still handsome as the devil, which was one reason why she had avoided going anywhere near his auto body and repair shop in Chesterton since he had opened it a little more than a year ago.

Back when they were younger, Korey had been the kryptonite to her Superman, and she had been powerless under his spell. Though decades had passed since those days, Cynthia feared she would be powerless again if she got near him—and she didn't need the confusion he could bring to her life. Korey was not the right man for her now, just as he hadn't been the right man for her back then. But there was no avoiding him today.

"Thanks for coming, man," Derrick said, stepping forward. He and Korey shook hands, then embraced and slapped each other's backs.

They were quite the contrast: Derrick in his chic, immaculate suit, and Korey in his oil- and greased-stained navy blue shirt and pants, with grime on his hands and dirt under his nails. But even in his shoddy attire, Korey was by far the sexier of the two.

Hands down, she thought.

"Looks like I've got myself in a real fix, Korey," Derrick said. "I accidentally rear-ended this beautiful lady right here." He gestured to Cynthia.

Korey turned and looked at her. His dark eyes regarded her coolly and then shifted downward by several inches. She followed the path of his gaze, instantly getting an eyeful of her own cleavage. She was spilling out of her top. No wonder he was staring! Now self-conscious, Cynthia quickly raised her hand to cover her breasts.

"Are you sure it was an accident?" Korey asked softly in a heavy baritone she remembered all too well. He was looking at her, not Derrick, as if he was posing the question to her, not his friend.

She looked away, choosing to focus instead on the flower shop across the street.

"What? Are you trying to say I hit her *on purpose?*" Derrick asked with a chuckle.

"No, nothin' like that, man." Korey shook his head, still gazing at her. "Nothin' like that."

Damn it, stop staring at me!

She knew Korey was judging her, as he always had and always would. She could read his mind even now, after all these years.

Still playing the same ol' tricks, Cindy? Still runnin' the same ol' game? Aren't you getting a little old for this? Isn't this getting a little bit tired?

Well, to hell with you, Korey, she thought, raising her chin defiantly and meeting his gaze. She had nothing to be ashamed of. She was a grown woman who lived her life on her own terms! His judgment meant nothing to her. He wasn't going to make her question herself like he had two decades ago. She wasn't that girl anymore.

"So," Korey said, finally returning his attention to Derrick, "let's take a look at the damage." He strode toward her Lexus. "Where'd you hit her?"

"Back bumper," Derrick said, pointing at her SUV. "I left quite a scratch too."

Cynthia watched as the two men leaned down to examine her car. She crossed her arms over her chest and tapped her foot restlessly as they consulted each other, ignoring her. She wondered why Korey didn't acknowledge that he knew her.

So be it, she thought. She wasn't going to acknowledge him either. She could pretend they were total strangers if that's what he wanted.

Korey dropped to one knee and traced his finger along the gash in her bumper, giving Cynthia plenty of opportunity to further examine him in profile: his long dark eyelashes, high cheekbones, and full lips. The diamond stud he used to wear in his left earlobe was gone. She could remember sucking on that earlobe when they parked in the deserted lot behind an old drive-in movie theater outside of Chesterton. And she could remember eighteen-year-old Korey sucking on a lot more than that while they made love in the backseat of his mother's 1987 Chevy Cavalier. Those passionate moments they shared were not only hot and heavy, but done in secret. Not even her sisters knew about him because Cynthia worried the information eventually would find its way back to their mother. Yolanda Gibbons would have killed her if she knew Cynthia was fogging up the car windows with the likes of Korey Walker.

Cynthia thought back wistfully to those clandestine nights. Just the memory of Korey's hands and mouth on her skin made her shiver. And another appendage besides his hands had been just as memorable. One night, she had playfully nicknamed it "Big Korey." From then on, the nickname stuck, and all she had to do was whisper it in his ear to get his engine going.

She watched as he now stood up. "Yeah, that's a pretty bad dent, but . . ." He winked at Derrick. "I can fix her. It's no problem, and you won't even be able to tell the difference."

"Good! And I get the friend discount, right?"

Korey laughed and nodded. "Yeah, man, you get the friend discount. Though with all the money you make, I should charge your ass extra, not less."

Korey suddenly turned to look at Cynthia, and she felt her body temperature rise again under his warm gaze. He walked toward her, reached into one of the pockets of his stained blue short-sleeved shirt, and pulled out a business card. He offered it to her.

"You can bring it in anytime next week," he said. "I'll take care of it personally."

"Thank you." She took his card and quickly tucked it into her purse.

"We're the auto repair and body shop that's not far from Stan's Bakery. We're on the corner of—"

"I *know* where you are," she said then grimaced. She hadn't meant to admit that.

"Oh, you do?" He inclined his head. "I'm surprised to hear that . . . considering that you haven't paid me a visit the whole time my shop's been here, Cindy."

Derrick furrowed his brows. "Wait! You two know each other?"

"I haven't had a reason to visit you," she said breezily, tossing her hair over her shoulder and ignoring Derrick's question. "Why would I?"

"Oh, I could think of *plenty* of reasons." Korey took another step closer to her. She saw a shadow of an impish smile tug at his lips and the heat in his dark eyes intensify. "You and I have a lot of history."

She gritted her teeth at those words.

Cynthia had pushed that "history" out of her mind years ago when she found out that Korey was engaged to Vivian Brady, Cynthia's old arch nemesis in high school. Vivian had been the ring leader of the pack of girls who had ridiculed Cynthia endlessly about her mother, Yolanda—"the biggest gold-digging ho in

Chesterton," as Vivian and her girlfriends liked to call Yolanda back then. Korey marrying a girl like Vivian had felt like the ultimate betrayal to Cynthia, especially when she figured out later that he had been cheating on her with Vivian while they were together. It definitely made her feel less regretful about dumping him and getting engaged to her first husband, Bill, a millionaire who was fifteen years her senior. She had chosen Bill instead of Korey because he was handpicked by her mother.

"Bill is the *right* kind of man for a responsible woman who wants to ensure her future," her mother had said at the time.

Cynthia had since heard that Korey and Vivian were divorced, just like she and Bill, but that didn't change her feelings about Korey's betrayal. He had hurt her indescribably. She would never forgive him.

"I'll bring my car in on Wednesday," she said curtly. She then strode toward her SUV, forgetting Derrick, her big catch, and Korey, the first and last man to ever break her heart. Seconds later, she put her key in the ignition and pulled away, leaving the two men standing on the sidewalk, looking dumbfounded.

Grab the Hottest Fiction
from
Dafina Books

Grab These Novels by
Zuri Day